PRAISE FOR *IN THE FALL THEY LEAVE*

"To the names of Irène Némirowsky and Pat Barker, add that of Joanna Higgins: women who write about war from the point of view of civilians on the home front and who dramatize the complex and morally fraught interactions between ordinary people and their country's occupiers. The country is Belgium, the war is World War I, and the ordinary person is a nurse, Marie-Thérèse Hulbert, who in the course of the novel becomes quite extraordinary. Perhaps this splendid novel's most impressive feature is the way it combines an epic sweep with the intimacy of Marie-Thérèse's inner life. Readers will cheer her on, warn her of dangers, and repeatedly ask themselves, 'What would I have done?'"

—John Vernon, author of *The Last Canyon, The Book of Reasons, LaSalle*, and other works

"The writing is superb. Poetic. Elegant. The character renderings are sublime and lively. There's a fusion of word and image and sight and sound and thought. It's filmic and alive."

—Jerry Mirskin, author of *Picture a Gate Hanging Open and Let That Gate Be the Sun, Crepuscular Non Driveway: Poems*, and other poetry

"This gripping, character-centered novel gives readers insight into the humanity of some despite the danger and costs, and the brutality of WWI. It reminds us that not all heroes are found on the battlefield."

—Sara-Jo Lupo Sites, MLS, Head of Youth Services, G.F. Johnson Memorial Library

"On the face of it, Joanna Higgins' newest book is a story about World War I. But like all great novels, one must ask what is it not about? It's about war, but also about friendship and betrayal and art and nation-building. The writing, moment by moment, is so exquisite and precise it practically makes the reader hold one's breath. The novel is fast-paced but never hurried. Among Higgins' prized works, this may well be her masterpiece."

—Liz Rosenberg, author of *Beauty and Attention, The Moonlight Palace*, and numerous children's books as well as other works of prose and poetry

"In her novel *In the Fall They Leave*, Joanna Higgins captures the trepidation, fear of failure, and doubt that haunt every apprentice of nursing. Equally as well, she describes the hope-filled faith, courage, and dedication that guide aspiring nurses on their journeys."

—Donna Tomasulo West, PhD, RN, Clinical Assistant Professor, Decker College of Nursing and Health Sciences, Binghamton University

IN THE FALL THEY LEAVE

Joanna Higgins

Regal House Publishing

Published by
Regal House Publishing, LLC
Raleigh, NC 27605
All rights reserved

ISBN -13 (paperback): 9781646032983
ISBN -13 (epub): 9781646032990
Library of Congress Control Number: 2022935693

All efforts were made to determine the copyright holders and obtain their permissions in any circumstance where copyrighted material was used. The publisher apologizes if any errors were made during this process, or if any omissions occurred. If noted, please contact the publisher and all efforts will be made to incorporate permissions in future editions.

Cover design © by C. B. Royal
Cover images © by TBD

Regal House Publishing, LLC
https://regalhousepublishing.com

The following is a work of fiction created by the author. All names, individuals, characters, places, items, brands, events, etc. were either the product of the author or were used fictitiously. Any name, place, event, person, brand, or item, current or past, is entirely coincidental.

Printed in the United States of America

For Jerry,
Christopher and Kaili,
and in memory of John Gardner

When every autumn people said it could not last through the winter, and when every spring there was still no end in sight, only the hope that out of it all some good would accrue to mankind kept men and nations fighting.

—Barbara W. Tuchman, *The Guns of August*

Simplicity is the highest goal, achievable when you have overcome all difficulties. After one has played a vast quantity of notes and notes, it is simplicity that emerges as the crowning reward of art.

—Frédéric Chopin

ULTIMATUM

BRUSSELS, BELGIUM

Newsboys charge the platform, their cries a racket of startled birds. *Allemand Ultimatum...Alle-mand Ulti-matum... Ulti-matum!... Allemand Ulti-ma-tum!* Papers flap above heads, explosions of white wings. Disembarking passengers press forward. Clots form. Movement stalls.

"What is it, monsieur?" Marie-Thérèse all but shouts.

The elderly man is a little deaf. He is also laconic to a legendary degree. "*L'Allemagne encore,*" he says, his eyes on the arrivals from Ostend.

Germany again. Fragments of an old history lesson rise murkily through layers of other old lessons. The Franco-Prussian War, the cause of which does not rise murkily. She recalls, though, that just over a month ago, a young Serb shot the Archduke of Austria and his wife, Sophie, while they were in an open car on their way to visit a hospital in Sarajevo, the capital of Yugoslavia. Both died. That event sent the Brussels newsboys flying then too, shrieking and flapping their papers. And ever since, newspapers have been warning of a war potentially greater than any previously fought.

"Does it have anything to do with us? Aren't we neutral?"

"*Efficacité.*" Extending his right arm, he slashes at the air.

"Do you mean Germany's efficiency?"

He gives a curt nod.

"So, maybe she decided to stay in England. I don't know if I—"

The old man surges forward, waving his cap, Marie-Thérèse in his wake. Approaching a tall woman in cream-colored linen, he holds his cap over his heart and bows.

"*Bonjour,* Monsieur Wojtasczek," she says and, turning to

Marie-Thérèse, "Mademoiselle Hulbert. You came too. How nice."

Trained in observation, Marie-Thérèse detects an incipient frown held in check. She detects withheld criticism—and a miasma of disapproval. *You came too when you might have been doing something useful such as studying or even taking the dogs for their walk? How nice.*

"I had some free time and I…so I asked the gardener, but I should not have presumed… *Pardonnez-moi, Matrone, s'il vous plaît.*"

"No, no, it's fine."

They retrieve the matron's trunk from a baggage cart and then in breezy sunlight on the Place Rogier, the gardener waits in line to buy a newspaper. The matron asks about her two dogs, and Marie-Thérèse, still shaken, rattles off their latest exploits.

"I'm glad they're well."

In the back seat of the school's Landaulet, the matron raises her newspaper. Marie-Thérèse wishes she had one to hide behind. Why in the world had she asked to go along to the station? True, she was excited to begin her third and final year at the nursing school. True, she'd been free that morning, and a thunderstorm at dawn had swept through, leaving behind glitter and balmy warmth, and she'd felt some altogether uncharacteristic surge of euphoria. And further true, she worshipped the woman and was anxious to see her again, given all the war rumblings. And so, voilà, yet another mistake.

How ironic. She'd failed at her piano studies because she hadn't been impulsive enough. "Your playing is too stiff, mademoiselle. Take more risks!" But risk-taking meant mistakes, no? They were kind enough and tried to explain—and demonstrate. All of it lost in the pulsing roar beating in her ears.

She pries a speck of lint from her gabardine skirt. *Mistakes…* she hates them. And the foreboding they bring on. Turning to the window, she blinks away gathering tears. The boulevard, strangely, has become a parade route of sorts. Automobiles, horse carts, trams, and even bicycles trimmed with flowers and ribbons. Lampposts, too, and horses' bridles. Little girls wear crowns of marigolds. A bicyclist, just then passing the slower-moving Landaulet, is carrying two strings of onions in his right hand, each woven with yellow and red ribbons. Church bells clang at every block. Newsboys chant at every corner. Along sidewalks people are embracing or gesticulating in apparent argument. Belgian flags drape windowsills, balconies, and shop fronts, their vertical red, yellow, and black bars rippling like sails. And sheets of newsprint are skidding and tumbling along sidewalks.

Ribbons, flags, people, newspapers, traffic. Everything that day, August 1, 1914, in motion.

Why are people celebrating?

She's afraid to ask.

History Lessons

J ust outside the lecture hall, a crow screeches some staccato outrage. The matron's part-wolfhound, Jackie, responds with his window-shaking bark. On and on it goes—screech, bark, screech, bark. Donnie, the shepherd mix, joins in, and it's a Three-Part Invention.

"*Merci, messieurs*," she says when they all finally stop.

Someone in the assembled group laughs, then a few others. Tension crackles apart, and the day becomes what it is, under it all a fine, rose-scented August afternoon. The school and clinic were once four row houses in an old Ixelles neighborhood with mature gardens. Leaves are making their forest sounds. Marie-Thérèse takes a deep breath and observes the matron for clues. There are none. The woman's transcendent calm reminds her of the Académie's Madame Gonczy, the way the renowned pianist could walk onstage, take her time adjusting bench and gown, then sit there for the longest while in that ponderous silence until finally, with indifference almost, extending her arms and from some thread of sound begin weaving a tapestry of perfection. The memory reawakens Marie-Thérèse's headache.

"It is good to be back," the matron begins in French, "despite this morning's disturbing news."

But the woman doesn't appear disturbed in the least. Her hands are loosely clasped on the lectern, her voice steady. Her oval face, with its high forehead and swept-back, light brown hair in its coil, radiates the usual serenity, the only difference being an addition of peach tones, after her month-long stay in England. She's in uniform now—the white cap, cuffs, and apron, the lake-blue blouse and skirt. Obviously, she's following her own dictum, Marie-Thérèse thinks. *Never show fear.* Glancing at her own hands cupped on her chair's writing surface, she observes how the thumbnails are going hyacinth-blue, up near the cuticles. And the fingers are cold and minutely trembling. At the Académie, she always had to soak her hands in warm water before any lesson or performance. And practice a breathing technique that never quite worked to quell fear.

Nor does it now.

"I've placed copies of today's editions in your sitting room," the matron continues, "but for now, a summary. Germany has just given Belgium an ultimatum declaring that Belgium must allow German armies to pass through on their way to France. Germany is saying that France attacked first, and so Germany must retaliate for its own self-preservation."

Has her left eyebrow lifted a little in skepticism? Marie-Thérèse believes so.

"It is unclear whether any such attack has taken place. However, to allow Germany to pass through will violate Belgium's neutrality. Not to do so, Germany says, will make Belgium its enemy. So, my dear students and staff, we are in a predicament. King Albert is to give his response as early as this evening, and then we may know more."

Marie-Thérèse glances at her roommate, seated on her right. Rani, an excellent student in every other respect, unfortunately can't help showing anxiousness. Hives betray her. And there they are—blotchy crimson patches marching right up to her red-gold hairline. She's staring at the matron with the intensity of someone trying to absorb a difficult lesson.

"We will convene again when there are further developments. Meanwhile, I will be working on a new syllabus emphasizing areas we have already covered but must augment—amputations, bullet wounds, and blood transfusions. My dear students and staff, by this evening the situation may have been resolved diplomatically. But you know how I believe in being prepared. We may not have control over events, but we can control our responses to them."

She restates the words in English, then reverts to French. "Whoever wishes to discuss this matter with me in private may do so between the hours of two and five o'clock this afternoon.

Reserve a time on the sign-up sheet. Some of you may wish to consider taking a leave of absence. Our dear French, German, and English students might well consider this option."

The same words issue forth in calm English.

"I want to go!" a woman calls out in English. "Sometimes you're so mean!" The woman's laugh devolves into a gasping hack.

Marie-Thérèse doesn't turn as many others do. It's just Charlotte, a resident patient who became addicted to morphine during treatment in England. The matron has been trying for years to wean her off the drug. This interruption is likely just another ploy to get her small dose ahead of schedule.

As the matron and a sister lead Charlotte out of the lecture hall, Liese, in the row ahead, turns to Marie-Thérèse and Rani. "Sounds like you two will be missing out on some excitement around here. Not to mention your certificates. How unfortunate!"

"We might not have to leave," Rani says, more to her desk.

"Well, but it doesn't look good, does it?"

New students, forgetting Liese's name, will often add, "You know, the pretty one." Marie-Thérèse thought of her that way too. Liese's prettiness called to mind cherubs painted on nave ceilings—the plump pink cheeks and golden curls, the insouciant eyes. Liese was the first to extend friendship, and Marie-Thérèse, still stunned by failure and sorrow, found comfort in confiding in her. In no time, all that delectable information spread like some contagion throughout the school: her failure at the prestigious Académie; her rift with her mother, once a prima ballerina, no less; and then her terror of failing at nursing. For the rest of that first year, Marie-Thérèse had to endure stares and whispers and almost left. So that was The Pretty One, she found out the hard way. Trading in confidences in order to build other alliances.

At the Académie there'd been little time for friendships or even machinations of the Liese kind. Though polite and encouraging to one another on the surface, under that halcyon sea lay cold depths of ambition and, in Marie-Thérèse's case, debilitating doubt and fear. For the most part, she lived like some solitary cave dweller in her practice room. Those who joined quartets or trios had it better, she realized, enjoying a camaraderie of shared striving. At times Marie-Thérèse wishes she had taken that path. She might still be there.

No. Their smiles said it all when she told her instructors she'd be leaving.

But that water has flowed under the bridge. Against all expectations she's come to enjoy her nursing studies despite the occasional doubt and fear induced by mistakes. At the Académie you can fail no matter how hard you work, but here at the nursing school, persistence, study, and attention to detail can lead to success. And so far, to her surprise, she's been succeeding.

Liese breaks into these thoughts. "Well, let me know if you two need any help packing."

Dismissed by a sister, students and staff are leaving the lecture hall.

"*Merci*, but neither of us will be going anywhere just yet. Right, Rani?"

Rani's lips are curled under. She's still looking down.

Later they see Liese's name on the sign-up sheet.

"I hope she leaves," Rani says.

Marie-Thérèse agrees. Her own mean-spiritedness tells her she hasn't really forgiven Liese. But it does help to regard it all as a good, if painful, lesson.

WEEDS

Please have one, mademoiselle," the matron says, after pouring their tea.

The round table in her front window is set with teapot, cups, and the English wheat biscuits offered at student conferences. The matron brings them from England and probably had them in her basket that morning, Marie-Thérèse is thinking. Now, afternoon sunlight filtering through lace curtains creates figured shadows on flowered porcelain and white linen—and the precious biscuits that might be all gone by day's end. Carefully, she places one on her plate.

"So, you are uncertain?" Although they often converse in English so Marie-Thérèse can practice the language, today they've chosen French.

"I hope to stay at the school, but…"

"Yes?"

"My father, you know, is German, and my mother French. And the newspapers…they're saying the king is not going to agree to the ultimatum."

"He does seem set against it. But we will know soon."

"My family may want to remain in Brussels…all my father's eye patients are here…but if Father thinks we should leave, then I must as well. I would rather stay, though I realize it will be hard. War casualties…I'm not sure I have the necessary… fortitude."

"We can't know our strengths until tested. I do know that you are a thinker. That's good, but excessive worry is not. Think of worry as weeds that want to take over a flower garden. When I received the telegram about the situation here, I was weeding my mother's rose bed. Roses need so much coddling. Weeds, though, thrive in any bit of soil and in drought and even flood. Like one's worries. If you and your family decide to leave, I hope you will be able to return. You will always have a place here."

"*Merci, Matrone*. But this ultimatum… It may come to nothing?"

"I will not offer easy assurances."

"If there is war, will you stay?"

"Yes."

"*Pardonnez-moi, Matrone*, but it might be safer for you in England, no? And if England enters the war, the hospitals there—" Marie-Thérèse stops herself. Arguing!—with the matron. Heat floods her face.

The woman looks out at the rue de la Culture through the lace curtain. "Do you know, my mother said nearly the same thing before I left. That I could work in a hospital there." She regards Marie-Thérèse again. "But I am needed here. All the more so if war is declared."

"I am pleased you will be staying, Matron."

"*Merci*, mademoiselle."

It seems a dismissal. Marie-Thérèse pushes back her chair and stands, then attempts another tangled apology for going to the station that morning.

"Mademoiselle Hulbert, it was of no consequence. Please remember that if you need to finish your studies elsewhere, I will write you a strong recommendation."

"*Merci beaucoup, Matrone*." The matron never offers glib compliments. Marie-Thérèse tucks those words away for hard days. After replacing her chair, she turns to go.

"One moment, please. Could you walk Jackie and Donnie this evening if you have an hour to spare?" She offers the smile usually reserved for patients.

"I…yes! I will be delighted. *Merci. Merci beaucoup!*"

"Tell monsieur so he won't worry they got out on their own."

"I will do so now. Thank you again."

"Oh, and please take your biscuit for later."

The gardener is holding a minuscule piece of paper up to his eyes while a pigeon struts back and forth on the coop's plank counter. Its feet, she notices again, are so extraordinarily red.

He drops the paper on the counter, and as he seems in no mood for even minimal conversation, she picks it up and deciphers its tiny print. *Ponts de Liège détruits.*

"They destroyed the bridges, Papa?" she says, using their pet name for him.

"We did."

"*We* did? So that means… Does it mean we are *not* agreeing to the ultimatum?" *Of course it must. Don't be stupid.*

He hands her the pigeon and then, with knobbed and scarred fingers, rolls up the paper. The bird seems just a few bones and feathers and a tiny, quick-pumping heart, its round eyes shiny as obsidian. The gardener finally gets the paper inserted in the tube, and the tube fastened to one of the twig-like legs. Then he takes the pigeon outside and brings it to his face. "*Idź z Bogiem,*" he says. Go with God.

The bird flaps upward. Rising above the trees, it turns eastward. When they can no longer see it, she tells him about coming for Jackie and Donnie later. After a moment she adds, "Does it mean war, Papa?"

He probably was a soldier once. She's heard there's an old saber over the mantel in his cottage. And he keeps his white hair and mustache evenly clipped. A cross-hatching of nicks and scars on both face and hands and one rather large scar through his left eyebrow add to the impression. Also, there's the way he wears his workman's clothing belted and neat, even the brown boots polished. Marie-Thérèse has never asked him about his past. There's something too reserved about him. And possibly tragic. She's read somewhere, or at least has gotten the idea, that those who've seen much often say the least.

"When they want," he says now, "they take."

WRONG NOTES

Marie-Thérèse lets herself into her family's home, and there is the housekeeper, Francine, at the far end of the hall, holding dinner plates. Marie-Thérèse has startled her.

The woman isn't tall and over the years has grown stout. Her black hair is still worn pulled straight back into a bun level with her ears. White streaks stratify the once-solid black. The bun itself, once plump, now appears deflated.

Since Marie-Térèse's defection, Francine has never offered a greeting.

"*Bonsoir*, Francine. How have you been? You look well. Are they at home?"

"Only madame. Do not upset her. She is very nervous today."

Madame. Francine was only thirteen or fourteen when employed to help Marie-Thérèse's mother at the ballet, who, at the time, wasn't much older than Francine. As Mademoiselle Adrienne rose in the ballet corps from chorus to soloist to prima, Francine's fortunes ascended with her. Now she rules the household.

"May I let them stay inside? They're quite thirsty."

The housekeeper glares down at the two dogs through the thick lenses Monsieur Hulbert has fit for her. The panting dogs are flopped on the cool marble of the foyer and seem to be smiling up at her.

On any other day, the black sheep of the Hulbert family might have laughed at the juxtaposition.

"Are they yours?" Francine asks.

It would not surprise me, Marie-Thérèse hears, *you having two such mismatched mongrels.*

"Oh no, no. They belong to… Ah, the school."

"Some school. I will get them water. Go see your mother but do not upset her."

"*Merci*, Francine. They're tired and won't be any trouble."
She loops the leashes around the newel post, hoping they won't
pull it down.

Passing the dining room, she glances in at the blue hydran-
geas on the sideboard, the candles to be lighted. In a salon, glass
doors open onto a stone terrace where three stone steps lead to
a lawn. Madame Hulbert, wearing white that appears lavender
in the shade of the arbor, sits at a round wrought-iron table.
There are dangling clusters of immature grapes, still chartreuse,
above her. Francine refills Madame Hulbert's cup after moving
aside a sheet of newsprint. Then she splashes out tea for Marie-Thérèse.

"*Merci*, Francine." In the Hulbert household, Marie-Thérèse
is well aware, the woman can be as grumpy as she pleases as
long as it isn't with madame or monsieur.

"*Ce n'est rien.*" Francine turns back to the house.

Evening is coaxing the scent of moisture from lawn, vegetable bed, and Francine's herb garden. Sparrows chirp fiercely in
a shrub. To Marie-Thérèse, it sounds like they're arguing.

Which brings to mind the tirades. *It is so hard to abandon one's
hopes for a child. To see that child throwing away her gift as if it were
no more than a few potato peelings. When you become a parent, you may
understand. Only I hope you won't have to go through this.*

Yet during those tirades and arguments two years ago, there
was at least hope of convincing the other. There was, at least,
emotion.

Now the words are simpler. "*Bonsoir*, Maman. *Comment al-
lez-vous?*"

"As you see."

What Marie-Thérèse sees is a still-lovely woman whose oval
face is smooth, whose dark hair, with its feathering of silver
at the temples, still gleams in its low chignon. Her skin always
reminds Marie-Thérèse of apples, nearly white apples, as if
light were radiating through them. Twenty-six years ago, Mademoiselle Adrienne was at the pinnacle of her career with the
Belgian Ballet, yet remnants of that time still wreath her like

some vivifying mist. As a child, Marie-Thérèse was oblivious to it, but as she grew older, it became obvious. If anyone ever "trailed clouds of glory"—in the English poet's words—it was her mother.

Though her own thicker bones are a legacy from her father, Marie-Thérèse inherited her mother's height as well as her dark hair and fine-grained, pale skin. Both of her brothers, in contrast, have their father's bronze hair and ruddiness. Her decision to leave the Académie—and her mother's beloved world of the arts—might not have been so hard on Madame Hulbert if her daughter hadn't resembled her quite so much. Or so Marie-Thérèse often thinks.

"I found myself nearby," she says now, "and wanted to stop. The news is awful. What does Father say?"

"How was it that you found yourself nearby?" Madame Hulbert emphasizes the final three words of the question.

"I, ah, I…I was asked to walk, to take for a walk, the two dogs that belong to the school."

"Dogs."

"Yes, well, and I've read the newspapers and was, I mean I am, concerned. What does Father say?"

"Will it make any difference?"

"*Pardonnez-moi*, Maman. Perhaps I should not have come today and…disturbed you further. I'd better go. I will telephone."

"Did you walk all that distance from the school?"

"*Oui.*"

"Your father and your brothers are at soccer. Imagine. On such a day. If you can wait, they should be home within the hour. Why not have dinner here and then he will drive you back."

The thought of waiting in the quiet house with the two censorious women sends her heart skipping. She's glad for an excuse. "I have duty soon, Maman. Perhaps I can arrange something for tomorrow."

"Ah. *Duty.*"

Marie-Thérèse turns to see what her mother seems to be

gazing at. The plum tree, its branches arcing downward, heavy with ripening purple and green-hued plums. This tree dates back to the time when her parents first met after Mademoiselle Adrienne had just performed the dual role of Odette/Odile in *Swan Lake*. Most admirers brought armloads of roses, but Marie-Thérèse's father, a student from Berlin then, had a small plum tree snowy with blossoms, its roots wrapped in rough cloth. He had seen the performance several times. That moment backstage became a family story, how he said the tree reminded him of her, and Mademoiselle Adrienne replying with hauteur: Why? Are my feet so ugly?

Madame draws her gaze back to her daughter. "I have been thinking, *ma chère*, that if war is declared against us, you will be surrounded by wounds and death far more than you are now. It will be a…danse macabre. Reconsider, I beg you. They will have you back. I have spoken to them."

"Maman!" Astonishment and pain erupt from the word.

Madame chooses to ignore it. "I was going to surprise you with this news when you next came to dinner. But my thoughts are so roiled today. You might be sent to a battlefield hospital if it comes to war. What then? A danse macabre for certain and not on any grand stage. It will be dangerous. It will be terrible and demoralizing. Please return to the piano, I beg you. Your teachers will welcome you back. They are holding the door open for you."

Because you and Father support the Académie.

"I have been thinking that you can spend some weeks at home, getting back into practice. We will find a teacher to help you prepare…Monsieur Coussens was quite good, no? And when you regain confidence, you can return. And if we should have to leave Brussels, well, we will find another instructor for you."

But I never did have confidence, Maman.

"One day you will look back on this moment and realize how happy you are that you decided to go back. You know, many times while in some pique I was tempted to leave the

ballet out of spite. Had I given in to that childish impulse, I
would be a bitter woman today, perhaps blaming everyone else
for my failure. But instead, I vowed to work harder. I drew
strength from within. And now I can look back on triumph,
not failure."

"Maman, Madame Gonczy didn't invite me into her master
class. Remember? Year after year. You of all people know what
that means. What if you had never made soloist year after year
after year? How long could you have gone on, being passed
over like that?"

"*Oui, oui*, the great Madame Gonczy. I spoke with her and
asked the question outright. Why did she not allow you in? Her
answer was that you had potential. She said she was sorry you
left. She all but said, *ma chère*, that you needed to work harder."

"You…spoke with *her*?"

"I did. I made an appointment and went there. She said she
remembered you with fondness. She said that you had potential."

Marie-Thérèse remembers different words. *Mademoiselle Hulbert, I wish you well in whatever you choose to do. It has been a pleasure
knowing you. Bonne chance.*

"And so, you…asked if I could return. Oh, Maman."

"Don't sound so grateful, *ma chère*." Madame's eyes fill.

"Maman, I must go. I'm so sorry. I just wanted to… Please
tell Father I will telephone, though not tonight. It will be too
late when…"

She stands and so does her mother. Then Madame Hulbert
embraces her daughter. "I want only what is best for you. Do
you believe me?"

"*Oui*, Maman."

"Do you have money for the tram?"

Marie-Thérèse nods though she has none.

"*Bien*. If you need more, ask Francine."

"I will."

"And, Marie-Thérèse, promise me you will reconsider."

"*Oui*, Maman. *Oui*."

She gets the prancing dogs outside and closes the heavy door behind her. In trees and shrubbery along the rue Belliard Stratt, birds are chirping their piercing evening songs. Sunset light sets beveled glass aflame, bronzes the ornate stone facades of row houses, and transforms flowers in front gardens and window boxes into fountains of color. It should be beautiful.

She and the two dogs race along the streets, Marie-Thérèse not caring what they must look like, flying along like that. Yet she can't outpace the ghost words keeping up with her. *But, Mama, I was only a talented mediocrity. My teachers saw this and thought it best I leave sooner rather than later.*

They do not know everything, teachers. I worry that you have leaped into nursing without understanding what it entails. You felt disappointed in one area and jumped, without much thought, into another. And you will be trapped in an unsuitable profession. You will lose your gift and become despondent. How many times did I think I wasn't good enough? I will tell you. Sometimes every day. Often after every performance. But did I give up? Non! If you expect constant praise from your teachers and fall apart when you do not get it, that is what a child would do. Not a true artist.

I must not be a true artist then.

At ten years old, she had been able to transform pages of tangled notes into gorgeous sound—the playing her mother must remember. Madame Hulbert hadn't heard her at the Académie, though, in the salons of her instructors, the careful, vapid attempts at grandeur. Anticipating the next mistake and then invariably making it. The stone of dread in her stomach. The wooden fingers. The shameful sounds. And then after so many years, her instructors finally withholding the lifeblood of criticism. Which meant she wasn't worth critiquing. Wasn't worth their valuable time. This, she hadn't been able to tell her mother—or father. It would have been cruel. Nor did she describe the way her instructors' smiles finally returned when she told them she'd be leaving. *Yes, you're right of course, mademoiselle. It will be good to get on with your life.*

What happens? Is it loss of faith or loss of ability?

Or are they interwoven?

And now to have to go through the agony of deciding all over again?

As she runs, she recalls her final performance at the Académie, how one wrong note had led to a jumble of them and then a loss of concentration—that white impenetrable wall—and finally to awful silence. She had to start over again. Her mother, father, Willy, and Jacques in the audience.

They want me back?

Impossible.

Yet she feels worse for her mother. That hope, and going there, to the pompous Académie, and begging.

As Mademoiselle Adrienne never had to do for herself. Nor would have.

AND STILL THE DAY IS NOT OVER

Rani looks up from her textbook. "You missed dinner. Where have you been? You look awful."

"I was walking Jackie and Donnie. I'm fine." Marie-Thérèse removes her shoes and lies down. The space between her temples holds a rushing stream pulsing through narrow channels.

"Well, you certainly look fine. And the day is not over for you, mademoiselle. You will never make it through. I'll get you something from the kitchen if Amalia doesn't chase me out."

Thinking nothing at all while lying in a quiet room is a gift. Soon, though, Charles Darwin comes to mind. Charles Darwin and his theory of species and individuals within species fighting for space. As her worries are doing. War. War with Germany. The Académie. Her mother.

I was weeding my mother's roses when—

You would do that with a…trowel? Marie-Thérèse has never weeded a garden or planted even a pot of flowers. You would weed with some sort of tool, perhaps. A spade? She tries to imagine this something in hand. This trowel or spade or whatever. But if you can't envision it, how can you dig at the large thistle that is war with Germany? She's trying to solve the mystery of the proper tool when Rani enters with a tray holding a glass of milk and a bowl of lentil soup.

"I told Amalia you took the dogs for a long walk, and she softened right up. She even added a cookie. How do you feel? You still look like you belong in the women's ward, in one of the beds."

While Marie-Thérèse eats to please her, Rani sits at her desk, its chair angled outward, and relates the news. In all, ten of the school's twenty-nine student and senior nurses have decided to leave.

"Liese?"

"No luck there, but Felicia and—"

"No! Not Felicia!" The quiet Polish girl is their bandaging genius. She quickly learns the complex and even beautiful bandaging patterns and spares no generosity when it comes to helping others, Marie-Thérèse always among them.

"She wants to go home. Papa told her there might be fighting along Poland's western border if Russia and Germany go at it in that area, but she wants to be with her family now."

Marie-Thérèse quells an inrush of guilt. "So that means we'll all fail the bandaging test."

"I'm glad you can joke about it," Rani says, though Marie-Thérèse hadn't been. "You must be feeling better." Rani regards her open textbook. "I think I have to leave too. I heard about the bridges. Papa told Felicia. He always talks more with her. By the way, you need to be in the ward in eleven minutes. Better change. *Quickly!*"

"Rani—"

"Hurry. You know how she is about punctuality."

Marie-Thérèse does. They get graded on it in each Form of Report card. She pushes herself up and looks for clean cuffs. "Why don't you think about it for a few more days? Not much can happen in that time. Maybe…maybe there'll be some unexpected resolution."

"I hope so. We're so close to finishing! Why did it have to happen *now*?"

"Or at all."

"*Oui.* This is awful."

Marie-Thérèse slips clean cuffs over her uniform sleeves and ties a fresh apron over the skirt while Rani names everyone who is leaving.

"Margaux should stay," Marie-Thérèse says. "It might be safer here. She's from Noyen. That's where Germany wants to go, isn't it?"

"I wouldn't know."

"I'm sorry. I didn't mean to imply—"

"It's all right. *Go!* Wait, don't forget your cap!"

She's relieved to find Julia on ward duty that night. The Flemish girl's efficiency and good will has made her everyone's favorite as a ward-duty partner. That night the two student-nurses are under the supervision of Sister Gauthier—Clara Gauthier, but "Sister" the title for a senior nurse at the clinic and in the city's hospitals. In her first year, Marie-Thérèse learned that using the title now, for a secular nurse, alludes to a time when nuns were the only nurses despite their having little or no training. Then, ministering to the diseased and dying was lowly work, which few, apart from the nuns, were willing to take on. In fact, a stigma was often attached, and the sister-nurses, in their heavy garb, were frequently shunned by the healthy.

Immersing her hands in a solution of methylated spirit containing five cc of tincture of iodine and then drying them with a sterile cloth, she recalls how Florence Nightingale changed everything by making nursing a secular vocation in its own right, with training and protocols and strict emphasis on sanitation. Before those reforms, the mortality rate in field hospitals was greater than on the battlefield during the Crimean War. Still, the title of "Sister" persisted. Marie-Thérèse has developed a great respect for those early sister-nurses. Poorly equipped as they were to handle complicated cases, they nonetheless offered what comforts, physical and spiritual, they could to people who might as well have been among a pariah class.

How strange, she thinks, that in both of her endeavors thus far, *hands* have been so important.

A thought causing her to glance up at the wall clock's minute hand, just rounding to the top. Silently, she walks to the bedside where Sister Gauthier is talking with Madame Heinbokel, a heavy woman whose festering right foot is bandaged. She'd stepped on a nail in her barn, and the throbbing pain is beating inside her "like a drum," she often says. Yet she usually strives for cheer. "And why not, mademoiselle, on holiday like this and treated like our own queen herself!" But every so often, her eyes shut in a quick wince.

"Does your foot feel any better this evening, Madame Hein-bokel?" Marie-Thérèse is using her calm and much-practiced nurse's voice.

"I'd be lying if I said so. I just told Sister I hope you're not planning to take it."

Marie-Thérèse glances in Sister Gauthier's direction, realizing too late that she just made a mistake. Dread settles in her stomach and her hands begin trembling. Distantly she hears Gauthier saying, "Of course we're not! What a thought. You'll be back feeding your chickens in no time, madame. And now Mademoiselle Hulbert is going to change your bandages. Soon you will feel much better."

Marie-Thérèse stiffens.

Explain.

No, first get what you need.

No. Explain first, and then get everything.

Marie-Thérèse! Here you are, having to remind yourself like some first-year.

"Madame," she says. "I will get the basin and fresh bandages. Then I am going to unwrap your foot and give it a little bath. After that I will dress it and wrap it back up—"

"Like pork in cabbage!"

"*Oui. Exactement!*"

"Will it hurt? Oh, of course it will. Just like this morning."

"Somewhat, madame. There will be some pain."

She returns with the items on a cart and helps the woman sit up. Then she maneuvers her so that both feet are dangling over the side. *Everything is physics.* She places a rubber pad on the bed, then unwinds the old bandage and lets it fall into a pail. *Never anything soiled on the floor.*

"It's hurting more!" Madame Heinbokel cries, her eyes squeezing shut.

"*Pardonnez-moi*, madame. You may lie back again."

Marie-Thérèse holds onto the woman's right leg as her patient leans back, and then she rests the ankle on the scalloped part of the basin's rim. The foot is puffy and swollen and a deep magenta color. The wound, just behind the large toe, is still frothed with pus and has a foul odor. Careful not to exhibit any sign that might be construed as disgust, she takes a vial of hydrogen peroxide solution from the cart and, with her left arm bracing the leg and holding a cloth at the heel, slowly pours the solution over the wound.

Madame Heinbokel gives a prolonged wail, causing others in the ward to regard them. She tells God that Mademoiselle Hulbert is trying to kill her.

"I'm afraid, madame, that you will live many more years to tend your chickens and pigs and vegetable garden. No eternal rest for you, at least not yet." She dries the foot with a sterile cloth, "bipps" the wound with the bismuth iodoform paste, and then applies the iodoform gauze with tongs before re-bandaging the foot reasonably well.

In the relative privacy of the nurses' office, Sister Gauthier critiques the interaction, beginning with the bandaging. Marie-Thérèse began from right to left, instead of just the opposite. It probably would hold all right, she adds, but Mademoiselle Hulbert must get it absolutely correct the next time.

"*Oui. Merci.*"

"The correct things: You were careful with the foot bath and did not have to change the bed linens with madame in the bed. Also, you made a joke at the right time, which is always beneficial. At another point you laughed and were cheerful in an appropriate way. And the wound dressing went well although when you first began to explain, you sounded stiff as a puppet. I, at least, heard fear in your voice. That must not happen. Nor should you glance at me in confusion or uncertainty if the patient can see you. Turn away if necessary and give me some indication of what you need to know. How many times must I remind you of this, Mademoiselle Hulbert? The patient is *always* hypersensitive to the least sign or tone that might indicate some terrible future we are trying to conceal from her. Later she will brood over it and work herself up. It does not help the healing but in fact hinders it."

At least, Marie-Thérèse tells herself, it's criticism. *"Oui,* Sister."

Sister Gauthier, a petite woman just over five feet tall, has been overcompensated with a basso profundo voice that often makes student-nurses quail in her presence, and laugh when not. Gauthier has to work to keep it in check, especially in the wards, where such a voice can frighten patients or, at the very least, wake and annoy them. "You did well, Mademoiselle Hulbert," she says now in her low rumble. "Write up your notes on Madame Heinbokel and then you and Julia go around the ward taking vital signs. Each of you observe the other. Leave Madame Du Lac to me, she remains in isolation. Also, Madame Deitlin. You two can observe me with her. The heart is weakening, the discrepancy between apical and peripheral pulse increasing. I may have to telephone Doctor Depage. In fact, I will, as a precaution.

"Oui, Sister."

"Then both of you see if you can talk awhile with Madame Prennet. She's been rather low."

Peripheral vision catches a flash of light somewhere. *Another bridge?*

"Heat lightning," Gauthier says. "Go on, now."

After she and Julia finish taking vital signs and noting results, they approach Madame Prennet's bed. The young woman's eyes are shut. The bones of her face lift her sallow skin, Marie-Thérèse observes, much as poles raise the canvas of a tent. Her breathing comes in long shallow breaths that alternate, irregularly, with shorter ones. The occipital bones hold pools of shadow. Marie-Thérèse and Julia stand at the bedside, watching the young woman breathe. They're about to leave the foot of the bed when Madame Prennet's eyelids began trembling and then open.

"Bonsoir, madame," Marie-Thérèse says. "How are you this evening?" But they know from the chart. The young woman's weight is in decline, her temperature low, her pulse weak. She has been diagnosed with cervical cancer.

Madame Prennet moves her head slowly from side to side on the pillow.

"Do you know what I did today, Madame Prennet?" Marie-Thérèse says. "This morning I went to the station and met the matron. She is just back from England and will visit you soon after your surgery."

Madame Prennet lets her eyes close again.

"Do you like flowers, madame?" Julia asks. "We will bring you some. There are roses and lilies in the back garden now."

Marie-Thérèse draws a breath before saying, slowly, "You have been waiting for tomorrow and now it is almost here. Time is like that, isn't it? Taking us to where we…need to be." She glances at Julia, who adds faint agreement.

"He did not come today."

"Doctor Depage?" Marie-Thérèse says. "He had several surgeries today, but you will see him tomorrow. He's an excellent doctor, quite in demand. But tomorrow is your day. You will see him then."

"My husband, Michiel."

"Ah! Your husband!" A waiter in a café, she recalls. "Possibly he was asked to work longer today."

"Is it a holiday? I have lost track of the days."

Marie-Thérèse's upper teeth clamp her lower lip.

Julia rescues her. "Madame, the weather has been very warm. Warm and humid. People do not wish to be inside. The cafés are full."

"That is so," Marie-Thérèse adds and goes into a story about the matron's two dogs, a topic Madame Prennet usually enjoys, but tonight she only stares into the distance as Marie-Thérèse describes how they begged for tidbits at each café they passed.

"What color are they?" Madame Prennet finally says.

"Well, you know Jackie. The big one. He's gray with some white. Donnie, the shepherd mix, has a white chest and tail and black tips on his ears."

"The lilies," Madame Prennet whispers.

"Yellow as butter," Julia says. "We will bring you some."

This isn't such a good idea, Marie-Thérèse thinks, unless they pick stems with many buds. The blooms of these lilies last one day and one day only, withering by day's end. "Or roses!" she adds with enthusiasm.

"*Merci.* You are very kind, but I am tired now."

In the nurses' office, the two students look at one another. "We can't predict," Marie-Thérèse says.

"But is she even strong enough for surgery?"

Echoing her own thoughts. "If anyone can save her, it's Doctor Depage."

Still, *cancer.* Photographs in textbooks depict cancer tumors as malformed masses feeding upon the body's clarity and order. Yet that parasitic chaos must have its own kind of order, if one could call it that. Its own impulse to be. Marie-Thérèse says a swift prayer that Doctor Depage will be able to excise the darkness and draw Madame Prennet back from the edge, as he has so many others.

A waterfall of thought, and a chill, keep her awake too long. She decides to resort to her old strategy at the Académie and soak her hands in warm water for a few minutes. But just as she turns on the lavatory light, someone grips her ankle. Shock rampages through her at the sight of Charlotte lying on the hexagonal tiles. Charlotte in nightclothes, her faded brown plait half undone.

Words emerge too fast, too alarmed as she leans forward to touch the woman's shoulder. "Miss Charlotte! Are you hurt?"

Charlotte smiles without turning her head. "Get it for me, dearie, won't you? Such a love you are. I'll stay right here and wait. Otherwise, you can't go anywhere."

"I must get help for you. Please let go."

"Look what I have!" The woman opens her free hand, displaying several coins.

And then Marie-Thérèse understands. "I'm sorry, but I don't have the key. Let me help you back to your room."

"I don't have the *key*," Charlotte mimics. "I know that! But you can get it. If you don't, I'll tell on you. I'll say you gave it to me and you won't get a sou." The whites of the woman's eyes are stained pink.

"You must be here for a bath, Miss Charlotte, aren't you? A warm bath! Let me draw it. There'll be lots of hot water now."

Charlotte twists around to clamp her free hand around Marie-Thérèse's other ankle. Coins scatter over the tiles.

"Just let me fill the tub, Miss Charlotte, and you'll see how nice the water is. It'll be so warm and soothing, and you may take as long as you like. And while you bathe, I'll get someone to open the cupboard." Marie-Thérèse goes on and on about the warm water, nearly hypnotizing herself despite the tremors still racing through her.

Charlotte finally loosens her grip. Resisting the urge to pull away and run, Marie-Thérèse inserts the plug and turns the taps on full force. After helping Charlotte into the tub, she rushes across the hall and knocks on the nearest door. "Get Matron!"

"*She* gave it to me, that one," Charlotte tells her. "She's very naughty, Edith. And she lies. Dismiss her." But the matron has seen the coins on the tiles.

Much later, Marie-Thérèse will remember this night coming at the end of a long and even terrible day, the first, really, of the war. She will remember the matron's nod, the unspoken *well done*, and Charlotte's sly smile and the brief silky warmth of bathwater on her own cold fingers, and how she and Rani talked nearly into morning, she not wanting sleep, finally. Only the words in the dark and the nearness of her friend.

FRIGHTFULNESS

The day is blue and white, with a strong wind from the southeast that turns the barley field at the Arit farm into a sea of green waves. The wind and rippling field and copse of rounded trees in the distance, which always reminds ten-year-old Elli Arit of broccoli crowns, make the previous night's strangeness seem nothing more than a fading dream. Then, there were flashes and thunderous explosions that drove her from the room she shared with her two younger sisters. Her parents were awake and whispering in their bedroom. The holy candle on the bureau threw flickers of shadow and light. It wasn't burned often, only on feast days of the saints and during storms. So Elli thought that what she'd been hearing was a thunderstorm in the near distance.

Her mother, holding her awhile, confirmed this. "Go back to sleep now." Elli returned to the tiny room where her two sisters were both breathing deeply. She lay down on her bed and waited for rain that didn't come. It had not rained in some time. Rain would be good. But the air outside her open window was still, not a wisp to disturb the room's humid warmth, and no sudden breeze heralding an impending storm. She thought it must be somewhere near Liège, where she and her family go on market days. If so, it seemed to want to stay there. The booming went on and on, a thudding she sometimes felt at her breastbone. Flashes gave quivering light to the ceiling and one wall. Her three-year-old sister, Margot, woke once, and Elli whispered that it was just a storm. Five-year-old Janine did not wake until morning. Everything was quiet then.

Now the wind shifts, and the waves rushing over the barley field change course. Some acrid smell wends its way through otherwise pure air. When she turns, she sees black smoke smudging the sky. Liège is that way. She thinks they must be burning something.

But the ewes and lambs in their enclosure are not bothered. Nor the black-and-white speckled hens pecking at grass and earth, sometimes plopping down and fluffing their feathers in the dust. Three of them run toward her.

"Bonjour, mesdames!" she tells them. "And where did you hide your treasures today, may I ask? Where must we go searching on this fine day?"

The three, squawking and clucking, run off in another direction. Such funny creatures! They always put her in a good humor, and for a while she forgets about the smoke to the east and the occasional taste of ash in the air.

That morning she and Janine collect eggs, refill water pans and buckets, and feed and water the rabbits in their hutch after raking out the dirty straw and replacing it with fresh and fragrant golden straw. Then after helping their mother wash buckets, pans, and funnels in the dairy, they're free to wade in the nearby stream flowing through the grove of trees at the edge of their farm. Little Margot naps while Madame Arit darns stockings and alters the school clothing the two older girls will soon be wearing.

At the stream, Elli and Janine dangle their feet in shallow water as they eat their *petite dejeuner* of cheese, bread, and apples. Beech trees, with their thousands of serrated leaves, transmute the day's light into a tranquil lagoon green. There's a breeze, high up in the trees, but down near the water the air is still and warm and humming with the drone of a bee now and then, or a fly finding its way through the green caverns. The low stream meanders through small stones and offers only a quiet burble where it separates around a larger stone, then knits itself whole and slides on. Somewhere above the beeches, a hawk gives its piercing, high *eeeeeee!* Nearer to the girls, a cicada needles away with regularity, making Elli drowsy as she stares at a patch of vegetation growing in silt. Would it taste like lettuce? Or a stalk of timothy? The patch blurs into an undefined shape, glowing at its edges. Then heavy eyelids close until Janine pulls at her arm, wanting to wade. Holding hands and stepping in moist sand where they can, they walk upstream to the hollowed-out place where one bank rises a bit. This is their playhouse. It faces a small pool formed by piled-up branches and two tree trunks lying in a V. Minnows dart back and forth in their amber few inches as if one creature. Above the brown minnows, a water spider skims the surface in jerky fits and starts to no seeming purpose, which makes the girls laugh. When the slant of sunlight through the beeches shifts to the west, Elli says they need to go home.

They dry their feet and put on wooden shoes and are at the wood's edge when they hear screaming. Then gunshots, shattering glass, and the bleating and squawking of animals. For a few blind seconds, Elli can't move. Then her sight clears. Before them, the barley field is still, the low sun bronzing everything except the smoke rising from their house and barn and sheds.

Bursts of gunshot come again, sometimes brief, sometimes lengthy. Elli lifts Janine and runs back through the woods to the stream and then upstream, slipping on stones. Finding the hollowed-out place, she heaves Janine down into it. The child, a mute sack in her arms a minute before, wrinkles her face, gathering herself. Elli drops to her knees and covers her sister's mouth. "*Non, ma petite soeur! Non!* We must be quiet as fish now."

The little girl's face is scarlet and every muscle in her body taut, but then she goes limp. Elli is a crouched statue, listening. Over the stream's burble she can still hear the strange clattering that must be gunfire. She grips each of her shoulders, crossing her arms over the wildness within.

It's night when Elli finally leaves Janine deep in the playhouse under the bank, covered with grasses and branches. She's told her not to move, not to make any sound. Above all, stay there. Elli will come back for her. With misgivings, Elli crawls through the barley field toward their farmhouse. By moonlight she can make out its shape, but the small barn, the coop, hutch, and other sheds are not there. Creeping closer, she sees that these are still burning, the wood and straw just heaps of red coals and an occasional shoot of flame.

She lies in the field awhile, her heart beating against the cool earth, but finally makes herself crawl forward again to the edge of the farmyard. Their chickens lie scattered everywhere, and the sheep and lambs in what had been their enclosure. The bodies of their rabbits are everywhere as well, two even in the front yard. In the house, piled-up furniture is still burning. She recognizes part of a chair back and the headboard of her bed. Also, a drawer from the heavy bureau that had been in her parents' bedroom. She sees the gleam of broken crockery on the stone floor. And in the dim light of the low fire, she sees her mother's body and Margot's, her mother half covering the child.

"Maman," Elli whispers, kneeling over the bodies. "*Maman?*"

When she looks more closely, she sees blood soaking Margot's smock and her mother's dress. Nearby are shards of broken wine bottles. The spilled wine looks like blood. She quietly calls her father's name but hears only the soft working away of the fire.

Her shoes crunch broken glass in the yard and then she is running toward their neighbors' house. But at the Sabourin farm, it's much the same—slaughtered animals on the periphery, objects burning inside the stone house, glass and broken crockery everywhere, inside and out, and barn and sheds still burning. But there's something more. A terrible smell she doesn't recognize.

Each house on the way to the village, the same, and everything that can burn, in the village, is either burning or already in ash. Bodies lie in the village square, all men, it seems, their bloody clothing black in the moonlight. And again, smashed beer bottles, wine bottles, windows, plates and cups everywhere. A rocking chair, intact, moves back and forth on its runners as if someone has just risen from it. She calls her father's name. The night breeze against her forearms is warm.

She goes closer to the pile and calls again.

Nothing. But still she stands there listening. The silence has an eerie thrum, as of distant voices.

No, not voices. Singing.

A German song she's heard before, sung by a quartet of farmers at a harvest festival. Someone played an accordion. Afterward, applause, and tankards of beer passed to the singers. Accompanying the voices this time is not an accordion but hoofbeats. She glances around for somewhere to hide. Except for the stone church, the village is all but flattened. She's afraid of being trapped in the church, so she runs between mounds of burning debris, then through a pasture before throwing herself down in field grasses. The singing is closer. She doesn't know whether to run again or to remain still. If she runs, they might see her and fire their guns. If she stays, she might be trampled by the horses trotting right over her. Only she wouldn't be. She'd be shot like a rabbit. The pulse in her throat is so forceful she's afraid they will hear it. Digging her fingers into the earth, she tries to stop shaking so hard. A storm is roaring through her and for a while there's only that until pops of gunfire break through the inner thunder.

Sparks sift down into the dry field grasses around her. A nearby clump catches fire, the patch of flame uncurling from its dark center. Soon a tongue of it will reach her sleeve. From the burned village come shouts and gunfire.

She crawls forward a few feet, pauses, then crawls forward again. To either side is only rough pasture. *Papa, what should I do?*

She can almost hear him saying, *Stay put, don't move a finger,* but this seems an impossible task because the need to run is awful. She does move her fingers, anchoring them more deeply. But when horse soldiers lope by just several meters behind her, she has to clench her teeth and hold back a scream. How can they not see her there, in the light from the burning pasture?

Later she will think that the fire saved her, the cavalry staying to one side of it, their eyes focusing ahead, to the next house, the next village, while foot soldiers, tired of shooting at bodies and mounds of fire, leave singing.

Moving stealthily back to her farmhouse seems to take hours. There, one curtain still hangs at a window from which all the glass had been shot out. She pulls the curtain down and covers the bodies of her mother and youngest sister. Where the furniture had been piled is smoking ash now. Moonlight reveals a small wheel of cheese on the floor, partially covered by broken glass. She picks it up and ties it in her shawl. Out in the yard a humped shadow amid the carnage is just visible. The shadow doesn't move when she approaches, so she thinks it must be dead too, whatever it is. Putting out her hand to touch it, she feels soft rabbit fur, the body warm.

Carrying both cheese and the rabbit close, she crosses the barley field and makes it into the woods. There she drops down and sleeps until something wakes her. Straining to identify the sound, she lies still, staring upward at sunlight piercing a veil of fog—or smoke—and forming rays. Soon it's quiet again.

"Papa?" she whispers.

But it's only the rabbit, moving about in old leaves, under a canopy of fern. Fear draining away leaves her weak. Her eyelids want to close again. But then she's running.

Their playhouse is empty, the branches and grasses scattered, Janine's indentation still there in the sand. The scene darkens and she has to sit down until the whirling stops. When she can focus again, she surveys the surrounding undergrowth and foliage. Nothing looks trampled.

"Janine!"

They found her. They must have. On the road when she came looking for me.

She hurries back through woods to the barley field. There's no sound except for chirping birds and a hawk's distant cry.

Clouds are moving in and the air feels heavier. Barley stems sway, darkening under cloud cover, then brightening again. A shape catches Elli's eye. She plunges forward through the tall barley stems.

Janine is standing in the field, all but hidden by the barley.

Elli moves one hand before Janine's unblinking eyes. "Janine! Can you not *see* me?"

It's not like her to be so still, so mute, and this frightens Elli more than if her sister were screaming and throwing herself about. And the stiffened little body seems heavier than normal.

The soldiers?

Or did she go to the house?

Pain twists its way down through her at the latter thought. Janine, looking for her, going to the house and seeing what Elli saw. She holds on to the little girl more tightly. Yesterday at this time nothing had yet happened. Her mother and sister and father had been alive, and their animals, and the day had been a summer day, warmer than usual, and there'd been no rain clouds.

Elli's teeth bang together as she says, "We will find someone, Janine. Someone who will help us." An instant's vision comes of her mother and father and Margot the way they had been just yesterday. She allows this picture for a moment, but then it hurts almost as badly as the other.

She leads Janine back to the stream and there tries to feed her some cheese, but Janine will not open her mouth. Elli wets the girl's lips with stream water and tries again.

"Janine, please! Maman would want you to eat this. You must live. For her and for Papa too. And for me."

She tries again, and this time the girl's mouth opens enough for Elli to poke in a bit of cheese. "Now swallow."

The little girl, staring straight ahead, does, and Elli cries out, again too loudly, "You can hear!" Looking at Janine more closely, she sees no bruises, no cuts, no marks of any kind. It gives her hope.

Elli has been to Liège on market days but knows, from the still-rising smoke in that direction, that they cannot go there now. Her mother's sister, their aunt Louise, lives near Louvain to the west, but Elli has never been there. Nor does she know how far it is. The town is near Brussels, her mother once said, where the king and queen live. In a picture book, its grand cobbled square and buildings looked like fairy-tale castles.

Papa, what should I do?

She listens for his voice, but there is only the wind now, high in the trees, and leaves making their water-sound.

She ties Janine's shawl more tightly around her shoulders. "I think we will try to find Aunt Louise. We will follow the sun westward and surely there will be someone to help us along the way. All right?"

Janine is staring at the stream water, the same shallow spread of amber as the day before, the same quiet music.

"Come!"

The little girl doesn't move.

"Janine, I can't carry you all that way. You're too heavy. You're a big girl now, and we must go."

Still, Janine will not move. Elli picks her up, settles her weight on her hipbone, and begins walking. Janine's shoes catch on undergrowth and fall off. Elli has to stop again and again. Finally, she puts them in the shawl tied around her waist, picks Janine up again, and goes on, the little girl's head tucked under Elli's chin, her thumb in her mouth.

Field gives way to field, most separated by hedgerows or streamlets. By late afternoon Elli comes to a narrow road that leads past burned cottages and houses. Janine's eyes are closed, and Elli has to keep hefting the little girl up. She seems far heavier now. The low rays of the sun are in Elli's eyes, and the countryside all around is settling into its dusty golden light. Her back aches. Her head aches. Every so often she stops to listen.

In an orchard she picks windfall apples and fills her shawl. Nearby farm buildings have been burned, though a shed remains partly upright. She is afraid to peer into it, but the rose-colored horizon and first evening star hanging above it tell her she must. Inside, there are only hay-strewn floorboards, a wooden wheelbarrow, one side gouged by bullets, and a metal bucket lying on its side. It, too, has been shot at, but the holes are near the top. After putting some straw in the wheelbarrow, she places Janine in it and covers her with her shawl. Then she takes the bucket into the farmyard. Treading between bodies of chickens and ducks, she tries not to look at them. At the well, she hesitates, but the water, when drawn, smells pure.

Janine frets in the wheelbarrow; she wants Elli instead. So

they lie behind it, straw heaped over them. Long after Janine falls asleep, Elli is still awake, listening to crickets and frogs and occasional explosive bursts somewhere that shake their way through the earth and make the top of the shed waver a little, against the distant stars. If they come, she tells herself, she will take Janine out into the orchard, and they'll hide behind the widest tree. But if they set fire to the orchard, they will have to run somewhere. She stays awake as long as she can, listening, until dozing gives way to true sleep.

At first light she piles more straw in the wheelbarrow, puts Janine in it, and sets off again after finding a sack of grain in the shed and scattering it for the two hens who wakened her, clucking. As the day clouds up, a mist begins falling. By midday it's a straight-down rain that soaks Elli's hair, the straw in the wheelbarrow, Janine, and their shawls. The wheelbarrow's metal wheel squeaks and makes a wavering trail in the road's mud. She walks on, Janine's face to one side on the wet straw, her thumb in her mouth, her eyes closed.

Holy Mary, Mother of God…

The prayer comes unbidden but she rejects it. Mary did not help. The candle did not help.

Sometime later she lowers the handles of the wheelbarrow and stoops alongside it, shivering, her head lowered in the rain. Above her, Janine is silent. When a hand touches her shoulder, Elli is instantly awake but unable to say a word.

SHRECKLICHKEIT

Are we holding them off?"

For the past week Marie-Thérèse has been hearing mortar shelling at night and often throughout the day, percussive blasts much like thunder, from the direction of the fortified cities of Liège, Namur, and Mons—to the east, southeast, and south.

The gardener finishes filling the pigeons' water trays. "They take revenge."

"But why? Everyone was saying they'd come through peacefully."

"Resistance."

"Ours, you mean?"

He makes his customary gesture when agitated, his right hand slashing the air horizontally, and says no more.

What he wouldn't tell her she soon learns from the newspapers. Whole villages leveled. Civilians killed. Livestock either stolen or killed. Barns and houses and cottages burned. For any resistance the invaders encountered, civilians were made to pay with their lives whether or not they had anything to do with it. The invading Germans, the newspaper articles state, were afraid of *franc-tireurs*—sharpshooters, snipers. At the first shout of *They're shooting!* machine guns were turned upon villagers. Incendiary bombs thrown into houses and cottages. And men dragged away, women and children too, and then everyone shot. These were not random shootings and bombings by panicked soldiers, according to the articles, but rather a campaign of terror designed to undermine the country's will. The plan, it was said, had a name: *schrecklichkeit*—"frightfulness."

It horrifies her yet she cannot quite believe it. Possibly the newspapers are exaggerating in order to inflame nationalistic passion and the will to fight. But in the days following the invasion, Brussels begins filling with refugees from the countryside—mothers with children and babies, old men, old women, but few younger men in the slow processions. Sometimes there are farm carts and goats and chickens in crates and wheelbarrows and handcarts with belongings in them amid the refugees trudging along on foot, carrying bundles, their expressions impassive until one of them is questioned by a reporter or townsperson. Then tears, sometimes, even weeping, and words garbled by emotion. At times, though, a refugee will manage to tell the most terrible story in a dispassionate and dignified voice. Story after story, and each one corroborating the next, and these stories making their way into newsprint day after day. The few young men among the refugees often ask how they can join the Belgian fighters. Where do I need to go? Direct me, please.

But it isn't until Marie-Thérèse begins hearing the stories firsthand in the wards that she's convinced.

There is Madame Kendahl, with burned hands, forearms, feet, and legs. Her hair has been singed off, and her scalp needs to be dressed as well. It's the first time Marie-Thérèse has ever seen such severe burns, the skin completely gone in places and the underlying tissue seeping fluids. When she first observed that, her stomach writhed with shock, but with Julia's help, she was able to dress the oozing flesh and give Madame Kendahl the replacement fluids she needed. Before the pain medication and sedative took effect, the woman told them what had happened. Soldiers shot her son and pushed her back into her burning house and closed the door. When she tried to leave, thinking they'd gone, they shot at her. They were drunk, she said. They were not like proper soldiers at all, and their aim was bad. There was a little cistern in a back room and she hid there until the following day. The pain was so terrible by then she could only lie in a bloodied pond, amid the bodies of her ducks. By the grace of God, someone found her and got her to the clinic, she didn't know how because she was unconscious most of the time, thanks be to God. Maybe an angel.

In the next days, Marie-Thérèse tries to find words to calm, if not cheer, the burned woman. "Madame, do you see the sparrow right by your window? See? On that branch?"

The woman doesn't bother turning her bandaged head. Her only interests are in retelling her story and sipping the broth Marie-Thérèse spoon-feeds her. If she likes it, she'll shut her eyes after the first taste, savoring it.

The gruesome burns still have the power to shock, and while dressing them Marie-Thérèse always recalls her mother's words about wounds and death. Yet does this work differ so very much from dancing in a ballet such as *Swan Lake*? Or *Coppelia*? In both, death plays a major part, but death transmuted into art and so…transcended? While here she's in the essence, the bedrock of life itself. It doesn't seem right to love one and disdain the other, does it? In time the shock of dressing the burns eases, and she begins looking forward to sitting with the woman and describing what her new cottage will be like, right down to the curtains and tablecloths. If Madame Kendahl dies, the words will hardly matter. And if she lives, well, new curtains and tablecloths are possible, no? The words themselves become a kind of dressing.

But then, her potato debacle, as she will later refer to it. Monsieur Pierre Durée is a farmer in his seventies, his frame narrow and still lumped with muscle. He too has been burned out, he narrowly escaping with his life. His burns, however, are not as severe as Madame Kendahl's, and so Marie-Thérèse approaches his bed with some confidence. While dressing his forearms and hands, she tells him that he'll be healed in time to harvest his potatoes.

Monsieur Durée all but levitates. "Don't talk to me about potatoes! I have no damn potatoes. Why didn't they shoot me too? Go away! Let me die!"

Others in the ward are watching. She begs the man's pardon but then can't think of any helpful words. There's spittle on his lips. His eyes are reddened and maniacal. Soon he's shouting again. His potatoes were all trampled into a pulp, his farm burned to nothing, his animals slain or stolen. Why did they do that? What did I do to them? Are they mad? And still she's incapable of uttering a single word.

Then Sister Depage is there, saying they're all so sorry his potato crop was ruined and his farm burned down and his animals killed. Those were the acts of madmen. On the other hand, everyone at the clinic is overjoyed that he's alive, and they can help him now. Marie-Thérèse inwardly cringes, waiting for the next eruption. But the old farmer is lying there, listening with the docility of a sweet child as Sister Depage examines his arms and hands and finishes dressing the burns. And all the while, she talks about farming. Types of cheese. Dairy cows. Different varieties of potatoes. Sister Depage, a society lady and the wife of Doctor Depage. Without any difficulty at all she takes his temperature. She lets her hand remain on his brow for a while. When he closes his eyes, she motions for Marie-Thérèse to follow her.

Julia and Rani glance up as she passes. Gauthier gives her a caustic look as if to say Marie-Thérèse has just disappointed the entire world.

In the nurses' office Sister Depage invites her to be seated. Then she pulls up a chair, quite close. Marie-Thérèse prepares herself for dismissal.

"You could not have known about his destroyed potato field, mademoiselle," she begins. "And you were correct in begging his pardon. But then...you froze. You didn't keep talking. They want acknowledgment. That was your mistake, the silence, not the words. You froze, which left a void for him to fill with rage. He was taking it out on you. At that moment you were the enemy."

"At least I may have served some useful purpose, then."

"Oh, I can assure you, we've all had our potato debacles!" Sister Depage gives a quick, wry smile.

Marie-Thérèse thinks her a beautiful woman, in a fine understated way. Her hair, brunette and wavy, is combed back and upward and pinned under her cap. The nose has an elegant curve. There's a sweet gaiety about her. And also, intelligence. As a first-year, Marie-Thérèse was astounded to learn that she was the wife of the clinic's famous director and surgeon. She might have chosen instead a life of leisure at the top echelon of society. Yet there she was, working alongside students.

"I'm afraid," Marie-Thérèse begins, "that I may not be suited, Sister. That I made a mistake in coming here."

"Oh heavens. If I told you how often I felt that way when I was a student nurse, and even as a senior nurse, you wouldn't believe it."

Madame Depage embarks on a story she has obviously told many times, to no diminishment of enjoyment. Once, as a younger nurse, she couldn't for the life of her get to a vein in a woman's arm—not just any woman's, but a titled woman and a friend. In retaliation the woman doused her with water flung from a glass and called her a dunce. "I was so angry I wanted to fling something right back at her. Water was dripping from my hair and face and, imagining what I must look like, standing there, mouth agape, I finally laughed. Then she was laughing too, and you know how sometimes laughter spirals out of control and becomes a force all its own? And so there we were, the two of us, laughing like crazed hyenas."

"Did you ever get to that vein?"

"I had to try the other arm, and it all took a while, but yes. I did." Again, the quick wry smile.

"Were you still friends afterward?"

"Of course! She loved having us to dinner so she could glory in the retelling of that momentous occasion. And garner all kinds of sympathy. Monsieur Depage and I were useful guests. So you see, Mademoiselle Hulbert, we all have had our potato debacles. Now go back and continue your work. You will make a fine nurse one day. I see it in you."

A fine nurse.

Resurrected, Marie-Thérèse returns to the ward and in the relief of the moment has an idea.

Two days later, off duty and not in uniform, as stipulated,

she's holding Donnie and walking toward Monsieur Durée's bed. Donnie appears to be smiling, his tongue lolling out, his eyes lively.

"Someone is here to visit you, monsieur. His name is Donnie." The farmer stares as tears follow channels and fall to the pillow. "Do you wish me to leave, monsieur?"

With bandaged hand, he reaches toward the dog. "Is he real?"

"Oh yes!" She moves closer. "And right now, he's quite interested in jumping all over your bed. So, I must hang on to him."

With her free hand she blots the man's wet temples, his face, and dripping nose. Donnie's tail thumps against her waist.

"He is real," the old man whispers, stroking the fur between the dog's alert ears.

"*Oui*, monsieur."

They talk about a dog he once had who looked something like Donnie. Then he goes on to say that his sheepdog, Sophie, is missing. He hopes she isn't dead. It's hard for him to say the word.

"Tell me about her, please. What is she like?" Her pulse and heartbeat quicken. But to her surprise, he speaks calmly, describing Sophie's intelligence, charm, and devotion. And all the while, he pets Donnie. "Bring him again," he finally says.

"I will, Monsieur Durée. Please rest now."

But Donnie's charm fails to work any magic with a mute child admitted to the clinic on the day, a Monday, when Belgium's governing officials abandoned Brussels, a day ominous in implication. All the Belgian flags were lowered from flagpoles and taken from buildings. The festive bouquets tied to lampposts and house fronts and vehicles were also removed. It was the gardener who brought in the child and her sister, conveying them from the countryside in the Landaulet.

When Marie-Thérèse stands alongside the little girl's bed, holding Donnie for her to see, the child seems in a trance-like state.

"He's very sweet," Marie-Thérèse says. "His name is Donnie.

You might want to play in the garden with him sometime soon. He loves to play and will return sticks if you toss them." The dog yawns, showing black gums and lips shiny as licorice. His tail thumps.

The child's skin is a healthy pink, with no scarring or contusions anywhere, and Marie-Thérèse has checked under the brown hair as well, hair soft as goose down once they'd cut out the tangles and washed it. Yet the skin has a waxen quality, as if the little girl were sealed over by some substance. Doctor Depage hadn't commented on it, saying only that she'd been traumatized and should be in a larger hospital where specialists might treat her. But as there were only so many beds and so many doctors, all of whom were now engaged in caring for the many wounded Belgian, French, and British soldiers, the child needed to remain at the clinic for the time being. "Do what you can for her. One never knows just what will work in these cases, difficult at best, but she's young, which is in her favor." Then the doctor left to take charge of the Belgian army's casualty stations.

Doing what they could for the girl—whose name, they learn from her sister, is Janine—consists of feeding and washing her, helping her to the lavatory, and taking her into the garden to watch the dogs play and also to see the pigeons. The gardener shows her Max, who brought word of the two children taken in by an old woman with pigeons of her own. In his abbreviated way, the gardener later reveals a few things about the woman. When a company of infantry passed her small holding, they kept to fields, moving fast, and didn't notice the house set among trees. But by then she'd gotten herself and her pigeons up into one of the oaks deeper in the forest. There they waited, with food and water and her drawn-up rope ladder, on a small platform made of a few inconspicuous boards. Who had helped her build such a platform ahead of time?

The gardener smiles.

"When you went out for the children," Marie-Thérèse says, "the soldiers might have killed you. How did you manage to avoid them?" He smiles again, this time revealing crumbling teeth usually kept concealed.

The pigeons, of course. Such small things. The gardener's rare smile. Madame Kendahl's appreciation for her soup, Monsieur Durée's extended hand, the platform in the tree, and a child pushing a wheelbarrow. These offer hope. And tamp down, for a time anyway, outrage.

VEIN

Rani isn't in their room. It frightens Marie-Thérèse, as always lately when Rani isn't there when normally she would be. A knock comes as she's changing into her nightgown.

"Marie-Thérèse!" Liese says through the door. "Matron needs you in the military ward. *Right now.*"

"Is Rani there?"

"We all are. Hurry."

The twelve-bed ward is filled with soldiers and not one of them asleep, in the general pandemonium of moaning and cursing. Nurses are at beds or rushing back and forth, carrying basins or pushing carts of supplies. Marie-Thérèse sees Rani at the far end of the ward, and her heart settles.

"That one," the matron indicates. "Vital signs."

Private Lafave, she notes on his chart, and then attempts to check his apical pulse rate, but at her touch, he whips his head from side to side. Soon he's shouting, "Richard! Richard!" His eyes are open, yet he seems to be dreaming. She takes a basin and cloth from a cart and, sitting alongside him, holds the cloth to his forehead and tells him that he's in Brussels, in a small hospital. He's safe now. There are no German soldiers in the hospital. She's a nurse and will stay with him awhile. She takes his right hand and finds the peripheral pulse. It's racing. "You are safe now, Private Lafave. Here you are safe." The young man's body shakes in spasms. "Where is he? Where's Richard?"

"I will ask in the ward about him, monsieur, only now you must rest. It's nighttime and time to rest. But you are safe." She lowers his hand to the bed linen. "See? You're in a bed with clean linen. You are safe now. Monsieur? Can you hear me? I am Mademoiselle Marie-Thérèse, a nurse. You are not alone."

Sudden inexplicable pain in her hand causes her to look

down. The top of the hand just behind the knuckles is darkening where the man's fierce grip has broken at least one vein. "Monsieur? Are you listening? You are safe here. You are not alone."

A sister arrives with a sedative. The man's pulse soon slows. His eyelids close, and his body relaxes. Marie-Thérèse slips her hand from his and stands. It surprises her that she's shaking so hard and her legs are so weak.

Hours later, the ward is finally quiet.

At another general assembly in the lecture hall, the matron tells them that the city of Louvain, fifteen kilometers to the east, has fallen to the German army. Its great cathedral and famous university, with its vast collection of books and medieval manuscripts, were severely damaged in the shelling. The matron, her posture as erect as always, her hair in its upswept coil, doesn't betray emotion until the word *medieval* and the lengthy pause after its first syllable.

"They will be here," she goes on, "tomorrow morning. My dear students and sisters, we must allow no prejudice. We will care for the wounded and sick, and lectures will continue according to schedule whenever possible. There will be no disparagements, no insults overt or covert. To do so is beneath our calling and our pledge as nurses. It would also be extremely dangerous for all of us here at the school and clinic and possibly for all the residents on this street. We will simply do our work.

"However, there is the matter of our own wounded. Tonight, they all will be gone. I am omitting particulars in this regard because the less you know, the better it will be for you if you are questioned, as you probably will be. Therefore, I cannot tell you anything more. Do you have any questions?"

Liese raises her hand. "Do you mean to say, Matron, that we must *lie* to the Germans? Won't that anger them?"

"No, you must *not* lie. You will say only that there are no Belgian, French, or English soldiers here. And that will be the truth."

"What if they ask if there ever were wounded Belgians here?"

The matron looks down at the lectern, a minute sign of annoyance they all recognize. Then she raises her head. "You may say that there were wounded soldiers here, but they left before the German army arrived. That, too, will be the truth. As to where they have gone, or how, you cannot say because you know nothing about it. Again, the truth."

"But what if they don't believe us? What if they take us prisoner?"

"Mademoiselle Dueltgen, we do not need histrionics just now. If you speak sincerely and simply, they will believe you. My dear students, Sisters, and staff, now is the time, should you have any misgivings whatsoever, to let me know if you wish to leave. Trains are still arriving and departing. However, the German commander may soon halt all civilian train travel to and from Brussels, at least for a while. So, please, think carefully in this next hour."

She doesn't mention Liese by name but looks directly at her.

Now is the time if you have any misgivings…

In the tram, raised voices chant, "Down with Germans!"—forming a counterpoint to the matron's words. Far from being cowed by the German strategy of "frightfulness," Marie-Thérèse has been noticing, townspeople are becoming emboldened, even to the point of vandalizing German-owned businesses and banks. They've also erected a barricade of barbed wire and heaped-up furniture and metal objects around the city, as if such flimsy obstacles could stop a German army. And that day in the ward, a second-year named Helene addressed Rani, saying, "You're probably on their side, aren't you? Maybe you can take care of them, then."

Sister Gauthier, overhearing, burst out, "We are not taking *sides* in this clinic. Do you understand? If you refuse to nurse anyone here, mademoiselle, you will have to leave."

Helene's sullen expression didn't change, but Gauthier bullied her into finally responding with a "Yes, Sister. *Pardonnez-*

moi." Marie-Thérèse saw how Helene's heart wasn't in it. Yet her ire was understandable. Newspapers have been urging every citizen to resist the invaders in subtle ways. Don't cooperate! Work slowly, not fast. Do what you can to thwart them. Drive your trams slowly. Hand over stamps or vegetables slowly. Don't give them the best cuts of meat; save it for Belgians. If they want a haircut, give them a bad haircut. Hide wounded Belgian soldiers. Don't allow them to be taken prisoners of war. *Strength in unity* is our motto.

While she has dinner with her family that evening, Marie-Thérèse's father declares that such forms of resistance in the name of patriotism violate common sense. He predicts further reprisals and possibly even the loss of their beautiful city. "I've been thinking," Monsieur Hulbert continues, "that we should probably relocate to Rotterdam for a time."

The table is quiet. "You will eventually feel at home there, my dear," he tells his wife. "Rotterdam has a cultural life. As for me, my skill is portable. I've also been thinking that it might be best to sell this house."

Marie-Thérèse observes her father as he speaks, his light hair and eyes betraying him now as German. How many people has he helped, as an ophthalmologist? Hundreds—Belgians, Germans, Dutch, and even French families from across the border. It's not in him, she knows, to poorly treat any disease of the eye. Or fit anyone with an incorrect pair of lenses. Yet how will he be received in the Netherlands?

"Marie-Thérèse?"

"I was hoping to finish my studies, but I understand." Then, a torrent of words. Yes, they should go, but couldn't they rent the house or close it up and then return, but if they went, perhaps they should go soon, just lock the house up and leave, the German army is arriving tomorrow and...

"Marie-Thérèse," her mother says. "Slow down, please. It seems we cannot keep this house now. Someone has already broken several windows. Surely they will do much more damage to an unoccupied house."

"When did this happen?"

"Two nights ago," Monsieur Hulbert says. "We found stones on the floor in the library, and shattered glass. They might have done worse. Well, they did throw in a burning torch, but we were able to stamp it out."

Madame Hulbert dabs her eyes with her napkin as water trembles in their glasses. Overhead, crystal pendants faintly chime. The rumble lasts a few moments.

"They have a new mortar cannon," Monsieur Hulbert says. "That might be it. They say it can fire a shell weighing nearly a ton at a range of some eighteen hundred meters or more. Imagine a shell weighing that much going that far. Louvain had no chance against such shelling. And here we are, provoking them like children."

"Father," Jacques says. "I *must* join our forces."

Monsieur Hulbert moves knife and fork to one side of his plate. "My son, the army has retreated toward Antwerp. It's been routed, along with the British and French. In any case, at sixteen you are too young."

"But I can find our army. I can learn to fight!"

Willy, two years younger than his brother, wants to know if the Germans will fire that new cannon on Brussels.

"They say they won't if there is no resistance. It's possible they'll pass through and continue on."

"Then, Albrecht, should we sell our house? If all this is... temporary?"

"Because while it is possible, it is unlikely."

"Father—"

"No, Jacques. I will not allow it. You are too young to fight. You will be going nowhere except with us. You have no idea—"

"Are you saying that because you're *German*?"

"Jacques!" Madame Hulbert cries.

Jacques throws his napkin at his plate and rushes from the dining room. As Marie-Thérèse follows him upstairs, that afternoon's lecture on bullet wounds flies into her thoughts—the enfilade wound, the transverse, and so many others. He really has no idea, but then, how could he? "Jacques? May I come in?"

"You already are."

He's lying on the silk counterpane, knees raised, arms crossed, and his face set in a mold of antipathy. His collection of childhood books and model ships are still on display, the cutters and frigates flying the colors of Belgium.

She pulls his desk chair to the side of the bed and sits but doesn't know how to begin. Jacques won't look at her. "I know you want to help our country," she says finally. "Father and Maman know that too. It's honorable, Jacques."

"*They* don't want me to."

"It's not because Father is German, though. What you said hurt them very much."

"What he said hurt *me*. I'm not a child! *You will be going nowhere except with us.*"

"Yes, he said that, but he didn't mean that you are a child. He's afraid for our family now. He wants all of us to be together. He needs to know that each of us is safe."

"But you, *you* want to stay at your school…and he'll probably let you."

"I don't know."

"And if you stay, you'll be helping wounded German soldiers while I want to kill them. It doesn't make sense."

"You're right. Little, now, makes sense."

"I want to find our army…and the king. I am not a *child.*"

"No, you're not. But from what I've been reading, our army has broken apart and is simply…running away. Would you like to hear what I think you can do to help?"

"Go with them."

"Yes, but first help with the house here and then help them find a place in South Holland or wherever Papa decides will be best. Be a good older brother to Willy, who's terrified now. I know he's trying not to show it, Jacques, but he is. Our parents have so much to worry about, and if you leave, there'll be that too. Do you see how important you can be to them? What real help you can give? Besides, our army can do little now until more forces join it. More British. More French. It has to re-organize, and that's going to take time. Meanwhile, you can be helping our family on a...personal level."

"While you help wounded Germans on a personal level. What a loyal Belgian you are. They're *Huns*."

"I see that I can't talk to you now, dear brother. Will you do one thing for me, though?"

"No. What?"

"Just let me know before you go off on your own some-where if and when you decide to do that."

"So you can tell them."

"So I can say au revoir and give you a great huge embrace."

"You can do that now."

She does. "Oh, my dear brother, I think that you're sad and angry because you are, in part, German and Father is German and your sister and brother have German blood. Is that it? Is that why you're so angry? And want to prove your loyalty to our country?" Jacques leans forward, linking arms around his knees, and lowers his head. She holds his shoulder while he sobs.

On the drive back to the clinic, Marie-Thérèse and her father pass boys and young men smashing store windows with shovels and lengths of pipe. "I think you should come with us," he says. "It's going to be extremely dangerous here even if the German command decides to spare Brussels. And perhaps, to please your maman, you might take up the piano again if only for your own enjoyment. You were a good pianist and might even improve. And then, one day, if we return, possibly you can resume your nursing studies."

She senses that he must have planned those words. "When you were a medical student, Father, did your choice of profes-sion offend anyone?"

"No one was offended. But it was different for me. I had no other talent or ability. Also, medicine...well, it's considered an honorable profession for a man."

"Maman is ashamed of me, isn't she? She believes I threw away something valuable for something worthless."

"Well, your maman…she believes that art can heal too, in its way."

"Father, our matron has said that I'm quite good at nursing."

"I'm sure you are. But as you can see, it's getting bad here and will only become worse. I'm speaking of the citizenry. The German military may…*may*…treat us more civilly. If, that is, we subject ourselves to their orders."

"I will do as you say."

"I would like to think that it won't make you very unhappy."

Boys are standing around a bonfire at the center of an intersection, singing Belgium's national anthem as flames leap up in the warm night. Monsieur Hulbert stops, puts the car into reverse, and turns into a secondary street.

"Such bravado."

She's thinking of the matron, of having to tell her, and only glanced at the boys who are just being boys. The aching sadness of her Académie days has set in, that debilitating awareness of how something urgently and deeply hoped for is not to be.

"They should be at home," her father is saying, his voice unusually sharp. "Instead, there they are, treating it all as a national holiday. Idiots!"

In front of the nurses' row house, he tells her he'll telephone as soon as he settles matters and finds a buyer for the house. "Within the week, I hope. Meanwhile, speak to your matron and make arrangements, *ma chère*."

"*Oui*, Papa."

"I hope we won't need travel documents. That might slow everything."

It's awful, she thinks, to find some small comfort in those words. Her hand aches with a dull continuous pain and she remembers the soldier's crushing grip—and her mother's comment at dinner. "What happened to your *hand*?"

When she looked down at it, she was surprised to see that the entire top of her hand from wrist to knuckles had turned blue-gray.

"Oh, nothing much, Maman. A small mishap."

Rolls

Matron, my father wishes me to leave with the family. I can stay for only a few days longer. I'm terribly sorry." They are in the matron's office with the door closed.

"I'm sorry as well, mademoiselle."

"But in the meantime, I will do whatever you ask. Extra ward duty, whatever you need."

"*Merci.*"

The matron appears calm as always, but has her glance drifted to the side just a little before centering again? Marie-Thérèse thinks so. "*Pardonnez-moi, Matrone.* I did try."

"I know you must have. *Bien.* Return to your work now. Do what you can."

Walking back to her ward, Marie-Thérèse tells herself to be like that. Stoic. Accepting.

Later that morning word spreads through the clinic that Helene and two other student-nurses, both English girls, have left the night before. At an assembly in the lecture hall, the matron holds no folder of lecture notes.

"Today," she begins, "our school and clinic will be under German supervision, as will all the hospitals in the city. In a few minutes we shall lower our Belgian flag and raise the flag of the International Red Cross. The occupiers will expect us to speak German or Flemish. Some may understand French. We will do what we can to surmount language differences. Our work, however, will not change. At least one German doctor will arrive here within the hour. It is imperative, my dear students and nurses, to treat this doctor with absolute respect. Allow me to repeat. We are to treat the German doctor, or doctors, with respect. If you cannot do this or if you have the least doubt, you must leave. Trains are still running. The mayor has constables walking about, cautioning everyone that if one person, just one, should fire a weapon, our city may be lost. And if even one person insults a German officer or infantryman or cavalry soldier, the consequences for all of us will be catastrophic. So you see, our situation is grave, and our comportment must be perfect.

"We are also expecting an influx of wounded German soldiers today. The afternoon lecture is canceled. Those of you who are still here should report to your assigned wards three hours earlier. We will keep our civilians separate and, as usual, our male and female patients. The wounded German soldiers will be placed in wards C and D, and also in the private and semi-private rooms on the third floor.

"I do not know which boulevards the German troops will be taking as they enter the city, nor do I know how many troops will remain here. I expect that a good number will stay; the others will pass through to France.

"We must, all of us, focus solely on our work as nurses, as healers. I am sorry to say that you will be overworked, but we may be able to acquire staffing help from some of the other hospitals, at least on a part-time basis. I will take no questions this morning except in private. Those who are staying, please spend some time, if possible, resting and composing yourselves for the work we have to do this afternoon and evening. I have great confidence in you, my dear students and sisters. I know that you will do your best. Now, may God bless us all and keep each of us, and our city, safe."

For Marie-Thérèse, the words transmute themselves into pain. They are for others, those words. She no longer belongs. Worse, she won't be able to help the matron now, just when she needs it most. She blinks back tears.

"Marie-Thérèse," Rani whispers, as others are leaving the hall. "What's wrong?"

She shakes her head. But the concern in Rani's voice makes it impossible to stop the flow, and she's ashamed, on top of everything else. Liese is lingering behind, scrutinizing the two of them. "Is there anything I can do?"

Pull yourself together, Marie-Thérèse!

She clears her eyes and focuses on Liese. "Thank you. It's just...nerves."

"Do you want to come with some of us and watch them enter? *Le Soir* says it's going to take hours. Imagine! We won't stay long, but this is a historic day. And after all, they're your people. Why not come along, both of you?"

"*Non, merci,*" Rani says. "We're going to rest."

In their room, Marie-Thérèse relates the conversation she had with her family. "I wanted to tell you last night, but you were on duty. And today I thought I should speak to Matron first. It hardly seems real. Leaving!"

"But isn't it possible," Rani says, "that your father might change his mind? After all, his patients are here and rely on him. You've told me how conscientious he is."

"I know, but with him, family comes first. He's so afraid for my brothers, especially Jacques. And he adores my mother and would die, literally die, if anything happened to her as a result of something he failed to do. I understand that. Still, it's so hard to...have to give up everything and the matron...and you, Rani...our plans and hopes. I need you to know that. That it's not my decision and I'm not...running away because I'm frightened. I'm not."

"I know you aren't. It might not be of much consolation, but I think I have to leave as well. This morning a small, stupid thing happened, yet it says so much. I couldn't fall sleep last night after being in the wards. I was so tired, but there were too many thoughts. When it grew light, I quietly dressed and went down to the patisserie. I thought it might be closed, but no, it was just opening. Well, you know how my French is flavored with a German accent. An old woman was there, and we walked out together, and she...spat at me. It's absurd to take it to heart, given everything else now, but she made a point of spitting in a way so that I would know what she was thinking: *German.* I suppose she might have spit at the rolls and ruined them, at least she didn't do that, but it was deliberate. What do I care? Just an old woman! But what if she does that to a German *officer?* There must be hundreds of old women like her in this city. Or worse. I don't see how anybody is going to be safe. And I'm so ashamed that they're doing this. *Why?*"

"The old woman?"

"No. *My* people."

"I've read that they just want more territory." Marie-Thérèse is conscious of using the third-person pronoun, as Rani did at first.

"But *why?* We're a large country. Why do we need more territory?"

"Maybe need isn't the right word."

"*Oui! Want*, more likely. You know, I was thinking about that when I couldn't sleep. How they talked about it at school, saying we deserve more territory because…because why? I couldn't remember because I always stopped paying attention. The teachers would go off topic and rant about it, and I'd use the time to think about more pleasant things. It was a patriotic idea, I recall. Sometimes other professors would come in to lecture about it. Had I paid attention, I might understand all this now. Well, I do understand! They just want more. Now I feel like such a…traitor for being so angry. And ashamed. And everything!"

Rani presses fingertips against her eyelids.

"You're not a traitor. How can you think of yourself as a traitor if you stay and nurse wounded Germans? Besides, the clinic needs you more than ever now. So does Gauthier. She hardly speaks German. She'll be able to rely on you."

"And more old ladies will spit at me."

"Let them. At least you won't shoot them."

"Maybe I'd like to, though." Her face takes on its blotchy heated look.

"Rani, please. Stay for Matron's sake. And really, your own as well. And maybe…I can come back in a few months and catch up somehow."

Rani puts an arm around Marie-Thérèse and the two lean

against each other, their heads touching. They sway from side to side a little until Marie-Thérèse says, "What about those rolls? Did you finish them off?"

"I only ate one."

"Well, that's something anyway."

They're honey colored and still crisp. Their scent reminds Marie-Thérèse of fields and sunlight.

"Can you get rolls such as these in Germany?"

"No."

"Then maybe that's the reason for this invasion. They want the patisseries."

"It must be."

"So, you see, Rani, you need to stay, if only for the rolls."

LOGIC

Herr Doktor Manfred Kuhn introduces himself in German by stating his name, place of birth, and credentials. Study in Paris and Vienna; specializations in bacteriology, public health, and in diseases of the ear, nose, and throat; positions at premier hospitals throughout Europe. He recites it all as if telling the assembled sisters and students the weather that day. He's moderately tall but slightly built, his goatee rust-red, his hair combed back from forehead and temples. There are pale bays to either side of the center peninsula of hair. Marie-Thérèse finds it hard to determine the hair's color because it looks sopping wet. A dark brown, possibly. She observes a sheen of perspiration along the brow line, but then the lecture hall is quite warm. The man's color is good, but his eyes behind the rimless eyeglasses appear reddened and the fleshy crescents underneath puffy and dark. Everything about him, from his voice to his detached manner, conveys disdain for his audience. Marie-Thérèse concludes that he must be displeased by his assignment. Such a lowly little hospital, given his exalted education, reputation, and experience.

The matron sits to the left of the lectern, her chin raised somewhat higher than usual. The table against the wall holds no welcoming flowers, in contrast to other times when visiting specialists give presentations. Marie-Thérèse glances at Sister Gauthier in the row ahead, her expression stony with incomprehension—and probably fear, given her weak German.

But surely, Marie-Thérèse thinks, this learned doctor deserves their respect. He's here on orders, no doubt, not personal inclination. Who can say what he thinks of the invasion? Maybe he's horrified. What man of medicine wouldn't be? Her own father certainly is. She decides to give him the benefit of the doubt and be calm in his presence and say no more than necessary. And she will help Gauthier, who must be scared half out of her wits by now.

The doctor goes on, in his monotone, laying out his expectations. In a word—*excellence.* Perfect personal cleanliness, perfect sanitation in the wards, and perfect treatment of patients. Nothing less. "For any infraction, a meal will be withheld. Serious infractions will earn dismissal. Inspections will be frequent."

A meal? They already understand the importance of perfection in the matron's school and Doctor Depage's clinic. Doktor Kuhn is beginning to sound like someone who enjoys making examples of people for the edification of others. Or, possibly for the pleasure of simply being able to do so. A chill raises gooseflesh on her arms.

"Tonight," he states with more animation, "twenty wounded soldiers will be in wards C and D. Sisters are to attend them after my examinations. Kitchen staff, be ready to prepare meals for any patients who are able to eat. Orderlies, remain on duty until dismissed. Student-nurses, see to the patients in wards A and B. You will be assigned work in wards C and D in due time."

While the matron restates his directives in French, the doctor closes his folder and unceremoniously, even rudely, leaves the lecture hall.

The sound of brass bands somewhere in the distance drifts into the ward, along with a fragrant breeze. Marie-Thérèse is sponging Janine's arms with a warm cloth and observes, with satisfaction, that her own hand is steady. "And Jackie," she continues, "found it necessary to roll in soil Monsieur the Gardener had just prepared for a new bed of lettuce. He rolled and rolled as if monsieur had been working all morning just for him. Oh, he had a fine time rolling about, and monsieur…" Marie-Thérèse pauses, sensing a presence just behind her. Angling her head minutely, she glimpses light gray trousers the color of lichens. "And monsieur, poor monsieur…"

"Please continue, Fräulein," the man behind her says in

German. "I also would like to know what monsieur did at that point. I know what I might have done."

"Monsieur the Gardener," Marie-Thérèse continues in French, "laughed at the ridiculous dog making such a clownish spectacle of himself. Then the gardener took off his cap and tried to shoo Jackie away, but before running off, Jackie shook himself mightily, getting bits of soil all over poor monsieur. And monsieur had to brush himself off and begin anew with his flattened lettuce bed. Thank goodness there were no lettuces in it."

She places the cloth carefully in the bowl, takes a small towel, and pats the child's arms and brow. The girl, as always, is looking at something only she can see.

"Do you speak German, Fräulein?" he asks. To her dismay, her hands are now visibly trembling.

"Yes, sir."

"Very good. When you are finished here, please step to the back window. I will await you there."

She restores order to her cart, then leans toward the child. "Mademoiselle Janine, all will be well. You will get better and will be able to play with your sister again. That will be very nice. I will come back to say goodnight."

At the window overlooking the garden, the doctor, in white coat and the gray trousers of a German soldier, asks her name.

"Madem— Excuse me! I am Fräulein Marie-Thérèse Hulbert, a student-nurse, in my third year." With effort, she keeps her arms loose at her sides, the palms open. She tells herself to look at him.

"Do you enjoy it here?"

"Very much, sir."

"Your matron is a good teacher?"

"She is an excellent teacher, Herr Doktor."

"Student-nurse Hulbert, tell me about the patient you were just now attending."

"Herr Doktor, the child's name is Janine Arit, and she is five years old. She came to us two weeks ago exhibiting no external injuries and yet was unable, or unwilling, to speak. We know that she can hear. Sometimes she pays attention to what we are saying to her; most often she does not. She has been seen by Doctor Antoine Depage, who gave the diagnosis of mental trauma manifesting itself in muteness."

"Yes. I have read her chart. You are thorough. Did her parents bring her here?"

"Her parents are…missing. The child and her sister were brought to the clinic by our gardener after the clinic was notified. The older girl, who is ten years old, is helping our cook now."

"Was the child's sister able to tell you what caused the mental trauma?"

Marie-Thérèse orders herself to maintain eye contact and show only confidence. She takes a long breath, exhales slowly and then explains, measuring her words.

"I am sorry to say that the old woman who found the child and her sister relayed a story of destruction in the countryside… farms and farmhouses burned, people and animals killed. The children's parents have not come to claim them. The child's sister told us that her mother and another sister were killed inside their farmhouse. Her father is missing. Their farm animals had been killed. Janine Arit, the child you just saw, may or may not have witnessed these…events, but according to her older sister, she left their hiding place and probably did see the bodies of her mother and three-year-old sister in the farmhouse."

It is the doctor who averts his eyes. Then looking directly at her again, he says, "Do you know who committed these acts?"

Tell the truth simply. "The child's sister told us that soldiers of the German army did those things. She seemed quite certain."

Arms crossed, he studies her as if waiting for her to continue. Finally, he says, "So far, Student-nurse Hulbert, I have been admiring your honesty and intelligence, but now I must take you to task for a lapse in logic, which will cost you one meal. You seem to have accepted at face value the words of a ten-year-old child. Yes, there was death and destruction. Yes, a five-year-old child is mute whereas before—presumably—she was not. I will accept that much. But it does not follow that *German* soldiers committed the savagery. Could not these acts have been carried out by retreating Belgians hoping to discredit the German army...and Germany? Could not these acts have been part of a propaganda strategy? Could not they have been committed by Belgian farmers intent on looting, in the wake of retreating Belgian forces? Reality, I have found, is much more variable and complex than we often allow, in our need to get at the truth of anything."

Could it be? Are such things even remotely possible? Marie-Thérèse suddenly isn't sure. What does she know about war and its strategies?

"You are not certain. I see this. You wish to protest that I am wrong, yet you are horrified by the possibility that I am correct. Is this not so?"

"*Ja,* Herr Doktor."

"I commend your honesty. I think we will work well together.

"*Danke,* sir."

Her hands are frigid, her face hot as she turns to go. But then he says, "One moment, please. I have another question. Why wasn't the child taken to a more suitable hospital, given her needs?"

"There were no available beds at other hospitals."

"Wounded Belgian and French soldiers were occupying them?"

"Yes, and some English soldiers as well."

"Were they here, too, wounded Belgian, French, and English soldiers?"

"For a while some were."

"But not now?"

"No, sir."

"Extremely wounded men have just...gone somewhere else."

"Yes. They are no longer here."

"Do you know where they have gone?"

"I do not, Herr Doktor."

"They were taken away?"

"I did not see them go."

"Ah. And so, you cannot say how or by whom they were removed."

Look at him. His eyes.

"I cannot, sir."

"I must tell you that there will be grievous consequences for anyone harboring wounded Belgian, French, and English soldiers. They must be sent to Germany as prisoners of war. That is the law."

"I understand."

"Very good. Will you personally tell me should any wounded Allies come here surreptitiously for treatment?"

Do not hesitate.

"Yes, sir."

"*Danke.* I have your word?"

"Yes, sir, you have my word."

"Student-nurse Hulbert, we need nurses such as you in Germany. Perhaps when you complete your training, we might further discuss this matter."

Smile.

"*Danke*, Herr Doktor Kuhn."

"Go back to your patients now. I have kept you long enough. But remember, be watchful. Be alert. Do you understand?"

"I understand, sir."

"*Gut.*"

He waves a hand, and Marie-Thérèse walks away, blind.

An Unspecified Task

Y*ou have my word...You have my word.* Sleep is impossible until, finally, a few hours of churning dreams, and then morning too soon. Along with the stomach-cramping awareness, again, of that conversation.

When she sits up, the room slides out of focus. She's afraid of fainting and wonders if she should stay in bed. But the matron will come up and question her. After the dizziness passes, she ventures to stand and then gets ready for the day.

That morning Madame Heinbokel, of the festering foot, doesn't offer her usual pleasant greeting, which always cheers Marie-Thérèse. Instead, it's "I suppose you want to get rid of me now. Make more room for *them.*"

She decides to respond only to the first part of the woman's querulous statement. "Of course we don't want to get rid of you, madame! Who would cheer us up? No one. May I examine your foot now, please?"

The woman gets herself upright this time, and Marie-Thérèse lets the old bandaging fall into a receptacle.

"It looks much better! The swelling has gone down, the color is perfectly normal, and...let me just see...yes! The wound is healing well. This afternoon we will take another little stroll. The circulation, you see..."

"It hurts."

"Can you describe the pain?"

"It's...all over. The foot, I mean."

"Sharp? Like before?"

"No, dull."

A memory of the earlier pain? They learned about this strange phenomenon, called phantom pains. But those occurred, usually, after an amputation, the nerve endings somehow remembering past pain. "Ah. A dull pain. I will note that on your chart."

Writing, she pauses.

"It is not a severe pain, is it, madame?"

"*Non.*"

"*Bien!* Your chickens must miss you. And your husband, Monsieur Heinbokel, as well, of course."

"He said he was going to volunteer when the German army arrived. He was going to speak to the first German officer he saw and volunteer."

"I see. And what of your son?"

"He refuses. Now he will have to run away. Otherwise, they will send him to Germany and put him to work. I will have to do everything myself, but how can I? With my foot hurting?"

Marie-Thérèse glances to her left. The doctor is at the far end of the ward, talking with one of the sisters. "I have an idea. There is someone at the clinic who knows people in the countryside. He may be able to find a helper for you."

"Is he German?"

"No, madame. Polish."

"I don't want a German's help."

Marie-Thérèse involuntarily steps back but is able to keep her voice neutral. "I understand. Please don't worry. He will find someone. Now, I am going to lightly re-bandage your foot, and later, with the help of your crutches, we'll take our little walk. Tell me, does your foot feel any better now?"

"Somewhat."

"*Magnifique.* You see? You are making good progress."

When she turns from the bed, there is the matron. From her stance, one hand loosely wrapped around the other and both resting against her apron, it's clear she's been there for several minutes.

She motions for Marie-Thérèse to follow her. In the nurses' office, Marie-Thérèse stands with cold hands linked behind her back, her stomach cramping again.

Gone are the peach tones in the matron's complexion. She looks drawn and preoccupied.

"Very good, Mademoiselle Hulbert. You not only treated

your patient's wound with deftness, but you also grasped the nature of her pain. You didn't argue with her, which a less sensitive nurse might have done. Nor were you dismissive. You responded to her as a whole person. This is difficult to teach. With you, it seems instinctive."

"*Merci beaucoup, Matrone.*"

"Also, these past months you have given me confidence that I can trust you." She lowers her voice. "Would you be able to help me with a task later tonight, after midnight? It should not take too long."

Midnight. An unspecified task. The matron is always exact and detailed.

"You hesitate. Perhaps I understand."

"Matron, I…I had to give him my word."

"Your word?"

"Last night. He asked that I tell him if any Allies come here secretly for treatment. They are supposed to be prisoners of war. *Pardonnez-moi.* It happened so fast, and I was trying not to show anxiousness. I know it was wrong of me, but it seemed I had no choice at that moment. So, if this task concerns—"

"Thank you for telling me. I should have expected this. Why did I not?"

"*Pardonnez-moi,*" she repeats, twisting her hidden hands together. She realizes she should have told her sooner, and in private.

"I understand. No need to apologize."

"Should I leave? Do you wish me to leave?"

"And everyone else! And then we will close this clinic."

The quaver of emotion, the vitriolic tone. This is a surprise.

"I need you here," the matron adds, her voice restored to calm and volume. Then looking beyond Marie-Thérèse, she says, in German, "Please come in, Herr Doktor Kuhn. How are you finding everything at our clinic?"

"Quite satisfactory, Matron. I've found, too, that you have several exceptional students, including Student-nurse Hulbert here, though she needs to review her logic studies. However, you were speaking French just now whereas both you and Student-nurse Hulbert speak excellent German. Please do so from now on. In fact, notices to this effect will be going up all over the city. We may as well begin implementing the rule immediately."

"Yes, of course. We were speaking French out of habit but from now on will make every effort to use the German language where possible."

The words aren't to his liking, Marie-Thérèse senses, but he won't correct the matron in front of a student. "I must also inform you," he continues, "that Brussels will soon be on Universal Time plus one hour, and all clocks at the school and clinic must be reset accordingly."

"Perhaps you will be so good as to notify me in advance."

"Of course. Now allow me to wish you a good day."

"*Danke*, sir. And to you."

He pauses. "And remember, Student-nurse Hulbert, no dining room tonight."

"Yes, Herr Doktor."

They stand there for what seems like too long after he leaves. Nausea is rising in Marie-Thérèse's throat. Could he have overheard them? How well does he understand French? Quite well, obviously, if he taught in Paris. The nurses' office seems to darken, and later she'll wonder if it was some kind of premonition and not just an effect of lightheadedness.

"What have you done?" the matron asks in German. Again whispering, Marie-Thérèse explains. When she finishes, the matron sends her back into the wards.

That night, on her desk, there's a tray holding cutlery and napkin, a wedge of Camembert, an apple, bread, and a custard tart with caramelized sugar on top. The accompanying note is in French. *He said no dining room but neglected to mention dinner. I remember my Logic studies. Destroy this note.*

She hates doing so but tears the note into pieces and flushes them down the commode.

Bayonet

Sister Gauthier pauses at the entrance to ward C. "You can do this, Fräulein?"

Her German is halting and incorrect, so Marie-Thérèse asks that they speak French, whispering if necessary. "I'm afraid that when you tell me to do something, I might misunderstand and do the wrong thing, Sister."

"It break rule!" Sister Gauthier says in her usual stentorian tone, though now in German. "We must never."

Marie-Thérèse suppresses a laugh. "Which is worse," she responds in German, "breaking some arbitrary rule or harming our patients?"

Uncomprehending, Sister Gauthier raises and lowers her shoulders in annoyance. Marie-Thérèse understands something else then. There's a hierarchy to rules. At the very lowest level are the foolish ones such as having to speak a certain language no matter the consequences. Of greater importance are the pragmatic ones. No soiled linen and bandages on the floor. Cleanse hands before working with a patient. Then the great one, for nurses, signified in the matron's refusal to kill a small spider a nurse pointed out on a white wall. The matron had scooped it onto a piece of paper and shaken it out the window. Did that rule supersede the Commandment about not lying, though?

Twelve German soldiers now occupy ward C, six on either side. Two windows at the far end are open to the late afternoon. On white floorboards under the windows, trapezoids of golden light.

Sister Gauthier explains in a pastiche of French and German. Infantry. All shot or shelled. Four amputees, the surgery done in a field hospital. All to be sent back to German hospitals as soon as they can be moved. "We dressed wounds. Introduce, read charts. One man, Reissner, shouts in sleep. Shouts often awake. Needs calm. He wakes everyone. We sedate."

While Sister Gauthier struggles linguistically, Marie-Thérèse takes in the beds, their symmetry, whiteness, and order. How can these men deserve such peace and care? One of them—or more—might have been among those who murdered the villagers, Janine and Elli's parents, other parents, children, animals.

Sister Gauthier takes hold of Marie-Thérèse's arm. "Fräulein?"

"*Je vais bien*," she says, though she is not, in fact, fine. In the first bed is an eighteen-year-old German private wounded, states his chart, at Louvain by a mortar shell. It shattered his left leg and left forearm. Both were amputated at the casualty clearing station. There are lesser though still serious wounds. A ricocheting bullet struck the upper right arm obliquely and broke up, and pieces bore their way through the arm, narrowly missing bone but tearing masses of cartilage and muscle. There are two other bullet wounds, a clean one in the upper right thigh and another along the neck that had furrowed through the top layers of flesh before going its way. That the private did not die in the field from loss of blood is a miracle. Or testimony to the efficacy of German doctors. The deceptive rosy color of his skin indicates fever, as do the swollen, parched lips. His closed eyes rest in orbs of darkness surrounded by prominent occipital bones. The ears, cupped outward, evoke youth, even innocence, but otherwise he appears more like an elderly man on his deathbed. His temperature, when last taken, was dangerously high.

Her knees and calves weaken.

"Good afternoon, Fräulein," he whispers, raising his eyelids slowly and then squinting with obvious pain. "I am...Private... Konrad Schalk."

"Good afternoon, Private Schalk," she responds in German. "I am Fräulein Hulbert, a student nurse."

After a long while, he tries for more words. "I am...from... Cuxhaven..."

Then he's sobbing in weak gasps.

"Private Schalk, are you in much pain?"

"*Nein.*" A whisper.

The morphine, she thinks, might be fraying his nerves. On the bedside stand are a bowl of water and a sterile cloth. She dips it in the water, wrings out, and places it over his forehead.

"*Danke,*" he murmurs.

"Cuxhaven?" she says in her nurse's voice. "Isn't that on the North Sea?"

"*Ja.*" Small gasps follow this exhalation.

She feels hypocritical saying that it must be a beautiful place.

"I am…was…a swimmer. International." These words elicit tears and more gasping.

Still reluctant to touch him, she carefully turns the cloth over. "Private Schalk, you are safe here. You are in a clinic in Brussels. We are taking care of you now."

"I was…swimming. I am…swimmer."

Delirious, she thinks, again attributing it to the morphine. "You were swimming? In a dream? It must have been a pleasant dream."

"In Paris. I competed…"

"Ah. Paris. How fortunate."

"Water…please?"

She has to raise his head and bring the glass to those puffy, sore-looking lips. The back of his neck feels scorched. She puts the glass aside and deftly turns the pillow over before lowering his head.

"*Danke.* You are…kind."

Now her hands seem to be burning, the fingers tremulous, as she checks the drains on each of his bandaged stumps and then checks the other bandaged wounds. Soon she'll have to change those bandages.

"Rest now, Private Schalk. Go back to your dream."

She's about to turn away but some impulse causes her to dip the cloth in water again and wipe the young man's face and brow. She changes the water in the basin, takes several clean cloths from the linen supply, and places a damp one over his hot forehead and closed eyes.

By the time she enters the curtained area around the next bed and reads the patient's chart, her hands are steady. It's all right to empathize, she tells herself, given that she'll be leaving soon. Private Berthold Kohnert, thirty-eight years old, has three bullet wounds, one in each arm and another in his torso. His jaw is broken and so is his left cheekbone, from being run over by the wheel of a gun caisson. Impossible that the shape of his face will ever be the same—if he even recovers. And in the same accident, he lost his left eye. With exception of his right eye and his mouth, the face and jaw are bandaged; his hands lie to either side, palms down. He seems asleep, and she's about to slide shut the curtain, but at the sound, he wakes, stares dumbly at her awhile, then motions to the bedside table. Looking there, she sees a pad of paper and a pencil.

Am I home? he writes in German. The letters break here and there.

"*Nein.* You are in Brussels."

He takes a long breath before laboriously writing, *I dreamed I was home.* He pushes aside the pad. It falls to the floor, and she quickly picks it up, wondering if she should bring him a clean one.

"Where is your home, Private Kohnert?" With reluctance she gives him the pad.

Mentz. On the Rhine. Do you know it?

"*Nein,* I am sorry. I do not."

Now I will die here.

"Your chart says that you will live, Private Kohnert."

It lies.

"You will live if you want to live." She reminds herself not to argue.

Are you German?

I am Belgian."

I wish German nurse.

He pushes the pad aside again, and again she picks it up.

"I will find a German nurse for you, Private Kohnert."

His eye is closed. He brushes at the air with one hand. She drops the pad in the bin for soiled bandaging and tells herself to remember to bring him a new one.

The next bed is also enclosed by a curtain. As she reads this patient's chart, sweat breaks out on her forehead, and she takes hold of the bedrail. Her skin has gone cold. She prays she won't faint. Gerhardt Haske, twenty-five, was stabbed with his own bayonet in the chest, arms, abdomen, and eyes. He had morphine at two that afternoon and is due to have it again at six. Bandages wrap head and eyes, shoulders, arms, and torso. The liver has been perforated; the kidneys are failing.

Mon Dieu.

Yes, his skin—what she can see of it—is jaundiced. The ankles, edematous. So his lungs are failing as well. He should be in one of the larger hospitals. But the German military must be practicing its own form of triage, using those hospitals for soldiers who have a better chance of surviving. Twenty-five-year-old Sergeant Haske, like Private Schalk, has been brought here to die.

A detail snags: *with his own bayonet.*

She swallows back nausea, understanding that he couldn't have inflicted those wounds upon himself. This understanding is terrible.

She inserts the chart into its holder and continues on. Vogler, Hinkle, Hausbeck, Ennst, Bauer, Reissner—men ranging from nineteen to forty-eight. Bullet wounds, head wounds, shrapnel wounds, limbs amputated. One demands German beer. Another asks that she write a letter to his wife in Frankfurt. Still another, with broken legs sustained when he fell from the ladder of a cannon as a shell burst nearby, asks if he will still be able to dance and if, one day, she might dance with him. This man has a heavy mustache, its tips groomed into small curls. Of course, she tells him. But he is far away, a small figure in a white bed on an August afternoon. The day's warmth eddies through the ward, again bringing the scent of roses.

Leaving, she pauses at Sergeant Haske's bed. Heavily sedated, he hasn't changed position. She takes his wrist to check for a pulse. It's there, a faint faltering beacon of life. She touches his neck. There too. She imagines something small, a child, trying to drag a wagon uphill. Elli pushing that wheelbarrow with Janine lying there, in wet straw.

She takes the sergeant's hand again, this time not checking for his pulse. "I am sorry for what has happened to you," she says in German. "But I must leave now. I will find a good German nurse for you. Her name is Fräulein Rania. She is an excellent nurse and will help you, Sergeant Haske. Do not give up. Have courage."

Then she turns to leave, her unstarched apron and skirt making no sound.

"Fräulein?" the soldier in the bed nearest the door murmurs. She pauses. His eyes are flickering in that painful way as he tries to focus.

"Do you need anything, Private Schalk? Can I bring you something before I go?"

"You…must go? I wish you…might read…to me."

She hesitates but then says, "I cannot, Private Schalk. You see, I must leave the clinic. But I will ask another nurse to read to you."

"*Danke*. You are kind. I will always remember…your kindness."

The ward blurs as she passes the nurses' office. In a lavatory, she washes her hands and face. She holds a cold cloth to her own forehead and eyes. Everything is telling her to leave at once. For her parents' sake and her own. Why she next walks out into the garden, she doesn't know. Seeing the gardener there, digging up potatoes, she's unable to speak.

He straightens and waits. His cap the same, his jacket, the trousers, all the same—his own uniform. He takes out his handkerchief, a bit of blue cloth crushed into a ball, and extends it toward her.

She laughs then, though it's more of a sob, as she takes it and wipes her eyes. *What does it matter now, a few germs?* Words finally jumble out. She needs to leave. It's impossible, all of it. She thought she could do it, this danse macabre, but no, she's not strong enough, she deceived herself, and on top of everything to have to *lie*, that she will not do, but it's all right, she's accustomed to failure, she will just have to find something else to fail at. Besides, her family needs her now. As she's speaking, Jackie and Donnie mob her, expecting a walk, and when they start barking—Jackie's a roar, Donnie's high and shrill—she tries to shush them. "Monsieur, the doctor will hear. Make them stop!"

"They want their walk."

"But I cannot. Au revoir, Papa. I wish you well. I must go now. *Merci!* Thank you for everything."

"In the fall they leave, the birds." He holds his cap over his heart. He bows his head.

"Monsieur, please keep them quiet. Jackie! Donnie! Stop this!" She takes a few steps, then abruptly turns and picks up Donnie.

In Janine's ward, the little girl is awake and staring at nothing as usual. In the garden below, Jackie is still barking.

"Janine? I have brought Donnie. Can you see him?"

Gradually, the little girl's eyes focus.

"Would you like to pet him?"

The girl's fingers move but not her hand.

"I have come to say goodbye, my dear. Your sister is going to take good care of you and so will the matron and all the other nurses."

Is the child frowning? "You are going to get well," Marie-Thérèse continues, "and one day I will come and see you again. You will be much better, and you will talk to me and say, 'Bonjour, Mademoiselle Marie-Thérèse.' And I will say, 'Bonjour, Mademoiselle Janine!' And we will be like old friends meeting again. Won't that be nice?"

"You're *leaving*?" Elli says, coming up behind Marie-Thérèse. "You're going *away*?"

Donnie wriggles to get to Elli, who is a figure frozen in astonishment and confusion.

"I'm sorry, Elli, but I must."

"*Why?* She likes you. We both do. She wants you to stay. You can't go too."

Too.

"See?" Elli says. "She's crying."

Marie-Thérèse transfers Donnie to the girl and lifts Janine from the bed. Holding her, she pats the child's back. Both girls are crying now and so is Marie-Thérèse. When she brings Donnie back down to the garden, Jackie whirls around, barking as he always does when greeting the matron after an absence however short or long. Monsieur frees a potato from loose soil and places it in his basket. He looks up.

"I'm staying. At least for a while longer."

"And in the spring," he says, "they return."

SECRET

Mademoiselle, your father wishes you to call him at
home."

They are in the matron's sitting room, off the garden,
and it is nearly 1:30 in the morning. On the table are a sketchbook, a box of drawing pencils, and the matron's telephone.

"Does he want me to return *tonight*?"

"He did not say."

Fear blanks thought as Marie-Thérèse lifts the telephone's
earpiece from its cradle.

He answers immediately. Then a muffled sound tells her he
must have cupped his hand over the mouthpiece. In the next
moment he's telling her that Jacques is gone. "When he didn't
come home from school, we were afraid something happened
along the way. I walked back to the school, taking his route,
and learned that he hadn't attended today. They didn't call us
because they assumed we had left Brussels. Or there may have
been another reason for not calling. We feared for Jacques's life.
The police say they will help, but there's so much disruption
they hardly have the means to do much at all. I think he's gone
to join our forces. Your mother is distraught. I should have
waited until morning to call you, but I had a thought and wanted to talk with you at once."

"It's all right, Father. I've been working in the wards. Jacques
left no note?"

"Nothing."

"Do you want me home now? What can I do to help?"

"Stay there. I told the police where you are, and they'll contact you if they find him. Or, he may even come to the clinic
himself. Or be brought there. And then you can contact us. I
will send an address. We're going to take Willy and leave in the
morning for Antwerp, assuming we can get through. Our forces

are still somewhere in the vicinity, and we'll try to locate him. I wrote all this in a letter for Jacques and will leave it here, but our house may be vandalized in our absence or even destroyed, and when he returns—"

"Papa, our gardener has pigeons. I'll ask if he can send a message to someone in the military. I'm not sure how but surely—"

"*Merci!* Be careful. Don't go about the streets now."

"*Oui,* Papa."

"I'll get word to you. Take good care, my dear. *Je t'aime beaucoup.*"

"I love you, too, Papa. *Bon courage.*"

Then her mother's voice. "If Jacques should come there—"

"I will let you know at once, Maman."

"Who can convince a sixteen-year-old of anything!"

"Or one nineteen."

A pause. "*Exactement!* Au revoir. "

"*Au revoir, Maman. Bonne chance.*"

She holds onto the earpiece a while longer, their voices fading pulses of sound.

The matron enters with a tray holding a pot of tea and two cups. "I'm afraid it must be bad news."

"My brother Jacques is missing. They think he's gone to join our forces. He's only sixteen and knows nothing about fighting. Nothing!"

"Do they wish your help, mademoiselle?"

"They want me to stay here in case the police learn anything or if he should somehow come here. They're going to look for him among our forces."

"I'm very sorry."

"*Merci, Matrone.* I only hope he's still alive. That he wasn't attacked by other boys and his body…thrown somewhere. If he's gone to join our forces, then at least he may be alive. For now."

"Be calm, mademoiselle. Be hopeful. For selfish reasons I'm relieved you'll be here for a while yet. We have so much work now." She pours tea and adds milk.

The hot tea is comforting, but the words tweak her conscience. "I need to tell you that I almost left today. I was in the military wards, and it all seemed impossible to care for such terribly wounded men. And I was also thinking of the girls and what they've been through. I was thinking...perhaps too much." Even now, guilt and fear, the one a cold and sorrowful sensation; the other, anxious and fraught. "I thought how staying will demand courage and self-discipline. Staying, I will have to learn to see every person, regardless of nationality, as someone to be healed. Leaving, even though it's what my parents will eventually ask of me, will amount to cowardice, won't it, given my doubts?"

"But you did not leave."

"No, ironically, *because* of the girls."

Jackie groans. His long legs twitch. Both dogs are on their sides, asleep in the warmth from the small fireplace with its grate of coal. In her tiredness Marie-Thérèse stares at the low fire. The matron, noticing, goes to the bucket holding pieces of coal the gardener wraps in paper so her hands won't get dirty. She drops two pieces on the fire. The paper blazes a moment.

"Mademoiselle, I hesitate to ask, but now I find..."

Marie-Thérèse waits.

"I need someone absolutely trustworthy. I know you have a tendency to talk a bit excitedly at times, but I also know that I can trust you to be discreet. And I know that I can rely on your skills."

The matron has assumed an uncharacteristic pensive pose, one arm folded, elbow braced on wrist, and fingers against her mouth. Marie-Thérèse also observes what she failed to notice before—the slight glassiness and redness of eye, the imprint of fatigue under each lower eyelid.

And then she knows.

"Tonight?"

"Tonight...and other nights."

"How many?"

"Three. But there may be others soon."

Fear jolts through her. "He said the consequences will be…
severe, Matron."

"There are higher laws, no? Do you need some time to think
about it?"

"You are taking an awful risk even telling me." Her face,
warmed by the coal fire, is now too warm.

"Yes. But, you see, if I'm called away from the clinic or…re-
placed, you will be able to care for them and have them secretly
removed. I'll tell you how. And there'll be someone to help. I'm
asking far too much of you. If you decline, I'll understand and
trust you will say nothing to anyone about our conversation
tonight."

Marie-Thérèse looks at the two dogs, their sides evenly rising
and falling in sleep. Street dogs once.

"Please tell me what is involved," she hears herself saying.

"We will secretly nurse wounded Allies and help them get to
the Netherlands once they are able to travel. They have been
left behind in the rapid Allied retreat or have gotten lost in
what is now, for all practical purposes, German territory. You
will have to lie…to the German doctor, to any German authorities, and at least for now, to your fellow nurses. You will have
to become wily and deceptive and guarded. Do you think you
have it in you to do that? Practice deception every day? It's far
too much to ask of you, mademoiselle, for you are a person of
integrity. I see it in your work. It's an awful thing to ask, but the
wounded Allies, if found, will become prisoners of war and *may*
be transported to Germany. Most likely they will die en route, if
they are actually transported there and not shot outright." She
lowers her gaze to the teapot.

Marie-Thérèse, hearing her father's voice urging caution,
closes her eyes a moment.

"*Pardonnez-moi*," she says finally, "I want to help. But I…
have failed my family once already. Especially my mother. My
being here at the school causes her daily heartbreak. And now,
Jacques…I'm so sorry, Matron. But you have my word that I
will never reveal our conversation."

"*Merci.* I will see you tomorrow then, though tomorrow is already here and you need your rest. *Bonne nuit.*"

"*Bonne nuit, Matrone.*"

At the door, Marie-Thérèse pauses. "Please don't ask that of Liese."

"No?"

"No. You must not."

"Can you tell me why?"

"I...confided in her once and she...betrayed that confidence." Words causing shame to flood through her. What is she herself doing right now, if not being disloyal? Not just to Liese but the matron. Above all, the matron. And betraying, even, her chosen profession.

"*Merci,* mademoiselle."

Closing the door, she resists an impulse to reopen it, saying, *I've changed my mind. I'll help.*

In the lavatory on her floor, she rinses her face with cold water.

Failure. My old friend. You're back, aren't you?

ECLIPSE

Where were you last night? You weren't here. I was worried. Were you ill? When did you get back? I tried to wait up but fell asleep. Wake up, Marie-Thérèse! It's late." Rani's face comes into focus. "Marie-Thérèse! Are you ill? What's the matter? You need to be up."

"I had a telephone call from my father. I took it in the matron's apartment. My brother Jacques is missing."

"Are you leaving then? Do they need you at home?"

"*Non.* They wish me to stay here a while longer. I'll tell you more later."

"Ah! *Bien!* Then hurry. After breakfast we have another lecture on bandaging, followed by practice. Also, I heard last night that more German patients have arrived. And that the doctor will be conducting an inspection. This is supposed to be a secret, but I overheard one of the sisters talking."

"An inspection?"

"I know! Another one."

"Why?" She's putting on her robe.

"Well, of course you know that Germans are exceedingly tidy, that's probably why."

"Then he'll be in the wards."

"Everywhere!" Rani has been speaking in German and adds an injunction about using that language, and nothing but, today.

"*Oui,* Maman." Marie-Thérèse gives a playful inflection to the word to mask uneasiness.

"I am happy you can joke about this, *ma chère petite!*"

"Rani, I'm happy you're here." This she says in her perfect German.

Rani regards her. "You *aren't* well, are you?"

"Au contraire. *Je vais bien!*"

"*Stop* that!"

Noticing the private's glance, Marie-Thérèse lowers the book and turns.

"Fräulein Hulbert," the doctor says, "you read very well, but might I ask that, next time, you choose a more appropriate author?"

Her face grows warm. She was just then thinking the story might be too dark for Private Schalk. "I will be happy to do so, sir. What do you suggest?"

He recommends Goethe, Rilke, and Heine along with a number of minor German writers. She keeps the book closed until he leaves the ward. Her mouth is dry from reading but also fear.

"Continue, Fräulein, please," Private Schalk says. "It is a very nice story."

"I don't think he wants me to continue with it."

"He said 'next time,' so it may be all right to at least finish it. We are at war with Russia, too, you see, and Chekhov is a *Russian* writer. That's why it's inappropriate."

A smile then. Private Schalk smiling. The fever has subsided, and the private's bony, pained face is reverting to its younger self.

When she finishes, after speeding the story along, he says, "I will think about this all day now. How the young student is so joyful about his revelation despite the darkness of the time. And how he expects to be happy in life, and life seems to him full of grand meaning. Well! He's quite naive, isn't he? I was like that too! And yet here I am, so happy that you have read this fine story to me. So happiness is possible after all. Some of the time, anyway. Thank you, Fräulein. I wish... Do you think you might be able to read me other stories by Herr Chekhov somehow? That would be very nice."

"We'll see, Private Schalk. Why not rest now."

"The day outside...how is it today?"

She goes to one of the open windows. Cloud shadow deepens the grays and russets of other houses and the greenery in other gardens, and then lifts. The colors brighten again. And in the sky, long narrow clouds, gray and white, slide by like barges on a dust-blue canal. A chimney swift arcs over rooftops. But then some repetitious sharp sound, as of something rattling against metal, breaks the tranquility. It stops, then comes from a different direction. In a garden two houses away, a man rushes from an open doorway and crawls behind a hedge bordering a rose garden. Two soldiers in gray emerge from the back of the house, aim rifles, and fire. There's a cry. The soldiers fire several more times, each taking a turn. One then walks over to the torn hedge. The day seems to be sinking into twilight. She rubs her eyes and looks out at the garden where, now, nothing is moving.

Mon Dieu. We must go there and help that man. But she knows that he cannot possibly be alive. Or has she imagined the scene?

"*L'eclipse!*" someone in the ward exclaims.

The eclipse. It was predicted, she recalls. A full eclipse over Eastern Europe, a partial one for Brussels. The rattle of gunfire comes from various parts of the city as the day darkens and lights are turned on in the ward. Other nurses take quick glimpses out of windows.

"An *eclipse?*" Private Schalk says. "Tell me, Fräulein, what is it like? Describe it for me, please."

"It is like night coming on, Private Schalk. Color…goes out of everything."

"Ah! I wish I could look outside. I have never seen an eclipse of the sun. Will it last long, do you know?"

"I don't know."

"But what is that sound? Gunshots?"

No useful prevarication comes to mind.

He squints as if in pain again. "Is there fighting nearby?"

"No, not fighting, Private Schalk."

"But then?"

"I think some men may be…shooting."

"Some men? It sounded quite close. Is it our soldiers or couldn't you see?"

Conscious of the rule not to impart anything negative, she says, "I couldn't see clearly, Private Schalk."

"Could it be Belgians?"

"I don't know."

"Probably not Belgians."

"I may be able to get permission for a chair and someone to help move you into it. Would you like to look outside?"

"*Nein. Danke.*" Closing his eyes, he turns his head to the side.

"Then rest, please. I will read to you again later."

"*Danke*, Fräulein."

She takes the book of stories to the nurses' office and after cleansing her hands, goes to check on Sergeant Haske and administer the prescribed morphine. His position hasn't changed, but his ankles are even more swollen. A blood pressure reading is very low. She understands she should have the matron called but instead keeps her fingers on the man's wrist and senses life ebbing away, long moments between each beat, then longer, then for an extended period nothing until, finally, the smallest beat, pianissimo.

Mon Dieu! Too much morphine?

Terror stills her. The glass syringe is on the tray, a film of liquid within its cylinder. It doesn't tell her how much there was, initially, for it's on its side.

Too soon, surely, for the morphine to have killed him, no? "I am here, Sergeant Haske," she whispers, more to calm herself. "I will stay a while longer."

A thought forms in that hiatus. Beethoven's use of opposites wasn't just a trick of composition for its own sake. Loud/soft; fast/slow; major key/minor key; light/dark. Both Chekhov and Beethoven would have understood: the German wounded—and dying—in sunlit wards and rooms; the Allied wounded and dying, hidden away in dark nooks and cowering in bushes. And the line of emotion flowing through it all, binding them each to each.

She slides one of the curtains open, and then Private Kohnert's as well. They are friends, she's learned. He raises himself up a little so he can see around the mound of his bandages. "Is he going?"

She nods. A small lie. He's already gone, but Death, that mystery, lingers, it seems, all but tangible.

After a while, she closes Sergeant Haske's curtain, and as she's about to close Private Kohnert's, he asks her name. She tells him.

"*Danke*, Fräulein Hulbert. You cannot know what a good man he was. But he was."

The matron is with Sister Depage in the nurses' office. They appear to be reviewing a patient's record. "*Excusez-moi*," she says when both look up. "I'm most sorry to say that Sergeant Haske has…passed. Also, Matron, I have reconsidered the matter we discussed earlier. Perhaps we can talk further when you are free this evening. *Merci.*"

In the back passageway the matron unlocks a door and switches on an electric light, revealing a stairway. Then she shuts and hook-locks the door from inside, and they descend the stairs. An earthy, acrid smell grows stronger as the air becomes cooler and damp. On the cellar's stone floor, racks hold wine bottles. At intervals, massive wooden beams support the house's upper stories. Here and there the stone foundation is cracked and wet. Against a wall of rough-hewn planks stands a wooden table. The matron hands Marie-Thérèse the tray with bowls of beef tea and then moves the table to one side. She pushes on a plank, causing several to move inward, creating a doorway.

Inside the hidden room, she turns on another electric light. Beyond a pile of coal, there are several cots. Two men are asleep. Two awake. Here, there are no charts. No bedside tables. No cabinets. Lingering in the air of this closed-off room is a faint foul odor masked for the most part by the sulfuric smell of coal that irritates the nostrils.

"I don't use names," the matron whispers, and then shows her the pails for used bandages as well as a carpenter's chest filled with clean bandages and dressing in a hidden compartment.

"Good evening, messieurs," the matron whispers to the two

who are awake. "This is Mademoiselle Camille, an excellent nurse."

They feed the men the beef tea, then change bandages. One of them is quite young and brings Jacques to mind. His abdominal wound, she suspects, must be infected deep within the tissues, perhaps by bits of cloth and bullet fragments. There's a drain for the suppuration. He whispers that he was left behind with some others in a casualty station after it was overrun by Germans. They shot at them, looted the supplies, and then pulled down the tents before rushing after the Allies. That night he crawled out from under the canvas and made it into a wooded area, where a villager found him.

"I wanted to die in the woods."

Marie-Thérèse says a quick prayer that he doesn't die here, in a cellar.

They offer a few comforting words to each, hide away all supplies, gather the bowls, and finally turn out the light and reposition the table against the secret door.

"They know not to cry out or even talk," the matron whispers. At the top of the stairs she unhooks the door and slowly opens it. The hallway appears empty, but then they both notice it—cigarette smoke. *Charlotte.* The matron motions for her to wait on the landing. In the dark Marie-Thérèse feels for the hook and places it in the metal eye, then stands there, holding the tray and shivering. In her thoughts she plays the first of Schumann's "Scenes from Childhood." Then another, and another, until she makes it through all thirteen.

Finally, a soft tap on the door.

Deception

ZEPPELINS BOMB ANTWERP
The day's headlines.

They weren't there, she tells herself. Her father and mother, Willy and Jacques. Maybe for a while they were but not then. They would have had warning. They would have left in time.

But the queen hadn't. Queen Elisabeth and her children in the palace.

Other words, other images in that edition of the newspaper insert themselves into the nightmare. How the Germans devised a diabolic method of looting and destroying residences. At every twenty homes, on any given block, twenty soldiers line up, one in front of each doorway. Then twenty other soldiers simultaneously run into those houses to gather blankets, food, wine, and anything else of value. After they emerge, the ones waiting outside toss in petrol bombs, exploding twenty buildings simultaneously. *Efficacité!* Then the detachment moves on to the next twenty houses.

Why?

Marie-Thérèse pushes the newspaper aside. The tablecloth has a lace border of repeating, stylized flowers. She runs her fingers across hundreds of tiny knots making flowers.

Then takes her hand away.

I am German too.

Rani leans into the room. "There you are! Don't you want lunch? There's strudel today. Papa brought the cook—" Her glance falls on the newspaper.

Each side of the cloth has twenty-two interlinked flowers, and the cloth makes a square, so eighty-eight flowers in all. Two parents, two brothers, also an even number. Perhaps there's safety in even numbers.

But no. *Twenty residences at a time.*

Rani places an arm around Marie-Thérèse and they stay like that for a few moments. After Rani leaves for the wards, Marie-Thérèse loses herself in the "Pathetique" until someone begins pounding on the piano's treble keys.

"What is it, Liese?"

"I need to talk to you." This, in French. She's closed the door to the hallway.

"Fine, but why interrupt? You might have waited a bit." Nothing had been inhibiting concentration, strangely. Nothing locking her out.

"The doctor asked me to spy...on Matron."

"He asked all of us, no doubt." Her hands still throb with life.

"Are you going to?"

Marie-Thérèse closes the keyboard cover to give herself time. "If you have doubts about what to do, maybe you should consider leaving until all this is over."

"But tell me, are *you* going to spy? I don't want to be the only one being disloyal to her."

A test? And she sent by the doctor? Or...the matron?

"They're in command here now," Liese continues. "And not Matron. The question of loyalty is confusing."

"I agree."

"So, what are you going to do?"

"What's there to spy *on*? The contents of our supply cabinets?"

"Don't be evasive. You know perfectly well. If we see her doing something that isn't right, we're supposed to tell him. Hiding people, for example. I'm not sure I want to. Tell him, I mean."

"Then don't."

"You're still not answering my question, so that means that you probably *are* going to spy. Are you also going to tell the doctor about this conversation?"

"No."

"I've been thinking about how the clinic is supposed to be neutral. A Red Cross clinic. But if she takes in enemies of

Germany, she's violating that neutrality because at the same time this is German territory. Oh, I don't know! I'm all mixed up. I don't know what to do. He made me promise, but I still don't know what to do!"

Liese opens the keyboard cover and bangs on the keys again. Marie-Thérèse puts her hand over Liese's. "Think. If this clinic is a neutral zone, we should be able to treat anyone and everyone, no?"

"Are you saying we shouldn't spy?"

"I'm just following your words to their logical conclusion, Liese. It's—"

"You still won't tell me what *you're* doing!"

Despite her dislike—and distrust—Marie-Thérèse feels sorry for Liese. She possibly isn't lying. Yet this agonized Liese seems so unlike her.

"Don't worry so. There's nothing to tell him."

"How can you know that? Are you a spy, Marie-Thérèse? Please answer me. I can't stand looking at everyone and wondering what they're thinking…and saying to him. Don't we have to protect ourselves? If she's putting us at risk? They can burn this place down and us with it."

Liese, Marie-Thérèse senses, is capable of working both sides to glean favor. And doing it for the excitement. On the other hand, her distress may well be real.

"Pardon me, Liese, but I wish to keep my affairs confidential."

"Of course! So, what is Rani going to do?"

"She hasn't told me."

"And I should believe that. You just don't want me to know what you two are up to."

We will have to practice deception. It's ugly, deception. And yet, haven't they taken the Nightingale Pledge, promising to nurse *all wherever they may be and whenever in need?*

All.

"No one can serve two masters, Marie-Thérèse. It says so in the Bible."

"Yes. Then maybe we should serve the higher one."

"And just who is that? *Germany*. So that means you're a spy and we should be too."

"I'm a student nurse, Liese, who's trying her best under difficult circumstances. If this is all so upsetting, why not work on getting travel permission to go home for a while?"

"Because I don't want to go home! I want to finish my studies too. Thank you for nothing. I'm going to talk to Rani anyway. After all, *she's* German. *Auf wiedersehen!*"

For a few minutes Marie-Thérèse goes on with the "Pathetique," then gives it up.

While walking Jackie and Donnie, her thoughts rush from one worry to the next as if trying to extinguish fires that pop back up the minute she goes to another. Her family, the Antwerp bombings, Liese; her family, the Antwerp bombings, Doktor Kuhn. At tram stops, blaring posters tally in bold Gothic script the latest German advances and victories. Liège taken, the forts around that city destroyed, and around Namur as well. Louvain taken, its cathedral and university and library destroyed, Brussels occupied, and Luxemburg invaded. German flags fly where once Belgian flags had, the yellow, black, and red colors the same but the bars horizontal instead of vertical. Few civilians are about now. Instead, German soldiers and officers occupy most of the outdoor café tables, reading newspapers or talking, glasses of beer or cups of coffee before them.

All so extraordinary. She wonders if it will ever seem otherwise.

It's never as bad, despite the wounds, as the frightening return to her own room and the fear of meeting someone spying, the late-night quiet which intensifies the smallest creak, the dim hallway and need to traverse it to its end, then silently climb two flights of stairs to her floor, side-stepping the squeaky board, and then opening the door to the hallway and entering the lavatory, always anxious that Charlotte might be lying in wait, and then, finally, carrying her uniform and wearing the nightclothes she had on under it as she enters her own room while holding her breath.

That night Charlotte isn't in the lavatory, but Rani is sitting up in bed, fully awake. "Where were you? You weren't on ward duty tonight. And why are you carrying your uniform?"

Marie-Thérèse hangs everything in her wardrobe except the undergarments she drops in the laundry hamper. She gets into bed and tries to stop shaking.

"Marie-Thérèse?"

"I...remembered something. I threw my uniform on over my nightgown and went back down. Actually, I was worried about the drug cupboard. I always worry about forgetting to lock it. I had to go check."

"Were you with the doctor?"

"The doctor!" She offers a laugh. "At this hour? Goodness, Rani!"

"Or Liese? She told me you're spying on the matron. Is that where you were? The two of you?"

"Oh, for heaven's sake. I would never tell Liese anything of importance. You know that. And I'd never spy on Matron."

"I said that was absurd. And I told her I'm not going to spy for *anyone*. Not her, not the doctor, not anyone!"

She rolls back to face Rani. "Please don't say too much to her. You know how she is."

"No doubt I've already said too much."

"Tomorrow just try to gloss it over. Say you were upset and speaking out of...I don't know, exasperation. Exhaustion. Something."

"Three weeks ago, the only thing we had to worry about was *studying*. How innocent it all was and how happy we were, though we couldn't appreciate it, could we? We thought we had it so hard. And we worried about such trivial things, like a mark on our Report Forms or a comment by Gauthier. But now! Now I'm so worried about this war and how our school has changed, and all the shooting out there, and I'm worried about you, too, and your family. Marie-Thérèse? You wouldn't tell even if you *did* see anything suspicious, would you?"

"Of course not. But I've seen nothing."

"I don't know if I have or not. She seems so tired lately. I wonder sometimes if—"

"She would never endanger us, Rani."

"No. I know that."

She hears Rani turn over. There's no cheery *bonne nuit.* Marie-Thérèse's pulse slows eventually, but her heart hurts as if it has taken a blow. No wonder people talk about "heartbreak," as if that organ can break like some porcelain object. But it isn't porcelain or even delicate, more like a mechanical pump that can just quit. In other words, *break.*

Down on the street, automobiles speed somewhere. Farther away, a gunshot, then another. She thinks she hears Jackie barking. A scenario takes shape—the matron's apartment searched, the dogs barking wildly.

They will shoot Jackie too.

No. They won't.

Sleep. Or else tomorrow will be impossible.

REPORT CARD

The morning light is unusual in its clarity, each droplet of moisture on lawn, leaf, and petal a diamond. The lingering effects of malevolent dreams—in one she's in some out-of-control automobile speeding backward down a steep hill—shrivel away. No wonder medieval depictions of heaven often take the form of a garden, it occurs to her. And no wonder illuminators gilded their flowers and vines. This day is doing just that.

Seeing Elli near the pigeon coop, she calls, "*Bonjour*," defying the rule, as she always does with the children. Elli, holding a bucket, looks like a figure in a painting of summer foliage, with her sun-streaked hair in braids and green ribbons, the yellow dress, the light.

"Are you in charge of the pigeons now, Mademoiselle Elli?"

"*Bonjour*, Mademoiselle Marie-Thérèse. I do not sleep much, and it is better to be out here. "But…"

She strokes the back of a pigeon just then dipping its beak in its water tray.

"But?"

"Grand-père will tell you. I will get him."

Marie-Thérèse waits while Elli goes to Papa's cottage and knocks. The obscure shapes of worry and dread are creeping back. The scar through the old man's eyebrow appears almost like a fresh wound. The skin under his eyes is slack and dark, the eyelids swollen.

"Papa, what happened?"

He removes his cap and bows as usual but looks much older and all but devoid of spirit. "They come for them tomorrow."

"The girls? Someone is coming for the girls?"

He lowers his head, cap still held over his chest.

"Elli, what happened?"

"A soldier came. I hid but later Grand-père told me no one can have pigeons. It is now a law."

"You hid when a soldier came? That is not such a good idea, Elli. You—"

"I will always hide when they come."

The city is full of carrier pigeons, Marie-Thérèse is well aware. Many of them prized champions, winners of prestigious sporting competitions. The Germans wouldn't destroy them, would they? Not unless they want a true uprising.

"They shoot pigeons that fly," the gardener finally says.

"This they say."

"Then that means they won't shoot them, Papa. They'll keep them safe somewhere."

"Their deeds know not their words."

"Will you be able to see them? Where will they be? Did they say anything about that?"

"The soldier took Grand-père's bicycle," Elli says. "But he must bring feed to them somehow."

"So, you see? They will be safe. Do you know where he is to go?"

"I wrote it down, what I heard."

"*Mirabile!* You are such a clever girl!"

The girl and the elderly man remain morose. "Papa, it will be all right," Marie-Thérèse goes on. "If you are to bring them feed, it means they will live."

He picks up Marcel and holds him close to his chest. "I will not allow."

"Monsieur! No! You must. *S'il vous plaît.* Elli, you and Grand-père take care of each other. I will tell the matron, though she may already know. And please, both of you, never anger them. Papa, you are shrewd and know how to be patient, yes? Now it is time to be both patient and shrewd."

"A wolf."

"Not too much the wolf. And, Elli, you must not be a rabbit when they come."

"We will both be wolves."

In the civilian ward later that morning, she sees that Madame Heinbokel has been discharged. She hopes she still has her chickens. She pulls a chair closer to Janine's bed after sponging the little girl's face and forehead and then raising her to a sitting position.

"Should we walk today, my petite one?" she whispers in French. The little girl's expression remains stony. "Let me comb Her Majesty's beautiful curls, and then we shall take a tour, yes?"

Janine raises her left thumb to her mouth.

"Ah, I see you wish to be carried. I shall do that to please Her Majesty, but just once more. Tomorrow Her Majesty must put on her magic slippers and walk to the windows herself, with her faithful servant. *Uppa!* Here we go, into your golden carriage!"

Janine settles on Marie-Thérèse's arm, leaning into her, and Marie-Thérèse walks back and forth awhile. At first she's afraid to go to the windows in case of more shooting nearby. But the day draws her, and soon they are there, in a bath of sunlight. Liese approaches as Marie-Thérèse is describing the antics of the queen's royal pets.

"Why are you always carrying that child about, Marie-Thérèse?" she asks in German. "Maybe you should get one of your own."

"Well, I have," she replies in French. "*This* one!" She nuzzles her cheek against Janine's.

"Probably not for long. Especially if you keep speaking French the way you do."

The next morning a dream of explosions gives way to very real thuds. Rani, in her dark-blue suit and straw hat with daisy appliqué trim, is tossing books into her trunk. The hat looks about to fall off. Her other hat, a gray brimmed one with a pheasant feather, is on her bed, along with her hatbox and valise. Textbooks lie scattered on the bed and floor. It is twenty minutes to six in the morning. "What are you doing, Rani?"

"You have eyes, *non*? At least Liese thinks you do." Rani stuffs clothing around the books in the trunk, pushes in four more books, and then presses the top down over it all.

"What do you mean by that, for heaven's sake?"

"I don't know. It doesn't matter."

"Rani, you know better than to listen to Liese. Does your family say you have to return?"

"*Non!* I do."

Marie-Thérèse dresses quickly. "I'm sorry if I've upset you in any way. Please don't leave on account of me. Or Liese! You know how she is."

"It's not just her. Yesterday a patient in the civilian ward wouldn't let me attend her because I'm German, and another one called me vile names. I suppose they were talking about me and when I came into the ward, they just...went on the attack. And then later, Liese was implying all sorts of things, I don't even know! I stopped listening, telling myself it was just Liese. But then you came in that time, holding your uniform; obviously you had been up to something but wouldn't tell me anything. Instead, you made up a story about the drug cabinet, of all things. Never before have you gone down to check that cupboard. Why make up such a story? Because I'm *German.* Well, of course! *I* burned all the books in Louvain. *I* destroyed the cathedral, and so naturally you won't talk to me! So, I'm going home. At least I won't be spit at there and called odious names. And not trusted!"

"Rani, Rani, you're overreacting. You're upset and seeing things all one way."

"I know what I'm seeing. I earn excellent marks in observation. What I see is that I'm not wanted here. Neither in the wards nor in this city. If the only thing I'm good for is to spy on people, I refuse. I have more self-respect than that. I'm going home and will volunteer in a German hospital. That's what I am going to do."

"Are you forgetting that I'm German too?"

"My memory is functioning quite well. So, have you been spit at yet?"

"It's just that my French accent—"

"Good for you and your accent. Goodbye, Marie-Thérèse."

"Wait, please. You're leaving all these books?"

"I don't have room. Keep them. Or have the school send them to me. Whatever you prefer."

"I'm coming with you to the station at least."

"Please don't."

"I want to."

"I don't want you to."

"I'm coming with you. You can't stop me."

Marie-Thérèse reaches for a shawl and follows Rani down the stairway, the trunk bumping at each step. "Why not have breakfast first? You know how you like breakfast. Does Matron know you're leaving? Have you told her? Why don't you give it one more day? You may have had a terrible night and now are throwing everything away. All your hard work! All your achievements! Just one more day…please, Rani?" To her ear, she sounds like her mother.

"Why would Matron care?"

"Listen to yourself. You sound like a four-year-old throwing a tantrum."

"Maybe I want to throw a tantrum."

Ignoring the dining room, redolent of bacon and fried potatoes, Rani goes through the nurses' sitting room and out its street door.

"At least let me carry your valise and hat box."

"I can manage."

"What if the trains aren't running?"

"They are. They're taking the wounded back."

Marie-Thérèse slips into the patisserie and begs the proprietor for two rolls, promising to pay for them later in the day. Then she has to run to catch up. Rani has reached the tram stop and stands there, looking down the street for the tram.

"Please keep your French bread."

"Goodness, Rani! I had no idea you had such a temper. You're letting some baseless anger take over your usually excellent brain."

"It's not baseless."

"I suppose not, from your perspective. But anyway, you need something to eat on the way. Take these."

"The wounded on board have to eat. I am sure there will be something for me."

Marie-Thérèse knows the conductor on this tram and again finds herself begging. The woman looks from one strained face to the other and brusquely motions her on.

They sit alongside one another in silence as the tram clatters toward the city center and the Gare du Nord. Marie-Thérèse resists an urge to straighten Rani's hat. After a while she says, "I will miss you so much. I wish you'd change your mind. Right now we could be having breakfast. Why don't we just go back."

Rani is staring out at shops and cafés, some just opening. German posters cover walls and the sides of kiosks. "*Nein*," she says, without turning.

As the tram crosses a square, Marie-Thérèse notices several older men kneeling and scrubbing the cobbles with brushes while another sweeps up horse droppings and tosses them into a barrel on a cart. "There've never been elderly men cleaning the streets like that," Marie-Thérèse muses aloud. "And on their hands and knees!"

The conductor, passing their row, says, "They have to do that now, the old ones." She scowls, stooping a little and looking out the window.

At the station stop, Rani blocks exiting passengers as she struggles with her trunk, valise, and hatbox. Finally, her trunk bumps down onto the pavement. People stream around the two of them as Rani rearranges her things. Then she's pulling the trunk by one leather handle. The brass fittings on the corners scrape against the pavement as she leans forward against its weight.

"That looks so heavy. Please let me help you."

"It's not heavy."

"The matron really does need you. I'm not just saying that, Rani. You're one of the best students, and she's so shorthanded now. Look how many have already left."

"I don't blame them."

At the ticket counter, Rani tells the clerk her destination and then turns to Marie-Thérèse. "You know, if she *is* harboring wounded Belgians, good for her, but you're all going to pay for it. There's no thwarting Germany, as you well know. I don't want to be blamed for another of their victories. As for you, you're going to regret whatever you're doing if it's secret. And if it is, no doubt it's illegal."

The clerk's eyebrows are raised. Fear spiraling through her, Marie-Thérèse prays that he's Belgian and not one of the implanted German officials. Rani extends her hand, and the clerk slides a packet of tickets through the opening at the bottom of the grille. Knowing she shouldn't, Marie-Thérèse keeps glancing back as they walk toward the train platforms.

"Please, Rani. You've just had a bad night." Rani increases her pace. At a waiting train, a porter takes her trunk. "Why not wait a day? Give yourself time to reconsider."

"I have no choice!"

"But you do. Just one more day. We can talk and—"

"No."

"Your hat…it's about to fall off. Here, let me fix it."

Rani does it herself, mashing it on harder.

The platform is filling with soldiers carrying stretchers and pushing wheelchairs. Some of the wounded are alert. Others appear comatose. Still others are walking about and smoking, a few even laughing, their bandaging worn like casual badges of honor.

Rani addresses a stretcher bearer who, in turn, calls to an officer. "Captain Kirchoff, nurses!"

The middle-aged officer strides over to them and asks how far they'll be traveling. Marie-Thérèse attempts a hasty correction, but he waves a hand in dismissal and turns to Rani. Allowing her only a minute to introduce herself and explain, he issues rapid instructions before swinging around and ordering a private over. The young soldier runs up and takes Rani's trunk. As she turns to follow him, Marie-Thérèse grips her in a sideways embrace. "Write to me, please. I will never blame you for anything. And I will miss you terribly."

Rani pulls away and hurries after the private, then disappears inside the baggage car. But as the train slides forward, her face appears at a window, then her hand, touching the glass.

Marie-Thérèse raises her own hand, the one holding the rolls. Trotting alongside the train, she extends the bag upward. The window opens and Rani reaches down for it.

By the time the last carriage is out of sight, the platform is again crowded with wounded soldiers and stretcher bearers. On a luggage cart, bodies lie cocooned in gray blankets. There are too many to count.

"Fräulein Hulbert? *Fräulein Hulbert!*"

Private Schalk, on a stretcher carried by two soldiers, is motioning with his hand raised just a few inches. "I am going home! I am going home to a hospital. So maybe I will not die. It is something to think about! Where are you going, Fräulein Hulbert? Do you go to a new hospital today? Is it possible we will travel together? That would be very nice." One of the stretcher bearers laughs.

"She is an excellent nurse!" Private Schalk tells them. "I was most fortunate."

Now both are smirking.

"I will miss you, Private Schalk," she says, a tinge of defiance in her voice directed at the other two. "You brightened my days."

"And you, Fräulein Hulbert, brightened mine!"

The stretcher bearer at the head rolls his eyes. "True love," the other says.

"Pay no attention to them," the private says. "They are being silly because they are happy to be going home too."

"No, Fräulein," the one at the head of the stretcher says in a serious tone. "It is just that we are envious."

She raises her chin as the matron might have and looks directly at the young soldier still whole of body, still jaunty with pride and well-being. "As well you should be. Private Schalk is a courageous man and I am an excellent nurse and we do like each other. We are friends."

It surprises her to realize that this is true.

"And nearly the same age! I would very much like to write to you, Fräulein, if you would please allow it. You can write to me in Cuxhaven. The postmaster will know how to find me."

Carriage doors of a new train are opening, and soon Private Schalk, too, is gone.

In the fall they go, the birds. She stands there feeling the same desolation as if actually watching them all rise upward, circle, and then move as one southward. Tiny things against a tumult of fast-moving cloud.

In the room she shared with Rani for nearly two and a half years, there's a spill of textbooks on the floor and several on the bed. *Bacteriology: Dust and Its Dangers. The Story of the Bacteria. Textbook of General Therapeutics. Poisons. Nursing and the Care of the Nervous and Insane.* Marie-Thérèse owns the same costly books and can only think how Rani must have hated leaving these behind, though she did take her essential anatomy and bandaging texts as well as the *Materia Medica and Therapeutics.*

She stacks the books and decides to send them to Rani's parents that day, with a note for Rani. Checking under her bed, she finds one of Rani's Form of Report cards dated the previous May. For *Thoroughness in work,* she received an *Excellent. Interest displayed: Very Good. Powers of observation: Very Good. Punctuality: Excellent. Neatness: Acceptable. General attention and kindness to patients, disposition: Excellent. Health: Very Good. Improvement (if any): Please remember not to run in the back passageway, Fräulein Hier.* And under *General Remarks: Your marks on tests for the most part have been high and praiseworthy. However, please spend more time on Anatomy next term.*

The dreaded Form of Report cards had come once a week during the previous term, when everything at the clinic had been running in perfect order. Since then there've been only one report for the whole of August and one for September. Rani must have taken the latest ones with her. She, the better student, always with more *Excellents*, and so having to buy more pastries for the two of them.

Marie-Thérèse slips the Form of Report card into the textbook on poisons, enjoying the sad joke. After she strips the bed of linen, though, it seems as if Rani was never there. She remakes the bed and places *Nursing and the Care of the Nervous and Insane* on Rani's desk.

The room feels a little better.

In Germany, it occurs to her, Rani will at least be safe.

Excellent work, Fräulein Hier.

SCARCITY

In one hand, Jackie and Donnie's leashes, the two dogs ambling along the pavement, pausing every so often to sniff at fallen leaves, lampposts, and flower planters. Her other arm is linked through that of an elderly man dragging his right foot after sliding the left forward. His head is bowed. His hair is white under his worker's cap. He's trembling, and these tremors pass into her arm.

At a marketplace a woman is selling chestnuts; another has a few potatoes. "Be quick," she calls out to Marie-Thérèse, "if you want them!" Farther along, a child holds out a brilliant yellow chrysanthemum stem. Her bucket is still nearly full. Marie-Thérèse finds a few coins and takes the stem while her companion waits, staring at the paving stones.

"Are you all right?" Marie-Thérèse asks when they are beyond the marketplace.

"I may yet live," he replies in French.

In the October warmth, leaves twirl down and lie in gold and cerise carpets. Puffs of cloud slide northward in no rush. A good omen, she thinks, as she holds her face briefly to the sun.

Traffic passes on the boulevard, for the most part German automobiles amid a few trucks and wagons but no bicycles. "Almost a summer day!" Marie-Thérèse says in German. "How fortunate to have such lovely weather!" Her companion doesn't reply. He's eyeing the carpet of leaves, which his feet rumple. Besides, he has no idea what she has just said.

A German officer at an outdoor table reaches forward to pet Jackie, who has wandered within range. Jackie immediately sits and extends his long muzzle.

"Ho! What have we here? Another Belgian beggar! Shall we feed him or not?" he asks his companion. "Are we allowed, Fräulein?"

"*Selbstverständlich!*" Of course!

He takes half a sausage from his plate and holds it between thumb and forefinger above Jackie's head. Jackie gives his throaty bark and Donnie his high yelp.

"Ah! *Two* Belgian beggars!" Jackie opens his mouth; Donnie jumps up. "Ah-ah! No jumping. You must be polite."

The two tease the dogs for a while before giving them bits of sausage and fried potatoes. The old man alongside her keeps his head lowered.

"What do you think, grandfather? Would you like some sausage too?" This witticism causes more laughter. The officer dangles one in his direction.

The old man salutes the soldier. "*Nein, danke*, mein Herr."

"Well, good, because they're all gone!" He tosses it to Jackie, who catches it.

"*Danke*, sirs," Marie-Thérèse says. "You have made them most happy."

"It's unfortunate you have that old man in tow or we'd invite you to join us, Fräulein."

"My uncle must take exercise for his legs."

"Well, come back this way when you're free. We're usually here, right, Walther?"

She promises to do so and then they are walking again, the man's arm in hers shaking harder now. She's noted the name of the café, the street.

A block farther they turn onto a smaller street littered with linden leaves. Ahead, a girl with a large doll stoops over the pavement, arranging stones in a circle. The dogs pull at their leashes. Soon they're nudging and whining at the girl. She gives each a pat before scooping up her doll, brushing away the stones, and then skipping away with the two dogs.

Marie-Thérèse and the old man enter a dark brasserie and take a table in back. With a trembling hand, the old man removes half a playing card from a pocket and sets it before him. The ten of hearts. A waiter approaches, full glass of beer in one hand, towel in another. "*Bonjour,*" he says sotto voce. Setting down the beer and masking his next action with the towel, he slips the matching half of the card from his vest pocket and places it on the table alongside the other. Then he deftly makes both disappear.

"Well, I must go," she says in German. "I will leave you to your conversation."

"*Merci*," the old man says under his breath, flour dusting his shoulders like dandruff.

Her legs are weak as she takes a different route back. Which way had Elli gone with the dogs? She forgot to warn her about the café and the officers. A mistake! And not a small one. But at the clinic there's no time to find Elli and ask. The doctor stops her just as she's entering the main door.

"Well met, Student-nurse Hulbert. I've been hoping to have a little talk with you and here you are. A somewhat pleasant day, no? I hope you've been able to enjoy it. Ah! A flower. Not for me, I suppose."

"If you wish, sir."

"No, no. I was joking. Keep it!"

"If you will excuse me, Herr Doktor, I have ward duty and must change."

"Please step into my office a moment. I'll explain your absence and there will be no penalty."

She takes a chair facing the desk in what had been Doctor Depage's office. The desk is still where it had been, against the far wall and facing outward. On it, a green-glass lamp. The maroon leather chairs are still in place before the desk. A marble-topped, round table and four chairs haven't been moved from their position near the wall to the right. Shelves of books fill the opposite wall. A Persian carpet, its ruby tones leaping up, covers most of the floor. She's surprised that the doctor doesn't look much better than when he first arrived. Surely, he might have recovered from fatigue by now, but no, there are the same signs of exhaustion—the puffy sag of skin under the eyes, the bleariness, even the perspiration he mops away with a handkerchief.

She's distracted from her observations by her own situation. Was the Belgian caught? Had Elli been questioned? The café, the dogs… She sits as still as possible, hoping that her heartbeat isn't audible. The doctor makes it all the worse by taking his time, seating himself behind the desk and arranging his hands over the blotter in a relaxed clasp.

"Student-nurse Hulbert," he says finally, "you've been looking rather tired. Have you been getting enough sleep?"

"I believe so, sir, although I often do stay up late studying."

"Yes, I'm sure. But with all the work in the wards and the clinic being understaffed, I'm surprised you have time to walk about. You have been gone for nearly an hour."

"The matron…"—*don't hesitate!*—"wishes us to have some fresh air and sunlight. Today it was my turn."

"She is most concerned about your welfare."

"Yes."

"Are you certain of that?"

"I believe so. She always has been."

He raises one hand to his beard and smooths its already smooth point. "Again, I find a lapse in your logic. What has been is not always proof of how something is now. Do you see that?"

"I do, yes."

"So then does this 'seeing' cause you to amend your answer?"

"I believe she thinks about our welfare as much as she does her patients'."

"Truly? Would it surprise you to know that I have been hearing some disturbing things?"

Would it surprise? Think!

"Yes, I would be surprised, Herr Doktor."

"You are intelligent…and observant. Yet in all these days you have not come to me with anything the least suspicious. Why is that?"

"Because I have observed nothing suspicious, sir."

"Nothing?"

"No, sir."

"If you are trying to protect her, it is noble but foolish."

It seems that her chest holds a snowstorm. "What have you heard, Herr Doktor?"

"It is not for you to question me. I will ask you again. Have you seen or heard anything suspicious?"

"I have seen nothing out of order. All is as it should be." She holds her chin level and keeps her eyes on his while curbing a temptation to say more.

"I have been told that your brother, Jacques Hulbert, has been missing and that your parents have been looking for him. Is this true?"

Who told you? Her throat closes to sound.

"Is this in fact the case?"

"He has been missing, sir, yes."

"And he went to join the Allied forces, a young man with German blood."

"We do not know where he went for certain."

"I have received word that he has been wounded and is being treated in a German field hospital. It states here that he has a birthmark to the right of his spine, on the upper quadrant of his back. Perhaps you recall such a mark?"

"A birthmark? Yes, I do seem to remember that he has one, but the wounds…are the wounds…"

"Serious? They are. Five bullet wounds. If he lives, he will be transported to Germany as a prisoner of war."

His face blurs.

"If you cooperate with my inquiry, I will do all I can in regard to your brother. It will be difficult, but I have some influence in higher military circles. Otherwise, I am afraid that you and your family may never see him again. Given his background, he will be tried as a traitor and executed. He is how old?"

"Sixteen."

"A pity. But all may yet be well. If you help me."

"I have already agreed, Herr Doktor."

"In word, yes. I will be starting a review procedure and will be asking each student to write a statement describing something she is proud of accomplishing during the preceding week as well as any areas for improvement. This statement will provide the basis for our weekly discussions. On a separate page, you must describe anything out of the ordinary you observed about the clinic and the matron's behavior as well as dates and times. You are not to judge their significance. Simply state facts. Your assigned time is a week from today at one o'clock in the afternoon."

"How will you help him?"

"I can have him transferred anywhere I wish."

"Even here?"

"Anywhere. Now, you have work to do. You may leave."

Before taking the flower up to the children's ward, she spends several minutes in a lavatory, retching.

Their deeds know not their words.

Nor do mine.

The matron, she believes, is wrong. We can't *always* control our responses to events.

Late that night, she turns from the back passageway into the stairwell and stops. Charlotte is sitting on the third step, her face sweaty, her eyes manic. "Me smelt a rat!" she says in English. "And here she is!"

Marie-Thérèse knows enough English to understand. The muscles of her legs lose their tension. Her stomach flutters.

"*Bonsoir*, Madame Charlotte. Are you not chilled? It's drafty here. I've just closed a window."

"The rat lies! Get it for me or I'll tell 'im."

"I don't understand, madame. Tell who?"

Charlotte switches to French. "The snooping doctor, who else? He asked me to be on the lookout and so I am. And what do I see but you, coming from somewhere late at night."

"Of course I'm coming from somewhere. I haven't been feeling well and went to see the matron. She made me a ginger drink to settle my stomach. Then I noticed the wide-open window and closed it."

"The caught rat knows how to lie!"

"Shall we go ask her, then?"

Charlotte covers her eyes. "No. I don't want to." Down come her hands, and there's the manic glare again. "Just get it for me or I'm going to tell him all about you."

"Get what, Madame Charlotte?"

"You know!"

"A warm drink you must mean."

"Don't you be playing dense, now."

"Oh! Of course. Your drug."

"Yes, miss, my med'cine."

"Madame Charlotte, I don't have the key. I'm not on ward duty and have no access to the cupboard. If you're feeling bad tonight, the matron will help you."

"She won't! No more tonight. She's a stubborn one."

"Then I don't know, madame."

"I need it!"

"Maybe they can help you in the ward."

"They won't."

Charlotte lowers her head and pushes the heels of her palms against her eyes. She gasps for breath.

"Madame Charlotte—"

The woman writhes away from Marie-Thérèse's hand. "Get it or he's going to know there're soldiers here, British soldiers!"

Marie-Thérèse freezes in place. "But there are no British soldiers here. They were taken away weeks ago."

"Even if there aren't, I can say there are and she'll be in trouble. You too. They'll lock you both up."

"Madame, the matron is your best friend. You don't want her to go to prison, do you? You'll be all alone then. And they'll probably lock you up too. All by yourself in a room. Or even in chains. They can do that, you know."

"Just…get it for me. I won't ever ask you again."

But you will.

She takes the woman's cold hand. "Come with me." To her surprise, Charlotte stands, and Marie-Thérèse leads her to her own room. "It's warmer in here. Come now."

She covers Charlotte with Rani's thick blanket and adds her own coat. Charlotte lies there, crying and shivering, her knees drawn up, the bunch of hair wild over the pillow. Marie-Thérèse finds the roll from breakfast she had stowed away and feeds pieces of it to her. Then, wrapped in her own blanket, she sits alongside her, stroking the woman's rough hair. It reminds her of Jackie's wiry coat. "Soon," she whispers, "it will be better. Matron will give you your medicine in the morning and it's almost morning now. I'll wait with you. You aren't alone. You'll have your medicine shortly. In an hour or two it will be morning and you'll feel much better. Soon it will be morning, madame, very soon now."

Marie-Thérèse closes her eyes for short intervals that become longer. When her alarm clock rings, she's lying on the edge of Rani's bed. The first thought of the day stabs through the fading fabric of a dream: *Gone—to tell the doctor.*

Looking through the glass of the door to the director's office, she sees Charlotte, disheveled, slumped in a chair facing the desk. But—miracle of miracles—the chair behind the desk is vacant. Marie-Thérèse, pretending she is on routine business, searches wards, offices, and finally, with no one to see her, runs the length of the back corridor, praying that she hasn't taken the dogs for an early walk.

The matron doesn't answer Marie-Thérèse's knock, but the dogs are in the garden.

Running where she can, she returns to the wards. And there she is, in the nurses' office, asking about Charlotte. Marie-Thérèse dares not grab her arm.

After their whispered words in the hall, Marie-Thérèse goes into the dining hall for breakfast.

"You look wretched, Marie-Thérèse," Liese comments. "Were you on all night?"

This can be checked. "No."

"Well, you probably need a lot more sleep then."

"And who doesn't?"

"True!"

If her nerves weren't so wild, still, she might have been able to put a number to all the insinuations in Liese's words.

There is no butter. No bacon. No jam. No eggs. And definitely no sausage. How can it all go on, she wonders. It can't, can it?

SPY

But it does.

In the park along the rue de la Culture, Marie-Thérèse follows the matron at a distance. Jackie and Donnie want to chase squirrels, but she won't let them. At one point the matron pauses to pick up a small branch, shakes rainwater from the cluster of leaves, and then places the branch on the lawn, just off the walkway where other leaves are turning into sodden clumps. An odor of decay permeates the damp air. Marie-Thérèse has to keep swallowing and is afraid she's going to start retching again. It happens often now. Sooner or later this will be brought to the matron's attention.

Why did she pick up the branch of oak leaves and put it to the side? So that other pedestrians won't trample the leaves? Or was it a sign meant for someone? To Marie-Thérèse's disgust, she finds herself hoping the matron is there to meet someone. Anyone. Then there will be something of substance to tell the doctor.

Truly disgusting.

She turns back.

November 3, 1914: She was at the park today with the dogs. She picked up a small branch with some oak leaves on it. She carefully put it to the side of the walkway, the branch end facing forward, the leaves fanning out in back.

November 5: A well-dressed lady visited the matron at about eleven o'clock in the morning. She used the matron's private entrance, off the rue de la Culture.

November 7: The same well-dressed lady visited again but used the public entrance. She wore the same dark-blue cloak as she had on November 5th. It was the same time of day, eleven o'clock in the morning. Later she walked across the park and entered a waiting automobile. The automobile had a chauffeur. I do not know what kind of automobile it was.

November 8: The matron took Donnie to a veterinary office on the rue de l'Abbaye.

As usual, she throws up her breakfast of dry toast and unsweetened tea. Butter and sugar are rationed, and what the clinic does have goes to the patients first. The British are now blockading North Sea ports, and so the occupiers take what they need from Belgian shops and warehouses. Marie-Thérèse hardly cares. All food is tasteless now. The occupiers are also closing down newspaper offices. That doesn't matter to her either. All she can think about, nearly, are Jacques and the matron.

Ten minutes before her scheduled review, she walks through the school's main corridor to Doctor Depage's former office three doors from the operating theater. At the door now stating *Doktor Manfred Kuhn,* she swallows saliva and takes a shaky breath before knocking.

"*Eintreten!*"

She opens the door and enters. Sister Knecht, a white-haired nurse, is sitting in one of the maroon armchairs. The doctor is seated at the desk.

"*Guten Morgen,* Herr Doktor. *Guten Morgen,* Sister Knecht."

As he extends his arm to take her papers, his hand trembles. "*Platz nehen,* Student-nurse Hulbert."

She sits facing the desk and folds her hands in her lap while he reads both pages and finally sets them on top of an open folder. Then he regards her.

"So. You are proud of a bandaging exercise in which you excelled."

"Yes, sir. I had not been able to do that form before last week."

He looks at Sister Knecht. "A third-year not able to bandage correctly? Why does that astonish me? Is it so difficult, Sister?"

"I think Student-nurse Hulbert meant to say that she had not been able to do it *perfectly* before last week. Whenever I observed her, she sometimes took too much time or else didn't apply enough pressure and so ran out of bandaging material before she should have. In her practical exercises she often does not exhibit enough confidence. Student-nurse Hulbert seems to have an excessive fear of making mistakes. I tell our students that that is like having to work while wearing shackles. You must not overthink. Your actions must become second nature, ingrained, a part of you. That comes through repeated practice. Practice leads to mastery. And confidence."

"Well said. I agree, of course. And so, Student-nurse Hulbert, your excelling in this form obviously proves the point. You must have been practicing."

"I have been, sir."

"Very good. But I see that your weekly mark for an examination has gone down significantly. The examination had to do with *materia medica*. Do you find that course too difficult?"

"No, not especially difficult. I did study but—"

"Obviously not enough. You must do better. Where lives are involved, no medical facility wants mediocrity on its staff. Nor do I. Do you understand?"

"Yes, Herr Doktor."

"If you do not raise this mark by the next time we meet, you will be expelled. That will be regrettable for many reasons. Do you understand?"

"I understand."

"I will ask your matron to retest you so that you can prove to me that you can do much better. Now..." He looks at the second sheet then raises his eyes again. "You say you were late for a lecture. You give several reasons. But still, I find it inexcusable. Your matron demands strict punctuality, and I applaud her for that. Again, lives depend on your punctuality. I'm certain you can do better in this area. It's simply a matter of paying attention to a timepiece. Do you have one?"

"Yes, I do, sir."

"Is it accurate?"

"It is."

"Is she usually punctual, Sister?"

"She is."

"You must have been lost in the clouds then. An exception proving the rule. Is there anything you wish to add?"

"Only that I will work harder to improve, sir."

"Very good. I believe you will. Congratulations on your bandaging achievement. You may leave now."

He closes the folder over the pages.

As she enters a lavatory beyond the operating theater, Liese is just leaving. "Oh no," she says. "Not again!"

Marie-Thérèse laughs. "Just the usual."

The Queen of All Poisons

Dread is a constant companion. Surely a telegram concerning her parents will arrive *today*. Or, surely the doctor will find the hidden ward. Or, Liese will betray all of them. Nights, she plunges into her textbooks when she can't sleep because of festering worries. She reads until the open book falls on her chest and stays there until morning.

She writes Rani, saying that everything is fine and the clinic is running smoothly—this, for the censors. She says she misses her. She doesn't rail against her for having betrayed her about Jacques because she probably hasn't. She doesn't mention how Papa is bereft without his pigeons and spends hours in the garden, fussing with wet earth, trying in vain to get a few late lettuces to grow. She does include details about the Christmas gifts they have been knitting and crocheting for the children of the neighborhood.

In all, her letter is a non-letter. She doesn't know why she even sends it. Then she does. The truth is, she misses Rani. Her absence seems a kind of death.

One afternoon, drizzle and fog at windowpanes, the gardener hands her an envelope bearing no stamps. An envelope that has been folded in half. An envelope with only her name on it but in her father's handwriting.

"How did you get this?" she whispers.

He shakes his head and walks back down the corridor leading to the garden door.

The letter is dated two weeks earlier. There are no greasy crayon slashes to indicate it has gone through a censor's office. She says a swift prayer that they found Jacques. The fact that her father, at least, is alive doesn't at first register—to her later shame. She only wants the words *Jacques is with us.*

After a moment she opens her eyes and reads.

We are safe, my dear, and in the Netherlands. Although we haven't found Jacques yet, we have several leads. We did learn that his unit was fighting in an area I will not name here. A number of wounded were taken prisoner, but a number also wandered off. I have been traveling about asking questions. It has been difficult. People understandably don't want to talk. But I did learn that a number of those wounded Allies found their way back—or were returned—to their regiments. So, we have hope. I cannot get back and forth into Belgium easily now, and this makes it all the more difficult. It is possible that Jacques may find himself at your clinic, though in that case he would probably be a prisoner of war. I will continue to make inquiries.

Your mother and Willy send their love. I do as well. God keep you safe.

She tries to be hopeful. But all she can feel is self-revulsion and fear. Yet at moments, some small flicker of energy and conviction tells her that Jacques *isn't* a prisoner. That the doctor lied. He might know about Jacques joining the Allies, but that's all. He made up the rest to snare her. Why not? Somehow the secret police may have snared *him*, maybe threatening to destroy his stellar reputation, and so now he has to set his own traps.

These instances of conviction might energize her for a few moments but ultimately don't help much. She has to raise that mark on the *materia medica* examination. She has to find something to write for her next review. Above all, she has to eat something and keep it down.

She's studying in her room when her textbook on poisons draws her eye. Opening it at random, she finds herself staring at a pen and ink illustration of a plant with a tall stalk of small flowers resembling the hoods monks have on their cloaks. *Aconitum napellus*. The flowers are described as purple. This variety of *Aconitum* has several common names, among them Monkshood, The Queen of All Poisons, and Devil's Helmet. Its toxins enter through the skin and cause vomiting, diarrhea, blurred vision, tingling of the skin, and eventually, multiple organ failure.

If you have cuts on your hands and brush against the plant, you could die. Warriors once poisoned the tips of their arrows with the toxin of *Aconitum napellus*.

How many people, she wonders, died while just preparing the arrows?

Later she goes into the garden and looks for such a plant. There are none, of course.

"I am pleased to see that you have significantly raised your mark on the *materia medica* examination, Student-nurse Hulbert."

"*Danke*, sir."

"So much is possible when one applies oneself. Are there any other areas where you have excelled?"

I managed not to throw up after breakfast today. "No, but my work has been generally satisfactory."

"You must be proud of your new examination mark."

"I am not so proud. I should have done that the first time."

"I agree. Areas for improvement?"

"I have written down that I wish to be better in each area in my examinations and also ward duty. Specifically, I wish to raise my mark in bacteriology and also be less nervous while being observed. I have a tendency then to mix up my words and talk too fast."

He is looking at her second page.

"I have a report here that you seemed distracted while on ward duty. Do you feel this is a fair assessment?"

He still appears ill, she observes. You see it first in the eyes, the thickening of moisture, the red tinge. "If I have been observed acting distracted, then it must be accurate and fair."

"That is a serious failing. Why did you not mention it?"

"I didn't realize that I had been distracted. It wasn't in any... critique."

"It should have been. Do you agree that distraction is a serious fault?"

"I do, yes." His fingers are still trembling. Could it be the onset of palsy?

"Then you must work on that area as well. I expect a better report next time."

Again, he regards the second page, which holds only two sentences. The paper wavers in his hand. *November 14: A woman in a Salvation Army uniform visited the matron today. She left after fifteen minutes.*

"Distraction, Student-nurse Hulbert, leads to diminished powers of observation. And that can prove fatal, as you well know. Now, return to your work and do better."

"*Danke*, Herr Doktor Kuhn. I will."

She decides to use the lavatory up in the student-nurses' corridor and hopes not to faint before she can get there. The corridor is fading out of focus, and there's the stairway yet.

That evening while crocheting in the sitting room, she's again thinking of The Queen of All Poisons. And then knows why.

St. Gudule, no.

In her hands the aqua wool blurs. She has no consciousness of her head tilting backward and her eyes rolling upward.

When she wakes, the matron is sitting alongside the bed. Marie-Thérèse knows that she isn't in her own room just from the different coverlet. It's a private room on the third floor, one of three kept prepared for ill students and sisters.

"Are you feeling somewhat better now, mademoiselle?"

There's a drip in her arm. Fluid and nutrients.

"I am, Matron, *merci.*"

"You were dehydrated."

"I'm much better now, I think. *Pardonnez-moi, Matrone.*"

"For becoming ill? There is nothing to forgive."

Her heart begins shuddering away. And just as Marie-Thérèse might have predicted, the matron takes her wrist, presses three fingers gently against it and, lowering her eyes, concentrates.

"Your heart rate is somewhat elevated." *Somewhat.* "What has made you unable to eat, my dear? You have no fever. Do you have pain in your stomach?"

Marie-Thérèse turns her head toward the wall and tears slip

out. The matron releases her wrist and places her arm back on the coverlet as if it were some delicate thing in danger of shattering.

"No, Matron." Embarrassed by exhibiting so much weakness, she sniffs, inadvertently making a rude sound.

The matron takes a cloth and blots Marie-Thérèse's face. "There is no physical pain?"

"No."

She palpates the abdomen and lower torso. "None?"

"No, Matron. I just haven't been hungry."

She listens to Marie-Thérèse's heart and then has her lean forward so she can assess the lungs.

"Perhaps I should have the doctor here."

"No, please. Don't call him. I just haven't been eating enough."

"Apart from the elevated pulse, your heart seems strong. Your lungs clear. It seems we are in another area altogether. Can you tell me anything that might help you alleviate this lack of appetite?"

Once again Marie-Thérèse turns away. "I'm sorry to be taking so much of your time. There is nothing, really, to say."

"Have you heard from your parents?"

"My father. They're still looking for Jacques, but they themselves are safe in the Netherlands."

"Your father must have to slip over the border from time to time."

"Yes."

"Is this what you worry about?"

"Yes."

"You could have a leave of absence to go to them when you are well."

"I have no idea where they are. But in any case, I need to stay here."

After a moment the matron asks why.

"There is so much work and I must be here in case Jacques…"

Words upsetting the equilibrium.

Blotting Marie-Thérèse's face again, the matron says, "It would seem, then, that you might be all the more interested in your meals and in remaining strong."

Never argue with a patient. She's breaking that rule.

"Your family has been away for several weeks, yet only now have you become ill from not eating. When something like this happens, we look for correlations. Is it something about the food, for example?"

"No, Matron."

"Then overwork?"

"No."

"What about anxiety? Are you over-anxious about something? The doctor's reviews, for example?"

"I do dread them."

"He can be intimidating. And, of course, you are anxious about your brother."

Marie-Thérèse senses heat flooding her face. "I worry about him, yes."

"Has the doctor frightened you in any way regarding your brother?"

"No," she finally says.

"Well. Your tiny portions in the dining room, your giving away your food to others, your being sick in the lavatories have not gone unnoticed. And it all seems to have begun around the time the doctor implemented his reviews. Possibly, I am seeing a correlation where none may exist. Perhaps, my dear, you are simply worn out by a general anxiety, given our situation."

Half of the white coverlet is golden from the sun, the other half a dusky blue. Artists, Marie-Thérèse thinks, usually show white by tinting in other colors such as blue or lavender. Such a safe pursuit, painting. She places her left hand on the golden part and says, "I am trying my best." Each word feels like a sharp stone in her throat. "I should perhaps…maybe I should leave."

The matron settles back in the chair.

Let them talk. But Marie-Thérèse doesn't dare.

The matron continues to sit there, immobile, and in the quiet Marie-Thérèse hears a bird chirping, a passing motorcar somewhere, then the pulse in her ears as if she were underwater. The room begins to thrum like her Bösendorpher at home, that resonance, the deep harmonics, a sound of fading thunder, a sound she has always loved…until that moment. The thought of Jacques standing blindfolded before a firing squad of grown men nearly crushes her heart.

She sobs and then the matron is holding her.

"Tell me."

Marie-Thérèse does.

While she talks, the matron pales. Sadness comes to her eyes, the light there dimming at the mention of the well-dressed woman and the one in the Salvation Army uniform. Marie-Thérèse knows then. She has imparted significant information. And put people in danger. Possibly many people. Above all, *her*. Marie-Thérèse goes on, saying she needs to confess to a priest because she has had awful thoughts about suicide. And betrayal is a sin too, and just as awful. "I should have lied. Only, I couldn't think of any lies that would sound plausible, and what I did tell him, I didn't think very important. I am so sorry, Matron. I don't know how I can go on with those reviews, but then I think of Jacques…"

"People not accustomed to lying," the matron finally says, "often don't do it well. I am sorry to have involved you, my dear. I will ask Père Maarten to come see you. But for now, let us analyze the doctor's threat."

Her reasoning makes sense. Jacques is young and strong, muscular from his years of soccer training. Germany needs workers in their munition factories and other facilities. They are a pragmatic people and won't squander healthy young men who might otherwise be useful to the state. Jacques speaks excellent German. They will like him at one of those factories. He's an intelligent boy as well and no doubt handsome. A woman who has lost a son to the army will be only too willing to take him in and mother him, making him good hearty meals. "The factory manager's wife, for example. It's possible. It's even likely. If in fact he is a prisoner of war—and the doctor in no way sub-stantiated that—this scenario is far more likely, I think, than any wasteful execution. And if he is not a prisoner, then there are other possibilities to consider. He may, at this moment, be in a farmhouse, being cared for by some good Belgian woman. Or he may be back with his unit. We cannot know for certain. Reality, I'm finding, is so much more complex than we can pos-sibly imagine."

Words eerily recalling the doctor's own when she told him about Janine and Elli. Yet Marie-Thérèse drinks in those words. Those possibilities. That hope.

"He mentioned a birthmark to the right of the spine."

"Do you remember such a birthmark?"

"Only vaguely."

"Then you cannot say if it is to the right or left of the spine or if it's even there?"

"I do recall a faint smudge, I think."

"Birthmarks are rather common."

"Do you mean that it's like with a fortune teller who says things that are readily known or generally possible?"

"Something like that, yes. Stating an exact detail gives it a sense of authenticity. Liars use that tactic, I've found. And, so, he gives you an exact number of bullet wounds."

"I didn't think about any of that, Matron. I didn't consider all the possibilities. I just assumed he had specific information."

"How could you have thought about any of it, in the mo-ment? The doctor is intimidating. He exudes authority. And honest people, I've also found, tend to trust what is told to them, especially by one who is a doctor of medicine. Skepti-cism is not their first reaction."

Marie-Thérèse is aware that the matron is not trying to as-sure her that all will be well.

While recovering, she misses the following week's review. She feels safe in the private room, protected by its closed door, its shifting sunlight. Gauthier visits, bringing soup and bread. It takes several small meals before Marie-Thérèse can savor the taste of food. One afternoon Gauthier arrives before the dinner hour, Elli at her side and in her arms, Janine. The small child opens her arms and Marie-Thérèse reaches for her. Then she's speaking French into her hair, telling her what a good girl she is and how happy she is to see both her and Elli, and how fine it is that they came to visit. Elli climbs in beside them, under the coverlet. Gauthier leaves, saying she'll return later for the children. Marie-Thérèse thanks St. Gudule that she is alive. That she hadn't killed herself with The Queen of All Poisons—or by any other means. The girls meld themselves to her, and they soon fall asleep there, in the sunlight.

REPARATION

Observing Père Maarten entering the room stiffly, carefully, as if trying to favor every painful joint, tells her that the poor man is arthritic. The priest is also breathing hard, after his climb up three flights of stairs. His bunched cheeks and eyes appear to be smiling as he wishes her good afternoon. With effort he sits in the room's one wooden chair, positioned to face the bed, and then takes a long time with the clasp of his satchel. Finally, he lifts out the purple stole of the confessional, unfolds it, and lowers his head to place it around his neck. Then the satchel must be placed with care on the floor, next to the chair. All that completed, he straightens the stole so that its panels lie flat. Finally, he removes his beret and has to lean down again to place it atop the satchel. Then, at last fully upright in the chair, he smiles and says in French, "When you are ready, mademoiselle." He appears prepared, now, to wait all afternoon if necessary.

Whispering the words, she makes the Sign of the Cross, and then rushes into the next words: the betrayal, her hatred of the doctor, her entertaining ideas of murder and suicide. It seems to take a long time; in actuality only a minute or two. In the ensuing silence, he sits there, head still lowered, in case she wishes to continue. But there are no more words to be said. The terrible words filling her for weeks are gone.

He takes a deep breath as he raises his head. There are the bunched cheeks, the somewhat small eyes, and emanating from his rotundness, a sense of peace. He begins by talking about forgiveness and how, as imperfect beings, we shouldn't think we are above making mistakes. God understands our failings as well as our desire to do good and avoid evil. He knows we will fail, on our journey. Didn't He fall three times on His way to Calvary? The weight of one's cross is heavy sometimes, too heavy, and we fall, we fail. Yet there will be others to help us, as with Simon of Cyrene. The important thing is to get up and keep on.

He continues speaking, but other words have snagged her attention: *we fall, we fail, the important thing is to keep on.* Finally, she's whispering the Act of Contrition and then hears him saying, "*Absolve in Nomine Patris, et Filii, et Spiritus Sancti*" as he makes the Sign of the Cross in the space between them. Then he sighs as he leans back and lowers his head again.

"*Merci*, Father."

She thinks he has fallen asleep.

After a while she says, "Father? You haven't given me any penance."

His head comes up. "Ah. I was just thinking. Please say a decade of the Rosary, any one of the Sorrowful Mysteries. And…" Again, a lengthy pause. "Finish every meal served in your dining room, which, given all the rationing, may well be a substantial punishment." He smiles—the eyes, the round cheeks, everything about him, pleased with this solution to the penitential requirement. Then he removes the purple stole and goes through all the previous motions, only in reverse, and with as much care as before. Finally, holding the satchel in his left hand, he uses his right to propel himself upward, off the chair.

"God bless you, my child," he says from the doorway and makes the Sign of the Cross again. Then lets himself out of the room, quietly.

She imagines him holding on to the banister and taking the steps slowly.

An idea forms, an incredible, terrifying, yet exhilarating thought, even if it does mean she will have to make another confession.

The next morning, soon after Gauthier brought in the breakfast tray and then wouldn't let Marie-Thérèse eat right away because Gauthier needed to take vitals and lecture her about not eating, the door suddenly opens without any respectful knock and there he is. White coat. Wet-looking, combed-back hair, the brown peninsula at the forehead, the brocade of perspiration at the hairline, the sharp wedge of goatee, and an accusatory assessment of room, breakfast tray, recumbent patient. Gauthier excuses herself.

He studies the chart and then replaces it. "You must be feeling better, Student-nurse Hulbert. You have regained weight, are able to walk without assistance, and no longer experience blackouts. I'm pleased by this progress. We need you back. You are a valuable asset. The clinic is egregiously understaffed."

Her jaw and mouth are shaking.

"Have you lost your tongue, though, in the process of recovering other functions?"

He hasn't availed himself of the chair. Instead, he stands at the foot of the bed, holding her chart.

"*Nein*, Herr Doktor. I was just now asking myself if I should tell you."

"Tell me what?"

"And apologize."

"What have you done? Apart from getting ill and causing others to have to take up the slack."

"I made up information. In my reports. I was so frightened because I observed nothing out of the ordinary but knew I had to say something. I wanted to save my brother. There was no branch of oak leaves, sir. There was no lady in the park or chauffeured automobile or woman in a Salvation Army uniform. None of it was true. I have to confess something else as well. Everyone here is lying to you. I am sorry to tell you this, but it's true. Everyone is afraid of you. You are a person of great authority, and everyone is afraid. Even Charlotte, our permanent resident patient. You are obviously aware of how she suffers from excitability and nervousness and occasional delusions. Even she has said how frightened of you she is. Whatever she may be telling you is probably one of her delusions. She revealed as much when some of us were knitting two weeks ago. It was a Friday, we were in our sitting room downstairs, and she just burst in on us. You might have heard how we've been making gifts for the children of our neighborhood? We do this in the months before our Christmas party for families. Well, when Charlotte described her fear of you, everyone else agreed. Several nurses said that they were creating little fictions for you. I am sorry to have to tell you this."

"Who was it that said they were making up these fictions?"

"I cannot say."

"Or won't."

"In every school I attended we had a code not to tattle on one another unless someone was getting hurt."

"So, you do not want to tattle on your matron either, I assume."

"I think...If I knew she was doing something potentially treasonous or in fact treasonous, I would tell you. That is a serious crime. But I saw her doing nothing wrong, nothing that she should not have been doing, nothing even the least suspicious."

"Yet you made some very definite statements."

"They were lies."

"You dared lie to me?"

"Yes. Because I saw nothing. Because of what you said about my brother I had to tell you something."

"You know, now, that these words seal your brother's fate unless you can give me information that is not a lie?"

"I will have to make up more things, then, because, truly, there is nothing to tell. And by the way, there are young women at this school who are very good at lying. You wouldn't think so, this being a nursing school and most of us Catholic young women. But you might be surprised to know what a group of girls in a confined setting are capable of, Catholic or not. There's quite a bit of meanness to contend with. And competitiveness and jockeying for favor. Even, at times, small acts of sabotage, such as assignments actually being stolen or hidden or—and this happens often—the instruments and items needed for a practical demonstration put out of order or even tucked away somewhere the night before a student has to demonstrate in front of a sister. I don't know what it was like at your medical

schools but here, well, it's difficult at times. One reason I decided to tell you all this is so that you won't get in trouble for
your reports and be punished for fabricating. You have such a
fine reputation. We were all astounded when you stated your
credentials. We thought you should be in a much better hospital
than our little clinic. As for us, well, the students talk about you
a lot...whether or not you're married, whether or not you could
ever be interested romantically in a lowly student. Some of the
students here pride themselves on their beauty and of course
have designs on you and want to please you at every turn. So,
yes, most everyone here is lying. If not everyone. Even the sisters, I suspect, if you asked them to spy too."

"Are you lying to me now?"

"No. But that's why I became ill. I'm not a liar and never
have been, and after I wrote those things, I couldn't eat. I was
vomiting after nearly every meal. I confessed everything to a
priest yesterday, and this is the reparation I must make...telling
you the truth. Also, telling you that I cannot lie anymore. And
won't. I realize you have Jacques in your power. This pains me
more than I can say. You may have a brother or sister and so
can understand. I prayed about this after I made my confession.
I prayed that maybe Germany won't execute my brother after
all. He would be a good worker for the Fatherland."

He raises her chart and rereads it. His face is abnormally
flushed when he looks up. "Student-nurse Hulbert, you are
walking well on your own. You are finishing your meals. Your
recovery appears complete. I am suspending you from the
school for three weeks. This will be a serious blot on your permanent record. When you return, if you do, I will let you know
my final decision as to your fate. Good day."

The door shuts before she can say *for telling the truth?*

HOME

The rue Belliard Stratt looks unchanged except for a lack of flowers in window boxes. The front facade of her house is not damaged. The window glazing intact. The large stone urns on either side of the door are still there, ready for new soil and spring planting. She sets her valise and box of books down and finds her key. But the pressure she exerts inserting it causes the door to swing inward of its own accord.

What she sees makes no sense. As she stares at the incomprehensible scene, details detach themselves and slowly resolve into meaning. The hall's black-and-white marble tiles are gone, except for a few shards. Much of the subflooring has been torn away. One wall has been stripped of its mirror, and regularly spaced holes in the plaster indicate where electric fixtures once were. The chandelier is gone. The stairway's banister and newel post. Many of the steps. And the carpet runner and brass rods.

While ill, she indulged a fantasy that she'd find Jacques hiding at their home, and she castigated herself for not having thought of it sooner and gone to check.

"Jacques?" she calls.

The silence begins to thrum.

"*Jacques?*"

Again, nothing.

"Jacques, it's Marie-Thérèse. Please don't be afraid. I'm alone."

She closes the door behind her, but that dims the light. Bracing one hand against a wall for balance, she negotiates the unstable flooring by sliding along a ten-centimeter-wide floor joist. Could her family have taken everything? An absurd thought. They wouldn't have ripped up the tiles and torn away the wall sconces. They left in a hurry to search for Jacques. The dining room, she sees, has been emptied of everything, including light fixtures and chandelier.

Theft. Not vandalism. Someone or several people taking everything of use—to sell or keep or burn for warmth. In her father's library, his sets of Shakespeare, Molière, Dickens, and Maupassant, gone. His Latin classics. All his books. And the shelves, tables, desk, rug, lamps, and his chair. The window broken and cleared of glass. They must have gotten in that way, from the garden, she thinks, and then possibly carried things out the front door. Who would stop them, this being a *German* residence? Dank air blows in from the window opening. Water stains scribble the wall. The room's door, too, has been taken, and much of its subflooring.

"Jacques?" she calls again. "It's Marie-Thérèse. Are you in the cellar? I don't know if I can get down there. Answer me, please." Listening hard, she hears only the scratching of a few dry leaves, or mice. Balancing on floor joists, she makes her way to the music room. There, no sheet music cases, no lamps, sconces, or chairs. No ceiling or floor molding. The piano, her piano, is gone. She closes her eyes. How had they gotten it out? With care? Removing the upper part and properly taking that out first, wrapped in blankets and upended on a trundle? It was worth a great deal of money. Had they sold it? Who would have purchased it? Who had money for luxuries now? The answer comes. The occupiers.

She opens her eyes and prepares to turn around and follow the floor joist to other rooms, but something on the floor of the music room catches her eye, an object glinting. She crosses to another lateral joist and strains her eyes. Wires. Copper wires. And scraps of felt. And splinters of the piano's white mallets. And then something else—the Bösendorfer's massive cast-iron plate, half-fallen through the floor. That, they obviously hadn't been able to extract from whatever was holding it suspended there.

Nausea rises as the scene leaps to life in imagination. Men smashing the Bösendorfer apart for its wood. The heavy plate falling and wires pulling away. If Jacques had been somewhere in the house when they came, he would have fled. Or, had he confronted and… She refuses to allow the thought. No. He hadn't been there. Or if so, had fled at the first sound. They hadn't trapped him in the cellar. He had run.

Mon Dieu.

She steps to the next joist and reaches the doorway.

He ran and was shot in the garden.

Floorboards creak. She grips the doorframe as blood beats at her temples.

A man is creeping along the hallway toward her. She ducks behind the doorway but peers out.

He has a bundle under his left arm and is negotiating the treacherous floor as she had, right hand braced against the wall, his eyes on his footing. She sees that his cap is pulled low over his forehead. He has a beard. His jacket and trousers are brown, the shirt once white. A dirty cloth is wound around his neck. As he nears the music room, she steps into the open without loosening her hold on the doorframe. "Sir," she says quietly, though everything within her is crying *Fool!* His head jerks up. He all but loses his balance. He is not, she sees, Jacques. His free hand goes to his right pocket.

"Sir, if you have a gun, there is no need. You are welcome here. This was once my home."

His hand reaches for the wall again as he stares at her.

"I have come to look for my brother. Is anyone else here?"

"*Non.*"

The answer causes her stomach to plummet. "You are certain?"

"*Oui.*"

"How long have you been here?"

He shrugs. "Three weeks?"

"Is there food?"

"Not anymore."

"Were you here when…" She gestures.

"*Non.* I found the window open. And some cheese downstairs."

"You are Belgian?"

He doesn't answer, so she knows. "I am Belgian," she finally says. "You may stay here as long as you wish, but it's not safe, especially if you go out from time to time. And people may come for the rest of the wood."

One shoulder rises and falls. He's studying the floor joist. Then he coughs several times, deeply.

"You are ill."

Again, the shoulder rises and falls.

"Are you a soldier?"

No response.

"My brother is not here?"

"No one but me."

She thinks for a minute. "You must come to a clinic where they will help you get well. Tomorrow you will find a parcel in the urn to the left of the doorway as you step outside. Open the door tomorrow afternoon, just a fragment, and get it. There'll be women's clothing, a razor and soap. A mirror if I can find one. Also, money for trams. And some food. Go to the clinic on the rue de la Culture in Ixelles. You may have to be kept in isolation, but you will be warm, and fed. Let me stress: They will help you. Do you think you can do that?" His head is lowered.

"Sir, my name is Celia. What is yours?"

"Alfons."

"Alfons, now we are acquaintances. Tomorrow, the parcel. Then leave here at about five in the afternoon. The trams will be crowded. You won't be conspicuous. If you must ask questions, try to make your voice higher. I will leave you now. I'm sorry I have no food to give you. There will be some in the parcel. At the clinic they will be expecting you. Au revoir, *mon ami.*"

He nods and moves along without looking at her but offers a soft-spoken *merci*.

She waits until it is quiet, then steps onto the same joist but turns in the opposite direction. Bracing herself, she slides along on the joist as fast as possible, every so often glancing back. The hallway remains empty and silent. Reaching the front door, she looks back again at the emptiness.

In her rented room overlooking the rue de Venise, she organizes her textbooks on the desk, hangs her few articles of clothing in a small wardrobe, and then plans her twenty-one days of exile. On a sheet of paper, she writes: *Study. Eat.* Two accomplishments have already given her a modest sense of control. She has told the gardener about the man Alfons and about acquiring this room in a pleasant *maison de chambres.* The proprietress of the rooming house, Madame Lalonde, needed to hear her story before allowing a room to be rented, so Marie-Thérèse explained that she hopes to transfer into a school of nursing in the area and must prepare for an entrance examination. She is from Ghent. She opened her box, there on the front stoop, and displayed her books. "*Cieux!*" the woman exclaimed. "How can one's head hold so much?" and ushered her up to her room and explained about meals.

But it's lonely, and there's too much time for thought to slip in during her walks, and before sleep. Images of her home come to haunt. Also, thoughts of the girls. The matron. The doctor. Jacques. Her family. Even Madame Lalonde, who may decide to check on Marie-Thérèse's story. Scenarios form and dissolve. Meals are difficult, the four other boarders—two men and two older women who are sisters—mainly silent at the table. The sound of brittle toast being crunched is awkward. But the days pass.

While walking back to the *maison de chambres* on the Sunday afternoon of her third week, she's shocked to see the gardener, Janine, and Elli approaching on the rue de Venise. When quite near, he releases their hands, and she stoops and opens her arms. "Oh, my dears, what a surprise! What a wonderful surprise! How did you know that I've missed you both so much?"

"We've missed you, too, Mademoiselle Marie-Thérèse," Elli says. "We begged Grand-père to bring us. We have something for you!"

Marie-Thérèse straightens, but Janine wants to be held, so she lifts her up while Elli goes to the gardener, and he pulls two folded sheets of paper from a pocket.

Drawings of pigeons. Elli's is quite detailed and realistic. Janine's is mostly wayward lines with prominent ones for feet.

"These are beautiful! Thank you so much, my dears. I will treasure them." She kisses both girls. "I am just so happy to see you and have these lovely gifts! Do you know, there's a park nearby? Let's go there and we can sit. I want to hear everything that you've been doing."

The day is neither too cold nor windy and suddenly feels like a holiday. And the talk is happy until Elli says, "Did you know that the doctor is ill, mademoiselle?"

"Ill? I didn't know. Is he now a patient?"

"Not yet. But he should be. You could make him well again."

Elli describes how Sister Gauthier had a tray of instruments knocked from her hands by the doctor, who was angry.

"I was passing ward C, on the way back to our ward, and saw it happen. Sister Gauthier tried to apologize in German, but it made him angrier. "And then he stumbled. I thought he was going to fall down on top of everything and cut himself and be even angrier. I ran back to our ward."

"He stumbled? How strange." Marie-Thérèse looks at the gardener, who says something in Polish.

"When I turned just before going into the ward, I saw him drink from a small brown bottle and then put it in his pocket. I think it is medicine. I think he must be ill."

"Yes, he may well be ill. Does he… Do you see him drink from this bottle of medicine often?"

"That time and one other time. Papa says he has a dybbuk in him, and I don't like dybbuks."

"Do you know what a dybbuk is?"

"A little devil, Papa told us, and that we should stay away from him."

The gardener has taken out his pipe and is filling it with tobacco.

"I think dybbuks are in stories and—"

"They are! Papa told us a story about a dybbuk."

"Ah."

"A dybbuk is making him do bad things, so we don't like him."

"I see. Well. That is certainly one explanation, isn't it?"

They walk a bit, the girls skipping ahead, which gives her a chance to speak privately with the gardener. Deciphering his abbreviated replies, Marie-Thérèse learns that Alfons has been taken across the border. But more men are arriving all the time. As for the doctor, he's *un ivrogne*. A drunkard.

"Oh, Papa. I had no idea. That's how observant I am! And all the while you knew."

And then, finally, the last day of her exile. That night she packs her things and prepares to face the dybbuk.

He doesn't invite her to be seated, so she stands facing the desk. When he finishes writing something, he looks up.

"Has it been three weeks already?"

"Yes, Herr Doktor Kuhn."

She looks for the signs she wrongly interpreted before. They are there: the glazed eyes and flushed skin, the perspiration though it isn't overly warm in the room, the trembling fingers. She isn't close enough to smell his breath but assumes the pungency of "spirits" would be there. Stunning, she thinks, that she failed to interpret these signs correctly. And failed to make the connection to his assignment here. All those credentials! Yet he was still useful, his superiors must have decided, if unreliable. Too unreliable for a large hospital.

He seems to have forgotten her presence. "I am prepared to work hard, Herr Doktor," she says.

He drags his hands over the blotter and hides them beneath the desktop. "But you will tell me nothing."

"I will tell you what I see, though it probably will just be ordinary things."

"You will lie."

"No, I will not make up stories anymore. I have already confessed to lying and have resolved not to lie anymore. We have to do this, you see, after confession. Resolve not to sin anymore. Therefore I will not."

He grimaces. "You are not lying now, Student-nurse Hulbert?"

"No, sir."

She feels somewhat bad for him, the dybbuk in command, and the man in danger of losing not just his position at the clinic but also his reputation and his life's work.

"You will have to take my word for it, Herr Doktor. I promise you that I will work hard and conscientiously in the wards. I will do my utmost to perfectly carry out your orders. You can rely on me. If you and Matron wish me to work longer hours, I will do so willingly and not stint on any effort. This I *can* promise you."

"You are so young. So pitifully young. Go. Resume your duties. But if you see anything suspicious you must let me know."

"At a review, Herr Doktor?"

"Haven't you heard? I am through with those. They took too much of my time. I am an honored man of medicine, of science! It was absurd."

"I agree. You are too important. I believe you made the correct decision."

"*Danke!* How I value your learned opinion."

One hand appears and he brushes the air. At the door she resists an impulse to turn and thank him.

"Close the door. Don't leave it ajar. *Close* it!"

It shuts with a soft click. And then, heart striking joyful blows, she rushes upstairs to find the children. *Not expelled.* Maybe he forgot what he'd said before. Maybe he no longer cares. The reason doesn't matter. Only that she is home.

CHOCOLATE

October's honeyed light gives way to sullen skies and squalls that darken buildings, squares, and boulevards. The city's leafless trees, Marie-Thérèse observes, are black etchings. Lawns in parks and median strips offer the only brilliance—areas that will become vegetable gardens the following spring, she thinks, should the shortages continue. Already coal is being rationed as well as electricity, sugar, lentils, flour, and even potatoes. She's read that because of the block-ade, the occupiers have been emptying Belgian stores, homes, and farmyards. One day the gardener stood for hours amid a crowd waiting for a promised Atlantic herring apiece from a fish warehouse. When he returned with it to the clinic's kitchen, he was unusually loquacious, saying, "No miracle of the loaves and fishes today." The usually talkative German cook took the herring without a word. The gardener's witticism has become a near-daily joke in the dining hall, and she laughs along with everyone else, disguising apprehension at the thought of the coming winter.

Their Wednesday and Friday sessions creating Christmas gifts for the children of the neighborhood offer a welcome respite. Marie-Thérèse regrets never having learned to knit, but Febe, a second-year, taught her an easy crochet stitch that will do as well, she promised. This year, Marie-Thérèse's efforts re-sult in an aquamarine wool shawl to which she attaches tassels using three evenly cut strands of wool drawn through openings and then folded over and tied. After she attaches the final tassel, she raises up the finished shawl for those present to see. They laugh at her amazement.

If only I could show you this, Maman. But it would only be more wounding, wouldn't it?

While crocheting, her thoughts sometimes ramble in a

hopeful vein. Jacques *will* be found. The doctor lied about him. In fact, the doctor knows nothing at all about him or the clinic. Her "confession" worked. But often she can't escape a wrenching certainty that he does know a great deal, and someone in fact is betraying all of them. This thought draws other dark musings along with it. What happened to her family? Why hasn't she heard from them again? Or were the letters lost or stolen. German officers are in charge of postal offices now, but that hardly ensures that letters won't be stolen or destroyed. Her father, though, probably wouldn't have used a postal office. So, what happened? To counter these dark meanderings, she reminds herself of those she helped escape. Fourteen Allies so far. *Fourteen lives saved.* Possibly.

One Friday evening, glancing up from her careful loops, Marie-Thérèse notices Liese's small knitting needles flashing at some fantastic speed as she goes about creating multicolored wool stockings. Sister Gauthier tells her—in French, since the German doctor is nowhere near—that it's too bad her bandaging skills aren't half as good. Liese laughs and agrees. Their tiny coal fire gives off a bit of warmth, and despite her worries, Marie-Thérèse can sometimes convince herself that there isn't a traitor at the clinic and that all will be well.

The folded shawls, stockings, mittens and caps, the patched shirts, pants, and dresses grow into several stacks on top of the piano that she sometimes plays for them while they knit. At ten o'clock the ceiling light and table lamps flicker before going out, and nurses leave for their rooms or ward duty carrying oil lamps, which always reminds Marie-Thérèse of how, during another war, Florence Nightingale had carried hers.

By December 4 the Ixelles ponds are marble plates dusted with snow. This they hadn't been able to count on and so regard it as a gift. At one of the ponds, several sisters and student-nurses, along with Charlotte, stand near a bonfire along a path the matron is known to take while walking Jackie and Donnie. And that day she does, to their relief. Seeing them, she stops abruptly, her face tightening before releasing a smile. She's forty-eight years old that day and looks like an aristocrat, in her light-blue suit and gray fur stole, walking her dogs on a chilly but windless afternoon.

"Happy birthday, Matron!" they call out in English.

"*Mon Dieu*. Who is left at the clinic?"

They relay—it's more like boasting—all they had done in order to create this surprise, even finding and bringing her ice skates as well as a pair for Elli. It's then that Marie-Thérèse realizes the flaw in their plan. They assumed she would walk in *this* park, as she usually did, but there are others where she occasionally takes the dogs. The gardener must have hinted that she needed to be here today. And she must have deduced the reason. Nonetheless, she pretends surprise.

The gardener brought a few pieces of wood in a cart—Elli and Janine seated on top of the wood—and now frugally feeds their small bonfire. Jackie and Donnie sit tethered to a bench while all of them but the gardener put on skates and go out on the perfect ice. Marie-Thérèse helps Elli with hers and watches while the girl, holding her sister's mittened hand, skates tentatively back and forth along the edge of the pond. When the girls return to the bonfire and the gardener, Marie-Thérèse sets off. It seems odd and not right, at first, to be out skating, with the country at war. But the disorientation soon gives way to happy memories. Skating her with her family on Sunday afternoons. Then returning home and sitting by the fire, contentment settling over them like warm quilts. Now her ankles wobble until muscles somehow remember what to do, and then she's gliding along with everyone else in a counterclockwise rotation. It's such a familiar and beloved sensation that thought falls away, and soon she breaks from the circle, finds open space, and executing a swift turn, races around backward, skate blades carving linked slashes in the smooth ice. Then she executes an arabesque that all but knocks over two German soldiers.

"Brava, Fräulein!" one calls as he glides out of the way.

Awful. She begs their pardon and skates back toward the

revolving group. But one of the soldiers catches up with her, and then they are skating side by side. She's about to apologize again when he speaks first. "I am sorry if we frightened you off, Fräulein. You're a very good skater. It was a pleasure to watch."

"*Danke,* sir. But it was rude to be so careless." She glances at him long enough to observe that he resembles Private Schalk; possibly it's the irises' pale blue shading to gray and the prominent facial bones. But he's older than Private Schalk by several years. The military greatcoat paired with ice skates and a reindeer-patterned wool cap gives the moment a sense of absurdity.

"*Nein, nein,*" he says. "It was excellent."

She thanks him again.

"Is that your group, Fräulein, near the bonfire?"

"Yes. A little birthday party."

"Yours, may I ask? You looked so exuberant."

"Oh no. Not mine."

"A friend's then, of course. Or…one of the children's?"

She's being too evasive. "The gathering is in honor of the woman who heads our nursing school."

"Ah. So, you are a student? Or a nurse?"

"Merely a student nurse."

"Now I must apologize. Here I am, asking questions without having introduced myself. I am Leutnant Rudolf Fischer. From Coblentz. My acquaintances call me Rudi."

A second lieutenant. She introduces herself and tells him she is from Brussels. The day seems ruined.

After some light talk about the weather, the ice, and her nursing studies, he asks if he might request her father's permission to call on her.

She explains in rushed words: her family no longer living in Brussels; her father needing to practice his profession elsewhere.

For a while there is just the sound of skate blades against ice.

"May I ask your matron's permission, then? It would be a great honor, Fräulein."

Marie-Thérèse points her out—she's talking to the

gardener—then watches as he skates to the edge of the pond, hops onto the grass and strides, in his skates, right up to them. To Marie-Thérèse's dismay, the gardener doesn't salute or remove his cap. Janine is burrowed into Elli's coat.

Soon the lieutenant is back, again skating alongside her. "She gave her permission!"

Had she any choice?

They make another revolution of the pond, each of them silent.

"I must go now," she says, finally. "I promised the girls a turn on the ice."

"Ah. Of course. Then Saturday?"

After they set a time, he removes his cap, gives a quick bow, and then skates toward the opposite side of the pond, where his friend is taking off his skates.

Elli is again awkwardly skating back and forth near the edge of the pond while holding Janine's hand. Marie-Thérèse picks up Janine and glides around the pond with her in her arms. It's almost heartbreaking to see the little girl's tentative smile. She returns for Elli and together they make a slower revolution.

"He was a soldier," Elli says.

"Yes."

"He wants to see you again, doesn't he?"

"Yes, he does."

"We don't think you should."

"I know, my dears."

"Will you, then?"

"I'm afraid I must."

Seated on the bench and putting on her shoes, Liese says, "You're not crying, Marie-Thérèse, are you? For heaven's sake, what happened?"

"It's just the wind."

"There is no wind."

Marie-Thérèse changes into her shoes and then helps Elli. At the bonfire, she holds her hands toward the heat. Soon Gauthier presents a box of twelve chocolates to the matron—a gift from all of them—and then a single chocolate for each, with thanks to Monsieur the Gardener for his resourcefulness.

On the way back, only Liese mentions the incident. "You surprised us, Marie-Thérèse, showing off for those Germans like that. Well, but I suppose you needed to do *something* for your compatriots."

The gardener is behind them a few meters, pulling the children in the cart. "Of course!" she says. "My exact intention." And gives a foolish laugh. She thinks of the chocolate instead—silken on the tongue, its sweetness understated, its richness full and perfect. And so quickly gone. Like time before this time.

She wishes she had savored hers more.

COINCIDENCE

She pours slowly, the stream of coffee bumping the sides of the lieutenant's porcelain cup, patterned with wild roses. Before them on the table in the nurses' sitting room are a matching porcelain pitcher and small sugar bowl, each holding minimal amounts of cream and sugar. At the center of the table, a gold-rimmed dessert plate with six small sugar cookies nested in the wild roses. The cook has made them at the matron's request. Two bread and butter plates from the same set are at each of their places, along with newly polished teaspoons.

"*Danke*, Fräulein Hulbert. These look delicious. May I?"

She's forgotten to offer them. "Yes, yes, please." She takes the plate too forcefully and one slides off onto the tablecloth.

"It's all right," he says. "That one's mine. *Danke!*"

He's been glancing around at everything. The framed watercolors, the piano with its stacks of clothing, the books shelved along one wall, the figured carpet, the upholstered chairs and reading lamps.

Her smile, she hopes, disguises repugnance. She places a cookie on her own plate and wonders if she'll be able to eat it.

He reaches for a second. The remaining two look rather paltry on the plate. "You must have a very good cook here. Or did you make these yourself?"

"Oh no. I'm not much of a cook." She decides to pretend that he's a patient with whom she must be pleasant. Better, she'll pretend he's Private Schalk.

"And why is that, Fräulein?"

"Why?"

"You were thinking of something else, weren't you?"

"Yes! I was just thinking how you remind me of a patient who was at our clinic for a time, a kind young man."

"Ah. I am happy to hear that. A kind young man. And handsome?"

"Yes." Her ears feel too warm.

"Then we are off to a good start. Is he no longer at your clinic, this handsome and kind patient?"

"He returned to Germany in October."

"Very good! Then I have no rivals. Or do I?"

His question reawakens memories of loneliness at the Académie. And now, of course, again, who has time for all that?

Any possible lighthearted response eludes her. "No, Lieutenant. There are no rivals."

"That is difficult to believe. You know, I've been looking at your piano. A Bechstein, yes?"

"It is."

"They're very good pianos. Favored by Liszt. Does anyone here play?"

She always wondered but never asked how a Bechstein came to be in the nurses' sitting room. A donation, probably. Her first year at the school, she ignored it. But then, knowing her background, the matron asked if she might play a few carols and hymns at the Christmas party that year. After that, she began finding time to play for herself, despite the painful memories.

"It's a shame," he goes on, "if no one plays."

"I sometimes do," she finally says. He's in his dress uniform, with corded shoulder boards unadorned by any stars, which means that he is, in fact, a second lieutenant. Her hands won't stop trembling. Briefly she tells him about her time at the Académie, years that also precluded any attempts to learn cooking or baking. When she finishes, she observes a dramatically changed expression. Gone is the veneer of strained politeness. In its place, incredulity and excitement.

"It can't be! Is this true? You were there how long?"

"Seven years."

"Seven!"

"Yes."

"Then, please, you must play something!"

Gone, too, the superficiality. And he's doing what they frequently did at the Académie, the piano students, glancing at one another's hands, the length of the fingers, assessing their strength.

Waiting for him to call that day and then ushering him into the sitting room had been unnerving. She demanded that everyone stay away. She soaked her hands in warm water. Once he was actually sitting down and having coffee, she relaxed...a little. Now fear is again crackling through her, and her hands are growing colder by the second.

"You hesitate. But I have a feeling you are quite good."

"Oh no. I was only a mediocre student, Lieutenant, and that's why I left. And now I'm quite out of practice."

"You were there for seven years. You cannot have been merely mediocre. And I imagine you had lessons even before attending the Académie."

"I did, yes."

"Would you mind playing something, however brief? I would love to hear a bit of music."

Does he think she's lying? Under the table she squeezes her hands to get the blood flowing. "Would you like to hear anything in particular?"

"Oh, a hundred things but maybe...some Schubert? I am partial to Schubert because of the melancholic undertones in many of his compositions and also because he lived in the shadow of Beethoven. Had Beethoven not been born, imagine how we would now idolize Schubert. As it is, he's like the poor second cousin. Or, to fix the analogy, a sapling in the shadow of a towering oak."

Well, not exactly. Schubert... One of the waltzes? An impromptu? She apologizes for the stacks of clothing and quickly explains their presence while removing them to armchairs. Seated at the Bechstein, she still doesn't know what to play. *Schubert.*

Her hands decide for her—the "Phantasie"—and for several minutes she hides inside the music. When she raises her hands from the keyboard and finally turns, his head is lowered over his right hand, thumb on cheekbone, two fingers pressed against brow. She's made dozens of mistakes. He removes his hand and says, without opening his eyes. "You never should have left." He sounds tired now, even sad. "A few mistakes, yes, but your playing has a certain…élan."

Nurses have been peeking in and whispering. The lieutenant pretends not to notice the shuffling in the hallway or the whispering or the door that keeps opening wider. And the mortifying fact that someone is also giggling.

"Should we have a little walk?" he says. "There is still some sunlight. Oh, but you haven't had anything!"

"It's fine. I'll have it later." Needing her jacket, she excuses herself.

"Out!" she whispers to everyone after shutting the door behind her. "Don't you have work to do?" She runs up two flights of stairs and then back down. Three nurses are still there, and the door again ajar. Julia offers her serene smile as if to say she approves, though Marie-Thérèse knows she probably doesn't.

In the park off the rue de la Culture, old women are competing with squirrels gathering acorns under the oaks. The day is calm, the sunlight milky, and the women send the two of them— a German officer in uniform complete with greatcoat, and with him a traitorous Belgian woman—excoriating looks. Marie-Thérèse, trying to ignore the old women, prays they won't do anything even more dangerous. He notices the women as well, though he pretends otherwise.

Melting snow has left the lawns glittering. Some leaves still cling to the oaks; others lie in wet grass like pieces of maroon parchment. The cold air feels good on her face.

"Fräulein," he begins, "this coincidence…I don't know…it's odd and even incredible. My father, you see, is a great craftsman. In his youth he apprenticed at one of Herr Bechstein's factories. That's why I was stunned to see a Bechstein in your sitting room. I found myself wondering if my father might have had some part in building it. He loved music—and still does, particularly piano music—but his family was poor, and there was nothing for lessons. The best he could do was find a way to hear performances, often sneaking in during intermissions and then lurking at the back of the hall and finding an empty seat when someone didn't return.

"All this he told us, his three children, much later, after he became a successful piano maker. He had taken all he had learned at the Bechstein factory, moved to a different region, and then set up his own shop in a carriage house. His pianos became well known and respected in the area, and best of all, they were affordable for families of lesser means. When he had some time to spare, he tried to learn to play. You can imagine. He was nearing forty years old and had trouble with simple scales, never mind Mozart's "Eine Kleine Nacht Musik." But he tried and kept trying until we were old enough to take lessons and then outstripped him in no time. So, he pinned his hopes on us and gradually stopped playing. And for us he bought a Bösendorfer, of course, and found us the best teachers. Evenings after dinner, he would listen to us practice, first my older sister Anna, then Margarethe, and then me. He never tired of listening and never minded our mistakes and repetitions. He would sit there so proud and entranced.

"You know, I have come to believe that hope is the cruelest emotion because the things one hopes for are so often withheld. Think of the myth of Tantalus. A good depiction of futile, agonizing hope. In the end we all disappointed him, I most of all. Anna did become the organist and musical director at our church, though. Margarethe gives lessons, and on Sundays both families go to the house and play for him. Still, he wanted so much more. He wanted what he had heard as a child, that grandeur. He wanted what lived inside him but could not find a way out. Well, there are the grandchildren."

"And you," she said after a few moments, "what did you want?"

"To go away. I couldn't bear the burden of his hope. In his eyes my sisters failed, though he would never tell them that. I just knew that's how he felt. So it was up to me. And I…well, let's just say I wasn't good enough to even enter a conservatory, never mind managing to stay in one. While I listened to your playing, I thought of him and how you should have been his daughter." These words strike her as bizarre.

"I'm afraid I would have disappointed him too."

"Yes, well, leaving the Académie. I suppose so."

So many thoughts. That father. A son's guilt. Her own mother's pain and hers as well. And art—what *is* it that draws one? What force? And why can't so many aspiring artists be good enough?

"You're awfully quiet, Fräulein Hulbert. What are you thinking so deeply about?"

"Oh, a bit of everything." Briefly, she tells him about her mother and the divide between them and how she can alleviate patients' pain but not her mother's. Abruptly changing the topic, she asks why he chose the military; it seems so radically different from his previous life.

"Well, you perhaps know about our military reserve groups? All young men must train in a reserve group and then when the group is called up, we go."

She hadn't known. "What is your specific task, Lieutenant Fischer, in the army? Do you have one? Are you…infantry?"

"Oh no, just liaison work, a message boy in essence. It's hardly worth a person's time. But I have to see my term of service through and then will do something else."

"Could you go back? I mean to your father's factory?"

"After I stopped taking lessons, he asked me to consider it. I could manage a section, or learn the financial aspects, or become a salesman. Any number of things. I actually did consider it. Until looking in his eyes and understanding what I'd be seeing each day. That defeat and loss. So, no, I don't think going back would be good for either of us. When we children were young, my father was so happy taking us to concerts. He had so much hope in those days. But now…actually, I would very much like to study astronomy."

"Astronomy!"

"Yes. I had an excellent course at university, but then our reserve unit was called into active duty and so here I am. While at university, I read about a sixty-inch reflector telescope lens being built in California, in the United States, at the Mount Wilson Observatory. I would very much like to go to California after this war and continue my studies."

California. And if the United States should enter the war on the side of Britain and France? She suddenly feels bad for the lieutenant.

"Do you enjoy nursing, Fräulein?"

"I am beginning to enjoy it very much."

"Are you afraid of making mistakes, as at the Académie?"

"Always."

"Do you make many?"

"Unfortunately, I do."

"May I ask another favor, mademoiselle?"

Mademoiselle.

"Could you please call me by my Christian name if that won't...bother you? I prefer Rudi."

"Yes, I can do that." It brings Rani to mind.

"*Merci.* Now a second question. Would you prefer we speak French...at least here in the park?"

"You speak French, then?"

"*Mais oui.* And some Polish. My father loves Chopin, of course. We had language lessons as well as vacations in France and Poland. My poor father tried to leave nothing to chance."

They talk on and on, in French, until she glances at her watch and then they're trotting like ponies back through the park, past the outraged women, and out through the main gate. The sun is setting in gray gauze. Finally, at the door to the nurses' residence, while he's trying to express how much he enjoyed the afternoon, she's thinking there's hardly time for her to change.

Later she'll chide herself for not having prepared an answer.

"Mademoiselle, I am hoping, that is, if you wish, I am hoping we...what I mean to say is that I hope you will have some free time next Saturday and…if you wish…if it is possible, that is…we might have another visit. There is no need for coffee or tea and those excellent cookies your cook provided. We might stop at a café if you wish, of course."

All those words stated, he lowers his head.

No, she's thinking. *No.* Everyone will hate her. Also, she might slip and reveal something. Words form, in thought: *Thank you, sir, but my studies are so demanding that—*

What she hears herself saying is *Yes.*

Resolve

Their cook, Amelia, comes over to Marie-Thérèse in the dining room at lunchtime the next day and none too quietly gloats over the fact that five twenty-pound bags of flour and five of sugar unexpectedly arrived at the clinic's kitchen that morning. The driver wouldn't tell her anything. "But we know who sent them, don't we, Fräulein Hulbert? You must have had quite an afternoon!" She cackles with the evil gusto of a Baba Yaga.

Liese, across the table, smirks. Others begin calling out, "Brioche! Streusel! Cinnamon rolls!"

Marie-Thérèse states that she isn't going to eat anything the cook makes with that flour and sugar. But hardly fazed and so joyful to be able to bake again, the cook only pats her back and fairly shouts, *"Très bien!"*

Her resolve doesn't last. There's brioche, and sugar for coffee and tea, and cinnamon rolls, the holiday scent winding through the dining room and finding its way even into the lecture hall. *Cinnamon.*

"Do you think," she asks the matron in her sitting room, "that he might possibly have some motive? After all, Liese is the pretty one. She was there that day too." It's difficult to look directly at the matron, her own sense of guilt and unworthiness still so strong.

The matron studies her. "I've noticed that you have a tendency to demean your own qualities and abilities, mademoiselle. I've been wondering why. You're an exceptional student, a lovely pianist, and even a fine skater"—here, she smiles—"and yet you so often question your abilities. In addition to the qualities I just mentioned, you also strike me as someone with integrity."

Integrity. Absolutely not. A few weeks earlier all this praise might have toppled her. And it would have provided emotional sustenance for weeks. Now it only augments the sense of guilt. "What motive do you think he could have?" the matron goes on. "Did he ask about the clinic?"

"No. Just my family, mainly, and my choices. He said his father wanted him to be a pianist." She relates his story. "I don't know. Could he have been fabricating in order to…build trust, create some bond between us? The coincidence seemed so remarkable. Too much so."

"But sometimes life is like that, no? The striking coincidence one can hardly believe. Let's assume that what he said is true. So then, his only motive might be that he's drawn to you because you have so much in common and also because you are a beautiful young woman. Not merely pretty. You have something deeper."

Heat infuses her face. "But I feel that if I continue to allow this man to visit or if I go to events with him, it will be a betrayal of everyone here as well as of my country."

"Whether you are betraying yourself should also be of concern. And too, there is this question: Do you want to take the whole person into consideration or do you want to judge based on a generality?"

"I understand," she says finally. "I judged Private Schalk on a generality at first and then got to know him."

"So you have much to think about."

Marie-Thérèse puts a bit of sugar into her tea.

"Mademoiselle, can you help me later tonight?"

A chill finds its way into her hands. "There are more?"

"Just a few."

"When you didn't ask my help, Matron, I assumed, partly, that they were all gone. Or that…you didn't trust me anymore."

"I do trust you, and I'm sorry to have to involve you again. If you don't wish to, only say so. I will manage."

"Please, don't ask Liese."

"I remember you cautioned me before."

"Actually, I'll do it."

That night they nurse four wounded soldiers in the cellar,

the soldiers' relief at being momentarily safe making them careless. She has to keep asking them not to talk so loudly, groan so
loudly. In fact, please try to keep quiet altogether. This causes
the least wounded one to snuffle in laughter and then flirt. It
wasn't meant to be easy, she tells herself, and resolves to do
what she can in reparation.

Freezing rain and drizzle scour the city. Snow squalls blow in
from the North Sea. Walking Jackie and Donnie, Marie-Thérèse
overhears people complaining in low voices about the rationing;
the confiscated pigeons, bicycles, and telephones; the electricity restrictions, travel restrictions, and curfew; the forbidden
telegraph cables, newspapers, and French language. They com-
plain, too, about how Belgian men are being sent to German
labor camps and how there are German officials in every public
office now, and old men still clean the streets on hands and
knees in the cold and wet, pushing themselves up awkwardly to
salute passing German officers. Those old men standing crook-
edly become an indelible symbol of the Occupation. While
walking with the lieutenant, she senses people not daring to spit
outright but doing so with their cloaked though contemptuous
looks. Nor does she like seeing the ubiquitous posters declaring
in bold lettering the latest German offensives and victories in
France. Often there are blank places on walls showing streaks
of glued paper where posters had been. "People are tearing
them off," he says. "I've heard there will be severe penalties."
She recalls those words when visiting the children in the gardener's cottage and seeing a pile of twisted papers amid the
broken-up branches near his hearth. She knows, then, that taking the posters isn't merely an act of sabotage. "Papa," she says,
"do you think you should?" She indicates the twists of paper.

"Lies burn brightest but only for a short time."

Interspersed among the German war proclamations are
notices of free concerts and theatrical events for the people
of Brussels. Classical music, opera, plays, popular music—so
many free events, and several each week. Townspeople have
been scorning these enticements. Marie-Thérèse is of that

mind as well; yet drawn to the music, she attends several performances with the lieutenant despite a deepening sense of
guilt. Why go, she asks herself repeatedly, if it makes you feel
bad? But she knows why. Because it's so good to hear music
performed beautifully. She'd nearly forgotten how much she
loved it. And too—honesty bringing the scald of shame—she
has begun to enjoy Rudi's company, his knowledge of music
and rueful appreciation, his overlooking the insulting glances
and halfhearted salutes, his—she ridicules herself for thinking
this way, but there it is—essential decency. For a few weeks,
enjoyment and distress create a stalemate. Eventually, though,
distress wins out. She resolves to refuse any more invitations.
But as with the cook's breads and rolls, this resolve soon fails.
Until the evening of a Christmas concert that should have filled
her with hope and delight.

Garlands of fir branches drape walls and stage front. Five
musicians—three in German army uniform and two Belgians in
formal civilian clothing—take their places onstage in an ornate
chamber hall within the grand Hotel de Ville. As they raise their
instruments, the two cornets, a French horn, trombone, and
bass trombone catch the light and appear silver in places, gold
in others. There is no conductor, but one of the Belgians signals
with his eyes, and the program opens with Johann Sebastian
Bach's "Arioso" from Cantata #156. It's too much—the dense-
ly woven beauty, the acute sense of aliveness, the awareness of
deepening love for the man alongside her, and, too, grief over
the war, her own guilt, fear, and anxieties. An effortless spill
of tears then, sliding unchecked to her cloak. A Charpentier
prelude follows the Bach, then two sixteenth-century Flemish
songs. The audience of mainly German soldiers and officers
applauds with enthusiasm after each piece. Surreptitiously,
she stanches the flow while the quintet closes with several of
Thomas Morley's Elizabethan madrigals.

Rudi waits until she takes a deep breath and nods, and then
they're walking out of the gilded hall, his arm bracing hers.

They both notice the poster that had been obscured by the

crowd when they'd arrived for the concert. It's right there, facing them as they step out into the cold. *View the ruins of Louvain! Sunday Railroad Excursions. See the former Halles Universitaires and Cathedral. Trains departing...*

Neither one comments.

As they make their way to a table in a far corner of a crowded café, an officer calls out, "Fräulein! Where are your two amusing dogs? Or have they been transformed into your handsome lieutenant?"

"Better that way," another observes, "than the other."

The lieutenant offers a salute which the seated officer ignores. "Fräulein," he goes on, "why didn't you come back and see us?" He turns to his friends. "She had two ravenous mongrel dogs with her and an old mongrel man. Quite charming creatures—the dogs, that is. We fed them all our sausages. The old man we did not feed, needless to say. How is your uncle, Fräulein? He hasn't died yet, has he? I wouldn't have given him two more days."

"He is still alive, sir."

"And how is it you never returned?"

"I had to be elsewhere, sir."

"Yes, I *see*."

Officers at other tables join in the laughter.

"Well, go on, you two. It's clear that youth trumps age. Lieutenant, I commend your taste and wish you continued success. Though beware of her charms. You don't want to end up at the end of a leash."

When they finally reach the table, Rudi apologizes. His forehead is scarlet. "It's among the things I don't like about military service," he finally says. Her own face feels icy, her eyelids swollen. As she sips mineral water and he coffee, a waiter brings the slices of *Zwetschgenkuchen* Rudi ordered.

"This is wonderful," he says of the supremely expensive cake. "So many plums! Please, Marie-Thérèse, have some. You're quite pale. You must be hungry."

She regards her slice, rich and moist with Damson plums.

After a moment, she sections off a small piece with her fork, raises it, pauses, then places it on her tongue. It seems an act of further betrayal, and the sweetness an assault. She places the fork on the plate.

"But you haven't really tried it! It's excellent!"

"*Danke*, it is, but you see I'm not used to so much sweetness anymore. Will you please have it?"

"We'll get you something else! Waiter!"

"*Nein, danke.*" She slides the plate to his side of the table. "Are there…many plum trees where you live?"

"You know, that's a question I can't answer. I suppose so. I never paid much attention to things like that." He begins on the second piece. "Tell me about your uncle."

"My uncle? Well, there's one in London, my father's brother, and two in Paris."

"So, your uncle must have been able to get travel papers, surely not an easy feat. Good for him."

"Oh! I see. You're referring to that elderly man they mentioned." Her hands have gone cold. Her temples throb. "He wasn't an actual uncle," she continues after taking a sip of water. "Just a former patient. He seemed rather weak and unsteady, so I offered to help him get home."

Patient. Home. Dangerous lies?

"A chance meeting then."

"Yes. I didn't know his name, so I just referred to him as 'uncle' out of respect."

"Ah. Of course."

"The uncle who lives in London, my father's younger brother is an osteopath. Medicine seems to be in our family." *Why am I saying so much? Stop it!*

"I imagine you've visited London quite often, then."

She smiles as if it's the most natural thing in the world to be discussing an enemy country. "Several times. My roommate and I once considered working there."

"You have a roommate? Was she at the skating party? The blond one?"

"No. My roommate returned to Germany in August."

He scrapes up a few crumbs. "London is a fine city. I enjoyed the park, Hyde Park, I think it's called. We have parks like that in Berlin, of course. I once read that an English writer famously said—or wrote, I forget which—that when one tires of London, one is tired of life. I suppose every country has its London. I feel that way about Berlin." He finishes his coffee and glances in the direction of the officers' table. They're still there, louder now. "Ah well. Again, I apologize. This isn't such a pleasant end to the evening."

"There is need for an apology." She lowers her eyes first.

"We should go," he says after a moment. "We just have time before the curfew."

Snow is falling when they exit a tram, rounded clumps in no hurry to reach the ground. A candle burns here and there in windows hazy in the snow. It might have been peaceful, but Marie-Thérèse's pulse is raging. Turning to her when they reach the nurses' residence, he breaks the silence. "Next week, then? There's to be a Mozart sinfonia." The word *sinfonia* lilts upward in hope.

"Please forgive me, but I cannot."

"Then the following week, possibly?"

"No, I'm sorry."

He studies her face. "Was it that poster? The one about Louvain? You were so quiet and sad in the café and on the tram, I thought it might be that. I find it atrocious to be conducting *excursions* to a city we ruined. That isn't right. Nor all these... deprivations. I must sound like a traitor. But you understand, yes?"

"I do. You're not like that."

"Then what is it? You're simply not...attracted?"

This is excruciating. But then something catches her eye, a shape that resolves into the figure of someone on his knees, right there in the street. "It's...how you must follow orders no matter what. It simply wouldn't work, Rudi. Also, my family... there's too much against it."

He looks down at the snow a moment then at her again. "I'm very sorry, mademoiselle. I must accept your decision. But...it's hard."

"For me as well. I'm sorry too, Rudi."

"It's truly impossible?"

"I'm afraid so."

He takes her gloved hands in his. "Please. Don't be sad. You've made a wise decision. Allow me to just say that...I hope to see your name on a recital notice one day. I wish you well, mademoiselle. I've enjoyed your company so much. You will be in my heart." Raising one gloved hand, he kisses it, then walks away, cap and shoulders white in the snow, footsteps dark on the stones.

And you in mine. She stands there, watching, but he doesn't look back.

In the street the man reaches for his bucket and sloshes water over cobblestones, melting the snow. After clearing her eyes and blowing her nose, she goes out into the road.

"Papa, stop. This is absurd, in the snow."

He continues scrubbing.

"You're soaking wet. You'll catch cold. The matron can't allow this."

"She has to."

She gets a broom from inside and together they finish the block. She has to help him stand. "Papa," she says, inside the clinic. "Forgive me, please. There will be no more such outings."

He takes the broom from her and turns away. She thinks he nodded.

BIRDS

In the nurses' sitting room Marie-Thérèse studies the post-mark. Faint letters come clear: Cuxhaven.

Cuxhaven? Is Jacques in *Germany*? Or...*Rudi*? She tears open the envelope and pulls out a single thin sheet. *Greetings, Fräulein Hulbert.* Her stomach plummets. She scans down to the signature. *Konrad Schalk.* Private Schalk. The upright careful script evoking his schoolboy voice.

It is very nice here in Cuxhaven this time of year. I like to watch snow clouds out over the water. I can see the snow approaching from far away. It looks like a wall of haze and is most beautiful. At times seagulls fly in the snow! This is a remarkable sight that makes me happy. They are white and the snow is white, but the sea and clouds are gray. I think how fortunate I am to have my two eyes and this is a miracle.

My greatest wish is that this letter finds you well and happy, Fräulein Hulbert. I think of you often and remember how kind you were to me. Every day I read a story from the book you gave me. It was most clever of you to disguise its cover. No one here at the rehabilitation hospital asks about my book or tells me not to read Herr Chekhov. So that is very nice. Another patient has made for me a little bookstand. Pieces of wood come down and hold the pages open. It is a useful device! Now I can sit in my chair and read quite well.

I am writing to wish you happiness at Christmas. I hope you will be with your family on that blessed day and that there will be a Christmas tree in "my" ward. I will think of it that way and of you there. Do you still walk Jackie and Donnie? I wish one day to have a dog such as Jackie. Now, however, he would pull me off my unsteady feet. Yes! I have a prosthetic limb and am learning to walk again. This, too, is a miracle. Soon, I am told, my arm will be ready for a prosthetic limb as well.

I enclose for you a piece of driftwood from the North Sea. It is wrapped in gauze, which I thought you might find amusing. I hope it is not broken. God bless you and your family this Christmas.

Yours sincerely,
Konrad Schalk

The piece of driftwood has fallen to the floor. Unwinding its gauze "bandage," she sees that it has been broken. But the two pieces are porcelain smooth and nearly as white. Wrapping them back up, she recalls how she once mentioned that wounded soldiers might benefit from learning to knit or crochet. It could be therapeutic, she suggested, feeling productive. Everyone in the sitting room that evening snickered at the thought of German infantrymen fumbling with knitting needles or crochet hooks. Now she realizes it wasn't such a good idea after all. Anyone with Private Schalk's injuries would feel bad, being left out.

She rereads his letter and then finds herself repeating one of its sentences throughout the day. *They are white and the snow is white, but the sea and clouds are gray.* It seems almost a prayer.

A few days later, Janine wriggles down from her arms to stand at a window. Snow is falling and bare tree limbs hold white replicas of themselves. A sparrow is flitting from one branch to another, knocking off snow. Then it perches, fluffing its feathers and becoming twice its size. Janine makes a small sound that might be an exclamation. The bird fluffs its feathers again, shaking off snow. Janine tugs at Marie-Thérèse's arm.

"I see him," Marie-Thérèse says. "He's taking a snow bath!"

But Marie-Thérèse is really observing the little girl, standing there rigid with interest, her eyes fixed on the sparrow, her hands clasped.

When the bird flies off, Janine begins looking for others.

Marie-Thérèse begins chattering away about sparrows, and when no other birds appear, she expects the grille of detachment to lower. But instead, Janine indicates she wishes to walk back to her bed by herself instead of being carried. And as she does, her head turns from side to side, like the sparrow's.

Elli holds Janine's hand while the gardener carries sacks of grain and straw onto the tram. It's a Sunday afternoon, gray and cold, the streets quiet, the shops and cafés closed. Marie-Thérèse is tired, not having slept well the night before. Given Janine's renewed interest in the world, she asked the matron's permission for this outing. It was granted with some reluctance. But during the night Marie-Thérèse worried about all the potential variables, the dangers. Still, Elli was eager to go; even Janine appeared interested.

Others exit with them at the Exhibition Hall stop, and then it seems like some silent pilgrimage. At the entrance to the hall, a soldier checks the gardener's papers and smiles at the girls, who press close to each other.

Inside the large hall, the light is dim, the air heavy and somewhat foul. Pigeons burble, the pitch often rising as if in complaint. The gardener's allotted area is near one set of sliding doors.

Marie-Thérèse didn't anticipate the number of guards. They're walking up and down aisles formed by rows of sectioned off aviaries as well as standing to either side of the sliding doors. The ones walking the aisles sometimes pause to observe the birds. One guard is actually talking to them.

The gardener undoes the latch to his assigned aviary and begins speaking in Polish to his ten pigeons. Marie-Thérèse hands him a pail of water she drew from a spigot in the corridor. A brush and dustpan hang from the wire fencing, and he uses these to sweep old straw and droppings into the cloth bag he brought. When the floor and boxes are clean, the trays and pans refilled, he and the girls pick up each of the pigeons in turn, the gardener and Elli speaking to them and using their names. The birds haven't flown for nearly two months now, except for short flights in their narrow space. Marie-Thérèse is more concerned about the gardener and how much longer of this captivity he'll be able to endure. He tells her that the one named Bishop— who likes to fly in diagonals—isn't well. The pigeon didn't rush to the grain trays with the others. The gardener examines the bird and then each of the others, checking their eyes and holding his ear against their chests. In the old man's eyes, she sees what she does not want to see.

"Papa," she whispers. "Be calm, *s'il vous plaît.*"

A tremor has set in at one corner of his mouth.

"Think of the girls. If you must do something, do it when you're here by yourself."

Turning his back as a guard approaches, the gardener sets Bishop down on fresh straw. There's a shout, and guards are suddenly running toward the sliding doors at the opposite end of the hall. Marie-Thérèse lifts Janine and holds her shawl tightly against her right ear. The gardener picks up Bishop, tucks him under his jacket, then takes the bags he's brought and waves a hand, urging the three out of the aviary. Quickly they walk toward the unguarded door. Others are doing the same. At a burst of shooting, Elli begins crying. "*Ma chère petit,*" Marie-Thérèse says, "be brave now, for Janine. *S'il te plaît.*"

There's shooting somewhere, but the gardener ignores it as they walk fast within a group of others, Marie-Thérèse carrying Janine. Ahead, a waiting tram. As they're boarding, a guard shouts for them to halt. Glancing back, Marie-Thérèse sees him running toward them; another is aiming his rifle at the sky and shooting. Glancing upward, she sees a bird falling toward the earth, its wings askew.

The operator of the tram is the same one who conveyed them to the Exhibition Hall. Then, he proceeded as if everyone already existed in eternity. Now five people leap onto the tram, one after another, all shouting, "*Allez! Avancez!*" Just as Marie-Thérèse, the children, and the gardener board, the tram jolts forward and speeds away. Bullets clatter and ping. Before hunching down, Marie-Thérèse saw guards surrounding those who'd been left behind. Several blocks farther, the tram operator abruptly stops, jumps from the tram, and runs into a side street. They have no choice but to do likewise, though the gardener will not let them run to the next tram stop.

For the rest of the way back, Janine's thumb is in her mouth, her eyes blank. Marie-Thérèse kisses the top of her head and raises her shawl to cover most of the child's face. Elli closes her eyes and pushes in against Marie-Thérèse's side. Recalling Madame Depage's advice, Marie-Thérèse begins talking. "We've had a scare, my dear ones, but we're all right now. You see? All will yet be well, *mes chères*. Oh, a lovely tower now, I think it's a bell tower, and here is a garden, and now we are going home to see Jackie and Donnie, what have they been doing, I wonder, what do you think? Sleeping, perhaps? Your loyal pets are resting by the fireplace and waiting for us to come home." The constriction in her throat blocks other words. She has never before made such an awful mistake, the worst of her life, bringing them there. *Marie-Thérèse, don't give in. Keep talking.*

Holding them close, she begins again. The dogs, the day, and how good it is, being with them, even now, especially now, when they've all had a terrible fright. Janine lowers her thumb and holds on to Marie-Thérèse with both arms. Elli is burrowed in tight. Marie-Thérèse, whispering on and on, senses some fierce, even wrenching, sensation filling her. And then knows what it is.

"I love you," she whispers. "I love you both so, so much. And I'm so sorry for what happened. But look! Here we are, my dears, here we are, together." She gathers them even closer and holds on, her face against their heads.

Across the aisle, the gardener's expression is composed, his left hand loosely bracing a small bulge under his jacket that might be, for all appearances, some meaningless puff of fabric.

COLORS OF A DIFFERENT SEASON

Snow showers and squalls leave their few wet inches every other day. Bundled in her cloak, Marie-Thérèse leads three more "uncles" to rendezvous points in the city. Café doors are shut against the cold, outdoor tables stored away, and there are no lounging officers observing passersby. Marie-Thérèse is less afraid during these excursions until the day she and her "uncle" step aside to make way for two German officers walking abreast. The officers pause and one asks why the old man isn't carrying out his duty by cleaning the street. He points to a broom outside a shop entrance. Her companion responds, in poor German, that he has been ill.

"But you have no excuse now." The officer's breath smells of onions. He's a tall ample man, his face fuchsia-colored in the cold. His greatcoat reaches the ankles of his black boots. On his hands, gloves of black leather.

"No, sir, I have no excuse."

Marie-Thérèse's knees want to buckle.

"Well then, there is your weapon. The street awaits you."

"Yes, sir." The man salutes again and limps forward to take the broom. He carries it to the center of the street and begins sweeping at slush that hardly moves. Drivers of automobiles blare horns. Tires spray him with dirty water and slush. After a while, the officers move on but he keeps sweeping. He must be in pain, she thinks, his arm not fully healed. Slowly, fear is draining from her limbs and cold seeping into its place. After a while, the proprietor emerges, shouting that the man is ruining his broom and must stop. "*Chiens!*" he adds, under his breath.

No. A dog would never be like that.

After escorting the Allied soldier to his contact, she rides back to the clinic circuitously, staring out at the city under its cap of mottled gray cloud.

The thought comes that one day she might not be so fortunate.

Working with color is restful, the reds and blues, the yellows and greens—colors of a different season, a different time. And seeing those scarves and shawls taking shape row by row is also satisfying. But then there it is again. An image of the matron stopped in the street or on a tram. Or Marie-Thérèse herself apprehended. Or, if not those nightmarish scenarios, there's Rudi, walking away in the snow and not turning. *You will be in my heart.* It's like falling through the net of her crocheting.

"Marie-Thérèse," Liese says one evening. "You look quite drawn. You must be ill. You probably need a rest. Do you have any relatives still in the city?" The words sound sincere. That's the trouble with Liese. One never knows.

"If I'm ill, then I'm in the right place, no?" She smiles to make it a joke.

Liese glances toward the sitting room's open door, then gets up to close it. Seated again, she says, "Have you been seeing anything?"

"Quite a lot, actually."

Liese pauses in her knitting. "Yes? What?"

"Oh, just the other day, an abscessed carbuncle. I've never seen one before, have you? And one of the soldiers in my ward lost several lower teeth. He has no idea how. One minute there, the next not. He thinks he must have swallowed them. He was very distressed."

"Marie-Thérèse."

"No, Liese. I haven't. Have you?"

"Actually, yes. I saw *you* the other day, walking with some old man quite a distance from here. Who was that? And why were you with him?"

Marie-Thérèse frowns. "An old man? Oh! That was just someone who'd been cleaning the street. He was half-frozen and, I think, senile. He couldn't remember where he lived. Imagine! He knew the street name but not how to get there. He asked for help."

"And, of course, you gave it. You, so far from the clinic."

"I wanted to check on my family's home. But, yes, I did help him, naturally."

"You know, I was talking to Charlotte yesterday. She says she's been seeing things."

Marie-Thérèse steadies the crochet hook and keeps making her aqua loops.

"That's not so unusual. She hallucinates."

"I think it might have been something she heard, though. She was a little contradictory, yet seemed certain it was something odd. Voices…late at night."

"And you believed her?"

"She seemed coherent enough."

"It may have been auditory hallucinations."

"I know."

"Have you told Doctor Kuhn?"

"Not yet. I want to be certain before talking to him. He's so exacting. Though it might be a good idea, as I've said before, to tell him *something*. But I wanted to see what you think. Oh, I know you prefer to keep your own counsel, but again, I'm not sure I…well, you know."

Want to betray her? "Yes."

"If he should find out something on his own and realize that we've been telling him nothing, we're doomed. You know that, don't you?"

"I do."

"We'll go to prison. At the very least." Liese pulls at a strand of yarn, redoes it, and then is speeding along again, in red wool. "Have you heard from your family?"

"Just the one letter. Are you going home for Christmas?" she adds to change the topic.

"I want to. And maybe never come back. I hate this place."

"But why? You said you wanted to stay and finish."

"I'm afraid she's up to something, and they're going to find out. They're not idiots."

"She's not doing anything wrong, Liese. Besides, we're a Red Cross clinic, an international clinic. It's in Germany's interest not to destroy it."

"*It*, yes! That doesn't mean they won't destroy us, though, does it?"

Marie-Thérèse gives herself time to think before answering. "Nurses are in short supply now."

"I suppose so. You know those Sunday excursions to Louvain? I went on one."

"To *Louvain*? Why would you do that?"

"To see for myself. And I did. It was awful. There's nothing left of those ancient buildings, and nearly the entire town is gone. People were taking chunks of rock from the cathedral ruins. It was very sad. Someone else was selling postcards. That can happen here. Sometimes I can't sleep for thinking about it."

"Why not go home for a while? Spend the holiday if the matron can spare you."

"I should, not that she can spare anybody now. But look, here we are, talking about home, when you—"

"It's all right. I believe my family is well...somewhere."

"I hope so, Marie-Thérèse. I truly do. But I must ask you again, for my own sake but also yours and everyone else's—you really haven't heard anything odd, or seen anything strange?"

"No."

"Ah well. Perhaps before I leave, if I do, I'll talk with Doctor Kuhn. Then he can judge for himself whether or not to question Charlotte. It might help protect all of you, anyway."

"I don't know, Liese," she hears herself saying. It's a struggle to maintain a neutral tone. "I do know that last year before Christmas Charlotte was beside herself. You know how she gets around the holidays."

"All the same."

Marie-Thérèse pretends to be in thought, hand against chin, eyes directed at some middle distance.

"A good idea, no?" Liese says. "Just to be safe?"

"I'm not sure. To cause him to suspect something when it's

unwarranted, that might work against us too."

"I don't see how…if there's nothing. By the way, you're doing really well with your crocheting. Good for you! Maybe you
can try knitting something next. I can help you." She stuffs her
knitting and needles into a cloth bag. "So! I'm off to the wards.
Wish me luck."

"*Bonne chance!*" Marie-Thérèse catches the strand of yarn
with the tip of her hook and nonchalantly sets off again, making her loops in case Liese has paused in the hall to observe.

That night the woman with the severe ear infection is restless, and Marie-Thérèse convinces Sister Gauthier that the matron really should check Frau Gleffee's ear herself. "We don't
want the doctor to see some radical setback tomorrow, do we?
Worse," she adds in the nurses' office, "she could go deaf in that
ear." Gauthier is terrified of the doctor. Well, they all are. But
if he questions the staff concerning Frau Gleffee's condition,
Gauthier won't be a credit to herself. As Marie-Thérèse hopes,
Gauthier hurries to find the matron. And then, while Gauthier
attends another patient, Marie-Thérèse holds the chart, over
which she has clipped a brief note. The matron's face blanches
as she covers the slip with her hand, removing it in the same
motion. Then she walks over to Frau Gleffee's bed in her usual
unhurried manner and examines the ear while Marie-Thérèse
helps Gauthier bathe another patient. That is where they are
when Liese enters the ward.

Glancing up, Marie-Thérèse sees Liese follow the matron
into the nurses' office. Soon Liese is attending Frau Gleffee,
holding a warm cloth against the ear, attempting to draw the
infection out of its hiding place and to the surface.

That night Charlotte, lightly sedated, sleeps well. Marie-
Thérèse does not.

The following afternoon the doctor and two orderlies sus-
pected of being German soldiers in disguise inspect the wards
and supply rooms, the nurses' quarters and lavatories and office, the kitchen and pantries, the cellars, attics, and the matron's
apartment, along with the outbuildings. Marie-Thérèse notices

Liese's expression whenever the doctor is anywhere nearby. There's glow and amusement. *Is she infatuated with him?* If so, it explains why she hasn't left the clinic yet despite all those fears for her own safety.

For the rest of the afternoon, Marie-Thérèse goes about her work hardly knowing what she's doing, sensing the doctor right there, suddenly alongside her, anticipating him bursting into the ward and shouting for them all to line up. Hours pass slowly. At one point the matron smiles at her, in passing.

After her shift, she's afraid of finding orderlies in her room, digging through things. She gets her crocheting from the nurses' sitting room and goes to the gardener's cottage. The girls are there, but not the pigeon or its box by the hearth. In the warmth from a small wood fire, Elli is reading aloud from a children's book while Janine plays with a carved horse and cow, moving them into and out of an enclosure made of sticks. The fire in the hearth snaps from time to time. Drizzle streaks mullioned glass.

"The birds," the gardener says when Elli pauses at the end of a chapter, "have again flown."

Rocking, he lets his eyes shut. His hands hang limp from each armrest, wrist bones prominent, the first joint of each finger distended. His black trousers are tucked inside polished boots that reflect firelight. She finds the latter details disquieting. But no tasseled saber, in its battered scabbard, rests in its usual place on the two pegs above the mantel. She wonders if it's been confiscated.

Shaking away concern, she picks up the half-finished shawl in her lap. And while Elli pronounces each French word with flute-like clarity, Marie-Thérèse gives herself over, for the time being, to the colors of summer.

THE LOST CHILDREN

The door opens and the doctor peers in. Two men are lying in the isolation room, their eyes closed, their faces scarlet. Marie-Thérèse and the matron turn toward the doctor.

"I was told that you would be here," he says, addressing the matron. "Who are these patients?"

"The one on your right, Herr Doktor, is Herr Henri Lambert, a farmer from Mollem. The other is his brother Michiel. Two days ago, they arrived in the city with a wagonload of potatoes. Yesterday we admitted both."

As if responding to his name, Michiel opens his eyes and suddenly laughs. The matron shows the doctor a chart which he reads without touching as he stands just within the room. Michiel's laughter brings on tears and soon he's weeping in convulsive bursts. The doctor signals both the matron and Marie-Thérèse into the hall and closes the door.

"Maintain absolute cleanliness in that room and let me know at once if anyone, *any* patient or staff member, comes down with a sore throat."

"We alone have been attending these patients and will, as always, follow your instructions."

"Wipe down everything in the room with alcohol twice daily. Any instrument used there must be immediately sterilized. And it goes without saying, bedpans, basins, and linens as well. We cannot have an outbreak of rheumatic fever in the wards, and we will not."

"Of course not."

"The incubation period is two to four weeks, but if we can isolate anyone exhibiting symptoms of streptococcal infection, we may be able to halt any threat of an epidemic."

"Yes."

"Have all your nurses take their own temperatures twice a day and examine one another's throats. Do you know what to look for?" he asks Marie-Thérèse.

"Yes, sir. Matron has instructed us.

"I will repeat the lesson," she says, "just to be certain."

"And tell everyone to exert particular care regarding personal hygiene."

"Yes, of course. I will stress that point again."

"Very good. All the staff must follow these directions, with no exception. This includes the cook, maids, and orderlies. Even your gardener. Have one of your nurses check them at least once a day. And it goes without saying, although I will say it, that we must closely monitor each of our patients." He looks at the closed door. "We might have done without this. In a way I am sorry they were brought here, but of course we cannot have a run of rheumatic fever in the city or even in one of the larger hospitals, now, can we? So perhaps it is for the best."

"I agree."

At two in the morning the matron and Marie-Thérèse enter the isolation ward with bowls of broth and slices of bread. "Henri" appears to be sleeping comfortably. At her voice he opens his eyes, sweat no longer glossing his forehead, though his cheeks are still red with stage makeup. "Michiel" hasn't wakened. The lamp casts weak light, yet Marie-Thérèse sees that the towels she placed over the pillows are stained with makeup and must be changed.

"You did well," the matron tells Henri, whispering. "Are you sure you both weren't actors in a repertory company? Michiel's laugh was quite convincing."

She has rehearsed them well, Marie-Thérèse thinks. One of the symptoms of rheumatic fever is sudden uncontrollable laughter—or weeping.

"So good," Henri, an English captain, says, "that now our run will be extended."

Scabs and sores cover his head. His eyebrows are still thick and dark.

"For a while longer. But he didn't get a good look at either of you. He was too taken aback by your diagnosis. I may be able to come up with understudies for you both."

In the next bed Michiel thrashes, waking. He's eighteen years old, the matron has told Marie-Thérèse, and like many others in his battalion, was cut off from his unit and left behind in the general rout. A farmer near Flerbeck hid him—and, soon after, hid the captain—for several weeks in his hayloft, when it was safe to do so, and in the manure pile whenever German soldiers were in the vicinity. The two had finally been conveyed to Brussels under sacks of turnips and potatoes, both filthy and reeking of manure. The private now stutters when he tries to speak and so says little. His laugh, though, perfectly conveyed hysteria. He's from a village near Canterbury, in Kent, he told the matron, stuttering. Then he cried. Marie-Thérèse was given the task of shaving off his rust-colored hair and beard because of the fleas and lice. Both men's bodies have been bitten raw, the bite sores resembling the inflamed and sometimes bloody rashes of rheumatic fever.

Given what they've been through, it's astonishing they haven't, in fact, come down with a streptococcal infection. But at least, Marie-Thérèse thinks, the awful sores inspired the ruse.

"I want to show you both something," the matron says. She sits between the beds, facing them, while Marie-Thérèse stands near the closed door. The matron takes several flint pebbles from a pocket. "These are from Scolt Head Island in Norfolk. Do either of you know the place?"

"My wife and I went there several times on holiday!" the captain says. "I liked to do a bit of bird-watching. Sandwich terns, little terns, the arctic terns, the waders and wildfowl, so many species it was really quite marvelous."

"Did you ever walk across the mudflats at low tide?"

"Oh, indeed! Many times. My wife, Margaret, and I would take a picnic hamper and stay the day. May I?" He extends his hand.

She gives each of them a few pebbles to hold. The private

is crying again, though quietly. The captain studies his closely.
"I do remember these, yes, of course! Of little interest then,
but *now*!"

"M-m-may I k-k-eep them?" the private says.

"It's best if I do so for now. But you shall have them for
your journey."

The captain hands his back. "And you believe it's possible."

"I do, Captain. Tell me, are you from Norfolk?"

"No, Sussex, but we enjoyed traveling there, Margaret and I.
She loves to sketch, you see."

"So do I."

"Then we might have seen you out there and thought nothing of it. Imagine!"

"It's quite likely."

The captain's eyes are lively now, and Marie-Thérèse is relieved. Possibly there's strength in certain memories. Even courage. And he'll need both, given what he'll have to do for himself
and the private. Getting safely out of Brussels is one thing, but
then traveling through occupied country for another fifty miles,
or more if they have to take a roundabout route, quite another.
These two will be monks traveling to their home monastery a
few days before Christmas, or possibly even Christmas Eve.
Monks who have taken vows of silence. They'll have breviaries
and rosaries as well as identity and travel papers complete with
photographs and also handwritten notes in German, stating
their destinations in South Holland.

While they finish their broth and bread with a mere trace of
butter, the matron tells them that hope is every bit as important
as food. So they must have hope, which is not unlike faith itself.
Marie-Thérèse finds herself listening intently.

It's after three in the morning when Marie-Thérèse finally lies down, the luxury of non-movement so pleasurable she
doesn't want to relinquish it to the oblivion of sleep just yet. For
a few moments she allows her thoughts to flow where they will.
Those two and five in the cellar and two in a hidden attic compartment.
If it were *only* the matron, she thinks, it paradoxically might

not seem so impossible. But the matron—and she herself—are part of La Dame Blanche now, a small army of resistors that includes aristocrats, craftsmen, farmers, clergymen, fishermen, barge pilots, priests, a pharmacist, the gardener, some students probably, and who knows how many others. Given all that, absolute secrecy seems only a comforting myth.

At the sound of what might be footsteps, she jolts to attention.

Charlotte?

The doctor?

The bell at the Abbeye de Cambre rings four times. Then, in the quiet, she strains to listen again but hears only freezing rain striking the panes like bits of gravel.

You cannot go on like this. Sleep!

In the morning two other British men arrive in full daylight, entering through the clinic's main door. That makes twenty British soldiers from the Mons fighting and ten French infantrymen from the battle of Charleroi and a Belgian who doesn't give his rank or company and may be a deserter, all now part of a group called by its own code name: *Les Enfants Perdue.*

The Lost Children.

Joyeux Noël

On Christmas Eve, students roll the Bechstein into the dining hall, while Marie-Thérèse and several others decorate the fir tree the gardener found for them. Sister Depage serves pastries which astonish and delight everyone. There's even hot chocolate. At one point the matron and a third-year named Maurine slip out of the dining hall.

"Where are *they* going?" Liese asks.

Marie-Thérèse pretends nonchalance. "The wards?"

"Maurine was there all day."

"Well, you know. Always something more to be done." She immediately regrets the words.

"It just seems odd, their slipping out like that. I should probably mention it to him. He said anything out of the ordinary, remember?"

"Oh, Liese. Maybe Maurine just wants to talk with her. Maybe she can't get home for the holiday either and is feeling... sad."

"Charlotte told me she heard voices *again* the other night, at the public entrance. This time, she said, she went down to see. No one was there."

"That's not unusual. It might have been some emergency and the person taken up into a ward. Were you on duty? Or, it might have been Papa. He has to—"

"I checked the log. No one was brought in that night. And, no, I wasn't on duty. I was asleep. I still think we should tell him about such instances. I don't want to be killed for whatever *she* might be doing here."

"No one is going to be killed. No one is doing anything wrong."

"How do you know? I keep thinking they're going to destroy this place. I think it's a premonition. I really do, Marie-Thérèse."

Sister Depage comes up to them with her tray of pastries. Like the matron, Marie-Thérèse knows, she's excellent at observation. Marie-Thérèse asks where she managed to get so much flour and sugar, and the chocolate and milk. Sister Depage only smiles and urges them to have another. Liese asks about Doctor Depage, and treating them like patients, the woman edits out all but the most basic information. He's in France, somewhere behind the trenches.

"Was he able to get a letter to you?" Liese asks.

Sister Depage offers her impish smile. "They do manage to get through."

"How fortunate!"

Heat scorches Marie-Thérèse's face. She's relieved when Sister Depage moves on to others.

Liese steps closer. "I still think it's better to tell him something. We could say *voices*. Just that. Or even something about letters being conveyed from the front and probably not through any censor's office. It might help us later."

Marie-Thérèse stops herself from shouting Liese's name. When she finally does speak, it's in her quiet nurse's voice.

"I don't think it's right to cast suspicion on anyone without the least shred of proof. We'd be no better than those who… who destroyed Louvain. Don't you see?"

"That was different."

"A while ago, Liese, you were saying how you hated it here and wanted to leave. I think we're all overtired and prone to nerves. Maybe a short leave of absence would be helpful."

"My plan is to finish up and get out as soon as possible."

"You won't if she goes to prison. It'll be hard to find another qualified instructor, with everyone overworked in all the hospitals. *That's* what will happen if you go telling him made-up things."

"I knitted the girls stockings for Christmas."

"*Pardon?*"

"Elli and the little one. I made them stockings. To keep their feet good and warm."

"Oh! That was thoughtful."

"I have a sister Elli's age. I sent her a pair too. I hope she gets them."

Marie-Thérèse recalls that giving little gifts is another way Liese forges alliances. The stockings a strategy. Or is it? With Liese, one can't know. "I'm sorry you won't be able to spend Christmas with your family. I'm sure they'll miss you." And she is sorry. There's just something about Liese.

"Oh well, at least we'll be stuck here together. But again. Will you at least consider telling him about the voices?"

"No, Liese, I won't. I think it's unwise. Besides, do you really want to do that on *Christmas*?" By now the tree is finished, the tables set up for the following day, and a few students are singing. "Let's join them." Without waiting, she walks over to the piano.

Later, in the matron's office and the door closed, she begs her to have the remaining Allies removed and refuse to accept any more. The matron inclines her head as if in thought, but when she speaks, it's only to send Marie-Thérèse back to the wards. It's nearly midnight by then.

Marie-Thérèse wants to be joyful. More than joyful, she wants some firm, even brazen hope melded to faith that all will be well.

Soon church bells all over the city are heralding the birth.

On Christmas Day, she has to fight off sleep during the early morning Mass at Saint-Boniface. To her shame, her drooping head keeps snapping up at some swelling organ passage. She wishes she could be filled with a sense of His presence but feels only fatigue and foreboding. Yet Elli and Janine are on either side of her, bundled in warm coats from America. And Papa is there too, on the other side of Janine. He's forgiven her. And this, at least, is something. A large good something.

A complex fragrance of roasted carrots, parsnips, potatoes, and winter squash mingling with the deeper scent of roast beef drifts from the dining hall. Side tables hold dishes of plum

pudding and sweets—most of this bounty the result of gifts
from neutral nations and benefactors. The occupiers, it's ru-
mored, don't want food rioting and so allowed the donations
after the British briefly lifted their blockade. And all that making the clinic's annual Christmas party possible this year.

Marie-Thérèse notices that the children are wary and hes-
itant at first. The year before, their exuberance was barely in
check. While guests enter the dining hall, she plays Christmas
carols but thinks that it may take more than seasonal music to
raise spirits. When a girl of about five comes up to the piano
and watches, Marie-Thérèse breaks off and tells her, "Press this
key down while I play. Count to four each time and then press
down." Soon the child is depressing the C-natural key at four-
count intervals. Then Janine is there too, and Marie-Thérèse
gives her a C-natural in a higher octave. The first child looks
at Janine and smiles each time she presses her key. When Marie-Thérèse glances at the two girls again, she almost stops
playing. Janine's eyes are fixed on the other child and her mouth
is forming a shy smile. But as other children rush to the piano,
also wanting to play, Janine's hand slides from the keyboard,
and Elli leads her from the group. Whoever wishes to play gets
a turn, the old piano forgiving enough and ringing out discor-
dant merry sound. And in that maelstrom, an idea forms. *Mon
Dieu, Marie-Thérèse, you didn't see it before? You are so thickheaded.*

After the festive meal, Janine and Elli go to the matron's
table when their names are announced, both girls in red woolen
dresses and blue shawls. The matron lifts Janine up and an-
nounces that she and her sister are to distribute the gifts this
year. Then it begins, the grand distribution, as silence falls over
the hall. The matron calls a name, and the first child, a girl,
approaches with self-consciousness to receive her gift, passed
from Elli's hands to Janine's, and then to hers. After each child
has received a present, they all begin opening their gifts, finding
shawls and scarves and stockings, dolls, toy boats, caps, mittens,
mended dresses and boys' pants and jackets, some of these
things from as far away as America. An older girl has received

Marie-Thérèse's shawl and immediately wraps it around her shoulders, the aquamarine striking, with her blond hair, the long tassels dangling. By now children are shouting and running about.

Closing the festivities, Marie-Thérèse accompanies everyone singing the old carols in French, Flemish, English, and Latin. There is even the haunting "O Tannenbaum." Children sing several carols a cappella, momentarily transforming the dining hall into a church. While in a grand house on the rue Louise, Herr Doktor Kuhn raises his champagne flute to toast the Fatherland and its glorious future.

Leaving the civilian ward later that night, she encounters the gardener who apparently has been waiting in the hall. He bows, cap over heart, before presenting her with a wrinkled envelope. It bears no German stamp overprinted with *Belgien 3* Cent, only her surname and the address of the clinic. The handwriting is her mother's. She hardly notices that he's standing there, head bowed, as she eases open the glued flap and reads the missive's three sentences.

Ma Chérie,

Your father is ill. Please come at once. The bearer of this letter will tell you more.

She looks up. "Do you know where they are?"

"Breda."

"Is that a town or a village? I must get there as soon as possible, but I'll need travel papers for Antwerp, and that will take time, but what about after Antwerp? Can you help? Will you watch over the girls while I'm gone?"

"*Oui.*"

"*Merci, Papa!*" She grips his rough hand in both of hers. "*Joyeux Noël!*"

Winter Light

The gardener accompanies her to the Gare du Nord, the two of them using trams this time. It seems an age ago when they'd gone to meet the matron's train on that momentous day in August. And now, nearly six months later with no end in sight to the war, the armies stalemated along the Western Front, each facing trenches running over six hundred and forty thousand kilometers. At the Gare du Nord, no newspaper boys are shouting the news. There are just the ubiquitous posters proclaiming German victories. It strikes her again that Belgium might be an occupied country for many more months, even years, possibly forever. But just as on that August day, people are flowing through the station, only now, a preponderance of soldiers and stretcher bearers and wounded, the world reeling on in some almost ordinary frenzy while not far away, men are dying in scores every few minutes.

A child selling apples.

A woman selling eels.

Nine wrapped corpses on a baggage cart.

They find the right platform and waiting train. "Papa, take care of them. Reassure them that I will return. I will be a returning bird! And you must be careful, *s'il vous plaît.*" He bows, cap over his heart. She boards the nearest car and takes a window seat in a compartment, then looks out at him. He appears to be praying.

The car fills with military men in greatcoats, their voices like some rockslide in the confined space. Three officers enter the compartment, acknowledging Marie-Thérèse with a *Guten Morgen,* and hang their greatcoats on hooks near the door. The largest of the three pulls at the back of his uniform jacket and then all but falls backward into the seat next to hers. "*Oof!*" he cries, expelling a great breath. The other two, both thin and much younger, take opposite seats. One immediately shuts his eyes. The other is quite pale, she observes, except for hectic patches on his cheekbones. He lowers his head and gazes at his clasped hands.

The gardener is still holding his cap over his heart. As the train jolts and then slides forward, she places her right hand on the glass until her carriage is well beyond the platform. Finally, she leans back in sunlight and, pretending ease, lets her eyes close. But in the next minute the officer alongside her is saying, "Do you mind, Fräulein?" He holds a cigarette in one hand, a silver lighter in the other.

"*Nein, Nein.* Please go ahead." The man's drooping cheeks are flushed. His voice rather kind.

"*Danke!* Would you care for one?"

"*Nein,* sir, *danke.* I don't smoke."

"Ah. Good. Never take it up then. Right, Hans?"

The pale one agrees.

"He's not well, you see, and the doctor told him to stop smoking. I am being quite bad doing so in front of him, but what can I do?"

The two pips on his shoulder board indicate that he's a colonel. The younger men, she thinks, may be his aides. Odd that they would be traveling by train and not military automobile. But that might explain the one's sullenness. The colonel faintly wheezes as he inhales smoke and then expels it, a long, satisfied exhalation. She's tempted to offer some advice of her own.

"What a barbarian I am, though, not even introducing myself. This war has uncivilized me. I am Oberst Otto Bruning, from Cologne, not so far away in actual miles but a world apart all the same. And you, Fräulein?" She introduces herself and reaches into her valise to take out identity and travel papers. "I have no need for your papers, no need! Put those away. I am not some border guard, as those two well know." The sleepy one opens his eyes and laughs with the other.

She wishes the colonel were drowsy too. When everyone seems to settle, she takes out a textbook and opens it.

"Ah! What are you reading there, Fräulein? I thought you seemed a little bookish and, you see, I was right. Beware of bookishness! It ruins the eyes! Right, Hans?"

Hans, in eyeglasses, agrees.

"It is a medical textbook, sir, about germs."

"Ho! Are you a medical student? Will you become a doctor, then? Fräulein Doktor!"

The other two pretend they find this humorous as well.

"I am a student of nursing, sir."

"And you study about germs. You know, my family has a brewery in Cologne, so I can tell you anything you wish to know about yeast, which is a bacterium, no?"

He treats her to a lengthy disquisition on yeast and brewing and seems happy and far away in the remembering. Hans is looking down at his hands again; the other one has resumed his dozing. Marie-Thérèse asks question after question, probably annoying those two, but it's better, she thinks, than if the colonel questions her.

Finally he urges her to visit the brewery. Her whole family should come when things settle. And then she can see for herself how *good* beer is made. Is her family in Antwerp? He would be most pleased to meet them and extend the invitation himself.

Hans opens his eyes at that and gives the colonel a dark look.

She explains about her father's illness and how she's traveling to the Netherlands to help care for him.

"The Netherlands! Then you are an escapee!"

"*Ja.*" She laughs, hoping it sounds authentic.

"What about your studies? Are you giving them up?"

"I will resume my studies when my father recovers, as I hope he will."

"Ah. Very good. And where is it you study?"

She tells him.

Colonel Bruning frowns, his sparse eyebrows coming together. Hans is scrutinizing her. The other dozes on.

"You know, I think I have heard of that place, Fräulein.

Have you, Hans?" He grinds out the cigarette with his boot. Hans nods, still studying her.

"What I would advise, Fräulein, is to think about the benefits of a lengthy visit rather than a short one. Am I right, Hans?"

"You are, sir."

"*Ja.* It will be in the best interest of your family as well."

She arranges her expression to suggest confusion and diffidence. "*Danke,* sir."

He can't tell me anything more because it would be treasonous? Does he even know anything at all? Is he playing at importance?

Over fields, groves of trees, farm buildings, and waterways now, a flat winter light, the sun a platinum disk behind thin cloud cover. And here and there in fields, pigs, the survivors of devastated farms, rooting in snow.

As they approach Antwerp, he asks how she is traveling to Brabant.

"Friends of my family have arranged transportation."

"Very good. Then I wish you well, Fräulein. Don't forget my invitation." He hands her his card. "And don't forget what else I said."

She assures him she will not.

She's afraid he might insist on escorting her to these "friends of her family," but the three of them stride away and soon are absorbed within the gray mass of soldiers and stretcher bearers.

FARMHOUSES

Just outside the station's entrance, a peasant woman is sitting on a stool alongside a cart heaped with sugar beets. Approaching, Marie-Thérèse says, in a low voice, *"Bon après-midi, Madame Blanche."*

"Bon après-midi, mademoiselle." The woman stands and places her stool in the cart, then pulls the cart toward a horse and wagon waiting a short distance away. Seeing them, a man says something to the horse, pats its neck, and removes its blanket. Then he loads handcart, stool, and folded blanket while Marie-Thérèse climbs into the wagon's second seat. It all takes less than a minute. Soon they're passing through Antwerp, much of it piles of rubble. In a square, children in thick leggings and jackets are skipping around a lifeless fountain. The sky is low, the air cold, and as they leave the city, heading north, the wind picks up. Marie-Thérèse can't stop shivering.

Some forty minutes later they reach a small farmstead set on the snow-covered plain. After a meal of bread, cheese, and warmed milk, Marie-Thérèse is given a tiny room behind the kitchen. They ask no questions, not even her name. Nor does she ask them anything. The woman's face is creased, with thicker grooves across her forehead. She smiles often and darts quick glances at Marie-Thérèse, who senses her curiosity. The farmer's face is also creased and windburned. He keeps his eyes lowered most of the time. She admires the courage of this couple but is afraid for them. After all, they have a farm, however small, and there must be a cow, at least, in addition to the horse. And probably chickens. Much to lose, if not their lives as well.

She lies awake half the night while wind slams the farmhouse in waves. The wall alongside the bed feels icy to the touch. Sometime later she hears someone opening the stove door and throwing in logs. An image of the matron working in

the cellar comes. *I am familiar with that place, Fräulein.* When she
hears movement in the kitchen, she gets up and washes her face
after breaking a film of ice in the bowl on the washstand.

Decide.

But her will, too, seems frozen and she allows herself to
be carried from one thing to the next—another small meal,
this time bread and milk, a boiled egg and a small piece of
ham—then climbing up into the wagon again. The wind has
died, and the air is brittle. Clouds along the horizon are black
mountain ranges against a sky just beginning to lighten. After
about an hour, the farmer stops at a crossroads where a wagon
loaded with firewood is waiting. The farmer indicates that she
is to go on that one. He transfers her valise and wishes her a
safe journey. The two men nod at one another, and in the next
minute she's traveling north again while the first farmer turns
back. The perfect orchestration of it all astonishes her. *How
often do they do this?*

As the sun rises above the horizon, clouds in the east turn
pink for a few moments before becoming gray. She balls up
her fingers in her gloves. Her breath sends plumes out into the
frigid air. The driver's nose is dripping, and he swipes at it from
time to time with a blue handkerchief that reminds her of the
gardener. She's sitting alongside the woodcutter, in the wagon's
only seat, and the advised silence feels awkward. It also allows
for too much thought. *Keep going? Return? But my papers will be
wrong.* In either case, she will hurt someone no matter what
choice she makes. The shaggy horse clops on, giving a snort
every so often, its breath pluming. They pass farmhouses much
like the one where she stayed, small but sturdy on their open
expanses. Exhausted by her poor night's sleep and the unpro-
ductive thoughts, she finally nods off until nudged awake by
the woodcutter.

Ahead, a small guardhouse made of unpainted planks. White
smoke from a tin chimney curls upward in the still air. Just beyond the guardhouse, barbed wire fencing. The woodcutter
reins in the horse and waits. A guard in helmet and greatcoat

emerges from the hut a few minutes later. A rifle is slung over his right shoulder. The farmer salutes.

"Ah! Herman! Thank God. We're down to nothing in this damn cold."

The woodcutter jumps from the wagon and begins stacking wood along the hut's south wall.

"Who's the pretty young lady? Your daughter?"

"No, just someone who wants to go to Breda."

"She better have the right papers or she'll have to stay here."

The horse shakes its head and paws the frozen road.

The farmer laughs with the guard. By now Marie-Thérèse has her papers in hand and is praying that the trembling won't be noticeable. The guard is young, really just a boy, his forehead and jawline dotted with sore-looking eruptions. One makes his chin appear inflamed. She supposes he's trying to sound adult. His rifle looks adult enough. Anger simmers up through fear at the stupidity of it all, the terrible waste.

The air smells of wood smoke. The fields all around are white. As the guard takes their papers inside, she glimpses fried eggs on a plate.

An older guard steps outside and comes around to her side of the wagon. He looks from her to the photograph and then at the papers again. Finally he regards her again.

"So, you want to stay there for how long, Fräulein?" His left eyelid goes into a spasm.

"Until my father recovers, sir. I will be traveling back to Brussels, however, at some indefinite time."

"I see. Yes. It says that. Are you sure you want to go back? I hear it's dull there now."

"Yes, but I have work there, sir." Once more she regrets saying too much.

"Work! Why do you want to work? Why don't you find someone and get married?"

The younger guard, who has come outside again, sputters.

"I hope to, one day."

"That's better! You speak good German. Are you German?"

"Yes. I and my family."

"Why are they in Brabant?"

"They needed to leave Brussels."

"Why?"

"My father's office was vandalized, sir. Many of his patients left him."

"And so he chose a pigsty of a village?"

"It is only temporary until he recovers."

"Why should I believe you? Pretty girls lie." The eyelid twitches.

"You may know of a Colonel Otto Bruning. He is a family friend. I have his card. Would you care to see it?"

"Let me see."

She finds the card and hands it to him. He takes off his gloves and turns it this way and that. The card has beveled edges. The ink is dark. There is just the name and rank.

"Anyone can forge such a card. Did you forge this?"

"No, sir. He gave it to me prior to my journey." The implication—*In case I have difficulties*—seems clear enough.

"Very good," he says finally, handing back the card. "I wish your father a swift return to health."

"*Danke*, sir."

The younger guard opens the barbed-wire gate, and the woodcutter and his passenger proceed into a different country.

HOSPITAL

In the village square, a young man runs up to the wagon just as Marie-Thérèse is climbing down. "Willy!" she says after a disorienting moment. "You've grown so much!" She grips him in an embrace. "I thought I'd have to inquire everywhere. How did you know I'd arrive today?"

"I come every day. Today is the thirty-second day."

"You just *wait*?"

"Sometimes I help the farrier."

"Tell me. How is Father?"

Marie-Thérèse holds him while he cries.

"Oh, my dear. Is he gone? Am I too late?"

He shakes his head and then, all but running, leads her to a small house surrounded by a low stone wall. Behind the wall, a tiny garden, its foliage merely brown clumps showing some green near the earth. Inside, the parlor curtains are drawn, their worn fabric letting in random coins of light. A wall clock clicks each minute. A generous coal fire burns in the grate.

"Stay here," he says, then runs up a flight of stairs.

The room, with its settee and armchairs, is orderly and clean, but Marie-Thérèse detects a familiar odor. *Diarrhea.*

"*Ma chérie!*" Madame Hulbert cries, rushing into the room.

"Oh, Maman."

"*Dieu merci!* You will see him before he goes." Her voice rasps. Her eyes are glassy and reddened. The odor of diarrhea emanates from her hair.

Stepping back from their embrace, Marie-Thérèse sees her father descending the staircase. He doesn't look ill in the least. "Here you *are*!" he cries, striding toward her. "We had all but given up hope! The villager promised that the letter would be delivered, but it seemed so improbable. Francine! Look who's here! Put your soup on. She looks half-starved."

If not quite starved, she is certainly struck dumb.

From a doorway leading into the sitting room, the house-keeper, in her usual starched apron, gives Marie-Thérèse a little bow and a sad smile.

"And bread! She must have lots of your good bread."

"*Oui, oui,*" Francine says, in something of her old grumbling tone.

"Father, you're not ill? Then—"

"Come."

In an upstairs bedroom, Jacques is lying in a narrow bed, his eyes closed, his face dry and scorched with fever. To Marie-Thérèse, he appears all but unconscious.

"We didn't dare say anything in the letter," her father whispers, "in case it was intercepted."

Jacques! She whispers a prayer of gratitude and in a small lavatory across the hall scrubs her hands and forearms with hot water and soap for a full minute before reentering the narrow bedroom. "He has been like this for days," her mother says. "He takes some water and soup but nothing else. The doctor cleansed bullet wounds and set the bone of his right leg, but *four* bullet wounds…*Mon Dieu.* The doctor also gave him medicine for the diarrhea, but it does not stop."

"Four? Was he able to remove all the bullets?"

"Someone did, he told us. But he'll be here and you can ask him. He speaks Dutch and some French."

Two chairs are near the bed, telling Marie-Thérèse how her mother and father have been spending their days while Willy wandered about the village square, waiting for her. The thought that she almost turned back causes a streak of pain.

"I would like to make an examination, Maman. You may stay or wait in the hall, whichever you prefer."

Her father motions her close and explains that Jacques frequently soils himself and that the bedding was just changed but that it might happen again soon. "It's very bad, the dysentery. I take care of this for your mother."

"The doctor knows?"

"Yes. He gave us a bismuth solution for Jacques, but it isn't helping."

"May I see it?"

The matron lectured on bismuth as a treatment for dysentery, but a not particularly effective treatment. In fact, it could even be deadly, as the bismuth can coat the amoeba parasites in the intestine, and then they have nowhere to go, so they sometimes perforate the intestine. Patients often die.

"Father, can we have the doctor here?"

Willy leaves at once.

"Is there an apothecary in the village?"

"*Oui.*"

Please go and ask for emetine hydrochloride. If he doesn't have it, ask that he send for it. I will also need a hypodermic syringe and a bottle of sterile water. Explain that a nurse has just arrived from…France."

Marie-Thérèse follows him out into the hall. "You've been disposing the waste properly?" Her father had been a medical student. It strikes her as an unnecessary question.

"I dug a pit and bought lime."

"*Bien.* And everyone has been washing hands."

"Of course."

"We should have some methyl alcohol and iodine here as well."

"I already saw to that, my dear."

"Forgive me, Father. I'm a bit nervous."

He embraces her. "And rightly so. But look at you taking charge. I'm so proud of you, Marie-Thérèse."

When Willy returns with the doctor, she introduces herself in the parlor and speaking Flemish and some French while gesturing, asks if she might consult with him concerning her brother. She explains that she's a nurse. Wind has tufted Doctor DeKett's sand-colored hair, and to her eye he resembles an indignant bird. The mottled red face, intently focused eyes under their wiry, curling eyebrows, and thin lips already locked in disapproval add to the impression. She decides to say no more until after he examines her brother. Then in the parlor again, she asks if he might consider using emetine hydrochloride.

He shakes his head with vigor. He slaps his chest with the flat of his right hand.

She understands. Possibly fatal to the heart. The patient must be strictly monitored. Through gestures, she offers to do so. He goes on in a forceful jumble of Dutch and French and further gesturing. Keep him warm. Still. Diet, smooth and bland. Liquids. Blood pressure twice a day. He strikes his chest again. More, if contractions. He grips a wrist, shaking it.

From her valise she takes out the sphygmomanometer she'd brought and shows it to him.

He calls her *Juffrouw* Hulbert and from the tone of his voice might also be calling her a fool. When her father returns, she asks if the apothecary had the emetine hydrochloride.

"*Oui*. And what's more, the doctor telephoned while I was there."

Heat rushes to her face. The man would know she acted without his permission. Would he even return?

In the parlor she tells her family that the little house has just become a hospital with strict rules. To keep the bedroom and household absolutely clean—and give Francine some help—another maid must be found. All the soiled linen has to be boiled and more purchased if necessary. If the linen is too soiled, Willy will be in charge of burning it in the back garden. Then she explains about disinfecting hands, cutlery, plates, bowls, and cups as well as the bedroom floor and their shoes.

Her mother has only one question. "Will he live?"

Marie-Thérèse almost hesitates. "We'll do everything we can, Maman."

BRIO

Jacques? The doctor has a new medicine for you. Now you'll get better. Soon it'll be spring and you'll be able to sit in the garden. This is something to think about, yes?" She's predicting, she realizes, but it doesn't seem a bad thing.

"You came for my funeral."

"Ah, dear brother, I didn't come all this way to attend any funeral. Au contraire! I came to help you get well. And I vow to do so. I made the journey from Antwerp in a sugar beet wagon and also a woodcutter's wagon. People helped at every stage of the way and now I'm going to help you. Sometimes things seem so complicated and confusing, but actually, under it all, it's quite simple. Your body, for example, wants to get better and is trying very hard." She explains about his new medicine and how the blood pressure apparatus works. She talks about the heart and how it works. *As if I know.*

When she takes his hand it feels like a stone in winter. Blood pressure and pulse readings confirm her fear. The heart weakening, stumbling forward and pausing, stumbling forward again. Yet heat singeing his brow. *Is the fever killing him or the dysentery? Or both?*

Using half a grain of the emetine hydrochloride dissolved in sterile water, she prepares the hypodermic.

"There. Now you will get better."

In the parlor she tells her parents and Willy she'll wake them if there's any change or if she needs them. She keeps all dark thoughts to herself.

Madame Prennet, the cancer patient, died.

So did the bayoneted officer.

Sometimes the body doesn't want to get better. Sometimes it only wants its freedom.

Outside, the chalky light of a waning full moon makes

shadows in the back garden. Jacques drifts in and out of consciousness. Each time he moans, she places a cloth over his brow and says any quiet words pulled from the haze of her own exhaustion. A pet they once had. A soccer game. Boating on the largest of the Ixelles ponds. She takes his blood pressure and pulse every hour and notes the numbers.

Rising! But if it's too fast there'll be fibrillation or, worse, cardiac arrest. She watches for danger signs as she fights off sleep.

Sometimes he can swallow the water she gives him. At intervals purges of fecal matter gush onto the sheet. She bundles it up, wipes down the rubber mat, cleanses her hands and forearms, and puts another folded half-sheet on the bed.

On and on throughout the night. At dawn, the numbers are holding steady within the normal range.

Waking later in an unfamiliar room, she throws on a robe and rushes to Jacques's room. Willy is just removing the blood pressure cuff. "You fell asleep and Father carried you to your room. I can do it. I watched you, and Father also showed me. I wrote everything down."

"*Très bien!*" After looking at the numbers, she takes a new reading. *Still in range.* Her own heartbeat slows as she prepares another hypodermic.

By the fourth day Jacques is sitting up and able to eat by himself. The great purges have abated, and there've been no violent muscle contractions. When she stands out in the back garden to breathe fresh air, her mind is all but blank except for a single thought held there as if within a gilded frame: *Jacques will live.*

Doctor DeKett expresses no surprise, but she doesn't mind. Her own happiness at what seems a miraculous achievement is validation enough. At scheduled times, she administers the emetine hydrochloride, and the family keeps to its regimen of shifts and monitoring and hygiene. She even insists to the doctor, again mostly by gesture, that he send all of their stool samples to Rotterdam for testing, a request shocking Madame Hulbert into silence, though she complies.

One evening, the three of them at the dining room table, Marie-Thérèse tells them about their house in Brussels. Her mother grips the table edge and goes pale. Her father takes hold of his wife's arm. Willy is staring at Marie-Thérèse. Then Monsieur Hulbert says, "I was afraid of exactly that." A lengthy silence follows until he adds, "Sometimes people lose everything in a fire. This is not so different, no?"

"I didn't want to tell you."

"It's better to know."

An image of the stripped music room comes, the glint of copper wires, the scraps of felt, the cast-iron plate jutting out of the subflooring and reflecting a bit of light.

By the end of February Jacques can sit in a wheelchair. Sometimes his eyes are dull; at other times he's able to focus on conversations and even play a hand of cards with Willy. One afternoon a small dog follows Marie-Thérèse back from the village center. So many dogs wandering about now, a villager complains. Many lost or abandoned in Belgium and wandering across the border. This one has a black coat with black and brown markings around its face. His paws are narrow and all four legs are encased in dried mud that resemble plaster casts.

Willy helps bathe the dog outside, fleas and flea dirt falling from his fur, the water blackening and bloody with them. The dog shakes his coat nearly dry, and she combs out the remaining fleas. The small body with protruding ribs is pocked with sores both fresh and scabbed over.

Madame Hulbert isn't pleased. What if fleas get into the house? What if he has some disease and bites one of them? "But he wants to be here, Maman," Willy says. "He has no home. Jacques can give him a new name."

Marie-Thérèse brings out more warm water and soap.

The presentation takes place in Jacques's room, the dog wrapped in a towel, with only his face and ruff showing. "Look, Jacques!" Willy says. "Look what we *have*!"

Jacques has been gazing at the ceiling. Slowly, he focuses on the bundle.

"We must name him! What do you want to call him, Jacques? He's ours!'"

Marie-Thérèse watches her brother's face.

"Let me see," he finally says. Willy brings the dog closer and unloosens the towel.

"Brio," Jacques says.

Marie-Thérèse exhales. Brio: *Vigor, brilliance.* But then she wonders if he's being sarcastic.

"Brio it is!" Willy cries, hugging the dog.

That night Madame Hulbert, wrapped in a shawl against the chill in the house, knocks on Marie-Thérèse's bedroom door just as a church bell in the village is ringing midnight. It's Marie-Thérèse's turn to sit in Jacques's room, and she's been awake for a while. But the exhausted, distressed look on her mother's face causes her to abruptly sit up. Worse, her mother is apologizing and her eyes are filling with tears.

"Maman, what *happened*? Has Jacques—"

"No, no, *ma chérie.* He is sleeping well." Madame Hulbert sits on the side of the bed and extends her hands. Confused, Marie-Thérèse takes both in her own. Then Madame Hulbert is examining her daughter's hands as if she were the nurse.

"Once I hoped that these hands would create wonderful music on grand stages. Dreams die very hard."

"*Oui,* Maman. They do."

"I was foolish, trying to relive my life through you. It is a drug, you know, all that adulation from an audience. One simply...wants it again and again. *Needs* it. Sitting with your brother night after night, I've had much time to think. And I see now that you're able to create miracles of an entirely different kind, and no less magnificent. I was selfish, and I'm sorry. I was angry, and you, with me. I hope you won't be any longer." She exerts pressure on her daughter's hands. "Can you forgive me?"

"Maman, I wasn't angry, just sad. And of course I forgive you, though there's no need for forgiveness. You—"

"My not understanding, my withholding love, the vanity of requiring an artistic passion, imposing one's will...those are sins. Failures of the heart. You must not be sad any longer. You've found your true talent."

Words Marie-Thérèse has longed to hear, but these hold no enthusiasm. Just resignation.

Madame Hulbert leans forward to hold her daughter.

"Oh, Maman," Marie-Thérèse says, patting her mother's back as if she were little Janine in need of comforting. "*Merci.*"

GEESE

For news there is the tobacconist shop in the village, which carries newspapers from larger towns. Using a pastiche of French and rudimentary Dutch, Marie-Thérèse learns that the war, far from nearing a close, is worsening. The Allies have been mounting a large offensive in the Artois and Champagne regions, while in late January German Zeppelins floated across the English Channel and dropped their bombs on England. Now German U-boats have been attacking shipping in the Atlantic. "Torpedoing everyone!" the tobacconist says with disgust. "Allies, neutrals, even British passenger liners. And fighting now, in Poland and on the Mediterranean. Soon, maybe here. Who knows?" When the man's rage subsides, she asks if he's read anything about a clinic in Brussels. "No," he says. "Just about the scarcity there."

And then Monsieur Hulbert tells them at dinner one evening that he found a house in Rotterdam through an agent and also has been offered a position in an eye clinic. He refills their wine glasses and raising his own, says, "So now, my dear family, we can begin anew."

"Father, I—"

"Ah, ah, ah! Before you say anything, please consider that you will be able to continue your studies there in peace. So will Willy and soon, Jacques. We cannot move back, at least not for some time."

His words bring Brussels to the foreground again, along with a surge of anxiety, and longing for the girls.

Later, in his room Jacques says, "I will never find peace."

"Why do you say that, Jacques?"

"*Why*? When I was shot, I fell on top of someone who was cut right open by bullets. His insides sprayed all over me. Even in my mouth. Did I help our country? No. I fell on top of a dead man. Then I was captured. Then I was left to die with some others. We were supposed to be taken to Germany. I don't know why we weren't. Well, they ran away instead. I don't know why I didn't die like the rest of them. In my head they are crying for water. How can I give them any? So, no. I will never find peace. Why should I go to school and learn? Learn what? There is nothing more to learn."

Hearing these words horrifies her. Yet she knows that if he can talk about it, he can heal…possibly. Brio jumps up on the bed and settles himself alongside Jacques, but Jacques pays no attention to him. "For hours I listened to men dying, wanting water and dying. And now I should have peace? In the fine city of Rotterdam? I hear them screaming and then they are quiet and I am alone. Then they start screaming again, all of them."

"I'm sorry, Jacques. I'm so sorry."

"Well, you tried to warn me, but I wouldn't listen. I ran off and then I did…nothing."

"You may have inspired others."

"What good is that if I couldn't help them? I don't believe in honor anymore. I think I killed one German. Just before I was shot. I fired and saw three go down but others were firing too so I don't know. Still, I thought, I killed an enemy soldier! And then I was falling down on top of that dead man. I don't know his name. I would like to know his name. Even though he is in my dreams and is terrible. A mass of guts. I am so frightened of him in those dreams, yet if I knew his name maybe I wouldn't be. Maybe." Jacques covers his face and gives way to weeping, his thin body convulsing. She sits alongside him, an arm around his shoulder as he cries. Then he's saying, in short breathy phrases, "Nothing made sense before…how I am German and the Germans are fighting and killing us and we them. Nothing makes sense now. Least of all *honor*. Oh, I thought it was honorable to serve our king. You tried to talk me out of it. But I was stupid. I wanted to with all my heart. But I don't think that way anymore. I couldn't think that even if I tried. There's nothing honorable about…swallowing someone's guts."

"No, you're right. But, my dear brother, you followed your heart. You did what you felt at the time was the only thing to do. How could you have known? How could any of us?"

"You tried to tell me."

"Because I thought you were too young, too inexperienced. But love of one's country is still a good, Jacques."

"You know, I think I finally went because I was so...angry."

"Yes, you were angry."

"Well, I learned, didn't I?"

"We are all still learning, my dear brother."

In the next days, his wounds continue to heal, but his deteriorating mental state alarms everyone. There are outbursts alternating with sullen silences and refusals to join the family or eat. The nightmares continue, sometimes waking the household. Days, he rebuffs Willy and ignores Brio. When he does speak, he's curt and sarcastic. Marie-Thérèse's father is afraid that Jacques will find a way to take his own life. "I don't share this concern with your mother, but I'm quite afraid. I would like to move now. What do you think? Will a change of scene help?" Marie-Thérèse wishes she could talk this over with the matron. Her own instincts, though, tell her that Jacques needs a specialist in mental trauma and as soon as possible. The prospects for that will be good in Rotterdam. So, yes, she tells her father, they should go.

In the garden behind the small brick house, snowdrops have given way to crocuses, and those to early tulips, everything finding its way out of the dark sodden earth. She wants to take it as a hopeful sign, but progress in the vernal world, and its heartbreaking ephemeral beauty, only makes her dilemma all the more painful. Is it possible to save the girls, the matron, and Jacques? Or is she guilty of a kind of hubris in thinking that she can somehow accomplish all that? In fields surrounding the village, the newly tilled loam is chocolate brown against the chartreuse line of windbreaks. Spring breezes waft about the spicy sent of poplar buds. Birdsong and color. Streams and canals brimming. A heaven, in its way, but she's always tired...

tired, anxious, and restless. Dreams of frozen water and white, wind-blown curtains rob her of rest.

You're coming with us, Marie-Thérèse, aren't you? You really can't go back there now. It's too dangerous. Really, it's madness to go back! Come with us, and when it's safe, you can return then, if you wish. Doesn't that make sense? And you can help us take care of Jacques.

But I'm needed there. I can find a good doctor for Jacques in Rotterdam and then… You say you are needed there, but others are at the clinic, no? We have only you.

Those words, finally, the proverbial straw.

In early May they move into the new house in Rotterdam, one overlooking a small park and a canal running from Rotterdam, through Delft, and on to The Hague. When the house's casement windows are open, she can hear bargemen calling to one another. And can see livestock floating by or bales of wool, sometimes straw and hay, coal and produce, a ceaseless procession of goods and creatures plying both ways, all in some service to humankind. On sunny days flecks of light ride the water. Willy begins school and makes a friend named Kiels. Madame Hulbert has begun involving herself in the city's cultural life, and Monsieur Hulbert is relieved to find acceptance, not prejudice, at his new clinic. Marie-Thérèse, after interviewing several doctors, engages one who doesn't treat mental trauma with opiates. Jacques seems less truculent after his first session and agrees to go again. Despite her gratitude for all of it, Marie-Thérèse has to disguise her own unhappiness and uneasiness.

Nights, the two of them sometimes sit at a casement window, Jacques usually quiet. The inertia wears on her, and worry adds to the sense of malaise. She often wonders if her warning letter ever arrived at the clinic. Her father had to find a different courier; the one he hired previously had left the area—or was apprehended. Now, in Rotterdam, they may have to find still another and hope he's honest. An old dream returns. She's walking at night in an unfamiliar city, trying to get to some unknown place by walking fast, not taking an automobile or tram, which would have been more logical, but simply walking, leg muscles straining, the pavement underfoot hard, the light dim, the buildings dark and slick with rain, and she's making no progress whatsoever even though walking as fast as she can. A dream from Académie days.

One morning at breakfast she tells them.

"You want to return to your Germans," Jacques says. "You must be in love with one of them."

"No, Jacques. It's not that at all. I need to—" She stops herself from completing the sentence—*warn the matron.* Sadly, she can't trust him with that truth, given his state of mind.

"Finish my studies and then I'll return and work in a hospital here."

Deferential now, her parents politely argue. It's far too dangerous and difficult in Brussels. Couldn't she finish her studies here, in Rotterdam?

There is a bit of the truth, a mere crumb, she can give them, in response.

"Mon Dieu!" Madame Hulbert cries. *"Children?* You want to get two children?"

"And then return," Marie-Thérèse assures them.

A sudden din outside breaks the silence. A pack of dogs, it seems, have decided to start barking all at once. Brio runs from room to room, adding to the clamor.

"Geese!" Monsieur Hulbert says. "Wild geese!" They all stand to watch a large flock beating their wings and rising as one in the vaporous morning light.

THE MOUSE

She breathes in their scent and strokes their hair. It's hard to let go. But soon the girls are opening their gifts—paint sets, books, a piano lesson book, and a new summer dress for each. They're in a holiday mood until Elli mentions that she's still carrying her big doll about the district. She says this with pride. It's what Marie-Thérèse hasn't wanted to hear—that Madame Blanche is still active at the clinic. Dread shoves away the joy of homecoming.

Liese is still at the clinic. So is Gauthier and the matron. Madame Depage, though, has gone to America on a fundraising trip. No other students have left, and there are several new ones. The daily work of ward duty and study, the same. A new director has replaced Doctor Kuhn—an older man, Herr Doktor Klamer. As soon as possible, she asks the matron whether any hand-delivered letter arrived. With her eyes and a minute movement of the head, the matron indicates there'd been no such letter.

Anxiousness jitters through Marie-Thérèse when, later, she conveys the colonel's warning and urges the matron to consider leaving for a while. And if that's impossible, to at least stop taking in Allies. "Just for now, Matron. I beg you."

They're in the matron's apartment, in the front room that serves as an office, and the matron is spinning a pen on the desk's blotter. When she finally speaks, it's to describe how the occupiers have converted the house across the street into a barracks and command post. "Why just there? They could have any house! But of course I know why. They're watching us. I've ordered that those with rooms facing the street keep their curtains drawn. I think our cook is spying for them. She observes me so closely and recounts our supplies. But I can't let her go. That would be too suspicious." She rubs a cheekbone.

She pushes back hair, a forceful motion, fingernails dragging at the scalp.

The colonel was right. Marie-Thérèse hears herself asking how many are left.

"Thirteen."

"Matron, no. No!"

"Mademoiselle, you forget yourself."

"Au contraire. I remember everything. I remember how you'd say *just these few more.* Over and over. Just these few more. You're deluding yourself! Do you think they'll spare you? Did they spare the villagers? And farmers who had done nothing? *Did* they?" Her outburst horrifies her.

The matron finally replies. "*Non,* mademoiselle."

"That colonel...he knew something is going to happen here."

"That was three months ago...and it hasn't."

"He told me not to return. There was a reason."

"So, then, why did you?"

"Because Jacques doesn't need me now, but you do. And the children. I don't want you to go to prison. If you keep taking in Allies, you will."

"What can I do when they're brought here? Refuse? But you don't have to stay. Others are helping now. Nearly everyone."

"Liese?"

"Yes."

"Oh, Matron, that's—"

"I fear only our cook. Charlotte is with a family in Mollem for the time being. A nurse looks in on her."

And administers her daily dose.

"But Liese, Matron!" Marie-Thérèse can't stop the torrent of words, all questioning the matron's judgment. "She...she may have told him things. She may have invented. She said she might do that as insurance. I'm so sorry you asked her."

"But I can trust you."

The barb stings. "*Oui!* You can! Yes, I failed you once, badly, with Doctor Kuhn and now by not getting you word. You probably wouldn't have acted on it anyway. But, yes, you can trust me. I came back. I told myself it was to finish my studies, but I know the true reason. I want to get the children out and I want you to come with us. We'll invent a pretext."

"I'm afraid it's impossible. Work has resumed on our new clinic, and I need to oversee it, for one thing. But you can leave with them. I will give you your examinations early. I'm sure you will pass."

"Matron, you are so...*stubborn.* And you always have an answer and always must be obeyed even now, when you are wrong, *pardonnez-moi*, but you are wrong and will suffer for it. It must not happen, *s'il vous plaît*! It must not. I am going to help you with these patients and then we will get the necessary papers and leave."

"Ah. You are no longer the little mouse, are you? I heard it in your playing at times and now I see it. You are showing fire and heart."

Mouse. "Matron, if you saw me as a mouse, why in the world did you ever ask *my* help with all this?"

"I love all creatures, as you well know, and mice are fine... as mice."

"So, you chose me because I was the least brave? The most tentative?"

"And it worked, I think. Don't you?"

"You tricked me!"

"I felt I could trust you. But in another sense, it was a ploy, too, so yes, I suppose you're right."

"It was dangerous. And foolish. I might have revealed everything to the doctor out of my...mouse-ness! As it was, I probably said too much."

"Mouse-ness. I like that. But you didn't reveal the crucial things, did you."

"No."

"So, I was right."

"You always are." Would she hear the sarcasm? If so, Marie-Thérèse doesn't care, which proves, she supposes, that all mouse-ness has left her. "Except right now you're not. Those thirteen and *then* we'll go, Matron. It's a different world. You can teach there. And I will once again be your little mouse-student."

"Do you recall… No, I don't think I ever spoke to you girls about this, but years ago I made a vow. I told myself that someday, somehow, I would do something useful." She's smiling now. "Have more tea, please. Did I say that I'm very happy to see you?"

"You didn't. Thank you. But, Matron? If you stay, your usefulness may come to an abrupt end."

"We'll see, mademoiselle. We shall see."

THE SPY

A new patient is upending one of the men's wards. Not observing quiet time, up at all hours, demanding meals at odd times, and shamelessly flirting with staff, particularly the student-nurses. Black hair curling about his ears, bold eyes, audacious responses. Asked to return to his bed, he'll reply, often in French, "Only if you come with me!" Liese finds him charming. "Later," she might reply. Or, "Tonight!" He calls her a princess, an angel, and throws back his head and laughs at her responses, waking the ward.

Marie-Thérèse hates these displays. Yet she finds herself blushing in the man's presence, and then it's her turn to be noticed.

"Ah, you are new here, no?"

She responds in German. "I am a third-year student."

"But I did not see you before, mademoiselle," he continues in French. "Have you been hiding?"

"My name," she states, again in German, "is Fräulein Hulbert."

He repeats the words in stern perfect German and mimics her frown. "Such an expression, and you with such beautiful hair and skin too. Both of you! Princesses. It must be the air of Brussels."

She finishes making up a bed and turns to go.

"Mademoiselle! Forgive me. I do not mean to be brash. It's only...I am so happy I won't lose my hand. At least I don't think I will." He regards his bandaged hand.

"You should be speaking German."

"I do not wish to speak German, mademoiselle, though I can, of course. Indulge me."

"You are disobeying the rules. And I am not allowed to speak French."

"*Rules.* You're so serious. It spoils—" As Liese appears with a tray, he shouts, "There she is! My angel! See how good she is to me, mademoiselle? Unlike someone I've just met."

The matron approaches the man's bed and reminds her two students that the ward holds other patients as well.

"If these two are princesses, then you, madame, are most definitely the queen."

"And you, the fool in motley. Now, Herr Quien, kindly allow my nurses to do their work."

"Look at me! A poor sick fellow. How can I stop them?"

"You manage quite well."

Later Liese says, "Isn't he *magnifique?*"

"Too bold. I think he loves himself too much." It still shocks and appalls Marie-Thérèse that the matron revealed everything to Liese, justifying all of Liese's previous suspicions. Why *wouldn't* she tell the new doctor, in order to save herself? Or does she feel better now that she belongs to the matron's inner circle. And the matron gambling on this,too. *Oh, Matron, a bad idea. A terrible idea.*

"Too bold? You think so? That's good luck for me then, though he may not be here much longer." She gives Marie-Thérèse one of her coy looks. "And please don't get in the way. He noticed me first."

"He seems to notice everyone."

"It only looks like that. I know better."

"Be careful, Liese. It's against—"

"We're not full nurses yet. You're just envious."

During her shift Liese frequently gravitates toward Quien's section of the ward. Then Marie-Thérèse can hear the two of them laughing. Anyone in the immediate area is usually drawn into the fun. And whenever the matron enters the ward, she mimes clapping her hands, scattering everyone. But does so distractedly, Marie-Thérèse thinks, and without reprimand.

Marie-Thérèse studies her, from time to time, trying to see her as *Matrone.*

"Who is he?" she asks Gauthier.

"He's French, according to Liese. A coal miner."

"French! Why is he here? He's in danger. He could be sent to Germany."

Gauthier draws her lips together and tilts her head from side to side. "He seems friendly with them. They don't mind him, for some reason."

"He appears healthy enough. Couldn't he be treated as an outpatient?"

"I don't know."

That night, in the cellar, she questions the matron.

"We've been observing his infection," she says. "He could lose that finger, along with others."

"Isn't he afraid of being sent to Germany?"

"As a coal miner, he's needed here."

"Could he be transferred to another hospital? He's so disruptive. And crude."

"I've asked him to stop, but he's…irrepressible."

Asked him to? Not told him? So much seems off. "Who is he, Matron? Really."

She gives Marie-Thérèse a long look. "A spy," she finally says. "For France."

A spy. The matron now involved with spies from France. *Mon Dieu.* It explains, in part, her reluctance to leave, given that her "duties" have now expanded.

In her room, its drapery drawn against prying eyes from across the street, Marie-Thérèse can't fall asleep. What seemed simple before—*get her to leave*—now strikes her as immensely complicated. Not unlike a simple melody that in its variations becomes more and more complex and difficult and even unrecognizable.

In the next days, Marie-Thérèse and some of the others try to avoid Quien. It isn't easy. His flirting, his boisterous laugh have a strange levitating effect, especially on warm spring days, the windows open to soft air. He has an ability, Marie-Thérèse realizes, to neutralize stress and worry. "Look at her," he'll say, "the Winter Princess! She smiles, no? *Is* that a smile? The tiniest little smile? Or is it the beginning of a frown, which she is so good at. No! A *smile*. Don't hide it from us, my Winter Princess!"

Angry at herself, she'll hurry away. And every so often the matron appears, silently scattering everyone.

When Marie-Thérèse graduates to "Winter Queen," to Liese's displeasure, she begs Gauthier to schedule her on other wards, and she throws herself into her studies, cutting back even more on sleep. Her hope is to take her examinations and leave with the girls as soon as possible. There are tears in her eyes when she tells the gardener her plan. "You will have to save her now, Papa. She won't listen to me."

He offers the saying she takes to mean *meet force with force*. It gives her a bit of hope, though she's afraid his force will be no match for the matron's.

And then everything becomes even more complicated.

"He's here," Julia says one morning as she's stowing things from her cart. "Your beau. He asked about you."

The words incomprehensible.

"The one from last fall?" Julia says. "Don't tell me you forgot."

"As a visitor?"

Julia shakes her head and motions toward the ward. "He was admitted late last night. A bullet wound but not critical. Looks like he'll live," she adds, leaving.

Rudi. Lying in what had been Private Schalk's bed last October. His left arm bandaged from wrist to shoulder. It's just seven in the morning and the ward quiet. Marie-Thérèse slips Rudi's chart from its holder.

He was wounded when a bullet ricocheted off an automobile in which he was riding and entered his left arm at an oblique angle, causing a wide wound. Tendons were torn and tissue destroyed, but the ulna and radius somehow hadn't been shattered. She looks from the close-written words to the patient. *Rudi*. His face relaxed in sleep, but the moment he opens his eyes, perhaps sensing a presence, his expression tenses.

"Mademoiselle Hulbert. I was hoping you wouldn't be here. And yet I'm so glad to see you."

Words delivered without the least smile.

"Are you in pain?"

"Some. What have you been doing? Have you been practicing?"

"I'm sorry, no. But I've been teaching the little girl, Janine, to play."

"Like my sister Margarethe, you avoid the issue by teaching scales. It was finished for her the minute she hung out her sign."

Never argue with a patient. "I've been hoping it will help her speak."

"Has it?"

"No. The sound of the piano seems enough for her."

"Well, it might turn out all right. It's a language too."

Light words delivered without lightness. She takes a sterile thermometer from her cart. "Rudi, I must record your temperature."

He holds the thermometer in his mouth for the prescribed time, but she knows from the glassy reddened eyes and taut dry look of his skin that he has a fever. She places a damp cloth on his forehead. Other patients are stirring and soon breakfast trays will be brought in, waking Quien.

The bandage needs changing…already. She removes the bloodied gauze, cleans and then studies the wound.

"What are you looking at?"

A darkened smudge she's afraid might indicate the onset of gangrene. "We have been taught to be thorough. Do you feel chilled at all?"

"I was last night."

"I'll get you another blanket as soon as I finish with this." She follows the protocol for wound dressing, finally applying the treated gauze and then the bandage, doing her best with the correct pattern. But her jaw is shaking and her hands slow.

Rudi.

"At least I will be able to skate, no?"

Finally, a smile.

"Yes, you will be able to skate next winter. But for now, this might earn you a visit home."

"I thought so too but was soon informed otherwise. It's for the best, really."

"You know, you're fortunate. The bullet might have shattered your forearm. You might have lost the arm."

"*Ja*. A miracle."

He begins shivering in spasms. She gets another blanket and is just covering him when Quien comes up and demands an extra blanket as well. He's been calling for a nurse for some time, but has anyone rushed to his bed? No! And what's more, he's hungry, but is anyone bringing his tray? No again. And now, worst of all, he feels weak and lightheaded and is afraid he won't be able to make it back to his bed. He's a tottery old man who needs help from his Winter Queen immediately.

Heat scalds neck and face. Ridiculous man! "One moment," she tells him. Then finds Gauthier in the nurses' office. "Go help him or I'll never translate for you again."

"Me! I don't want to help him. *You* help him."

"He's going to fall over, maybe on purpose, and as ward Sister, it will be your fault. The doctor will hold you responsible."

Gauthier hurries out while Marie-Thérèse waits behind, hearing the commotion Quien is making. Surely no one in the ward is still asleep.

Her day has begun.

Sometime later that morning Gauthier pulls her into the office to say that Quien wants them to be wary of the new patient. He heard that he's a spy. "*Absurde*," she adds. "He just wants attention so he creates this fantasy. He also said he hopes there are no Allies here because he'd feel unsafe." Her French storms out, in its bass line.

Warm water soothes chilled hands but has little effect on the rest of her.

In the matron's sitting room, Marie-Thérèse says, "Did you examine Lieutenant Fischer's wound, Matron?"

"I did."

"And so you saw that blackened area." The wound had been debrided yet a thin margin of darkened skin remained. "Is it gangrene?"

"No."

"Could it be…gunpowder?"

"I believe so. He may have been shot at much closer range than stated by those who brought him here. Nor is the wound consistent with that of a ricocheting bullet, which tends to enter sideways and cause far more damage."

"Why does it say 'ricocheting bullet' on the chart then?"

"It's what we were told to write."

"Then someone might have shot him at close range? Could he have done so himself?"

"If he's right-handed, yes. Some do this in order to be sent home."

"I don't think he wanted to go home. And he isn't infantry, so it would have been hard to explain. Do you think someone else might have shot him precisely there?"

"I don't know." She rubs the bruised flesh under her left eye. "Mademoiselle, it's late. If you have no further questions—"

"Matron, I must tell you that Monsieur Quien has been saying odd things and quite loudly. He said he hopes there are no Allies here because he wants to be safe. And he used the phrase 'tottery old man who needs help.' He self-dramatizes, and yet *that* phrase? Has he seen us with the 'uncles'?" This seems more than enough to worry her. Marie-Thérèse decides to postpone telling her what he said about Rudi. "It's so confusing. I'm afraid I don't trust him, and I'm so concerned about you."

The vase of irises on the table has been catching her eye. Marie-Thérèse studies the flowers' lower petals again, with their dark veining on gold that pales to white and all of it surrounded by an iridescent lavender. The matron's closed sketchbook is nearby. Conveying the irises' complexity strikes Marie-Thérèse as impossible. She takes a last look at the flowers, and when she stands to go, sees something she failed to observe earlier.

"Matron. Your mother?"

The black mourning band around the matron's upper left arm is all but obscured by the sleeve of her blouse puffing up around it. It explains the darkened crescents under her eyes and the tinged glassiness Marie-Thérèse assumed was simply fatigue. *Now she can go back to England. And maybe not return.*

"I've been writing a statement for tomorrow, mademoiselle. I'm so sorry to have to tell you that Madame...Sister Depage... has died. Please say nothing until I can address everyone." She presses thumb and forefinger against the bridge of her nose.

"*Died?* In America? Was she...was it some accident?"

"I just learned that she was aboard the *Lusitania* when it was sunk by a U-boat. At least one torpedo hit the ship. For some reason she had decided to stay a day longer in New York and so changed her travel arrangements. Doctor Depage isn't sure why. Possibly for the fundraising, he thinks. As the *Lusitania* was so fast, it was scheduled to arrive in Liverpool at the same time, if not sooner, than the liner she'd first booked on."

Marie-Thérèse presses fingers against each eyelid. Posters have been touting this victory, showing a burning ocean liner, stern tilted above the sea, and a black U-boat in the foreground.

"Word came this evening. Doctor Depage is in Ireland. The ship went down off its southern coast. Madame Depage was listed as missing, but then they found her body in the sea, tangled in rope."

Tangled in rope.

Holding Marie-Thérèse, the matron whispers, "I'm sure she tried to help others first. Please bear this in mind. I'm sure that will come out. And now we must simply carry on, for her sake. She would not want us to be devastated."

Marie-Thérèse can't help it. She is devastated.

She keeps seeing Madame Depage in the sea off the coast of southern Ireland. Dark hair undulating about her white face, arms outstretched just beneath the water amid a tangle of rope.

The sea was calm that day, according to Dr. Depage, the May sun warm. But rescuers were reluctant to go out to the site. They were afraid of being torpedoed themselves, which often happened to rescuers.

Over the following days, Marie-Thérèse feels no easing of sorrow. In fact, it causes her to break every rule about how to speak with a patient.

"Why did you say, Rudi, that you hoped I wouldn't be here?"

"I was...hoping you'd be at the Académie instead."

She doesn't like the way his eyes flicked away. "Can you tell me, please, what happened to your arm?"

"As it states. I was in a car. Shots were fired. A bullet found it."

"A ricocheting bullet?"

"A bullet. I don't know."

"Should I ask the matron if you could have her gramophone for a while? You might like some of her records. We may be able to find you a private room."

"No, thank you."

"No? Rudi, I'm not supposed to be negative or argue with any patient, but you seem so preoccupied. I can assure you your arm is healing. Wouldn't some music help your mood?"

"I don't think anything would."

She pulls a chair close to the bed. "Can you tell me why?" She's nearly whispering. "Talking about it might make you feel better."

"It won't."

"Why not start with your wound? Did you shoot yourself?"

"No."

"Then obviously, someone else did."

"A doctor."

A *doctor?* "This doctor...wanted you here? In *this* clinic?"

"Ever since they brought me here, I've been arguing with myself, and so, yes, I am preoccupied. Do I tell her or not? Will it make things better or worse for them? What will happen to me? The easiest question of all. Dereliction of duty is punishable by death. But never mind. The important thing is for you to know there'll be more searches soon by the secret police. They have their suspicions but not enough evidence. There are outside observers. I was to be the inside one. Through you, I was to learn all I could. Even trick you into incriminating her. They saw us together and then created a little strategy. They promised me you wouldn't go to prison, but I don't believe them. Incidentally, that loud fellow here? I knew I'd seen him somewhere before, and then it came to me. It was in a café. He was talking with a tableful of German officers. It looked like some happy get-together. Don't trust him."

Because he is spying for France.

"Do I care about a few wounded Allies? This is a hospital. Everyone should be treated. I care only about you. When they figure out that I'm not cooperating, maybe they'll make up evidence and pay people to testify. They're relentless. But, really, Marie-Thérèse, you need to leave."

He takes her hand and is quiet for a few moments. But then, whispering again, he asks if she would go to Coblenz after the war and tell his father how sorry he was that his life hadn't turned out the way his father had hoped.

"Rudi—"

"You are about to say that it won't happen, that there'll be no execution, maybe only a prison term, that I might see my father again and say all those things myself. I know you, mademoiselle. But no. They will execute me. I'm resigned to it. It will be over fast and when you think about it, I haven't been doing very much with my life. Not cooperating with them will be something, anyway. Play him some Schubert and Chopin, mademoiselle. He loves those two composers. Say that in the end I was thinking of him and that I loved him and that I wished his passion could have been mine. If you promise to do this, I will die easy of heart."

"Yes, all right, Rudi. I'll play...the 'Phantasie'."

"Good." He closes his eyes.

She sits there a while longer, a prisoner of thought. Why

should this be happening now, and not earlier? Because she sent him away last fall and then was away herself? Had the "little strategy" been put into motion *before* the skating party last December? Were his words now part of some deception?

Gently, she removes her hand from his.

FISHMONGERS

The head of the secret police strides through the clinic, trailed by three deputies. In ward C the entourage halts at the back windows, where Otto Mayer gazes down into the garden. The Siberian irises are in bloom now, banks of them shading from white to deep purple.

Otto Mayer, in a civilian suit, does not behave with civility. After striding back through the ward, he opens cupboards in the supply room, pushes aside boxes and linens, knocking some to the floor and leaving them there, and then either slams the doors shut or lets them hang open. He paws through file cabinets, draws out handfuls of records, glances at one or two before tossing the clutch of papers onto a desk. He handles instruments and vials and bandaging material and linens all without gloves despite the matron asking him to wear them.

"I do not wish to."

While Mayer and his entourage rummage through cupboards and drawers, Gauthier and Marie-Thérèse, at the matron's signal, slip into the back passageway and rush to her apartment. The signal, two fingers placed against the jaw, means they should scan her rooms for anything amiss. What a time to do that! Of course she'd been careful, Marie-Thérèse thinks. She's always careful. Why check *now*? But she must have been worried, and, yes, there's a bit of paper sticking out from under the desk blotter. A list, they realize, of admissions, dated early that morning and including a number of British names. Gauthier rolls it up and then, using one of the matron's neckties, they suspend it inside the toilet's water tank. A quick look through desk drawers reveals no other incriminating evidence. At the sound of footsteps in the back passageway, Marie-Thérèse whispers that they should use the street door. Gauthier knows better. They'd be watching the street entrances. The two slip out into the garden.

"You talk to them," Gauthier commands.

Marie-Thérèse calls Jackie and Donnie, and when Otto Mayer opens the door off the back passageway, they're tossing sticks for the dogs. Donnie obliges. Jackie only watches morosely.

"What is this?" Mayer shouts. "Playing with dogs when you should be working? Why are you two out here so early in the morning?"

Hackles raised, Jackie trots toward the man. The matron calls him to her side and slides her hand over his great head and down to his collar. "All students are given some free time each morning when the weather is fine. We are having examinations, Herr Mayer, a stressful time." To the two young women, she calls, "If you have used up your twenty minutes, resume your duties, please."

"Wait. They must be searched."

She reaches them first. "I will do it."

She asks them to remove their aprons, which she then turns upside down. Marie-Thérèse's piece of bandaged driftwood falls from a pocket. After examining it, Mayer throws it toward a clump of irises. The two nurses remove their cuffs and shake their arms. Finally, they're told by Mayer to shake their skirts. Color rises to Marie-Thérèse's face. She envisions a row of Parisian dancers. Gauthier's face darkens.

"Shall they undo their hair too?" The matron's calm is icy. The faces of the guards are florid. Otto Mayer glances at the gardener's cottage.

"Who lives there?"

"Our gardener and general helper."

As he motions to the guards, Marie-Thérèse prays that Papa will not choose this morning to meet force with force.

That day in the clinic, the nurses can hear them moving from floor to floor, room to room. In ward C again, Mayer stops at Rudi's bed. "Who is this one?"

A deputy reads the chart. "Zweiter Leutnant Rudolf Fischer, sir."

"Are you getting good care here, lieutenant?"

"Yes, sir. This is a fine clinic."

"You find nothing amiss?"

"*Nein*, sir."

"And this nurse, she is satisfactory?"

"She seems well trained."

"Even for one who spends her time playing with dogs in the garden? I find that interesting. Well, I wish you a swift recovery."

"*Danke*, sir."

"How is his pulse, nurse?"

The guards laugh.

Rudi plays his part by letting his eyes close while Mayer questions other patients.

And soon they have other roles to play.

The two make their way through the district of Ixelles, each carrying an empty bucket. The taller one's head is covered by a kerchief worn low over her brow. Her blue dress is stained dark in places, her brown coat shapeless. The stockings thick and black, the wooden shoes worn and slanting. The shorter one wears a wrinkled cotton cap, a skirt and jacket patched with mismatched pieces of fabric. Their hands are dirty, the fingernails black-rimmed.

Rudi sways from side to side as he walks and holds his left arm close to his side. On a tram to the city center, the two keep their eyes downcast. A passenger makes a show of opening a window, which tells Marie-Thérèse that they are succeeding—at least for now. Fits of shivering come. She hides her hands in her jacket sleeves. *What if I'm wrong?* They change to another tram leading away from the city center, with its military officers, and come to the river.

The greatest misgiving of all, she's been thinking, is that it's a trap. All part of their little strategy. And his "confession" part of it too.

"What if there is no father in Coblenz?" she asked the matron. "How do we check?"

The matron already has—a simple inquiry to a seller of

pianos in Brussels and, yes, there is such a man in Coblenz, a Herr Christian Fischer, whose pianos are considered quite good despite their moderate price.

"I believe him," she said.

"The piano seller?"

"The lieutenant."

"You...talked with him?"

"I did."

Marie-Thérèse begged her then to come with them. She herself would return, take the rest of her examinations, and leave, somehow, with the girls and Jackie and Donnie. Meanwhile, the matron would be safe in the Netherlands. Even as Marie-Thérèse spoke, she realized it was impossible. A fantasy.

"Who will administer those examinations, mademoiselle? And certify them? Not just for you but everyone. Mayer found nothing. If I leave suddenly and without explanation, they will shut down the clinic and take everyone in for interrogation. Also, Doctor Depage charged me with overseeing the construction of the new clinic. There's that as well."

Marie-Thérèse now understands that the woman is beyond persuasion and forever will be. And she made valid points.

So, here she is now. Love—and faith—stronger than skepticism, stronger than fear. Taped to one thigh are medicines and bandaging material. To the other, German currency. And under her fishmonger's clothing, other clothing.

The barge is to leave at one-fifteen. It's nearly one.

Rudi asks if she's all right. She's nearly ill with fear but nods and attempts inane conversation. "And just look at this day! It couldn't be better. Sun and warmth and the river! It seems hopeful, don't you think?"

"I find it interesting that I have never fished in my life. And my name Fischer, no less!"

"You still don't sound like an old woman. You have to make your voice more guttural. Talk from the back of your throat more."

"A fishmonger!" he says, gargling the words. "Like that? And now I know the names of how many? Ten. Ten species of fish. In that occupation one must have great olfactory stamina. Or better yet, no sense of smell whatsoever."

"And don't use big words or long sentences." An approaching patrol soldier is walking leisurely, rifle angled against chest as he glances down into moored river craft along the stone-reinforced bank. Seeing them, he quickens his pace. They set down their buckets and take folded sheets of paper from under jacket and coat.

"These smell almost as bad as you two." The identity and travel papers bear the proper German stamps, photographs, and signatures, and after giving them cursory attention, he drops them to the side. "I should send you both into the river for a bath."

A breeze nudges the papers a few meters away. The young soldier is playing at arrogance, she decides, and so all the more dangerous. She glances at Rudi. *Be careful!*

"In fact, I think I will." He extends the butt end of his rifle against her chest and prods her toward the edge of the bank. Glancing behind, she tries to place herself between two of the boats.

"It's all right," she says, more to Rudi. "I can swim."

The young soldier is giggling. "Good for you! Then go clean yourself up, *Schwein.*"

Rudi comes up from behind, swings his bucket against the soldier's helmet and gives him a push. The soldier topples off the bank and onto a pile of canvas in the bow of a boat. His rifle splashes into the river. Two passing fishermen keep going, hurrying their pace.

Rudi gathers their papers and links his arm in hers. "No!" he says, pulling her back.

Her breathing is ragged as if she'd been running. "But, Rudi, he might be hurt. I need to—"

"He's not hurt. Look, he's already getting up. Quick. Let's go!"

Ahead, a clothesline strung along the deck of a moored

barge and on it four pegged white shirts and a blue one. She points to it, and they rush down a stone stairway to river level and board.

Lines are immediately cast off, and the barge eases into the river's main channel and then, soon, a canal. At a village near Vilvorde they take on baled wool that gives off an earthy pungency. At times deck hands pole or else a boy with a horse on the towpath pulls the barge along. Progress is soundless and smooth. Rudi and Marie-Thérèse are setting the galley's table with chipped crockery when two soldiers board to inspect the barge before it can enter a lock. Boots thud against the galley's ceiling as the soldiers move about the deck, no doubt stabbing bales of wool with bayonets. She was warned they would do this, looking for escapees. Her pulse quickens.

Soon they're clumping down the galley stairs.

"Foo! You two smell like dead fish. Don't you ever bathe?"

Marie-Thérèse gives a clumsy curtsy. "Yes, sir. Every two weeks."

They search cupboards and turn back quilts. They kick at moisture-swollen drawers under the berths and jerk them open. They survey the table, with its slab of cheese and loaf of rye bread. Then one of them studies their papers, peering from photographs to faces and back again. He does this for several moments. "Try once a week, Fräulein Stiller," he says finally, handing back the papers.

The soldiers climb back up, and then the lock's machinery lowers the barge to the next level.

"How many more of these?" Rudi asks.

"Two, then the river." She tries to disguise fear with a matter-of-fact tone.

"Is the river dangerous?"

"There will be patrol boats. You should lie down for a while. I'll wake you before the next lock."

"You did well, Fräulein Stiller."

"You did too." This isn't true. She's still seeing him swinging that pail.

They negotiate the second lock with no trouble. It's the dinner hour and patrols give the barges scant attention. The sun, low in the northwest, bronzes distant and near windbreaks. Fields are plum-colored. Ruined villages slip into view, their blackened bones and caved-in stonework in shadow. At sunset, they arrive at the final lock.

Two soldiers stumble onto the deck. "*Mein Gott!*" one says. "You're a clumsy oaf!"

"And you're not?"

They slash at bales, shout insults, and berate the pilot for having such high stacks.

"Get up there," the taller one orders, "and throw those top bales down."

The pilot, gesturing, tries to explain that there's not enough room on deck.

"Then in the water, *dummkopf.* Either they go or you."

Rudi appears on deck holding a bottle of wine and two mugs. His voice guttural, he tells them they're working too hard. They should sit and take some refreshment. There is German cheese and bread! Come! Rest! Eat! Who is here? Just us! So now, have something!"

Below deck Marie-Thérèse is shaking. She wishes he hadn't done that.

Soon both soldiers are following the domineering but motherly hausfrau down into the galley, where she tells her daughter to serve the deserving warriors of the Fatherland. Left arm held against her side, Frau Stiller hums a tune while pouring wine into mugs, humming that becomes "Ein Prosit." Soon they're all the best of friends—soldiers, pilot, deck hands, mother and daughter—standing and holding mugs, swaying to the tune and toasting cheer and good times, the barge tilting a little from side to side as night comes on and other barges line up, waiting their turn.

But then, shouting. "What is *this*? What is *this*? Up, out of there! Gelb! Fichte!"

The singing stops. Gelb and Fichte regard each other. They

look toward the sleeping alcove, then scan each other's face. One shakes his head.

"I will count to five and then begin shooting. *Eins...zwei... drei...*"

The taller one pulls the small one toward the stairs. "He probably will anyway," he says under his breath. The smaller one's rifle, catching against the steps, impedes their progress.

At *vier*, they're on deck, facing three aimed rifles.

"You are all under arrest."

They lead Gelb and Fichte away. The rest are taken to a guardhouse. An officer with a quivering triple chin asks why they detained his men.

"Kommandant, excuse me," the pilot says. "They were hungry and wanted some of our cheese and bread, so of course we gave them some

"And too much drink."

"They also wished it."

"Where are you going?"

"To Antwerp, to deliver the wool. A few mills remain open, sir."

"And then?"

"We take hides to Bergen op Zoom, Kommandant."

"And after that?"

"Sir, we return with flour and coal for the Fatherland."

"Who are *they*?" He gestures.

"The elder is our cook. The younger is her daughter, sir."

"You have a hag for a cook. I hope the food is better."

"It is mostly bread and cheese. Sometimes a boiled egg."

"If that is all, why do you need a cook?"

"She has been our cook since my father piloted our barge."

"In fact..." The officer is scrutinizing Rudi. "I have received a report of someone like her on the riverbank at Brussels, someone who attacked one of our guards. What a coincidence. Give me your ship's log."

The pilot returns, accompanied by a soldier.

"Ah. I see you were in Brussels at the time of the attack."

"She can hardly walk, sir. And she hurt her arm recently."

"She came up those stairs fast enough. Frau Stiller, allow me to inspect this arm of yours."

"Sir, may I say something?" Marie-Thérèse asks.

"Speak."

"We had to help her up the stairs. My mother is a patriotic German. I am as well. She is German through and through."

"As you are?"

"I am German, sir. Yes."

"All the same, let me see your arm, Frau Stiller."

Marie-Thérèse unbuttons Rudi's coat. The arm is bandaged from wrist to upper arm with tea-stained bandaging. The officer strikes the forearm with his fist, and Rudi falls to the floor in a faint. A soldier rolls him onto his back.

"So. It is hurt."

"She broke it in a fall."

"Now you will have to reset it. Hardly worth the trouble." His boot strikes Rudi's torso. "And these."

Another officer enters the guardhouse and shouts at the kommandant, who apparently is not a commander. "There's a line extending a kilometer at least! What's the matter with you! Everybody off schedule because of you idiots! Go," he orders the pilot. The officer who arrested them opens his mouth but then closes it.

Soon a sail is raised on the River Escaut, under a near-full moon, its silver bits scattered over the black plain.

In the barge's cabin, Marie-Thérèse examines Rudi's chest. Ribs are certainly fractured but not, she hopes, fully detached.

"Is the pain bad?"

"No."

Clearly a lie.

"I think we've used up our luck," he whispers. "I'll try to get across myself. The border will be the worst, especially if guards hear of what happened in Brussels...and know our descriptions. That was stupid of me and so was offering them wine. I apologize. If they arrest me, you will be as well. We'll both be

charged with treason. We must not travel together any longer.
Get off in Antwerp, change your appearance, and find another
barge. Or a different route altogether."

A change in plan at this point won't be safe, Marie-Thérèse
is thinking. The network itinerary and contacts have all been
prearranged. And she alone knows the right code words and
gestures that will get them to the farm outside of Rotterdam,
where he's to work as a laborer until after the war.

"But how will you get there on your own?"

"If I'm lucky enough to get across, we can meet later at that
farm. Please, Marie-Thérèse, don't return to Brussels."

"I have to get the children."

"Use your contacts to get them out. Don't risk your own life.
Don't go back. As for that farm, I can get there if you tell me
the right words and the persons to look for."

He wants the code words. He will remember the contacts.

"You don't trust me? I will never lie to you, Marie-Thérèse,
just as I would not spy on her. Please believe me. Remember
our plan? It still may work."

London—with the girls. And if being there proves too difficult and her family too resistant, well then, America. Somehow
it had seemed possible. Something an English novelist wrote
comes to mind. *It's not true that love makes all things easy; it makes us
choose what is difficult.*

Despite all misgivings, she gives him the codes. She describes
the contacts.

Embracing her as best he can, he begs her not to go back…
for any reason. He tells her he loves her and that she must
live. "We will meet at that farm. And we will get the children
somehow if you don't first. Go, Marie-Thérèse. I will wait for
you there."

She leaves the barge at Antwerp, and on the wharf, slips
into a labyrinth of stacked baled wool. Could she find passage
on another barge or ship heading to Rotterdam? How to explain? And her papers are wrong. Who will take her and risk
imprisonment, or worse? In a secluded corner, she removes her

outer clothing and with the skirt rubs at her face and teeth. She tidies her hair and hides it under a different cap she's stowed in a pocket. Then she gathers a few chunks of broken bricks and sinks her fishmonger costume, watching as bubbles rise up through turbid water. From the cloth bag attached to her thigh, she extracts several German marks.

All but obscuring the river are barges and tugs, trawlers and freighters and sailing ships, their masts glinting in the sunlight. Gulls shriek. Wind carries the scent of water and the calls of dock workers, the chinking of winches and chains and the subdued roar of steam-powered machinery in the distance. She walks east, just another hausfrau off one of the barges, going to the *Grote Markt*.

Asking directions in Flemish, she finds her way to the central train station, where she leaves the heat and wind for a lofty hall filled with soldiers and the ubiquitous stretchers and stretcher bearers. In vain she scans the sellers of goods. No one resembles the woman and her husband who'd conveyed her to their farmhouse in January.

A train will be leaving for Rotterdam in forty minutes, but there's the problem of travel papers. Another for Brussels will leave in thirty minutes. She thinks she can manage that one, with some flustered explanation about returning for proper papers.

The thought that she just may have ruined everyone's life at the clinic, as well as her own, is so terrible, she has to blank it out.

HAZE

Thunder breaks over the city and rain fogs the air. In parks and along streets, trees whip back and forth, limbs splintering, and branches falling on wrought-iron fences and café tables. Vehicles throw sheets of water to either side. She waits in a café, its electric lights flickering. Out on the sidewalk pedestrians are dashing about, some charging into the café. At a lull in the storm, she goes back out. There are no trams, so she runs through a litter of branches and green leaves pasted to sidewalks and floating in puddles. Soon there's another frenzy slashing at everything. The force of it seems to reduce all things to objects no more significant than the tree limbs and leaves underfoot.

In some dream-like contrast to the storm, ward C is quiet. Oddly, only four patients are there, the rest of the beds made up. "Where is she?" Marie-Thérèse asks Gauthier.

"Look at you! Go change. You're getting the floor all wet. She's away. Why are you back so soon?"

Once Marie-Thérèse found it humorous, how the absence of any German officer always restored Gauthier to herself.

"Do you know where she went?"

"No."

"Why is it so empty? Where's Quien?"

"Gone, and she followed him, probably."

"*She?* Who did?"

"Get into your uniform. I need you in A."

"Do you mean Liese? *Liese* left?"

"She's gone and took her things. On the same day. One can only assume. The cook is gone too."

"*Amalia?*"

"Do I have time for this?"

"*Non, pardonnez-moi*, Sister. I'll change now."

Her hands are shaking so hard it's difficult to get out of her wet clothing. When she returns to the ward, she dares another question. "Are there any more here?" Gauthier hurls her much-used warning look and says nothing.

There are routine things to do, which sedate rampaging thought. A Frau Rukeyser needs fluids and repositioning and assurances that her daughter-in-law is unlikely to be stealing from the family business, a *pension*. A Frau Sternburg needs oxygen and to have her vital signs noted every twenty minutes. Her alveoli are congested. She confides that her husband died and her two sons joined the Allies, but she hasn't heard from them in months, so they're probably dead too, everyone dead. Marie-Thérèse holds the woman's spotted and thickly veined hand. "It's difficult to get mail through now, madame."

"Stay with me awhile?"

She does while trying not to let her own dark scenarios consume her. When the matron enters the ward, Marie-Thérèse excuses herself. Soon they are in the matron's apartment, the dogs at their feet.

She begins calmly enough but then becomes her own storm. Sobs gust. Words fracture. When she's finally able to speak coherently, she tells the matron everything. "How many are still here, Matron?"

"One."

"Can he walk?"

"Possibly in a few days."

"Could you leave then? I know it's a futile question, and leaving might look bad. But, please, isn't there a way it could be accomplished?"

"There will be no need when the one leaves."

"Yes, but if you stay, you'll probably take in others."

The matron edges back drapery and looks out into the street. "They're there all hours now, by the light pole. Tonight, they're carousers who've had too much drink. Sometimes they pretend to be workers staring at a crack in the pavement. No work gets done. So obvious."

"Matron, you believed the lieutenant, but I…it seemed he wanted to save *me*. I had a strong feeling he might be a spy, after all, and that he's going to betray us…well, except for me. I can't shake the thought that it was his assignment to learn what he could about the network. I feel sick at heart and…terribly used."

"He could not have planned the incident with the pail."

"No."

"He could not have anticipated that so-called kommandant." Marie-Thérèse shakes her head.

"And he was truthful about his father."

"Yes, it seems so."

"Mademoiselle, I do not share your suspicions."

Yet that night the same nagging voice: *Then why tell me* not *to return? Had* she *told him to do that, to get me to escape?* These thoughts and a hundred others keep her awake. And anger—at both of them—anger alternating with shame and dread. It's awful to think that now their only rational course is to wait and do nothing extreme because if the matron left, inexplicably left, with Marie-Thérèse and the children, the entire staff at the clinic would probably be arrested, including the gardener. It's awful to think that her family has been waiting for her and no doubt sick with worry.

The abbey bell strikes four times. Her curtained window brightens with dawn.

Somehow the next day passes and the one after that. Another thunderstorm lashes the city, and afterward everything gleams. Jackie and Donnie splash through puddles, pausing every so often to drink. But Marie-Thérèse is always cold.

Rumors reach the wards. The architect Philippe Baucq has been exposed as the publisher of the underground newspaper *La Libre Belgique*. Hadn't she noticed him on the rue de la Culture, near the clinic? Hadn't she seen a copy of that newspaper in the matron's apartment? Yes. And the matron burned it on the coals in her fireplace. Another rumor concerns a woman named Louise Thuliez. She, too, arrested and charged with being part of a treasonous ring now fully exposed.

Fully? Marie-Thérèse recalls the couple in their little farmhouse and says a prayer for them. And who has done all this exposing? Rudi? Quien? *Liese?*

She takes the Anatomy and the Obstetrics exams and passes. She also passes the dreaded bandaging practical examination. But exhaustion has drained away emotion, and these victories seem meaningless. Evenings, the sun lingering until well after ten, she is sometimes able to read to the girls and give them brief piano lessons.

Their one escapee is gone, or so she believes. The cellar empty, the attic—possibly—as well. And despite her frayed state of mind, work in the clinic helps. In a few weeks they'll make the move to the modern and much larger clinic. All summer the gardener has been digging up roots and bundling them in cloth. Everyone is looking forward to the new clinic except Marie-Thérèse and the gardener. He doesn't want to leave his roses, his vegetables. She simply wants to take her remaining examinations and leave with the girls. But it's proving difficult to obtain travel documents through the official channels. She described the girls as her "charges." The reason, she thinks, for the holdup. Or it could be something else. A thought best not dwelled upon.

For the most part, the summer days pass uneventfully, fading away as dreams do, good or bad.

But then, one August morning before dawn, the haze lifts.

Meeting Force with Force

At the banging and shouting, Marie-Thérèse throws clothing over her nightgown, jams on shoes, and opens her door but has to leap back. A soldier pushes it fully open, shattering the mirror on one of the wardrobes. In other rooms nurses are screaming and soldiers shout at them to be quiet. The one in Marie-Thérèse's room overturns beds and desk chairs. Sweeps lamps from desks. Stabs at clothing in the wardrobe. Upends drawers. Kicks textbooks and papers aside. Then he orders Marie-Thérèse into the hall. Julia, still in nightclothes, is standing to one side of her open door, her face blank with shock.

This is what he knew.

"I must use the lavatory, please!" Marie-Thérèse leans forward, an arm across her abdomen and dry heaves over the soldier's boots.

He shoves her toward the lavatory door. She locks it and runs water in the basin. Standing on the bathtub's rim, she's able to crawl out the window and drop a meter or so to the slightly canted roof over the back passageway. Then it's simple enough to get to the opposite end of the four joined row houses, down a rose trellis, and into the back passageway through the garden door.

Just as the gardener, mattock raised, lunges at an officer. The iron blade of the garden tool gouges the man's right arm, causing blood to shoot upward. Another soldier brings the gardener down with a bullet to his chest. Three others have the matron in their grip.

"I can help your officer," the matron says. "He needs a tourniquet or he will die."

And then she's fashioning one. Another soldier, just arriving, appears confused at finding Marie-Thérèse kneeling over the gardener. He's the one who searched her room. "You will want to question him," Marie-Thérèse says. "Please let me get some medical supplies." The wounded soldier curses, and the one who shot the gardener shoots him a second time. Frothy blood spreads over the gardener's jacket as he tries to speak. Marie-Thérèse leans close.

He makes the same sound. It seems a name.

"Papa," she whispers near his ear, "in the spring they return, the birds."

She takes his bloodied hand as breath gurgles from his throat. After a few moments, she closes his eyes.

A soldier yanks her up and then across the street. The physical sensation of walking is absent. Some things are clear, others hazy: muted light, a long table, faces. She's told to sit and does so but senses nothing. Part of her knows that she is in shock.

A distant voice begins speaking.

Her name is spoken. Then, *garden, dogs.*

There's laughter and her name again followed by, *Who was she?*

Body and mind have entered some stasis. The words are so far away. *Get her some. Ja, Herr Mayer.*

Brandy burns through the numbness. Thought begins assembling.

"Who was she, Fräulein Hulbert?"

The room is a room again. The disembodied voice finds its source. Otto Mayer. His mustache bulky, hiding his mouth. A small circular pin on the left lapel.

"Sister Clara Gauthier." Saying the words causes her head to throb and eyes sting.

"That is correct. And you were recreating there."

"Yes."

"Taking a much-needed break at eight o'clock in the morning."

"Yes."

"Yes, sir."

"Yes, sir."

"What time did you rise that morning?"

"Six, sir."

"So then, two hours later you needed a rest from your arduous efforts?" The complicated response this demands is beyond her. She nods. "I take that as a yes. Am I correct?"

"Yes, sir."

"Do you know that someone saw you in your matron's office just prior to your playing with the dogs?"

"No, sir."

"Can you tell us what you were doing there?"

A young woman in military uniform holds a black pen poised over a notebook. She's blond. Her eyebrows are the thinnest of pencil strokes forming half circles, which make her look permanently astonished. Marie-Thérèse has to pull her gaze away and concentrate on the question.

"No one…is allowed unless…invited."

"But that is not what Clara Gauthier says. She says you were there. Tell us what you were doing in the office."

"We were…in the garden. Sir."

His clasped hands rest atop a file. "You are lying, Fräulein Hulbert. Do you know that you can be imprisoned for many years, if not worse, for treasonous activities?"

"Yes, sir."

"So then?"

"Only in the garden, sir."

"That is a lie. Tell me about the matron. What kind of woman is she?"

"A good person."

"A good person who serves her country?"

"She obeys the law."

"She takes good care of her patients?"

"Yes, sir."

And her *Belgian* patients?"

"We have Belgian…civilians. Also, German soldiers."

"Second Lieutenant Fischer was one. He spoke well of you. Do you know where he is?"

"No, sir."

"Has he tried to contact you?"

"No, sir."

"He disappeared from the clinic some days ago, did he not?"

"I did not see him go."

"Without being discharged?"

"I don't know."

"Is it because you were gone as well for a time? I have already been informed of this, so no need for further lying, Fräulein."

"I was going to visit my family but felt unwell and returned."

"Do you have travel papers to prove this?"

"No, sir. I did not keep them."

Mayer motions a deputy close and whispers.

"And, therefore, you did not visit your family?"

"No, sir."

"How did you travel to Antwerp?"

"Farm cart. To save money."

"How frugal. Can you prove this?"

"No, sir. A soldier just killed the man who took me there."

Mayer motions the deputy close again, and then the deputy leaves the room. Her eyelids are burning.

"Fräulein Hulbert, your father is German, and your mother French-Belgian. Has this ever caused you to question your loyalties?"

"No, sir."

"You speak excellent German. You spoke German at home?"

"Yes, sir."

"Your father is an ophthalmologist now living in the Netherlands. Why did he choose to move there last year?"

"There was...vandalism here. And many of his patients left him."

He opened the file. "I see that you have two younger brothers. Where are *they*?"

"One is in the Netherlands. The other...we are not sure."

"Why are they not serving the Fatherland?"

"One is fourteen. The missing boy is sixteen."

"Sixteen is not too young. Many young men that age have been serving. Has he gone to join the Allies?"

"I don't think so, sir."

"And I should believe you. Tell me about your activities at the clinic."

The man is fading in and out of focus. In her lap she grips her hands, which seem coated in hardening varnish. "Work in wards. Lectures. Study. Examinations."

"Is that all?"

"Yes, sir."

"Are you sure?"

"Yes, sir."

"There were two children at the clinic. Do you know where they are now?"

"No, sir."

"Do you think they may be in the garden, playing with the dogs?"

The laughter is too loud. "I don't know."

"Well, perhaps we can find them. Would you like that? To be reunited? I've heard that you are quite fond of them."

St. Gudule, help them.

"I beg you to understand, Fräulein Hulbert, that we have incriminating evidence against your matron and against you. She is a traitor to Germany, and you may be held culpable as well. By telling us what you know concerning her activities, *all* of her activities, you will exonerate yourself. If you do this, you will be free to leave after our conversation this morning. You will be free to reunite with those two children and live your life. I personally guarantee this. No harm will come to you, or to the children. My secretary is writing my words down as part of the official transcript of this interview. Do you understand that no harm will come to you?"

"Yes, sir."

"Otherwise, the children may be questioned and sent to Germany. Would you like that?"

"I would prefer…they reunite with their family here."

"How old are you?"

How old?

"Your age, Fräulein?"

"Nearly twenty, sir."

"So, all the better. You will be free to celebrate your twentieth birthday with those two children and have a long and useful life. Otherwise, I am sorry to say that by withholding information from us, you will be tried as an enemy collaborator and if found guilty may be put to death. Do you understand?"

He's receding out of focus again. *Think: he is only asking if you understand.*

"I do, yes."

"Good. Now, what can you tell me about Matron Cavell's treasonous activities?"

She forbids herself to avert her eyes. "Nothing, sir."

"*Nothing?* What if I told you she confessed everything? I will give you one chance to revise your answer, Fräulein. Your matron *has* confessed. Now it is imperative that we learn everything about her secret operation so that no one escapes justice. She implicated you, by the way. I will give you just this one chance to extricate yourself."

She confessed?

Bands of color pulse over the table.

"I can tell you…nothing more."

"How stubborn. And stupid. I am sorry, Fräulein Hulbert, but you are a stupid, stupid young woman. Take her to the prison."

What Might Chekhov Make of It?

She wishes she had taken the time to put on her apron that day, with Private Schalk's piece of driftwood. She wishes she had his letter that describes snow clouds and seagulls. Yet she has her own story to tell herself even though it isn't "very nice," to use Private Schalk's words. But she doesn't want to think of the gardener's pigeons and what might have become of them. She doesn't want to think of Jackie and Donnie. And often, not even of the girls. Or her family. Or the matron. And especially not of Rudi. Some days she leaves out so many scenes her life seems all but vanished.

At times she wonders what Chekhov might make of it. With so many of his characters, there's no fulfillment, in either love or aspiration. There's just the small doing, day after day. And the small and large hopes—and failures. And the not knowing. And the futile waiting. And longing. Her former hopes strike her as naive delusions. Concert pianist! A nurse as capable as the matron! Her failures, the true reality.

Yet something inexplicable causes her to resist despair. She paces her cell for exercise. She cleans her sink as best she can, using cold water from its one tap. She illicitly uses the French language if she's sure the person bringing the daily coffee and bread, the watery stew, the dry cheese is Monica. When she lies down to sleep, she sometimes allows herself to imagine the girls there, in their own beds. She tells them how much she loves them and then falls asleep bathed in a sensation of pure love.

But the next day it all starts again, the morning's thin coffee and bread, noon's watery stew or potato and cup of beer, and evening's hard cheese and bread she always savors, for it means life.

One day in the unvaried flow of them, she comes to the

conclusion that not everyone can live a grand and important
life, but everyone can live a small and nonetheless noble one
through resistance—to despair, especially, and to the occupiers.
Most of the time, particularly when she recalls the gardener's
determination and courage, she believes this. And it helps her
plan her final day. When they come to take her to the place
of execution, she will walk on her own without sobbing. And
wherever they order her to stand, she will stand and observe
them until they blindfold her. A harder thing—and she might
not be able to do this—will be to forgive them. But she will ask
forgiveness of everyone she has hurt, particularly her mother.
And the matron.

Herr Richter has a pleasant voice in the tenor range, a broad
face with shallow pits, and closely cut brown hair but a flounced
mustache like Otto Mayer's. And so, Marie-Thérèse is on guard.

"You must believe me," he begins, "she confessed everything. And they found a postcard from England written by an
Allied officer she had helped. I want to assure you of this so
that you do not foolishly withhold information, thinking you
will be harming her. That is not the case, Fräulein. By withholding information, you will be harming only yourself. You will not
betray her by speaking to us. She has betrayed all of you."

There are no hints of green to muddy the clear brown of
his eyes, and no eyeglasses to guard them. *What if he is telling
the truth?* Yet why were they supposedly giving her another
chance when Mayer said there would be no other chances? She
grips her hands in her lap, over the crusted bloodstains on her
uniform skirt. The man is sitting directly in front of her, on a
wooden chair that was brought in for him. "Of course, she is
British," he continues. "And it stands to reason that she would
want to help her countrymen and their allies. I can sympa-
thize…to a degree. As she saw it, she was being patriotic, and
one respects patriotism. Also, loyalty. But her patriotism and
loyalty conflicted with German law. You do see this, Fräulein
Hulbert?"

"She is a principled woman."

His eyes narrow somewhat. She senses his quandary—be stern and reprimand or continue to mimic kindness. "Execution by firing squad, Fräulein. That is the punishment for any treasonous activity. The authorities make it quite clear. Possibly you were so occupied with your work that you were not aware of the gravity of the situation. Tell me. Was that the case?"

"I was aware of that law, but she did nothing wrong. Nor did I."

"Germany makes no exceptions for status. A crime is a crime. And she confessed."

Marie-Thérèse doesn't want to believe this. Everything in her revolts against believing it. "She is a nurse who is…on the side of life."

"That's admirable, even noble. But in war, certain rules take precedence as a matter of necessity. Surely you see this."

"Was it a matter of necessity for Germany to invade a neutral country?"

"It was. We needed to get to France as soon as possible. Unfortunately, your country resisted, so really, Belgium is wholly responsible for all that ensued."

"What had France done to provoke such an attack?"

"Fräulein Hulbert, I would rather spend our limited time discussing your precarious situation. I understand that you are German, yes?"

"My father is of German descent; my mother, French; but actually we are Belgians."

"And you have been a student of nursing for how long?"

"Three years."

"Quite a while, then. Here is my thought. As a student nurse you were required to follow orders. That is obviously an important part of your instruction. Lives depend on your carrying out orders exactly. Is that correct?"

"Yes."

"So then there is a parallel with the military, a parallel that may be useful in your defense. Do you see it?"

"Have they sent you here to be my lawyer?"

"They have."

"And not an interrogator?"

"You already have been interrogated and we have your testimony, such as it is. It will not help you at the tribunal. If you tell us nothing, you will suffer your matron's fate should the tribunal find her guilty. You will face a firing squad."

"But if she told you everything, won't this cause her sentence to be reduced?"

"She was following no one's orders but her own, in violation of the law. How old are you?"

"I'm twenty. My birthday was a short while ago, I think. I've lost track of the days."

"Then you were nineteen years old during the time you carried out her treasonous orders. The tribunal will take that into consideration in addition to the context of your behavior. You were a student following instructions. I may be able to save you with this defense, Fräulein, but you must help me by telling me everything. Did you secretly nurse wounded Allied soldiers? Did you conspire with others to smuggle them into the Netherlands? These are the charges against you. Both are treasonous offenses. We have testimony that incriminates you. I propose to argue your age and your innocence, provided you tell me everything that you and others at the clinic did."

"I *am* innocent. I've done nothing wrong. You may say that."

He fixes her in a stare. "I need to know *everything* if I am to defend you. Others will be hoping for reduced sentences by telling everything they know. In fact, many already have."

"How reliable is that information when given by someone who hopes for a reduced sentence?"

"A good question. But we have ways of checking." He strokes his mustache with two fingers. "You are…let me put this delicately…a beautiful young woman whom I truly wish to help." He lowers his eyes then looks at her again and resumes his official tone. "Your death will be a waste. A sheer waste of skill and knowledge. And of life. Your life. Why should you sacrifice all that out of some sense of misplaced loyalty? No one, let me stress, is being loyal to _you_."

"In the fall they leave, the birds."

"What do you mean by that, Fräulein?"

"It's just a saying."

"And its relevance?"

"It may have none."

He stands. She does as well, though more slowly.

"Have me called, Fräulein Hulbert, if you change your mind."

He raps knuckles against the cell door but then turns. "You have a good writing table there. I will see to it that you have paper and pen if you promise you will not endanger yourself with the pen."

She assures him that she won't endanger herself in any way with the pen. The double-entendre makes her smile.

"Write down anything you remember. You need not give it to me, finally. You can choose. But you might decide to choose life, and I will do all in my power to defend you. It is entirely up to you. I will also see if they can get you some clean clothing."

But I want this clothing.

The cell door opens and then he's gone. Monica glances at Marie-Thérèse as she removes the chair. Then it's quiet again. She raises one end of her so-called table and swings it up and to the left and, voilà, her bed. She lies down, easing the pressure on muscles. It takes little to tire her now.

Shouldn't I choose my own life?

Is that what she did, by confessing? If, in fact, she did?

And yet they will execute her anyway. Did she know that?

Do they simply want me to incriminate her?

It occurs to her that she didn't ask when the tribunal is to meet.

It also occurs to her that she doesn't know the date or the day of the week. The month, she thinks, may be September.

Pen, Ink, and Paper

The morning tray scrapes against the stone floor. No surreptitious *bonjour* accompanies the scraping, so Marie-Thérèse knows that Monica didn't bring it. As she stoops to pick it up, her knee joints burn, and she has to push herself up with one hand. But she's pleased not to have dropped the tray, with its morning coffee and roll, nor to have fainted. Brief blackouts are occurring more frequently now. Sitting sideways at her "table," she takes her time over the coffee, the roll. She's taught herself to regard these moments as little islands in the flow of time, places of sanctuary. One doesn't fall into despair while sipping coffee, however thin and tepid, and chewing bread, however hard, when one is starving. Before she finishes, something else scrapes against the stones at the door's slot. A small wooden box.

It could be, she tells herself, a dream object. Meaning that she has fallen into a doze, right there at the table.

After she finishes her coffee and roll, she carries the tray back to the door and must stoop again to slide it back out into the corridor. If she neglects to do so, there will be no noon meal. These are complicated actions for her weakening body, and they demand, first, summoning will. A box is in the way. An actual box. Finally, the tray is outside the cell and the box is on the table. Removing its lid, she finds paper, pen, and ink bottle. These objects make a nice arrangement, evocative of the outer world.

The pen has a satisfying weight. The paper is of good quality. She begins, in French, with the first words that come to mind.

To fight infection, use carbolic lotion to wash the wound; then wrap it in gauze soaked in carbolic lotion. Or, the wound can be "bipped" with a bismuth iodoform paste smeared over it. There is also the process called debridement whereby tissue around the wound is cut away and the wound sealed.

For weeks her thoughts have consisted mainly of fragmented bits of memory and wide-ranging fears. To see evidence of coherent thought tells her that she is not, in fact, losing her mind along with her deteriorating body.

Emotional wounds are more difficult to treat. These need:
Bed rest
Sunshine
Physiotherapy
Talk therapy
Time

She has to rest her head on her arms a while. Sometime later, she hears the scraping on stones and Monica's soft *"Bonjour. Sun today. October second."*

A faint scent of food rouses her. She summons will and takes three precarious steps and then must make the hazardous descent to pick up the tray.

A puddle of something this time. A watery stew? Also, a tin cup of beer. Then her island again. And the slow savoring. She draws out the meal even more because she dislikes the risk involved in sliding the tray out into the corridor.

But again, she counts herself fortunate she doesn't faint, and soon she's back at her table and looking at remarkable words someone else, surely, must have written.

Even more remarkably, she adds to these words an actual date, *October 2, 1915,* and a place name. *St. Gilles Prison, Brussels, Belgium.*

The next morning, she continues forming letters, words, and, remarkably, sentences.

Our fatally ill patients must have experienced the shock of knowing they are about to die. At least some of them must have. Here it is now… death. Sometimes in those full days, it occurred to me to wonder how it must feel, realizing that death is only minutes—or a moment—away. Even though I witnessed death often, it always seemed remote, except for that time with Sergeant Haske, when it seemed so near…

Lost in that memory, she neglects her breakfast.

I could not fully enter into his experience, so how could I fully empathize?

Death was an abstraction, something we nurses defined as a series of physical occurrences culminating in the collapse of organs and therefore of life. This, I myself wouldn't experience for years yet, if fortunate. With my patients I could only keep my voice low and kind and do what I had learned to do for wounds and illnesses. When my patients died, my sadness was only temporary. Not as now, with Papa and how he died and how I was unable to help him. Or, too, when I won't be able to prevent my own impending death, or Matron's, which I pray will be fast. The thought of being pierced by dozens of bullets wrenches me with terror. How bad will the pain be? Will it be over in an instant? Or will I linger and bleed out? Will that be part of the punishment? And after death, what then? How will I be judged? What if there is no judgment? No peace? What if there is nothing? Will it be, simply, like sleep? Or will consciousness somehow still exist to torment as dreams often do? And that will be the hell of my religious teachings. Thoughts making me want to cry out. So far, I haven't. When hunger wakes me in the night, the firing squad is right there, just a few meters away, their rifles raised. Someone gives the order to fire…

There is no noon tray. Head on arms, she dozes through the time when the evening meal normally would have been brought, had she remembered her breakfast tray. But it's still on the table, pushed to the side. The lightbulb in the ceiling fixture dims, and so it must be nighttime. She's too tired to convert the table back into a bed and so stays where she is, head on arms. Slipping deeper into sleep, she's aware of some presence filling the cell. Then a stab of terror again until she realizes the presence is not the firing squad but the matron. The matron holding an oil lamp the way Florence Nightingale did when she visited wards during the Crimean War. Marie-Thérèse understands that the matron has had to bring this lamp because electricity has been cut off for the evening due to the rationing. The matron also holds a glass of water, which she extends to Marie-Thérèse. The water carries sweetness down through her, and the sensation is magnificent. "Matron," she hears herself saying, "I am so happy to see you."

Then the electric bulb is on full strength, and someone is shouting, "What is the matter with you? Do you mean to die here in order to get me in trouble? Are you ill? Always something! How can I do any work? Sit up! Sit up, now. What are you writing? What is that nonsense?"

Marie-Thérèse raises her head and focuses. The shouting person is the matron of the women's wing of the prison.

"*Pardonnez-moi.*"

"You are not allowed to speak French here. You know this. Do not provoke me further, Fräulein."

The prison matron's small nose tilts upward into a sharp point. It's red, as are her cheeks. Marie-Thérèse is seeing an angry elf in some child's story.

"*Bitte vergib mir, gnädig Frau,*" Marie-Thérèse says.

"That's better. Are you ill?"

Marie-Thérèse nods.

"Your stomach?"

Marie-Thérèse indicates her lower abdomen. "I think my appendix. Possibly a rupture."

"What does that mean?"

Marie-Thérèse explains in layman's terms. The prison matron's mouth crumples in disgust. "So, you *will* die, just to make my life miserable."

"She will know for sure if it's the appendix."

"She?"

"The matron of our nursing school. Matron Cavell. She can diagnose it."

"And you want me to bring her here, from her cell, I suppose?"

Marie-Thérèse leans forward and moans.

DECEPTIONS

S till moaning, she turns her head somewhat. *Matron.* Marie-Thérèse closes her eyes and reopens them. *Yes.* Emotion clots her throat.

"I was told they *all* would be released," the matron is saying. "Why is she still here?"

Those words, spoken in the same imperious tone she once used with Otto Mayer, are shocking. *She confessed to save us?*

The prison matron responds with equal hauteur. "Who tells me the why of anything? I have my work and I do it. That is all I know."

"What about the others?"

The prison matron resorts to sullen silence.

"Allow me to examine this prisoner in private."

"*Nein.* I must be here."

The matron comes to Marie-Thérèse's bedside and, blocking the prison matron's view, palpates the abdomen. Marie-Thérèse whispers in French that she only wanted to see her and say goodbye. "Did you really confess?"

"Yes. They said others already had. They said they'd let you all go if I did."

"You believed them."

She pretends to take an apical pulse measurement. "It seemed a simple choice."

"They tricked you, I think, by saying others confessed."

"But then, how many times have we tricked them?" She examines each eye. "How many times? Do you understand my meaning?"

"That's enough French, you two!"

Marie-Thérèse tilts forward, moaning. Under her breath, she asks forgiveness. The matron shakes her head somewhat, nods somewhat. Marie-Thérèse moans more loudly.

Très bien, the matron signals with her eyes then turns. "She must be taken to a hospital *at once.* The rupture must be repaired; otherwise, she will die before morning. I imagine you do not wish to have to explain yourself."

Guards enter. Two escort the matron out of the cell, one before her, one behind. Soon two others enter and lift Marie-Thérèse onto a stretcher and carry her through corridors, down staircases, and finally out into the courtyard, where they slide the stretcher into the back of a van and close its rear doors. The air is cold against her face. She wants to drink it. She wants it for the matron. She thinks that her moaning must sound authentic, for it is. Every so often she pauses to listen, but everything is quiet. She wonders what hospital they'll take her to and how she might escape. Will they post guards?

No doubt. She orders herself to think, but no plan forms. Cold sinks in. Her eyelids close again and again, each time for a while longer. She shakes her head to wake herself up. But that causes vertigo, so she lies still, trying to concentrate on listening for footsteps, for the engine to start, for warmth to seep into the cold box enclosing her. After some time, she knows.

Not to a hospital. No room in those hospitals for a traitor. They're waiting for me to die. Tomorrow, the prison's burial ground.

Her entire body is shaking. *Hulbert? Unfortunately, Student-nurse Hulbert died of appendicitis. We did all we could for her.*

Cardinal Mercier's New Year's Day words form in memory: *Endurance is faith. Endurance is an act of rebellion.*

She forces herself to sit up and slide toward the back doors. Then she brushes one hand across frigid metal. Fingers strike a tapered piece of metal.

Handle.

Surely locked, no?

As she eases the handle downward, it squeaks. Rigid, she pauses.

Still no sound from beyond the van.

She continues until the handle is vertical.

Knowing it must be locked, she pushes against it anyway.

It swings open, nearly pulling her off balance. Some distance away, a guard is pacing in front of the prison wall, under a lighted portico. She pulls the door back and waits for her heartbeat to slow. Then she nudges the door slightly open and observes the guard in his back-and-forth pacing, fifty steps in one direction, fifty in the opposite. When he's a few meters from the far end of the courtyard, she opens the door wide enough to ease herself out. For an instant, her skirt catches on something. But she's able to pull it free before the guard makes his turn. Then she edges to the side of the van and pauses.

She didn't latch the door. Will it start banging if caught by wind? Then he'll come over to check, and he'll see that she's not there. He might check anyway, she thinks, since she's no longer moaning. She peers around the back of the van. He's stopped to light a cigarette. She ducks back as he raises his head and looks toward the van. Her breath is making plumes she hopes he didn't notice. But then he's walking toward the far end again. She clutches her skirt close and, hunching over, takes careful steps toward the courtyard gate.

We will both be wolves.

Its two pillars have unlighted glass globes on top, but a waxing crescent moon reveals the shadowy shape of a guard standing against the opposite pillar. The figure's head appears non-existent. Rhythmic soft pops of expelled air come with regularity.

Sleeping. On his feet like a horse.

The buildings across the road are dark, the road empty. When clouds obscure the moon, she eases her emaciated frame through the space between the pillar and a wrought-iron picket, and then, bracing herself against the sides of buildings, keeps moving. The temptation to hide in a doorway and curl up against the cold is so strong she nearly succumbs. Farther ahead, a church. But when she finally gets there, she finds both its central doors locked. After panic eases, she notices a small door to one side of the main portico.

And that one opens.

The sanctuary light at the distant altar looks like a red star in a black void as she sits in a back pew, arms clutching her shoulders. Soon her head drops forward. When she opens her eyes, the church's stained-glass windows are a complexity of faint color. People will be arriving soon for early morning Mass, she knows, and might take her to a hospital—or police station.

She stands and after a while makes her way up the nave, gripping the back of each pew, then climbs the two steps at the Communion rail. In the sacristy, light emanates from a narrow stained-glass window. A bureau stands along one wall; chasubles and other vestments hang from a rod on the other. There's a scent of incense. She takes an armful of the chasubles and lies down against the base of the bureau. Another unholy act. After a while, she stops shivering, under all those colors of feasts and seasons. Her last conscious thought is that this is a good place to die.

POSTULANT

Prison? Yet she's so warm it hardly matters. When she wakes again, the room is dark. How strange that they would turn off the overhead light. And the pillow under her head is soft. She tunnels deeper into the mound of duvet and in that warm burrow falls back asleep. At one point she wakes, thinking she must still be in the sacristy, under all the vestments. Thought blurs into dream and dream, thought, back and forth, until she finally opens her eyes.

A nun is sitting near the bed, the right side of her face illumined as she reads. Her rounded black veil indicates that she belongs to the Dominican Order. The rest of her habit is cream colored. Marie-Thérèse slides an arm from under the duvet, prepared to see bloodstains on lake-blue. But no, it's unstained white cotton. The word comes slowly: *nightgown.*

"*Bonne après-midi,* mademoiselle," the nun says, at normal volume. She places her book on the night table.

"*Bonne après-midi*, Sister." Her voice is gravelly.

The nun pours water from a carafe and helps Marie-Thérèse drink. Then she repositions the chair, sits again, and says that Marie-Thérèse has been sleeping, off and on, for over three days. She's had some soup during that time. Would she like a bit more now?

It's liquid sunshine. Marie-Thérèse savors each spoonful and remembers Madame Kendahl, at the clinic, and her approval of the soup. Like Madame Kendahl, she can't get enough of the warm broth.

"*Merci,*" she finally says, lying back.

After the nun helps her to a lavatory, she sleeps again.

When she wakes, the nun is still there. The light is dimmer. Marie-Thérèse asks if she's in another section of the prison, a hospital ward possibly.

"*Non, non.* You are in a convent."

"Am I still a prisoner?"

The nun's laugh is a great whoop. "*Non,* mademoiselle. You're free to leave at any time, as we all are. But we do not advise it just yet."

Pieces are falling into place. "I'm putting you in danger. I must leave."

The nun shakes her head and smiles. There's something soft, this time, to eat. Rice and milk and—could it be?—butter. When she finishes, a sensation of having feasted fills her with warmth and clarity. She *must* leave. She can't endanger these good people any longer.

The nun takes the empty bowl and excuses herself. The room's one window holds a small rectangle of sky, pink with either sunset or dawn. But the window is too small. Soon, a different nun enters the room. Her eyebrows appear whitened with flour; her skin is pale and sagging. She wears eyeglasses, and behind them her eyes are large, watery, and blue-gray.

"*Bonsoir,* mademoiselle. *Je suis* Mother Gonzaga. *Et vous?*"

Her first impulse is to use Rani's name. Instead, she lies there as if struck dumb by that simple question.

"Have you forgotten your name, mademoiselle? Do you remember anything about how you came to be here?"

"I remember only up to hiding in a sacristy."

"*Bien!* Père Klei found you there. He took you for dead. When he saw that you were in fact breathing, something told him not to call any official. You were much in need of help, your clothing bloodstained, your hair filthy. We've had to cut it, I'm sorry to say. Someone left a flyer at our door describing you as a dangerous criminal who used her wiles to escape from prison. This, of course, explained your presence in the church. A reward has been set, quite substantial." Mother Gonzaga leans back, fingers linked over her ample waist, and smiles. "I commend you, Mademoiselle Hulbert. That was no small achievement, especially in your condition."

"You know my name then."

"Of course. It's on the flyer."

"I must leave. I know what they can do. If they come here, it will be terrible. You will all go to prison."

"I knew your matron. And I know that what they are doing is criminal."

"Is she…still alive?"

"*Oui*. Petitions are being circulated in England and throughout Europe. We learned this on our radio. So there is hope, mademoiselle."

Marie-Thérèse doesn't want to argue with this kind nun who obviously has a more sanguine view of human nature than Marie-Thérèse does at that moment. She touches the nape of her neck, the wisps of hair.

"Yes, it has been cut," the nun says. She goes on to describe how Marie-Thérèse resembles one of her favorite saints, Jeanne d'Arc, who also was a victim of political treachery. And, too, Marie-Thérèse resembles a postulant right after her tresses have been shorn. It is, Marie-Thérèse can see, a happy reverie. But they're wasting time. Her nerves are taut again, her senses acute. She dismisses the thought of trying to hide at her ruined home. But who in their network would be brave, or foolish, enough to offer shelter?

"Mademoiselle, I have been thinking," the nun says. "How would you like to join our convent, in a manner of speaking?"

Marie-Thérèse takes this in. "But you will be in constant danger. I cannot do that."

"If we refuse out of fear to do what is right, they will have won. But you already know that, yes?"

Her smile is beatific.

And so, Marie-Thérèse becomes a Dominican postulant dressed in black, with a black headpiece something like a veiled hat. She takes classes in theology with the other postulants, eats in the refectory with them, prays with them in chapel, rises for night prayers and dawn prayers, and rehearses for a Christmas cantata. An alien in a strange country. Since postulants keep silent except for brief exchanges in the refectory, she doesn't have to say much. She is from Bruges. She has wanted to be a nun all her life. A lie that strikes her as egregious. But she might not be harming these innocents, she decides. They haven't seen the flyer and probably have little if any interest in the convoluted political world and its war.

At night Marie-Thérèse buries herself under the duvet and grieves. When Mother Gonzaga visits again, Marie-Thérèse asks if she might inquire if Père Klei has heard anything about two girls who once were staying at the clinic in Ixelles. And if it isn't too much trouble, might he also inquire at the LaBreques' patisserie? The nun later tells Marie-Thérèse that he's done so but learned nothing except that the clinic is still open, though with a greatly reduced staff.

Snow appears in the small rectangular window, and snow clouds moving fast. She tries to see beauty in it. And hope. Soon after the Feast of the Epiphany, the postulants are to be taken by the Postulant Director—a young nun Marie-Thérèse likes because she sometimes whistles hymns while mopping their hallway—to a convent in Ghent for a retreat. Marie-Thérèse is to be Charmaine de Chantal, from Bruges. The stamps and dates on the identity and travel papers are current; the photograph might have been her own. "How did you manage this?" she whispers.

"Oh, quite simply. Our dear Charmaine has been given a different responsibility. She will be helping our eldest nun who, most sadly, has had a small stroke. Charmaine understands that corporal works of mercy are equally important in one's spiritual development."

"But the photograph."

"Ah, the photograph. Don't you think we all have a double somewhere?"

She hasn't noticed any such person in the group, but then the postulants all do resemble one another in their dark garb.

Identity papers. Travel documents. Photographs.

Marie-Thérèse looks more closely at the nun. And then asks

if she has learned anything more about the military tribunal. "Not yet." Her gaze slides away from Marie-Thérèse for an instant then back, and Marie-Thérèse experiences a crushing sense of finality. *She was tried...and convicted.*

On the morning they're to leave, Mother Gonzaga places a small envelope in Marie-Thérèse's hand. "Tuck it in your sleeve. Read it after you arrive in Middleton."

"In *Zeeland?* I thought we were going to Ghent."

The nun raises a finger near her lips. "You are. Then you will go on. Wait for instruction. *Adieu*, my dear convict. Go with God."

And Marie-Thérèse sees Papa holding Bishop aloft.

Sister Aquinas

On the tram and then the train, Marie-Thérèse's little group forms a funereal clump. Thoughts keep up their rush. Why Ghent? So far away? Why not a retreat at their own convent? Would postulants be coming from several convents? Was it customary, or all a ruse?

Ruse, she thinks. And if so, a clever one—sending a group.

Despite her heavy cloak, she's shivering. The train's military passengers hardly glance at them, but apprehension grips her each time the carriage door opens, emitting cold. The letter scratches at her forearm. She wonders if the nun included German marks. She wonders if she could get back to Brussels somehow and find the children. It hurts knowing that the thought is only a fantasy.

At the Ghent station, they draw a few glances but then pass through the center of that medieval city as if simply a flock of migrating birds. The wind is strong. Snow stings her face.

Finally, they exit a tram in a residential neighborhood where spacious mansions sit in private parks behind stone walls with imposing gates, one of which stands open. They walk through it and into a snow-swept expanse. To Marie-Thérèse, the massive crowns of specimen trees look like ornate black medallions, snow whirling around them. *Patience*, they seem to say. *Endurance*. And as usual, tears rise, hardly needing a cause.

Tea, cheese sandwiches, and pastries have been laid out on a long table in a paneled room where a fire burns in a marble fireplace between two massive doorways. Marie-Thérèse's group stands pooled together in a corner, far from the brightly burning logs in the fireplace. Older nuns are gathered there, chattering away. Marie-Thérèse observes that the eyes of the young postulants are darting from coffered ceiling, with its Biblical scenes, to oak paneling, to Persian carpet. Had someone donated the house to the nuns? Had any of her fellow postulants come from such a place and would being there now make her regretful and would she question her vocation? If so, Marie-Thérèse thinks, she herself may be responsible, given the world's unpredictable yet relentless causality.

Then, another strange thought. Why not just stay with her group? Join the Order and let everything be ordained for her, each large and small decision. No need to choose. No need to *think*. She might play the organ for them. Work in the infirmary. And learn how to pray. Truly pray, not just beg for things. Heaven on earth, no?

One of the older nuns claps her hands for silence, then welcomes the postulants and urges them to have their fill of the tiny sandwiches and pastries and to converse with one another. After seven that evening, silence will be mandatory for the entire week of the retreat. The postulants resume their conversations, and Marie-Thérèse finds herself telling lie after lie. And hoping her flushed skin won't give her away. Nor her unsteady eye movements. She's from farming country and not well educated. She hopes to learn in the convent and be of humble service. She enjoys domestic work but can play the piano a bit. She's not a very good singer and will have to learn. After a while the more inquisitive postulants turn away from the rather simple girl and talk instead with one another as if with old friends. Marie-Thérèse irrationally feels desolate at this unintended slight.

Following an evening service in a chapel with marble statuary and altar, the postulants are directed to a corridor with cells on either side, each holding a cot and wooden chair, a small black crucifix on the wall, and two black iron hooks for clothing. A folded cotton nightgown has been placed on the chair. An electric fixture on the ceiling offers light unsuitable for study or reading. After changing into the nightgown and placing Mother Gonzaga's letter on top of the folded undergarments, Marie-Thérèse kneels at the side of the cot but does not say the rote prayers of childhood. Instead, she asks for forgiveness.

Then, after augmenting the thin blanket with her cloak, she lies there listening to the wind. Too many memories, too much thought prohibit sleep. Being summoned for night prayers is a relief.

Despite the raging winds outside, the chapel's votive candles radiate peace. The still center, it seems, beyond the mutable, fractious, and imperfect. Beyond the always disappointing mortal. The chapel's marble, wood, mortar, glass, and lead might be bombed or burned, but what exists here seems beyond earth, air, fire, and water.

Pressing palms together, she leans forward into that power like a diver into the sea.

Breakfast consists of hot tea and warm rolls spread with a soft cheese and plum preserves. A nun at the front of the refectory reads from the Acts of the Apostles, the chapter having to do with the stoning of Stephen, the fledgling church's first martyr. He refused to recant what he knew to be true, and so townspeople stoned him to death. Marie-Thérèse doesn't find this story easy to contemplate while eating a fresh roll sweetened with preserves, but it does offer tempering and balance, telling them that everything exists at once, in a jumble. The benighted with the good; the tragic with the sustaining. How can it not be, in their fallen world? Therefore, they must not lapse into despondency at the benighted parts. Being humble, Marie-Thérèse is beginning to see, doesn't mean being weak and spineless and afraid. Rather, open to the possibility of good.

Endurance is faith.

Endurance is strength.

If faith is a form of humility…

Then humility is also strength…and endurance.

Euclid. Things equal to the same thing are equal to each other.

So. These nuns may in fact be more powerful than all the German forces.

The tea's warmth, and those thoughts, send the last of the previous night's demons fleeing. When a nun touches her shoulder as the postulants are filing out to the lecture room, Marie-Thérèse turns, as directed, into their cells' corridor. "I'm Sister Aquinas," the nun whispers. "Please get your cloak and papers."

Wrapped to their eyes, the two emerge from the convent into a world of white stillness and golden cold.

They don't converse on the tram, which is appropriate. One seldom sees talkative nuns out in public, Marie-Thérèse reflects. But at the Ghent station she's shocked out of her silence when she learns they'll be traveling east, to Antwerp, instead of north to Zeeland.

"Why?"

The nun quietly explains that this is Mother's way—to change plans at the last minute if necessary.

This is Mother's way?

"What about my travel papers?"

"I have new ones for you."

"Does she do this often, then?"

"No."

Marie-Thérèse studies Sister Aquinas's expression, the hazel eyes and ginger-colored brows, her long but harmoniously sloped nose. The tranquil expression. It gives nothing away. She tries to think what to do if this is some trap. Then reason prevails.

"All right," she says, and steels herself against all the German soldiers they're sure to find in Antwerp.

Demolished villages and farms, the rummaging pigs and sheep tell her they're nearly there. A young soldier enters the carriage to check papers. When he gets to their row, Sister Aquinas hands him both sets.

"And why must you go to Roosendaal?" he asks, not bothering to show respect by using her religious name.

"I am accompanying this postulant to her family."

"I once knew someone who became a postulant. She wasn't allowed to see anyone. No one could even visit her."

Under her cloak Marie-Thérèse grips her hands.

"Yes, that is how it is," Sister Aquinas replies in perfect German. "This young woman, however, needs time to reconsider her vocation. We have allowed her a leave of absence."

Smiling, the young man regards Marie-Thérèse. "You wish to change your mind, Fräulein?"

"I hope to understand God's will for me."

"I wish you luck with that!" He laughs as he returns their documents.

Marie-Thérèse's legs are so weak Sister Aquinas has to take hold of her arm as the two descend from the train.

On the platform for the northbound train to Roosendaal, they find an unoccupied bench, and the nun produces two rolls and some cheese from somewhere under her cloak. "You gave a good answer," she says as they have their *petite déjeuner.*

"*Merci.*"

"Do you truly feel that way?"

"I thought I knew...being a nurse, one as skilled as our matron. And before that, a pianist."

When the nun doesn't respond, Marie-Thérèse glances at her profile. The thickening of moisture glazing her eye, the reddening of rim.

"They killed her," Marie-Thérèse says.

The nun touches Marie-Thérèse's arm. "Not here. You need to remain in control. We have the border yet."

"Please. I have to know."

"It seems you already do."

"They executed her."

The nun's hands are clasped. She lowers her head.

"What about the petitions? *Were* there petitions?"

"Many. And all ignored. Now Germans are anathema to the rest of the world. Their old argument that they are fighting a just war bears no weight whatsoever. And Great Britain...well, Great Britain is grieving while every day adding thousands of volunteers to its ranks."

Perhaps all this Marie-Thérèse knew the moment the matron said, *It seemed a simple choice.* But hope is stubborn.

"When did they execute her?"

"October 12th."

"That soon!" It had been shortly after the matron came to her prison cell, then. The execution must have been carried out while Marie-Thérèse lay cocooned in Mother Gonzaga's convent. Safe, warm, and fed. Words rush as she tells the nun about the skating party they'd organized the previous December. How the pond at Ixelles had frozen into glass. How they'd had a bonfire and chocolates their gardener had managed to find. How expertly the matron skated and how happy she seemed after she learned that everything was being taken care of at the clinic. *Let them talk. They need to talk.* The lesson comes home, but at the same time she senses how futile her words are. How impossible to convey the woman's essence or the place she occupies in Marie-Thérèse's heart. The words no more than bits of sound immediately lost in the greater reverberating din of the station. And yet they ease, somewhat, the pressure on her heart.

The platform is growing crowded with travelers intent on their own journeys and paying no attention to the two religious women seated on a bench, in earnest conversation. But Marie-Thérèse emerges from her trance-like state and realizes that she's making the nun anxious by talking about the matron. She pauses, then asks, "How will you get back? You can't travel alone, can you?"

"I go on to Utrecht."

"To a convent? And then you'll find someone to accompany you back?"

The nun shakes her head. "I, too, am going home. You see, I am merely a professor of classics at the university. Now pull yourself together, my dear. It's time."

"Mother and you... You're part of..."

She touches Marie-Thérèse's arm again and then they're boarding.

Soup and Bread

As the train slows to a stop in a snow-covered field, Marie-Thérèse holds her prayer book and focuses on its title. *Devotions and Meditations.* Cold air wafts into the carriage as two German soldiers enter. One slams the door behind him, and then the two begin examining documents, working their way down the aisle, each taking a side. One of them is an older man with red brow, jowls, and nose. His mouth forms the horseshoe shape she's observed in the fleshy faces of men his age.

She's pretending to read as the younger soldier checks the documents of those on the other side of the aisle, uttering a *danke* in a flat tone at intervals. The one on her side says nothing as he works his way closer. When he reaches the row ahead of theirs, he takes a long time studying each of the four sets of documents. Finally, he pronounces that the dates on one set are inconsistent. Misprint or not, they're wrong. The passenger cannot be allowed to travel with such incorrect documents. Yes, he's aware that the date is correct on another line, but the inconsistency invalidates the whole. The document is incorrect and thus invalid and thus worthless. "You must leave the train immediately, Herr Brege."

Herr Brege meekly tries to assert that another guard allowed him to travel despite the misprint.

"But I am not that other guard! He is an idiot. Gather your things. You will have to wait for a southbound train here. Return to Antwerp and get new papers. It is your responsibility to see that they are absolutely correct."

Herr Brege puts on his coat and hat and takes his satchel from the upper rack. In no time he is standing outside the train. Beyond him stretches a long field bounded by a distant windbreak. Wind whirls snow into spinning tops. Marie-Thérèse's companion sits with her head bowed. "Frau Brege, these are in order. You will have to help your husband next time."

His horseshoe scowl deepening, the soldier extends his hand toward Marie-Thérèse's companion, then studies her documents. While gazing at the title of the prayer book, Marie-Thérèse wonders if reading is difficult for him. Judging by his silence, the other soldier has already reached the far end of the carriage.

"Do you stay in in Roosendaal then, Frau Aquinas?"

He pronounces the name A-quinn-is.

"Yes, sir. I will be at the Convent of the Sisters of Mercy."

"I see that here. Very good."

He thrusts the documents back and extends his arm toward Marie-Thérèse. It takes him long minutes while she waits, eyes downcast. Finally, he lowers the papers. "You go to the same convent and then on to your family. Why is that?"

"I am going to my family, sir, because I need time to reconsider my vocation. I have been given permission to do so by my Mother Superior." To her ear the words sound rehearsed, as they were.

He continues to scrutinize her, then finally says, "Well, Fräulein, that is probably a good thing. One should not rush, in a situation such as yours. The dates," he adds, "are correct."

But he doesn't return the documents.

"You are how old?"

"I am twenty years old."

"Yes, I see that here. What does your family think of you sacrificing your life like that?"

"My family"—she can't help it, tears are rising—"has been disappointed in me."

"Well, I would be too, Fräulein. Religion is all well and good, but on the other hand…What is it they say? Wisdom is wasted on the old? Something like that." This proof of sagacity causes the horseshoe to momentarily invert itself. He hands back the documents.

Marie-Thérèse's heart resumes beating. Her companion

grips her hand as the soldier questions those in the row behind them.

Some minutes later, the train passes over the invisible line demarking one world from another in the white light of a winter's late afternoon, the snow lemon-colored in fields and whipped, here and there, into dunes and the curving designs waves make, sliding up on shore and back, nothing straight, nothing imposed, and everything holding light.

The train slows again as it approaches what seems to be an encampment of some kind—numerous small, unpainted frame structures set in a grid pattern of streets. At one, a flagpole, and the flag of the Netherlands, its red, white, and blue horizontal bars all but rigid in the wind. The train stops, and Marie-Thérèse looks at the woman alongside her. "Another check?"

"I think they're stopping to allow someone from the camp to get on."

"Camp? Are the Netherlands at war now too?"

"No, not yet, at least. We're still neutral. What you are seeing is a refugee camp. Thousands of people have come across the border since last fall. There are camps all over now and some for British soldiers, even German soldiers. Also, families have been taking in refugees."

"*German* soldiers?"

"Deserters. They stay in their own camps, for the most part. We don't believe they pose a threat and so allow them to remain here. I suppose it could hurt our neutrality. Nonetheless, they're here. Some of the camps have their own post offices and infirmaries, even schools. They're very much like small towns."

Marie-Thérèse stares intently at the camp, wondering if some of those she'd helped escape might in fact be living there. Woodsmoke tilts toward the south. *Infirmaries. Post offices. German deserters.* "Is there…a refugee registry?"

"Yes, of course. And…you might be pleased to know this… the refugee infirmaries are always calling for volunteers."

They pass other camps, each flying the red, white, and blue tricolor of the Netherlands.

Built around waterways, Rotterdam is a large city, its design complex, and Marie-Thérèse has forgotten her family's address. But they easily learn it by inquiring at the grand and new Stadhuis, in an office on its second floor. There they also learn that records are kept of all the refugee camps, not merely those in the vicinity of the city. Their nun-and-postulant disguises elicit curious looks, but clerks are too polite to ask questions of their own.

This, too, seems another world.

The Hulbert row house is on a quiet block. Across the street a park, and beyond it, the canal Marie-Thérèse now recalls. A line of leafless trees, black against the blue sky, and a lawn crusted white evoke that peace she also remembers. Yet anxiousness rushes through her at the thought that they might not be there after all.

She turns the doorbell's brass key to the right and hears its attenuated, muted ring. After a moment, she turns the key to the right again and holds it there for a longer interval. A frigid wind blows their veils about. She's about to turn the key yet again when the door opens and there's Francine, squinting against the strident winter light and bunching her lips in annoyance at having to open the door in such cold. Marie-Thérèse anticipates, exactly, her words. *What do you want? If it is food, wipe your feet and come into the kitchen.*

"Francine, don't you recognize me?" With one hand Marie-Thérèse holds back her veil.

"Mon Dieu!" Francine says after a moment. Then she's shouting, "Madame! *Madame!* It's your *daughter.* It's Marie-Thérèse! Come in, come in, Sister, please!" Marie-Thérèse pulls the door shut behind them as Francine does her own version of a pirouette. "Where is your mother? I must find her! She might be napping. Go into the kitchen. There is potato soup. No! The parlor. No! Come with me."

Marie-Thérèse begs her companion to stay and have a bit of lunch, and then Francine is half-pulling Marie-Thérèse upstairs.

On a landing, Francine has to press herself against the wall as Madame Hulbert envelops her daughter. While madame sobs, Francine goes on about how Marie-Thérèse needs to eat something. "*Mon Dieu,* she looks like one of those wraiths in those dances of yours. *Pardonnez-moi,* madame. Let me pass. I must get to the kitchen."

And soon they're in the dining room, potato and leek soup steaming in white bowls, and a loaf of bread and mound of butter at the center of the table. Marie-Thérèse's father has joined them, and Jacques and Willy summoned from school. Marie-Thérèse is aware of her family's concern and wonders if she really does look like some ghostly image of herself.

Possibly so. Survivors often do.

THE MATRON

Other volunteers are now referring to her as "the matron," which often brings on profound sadness. Sometimes, though, she takes heart at those words and is even able to sign her notes of instruction with the letter *M*. And though not officially qualified to do so, she's been training the volunteers in the matron's methodology as well as occasionally giving brief lectures on basic nursing topics. Through her, she thinks, the volunteers are connected to the real matron and through *her* to Florence Nightingale. A humbling but nonetheless encouraging thought. *Matron Hulbert*, they'll say. *Ask Matron*. Was there ever a time when her own teacher had felt like an impostor? Possibly at first. Marie-Thérèse wishes she'd asked. It might be that everyone has to learn how to inhabit one's dreams. Fit oneself into them and then wear them until the dream and the person become one.

At times, she rereads Mother Gonzaga's letter, left unopened for weeks after her arrival in Rotterdam. At first, she'd told herself she knew what it would say: *She was executed by firing squad.* So why read those painful words?

She has since come to understand that there was another reason she refused. Left unread, the words couldn't destroy hope. Left unread, the letter held forth possibility. *She escaped, mademoiselle. Against all odds, she escaped as you yourself did. But we don't know where she is.*

And Rudi too. He escaped. It felt good to tell herself these things. And it got her through the weeks. But one day she decided that such thinking was dangerous. Had she come so far only to sink into delusion? She and Jacques had been talking, nights, sitting at the casement window overlooking the little park and waterway. She could see how hard he was struggling to return to rationality and self-forgiveness. So, in time, she made herself open the letter.

My Dear Mademoiselle,

Your dear matron went to her death with great dignity on October 12, 1915. She made her peace with God and faced her executioners with equanimity. I am told she wore her blue suit and fur stole and reindeer gloves. The night before, she told the Reverend H. Stirling Gahan, "But this I would say, standing in view of God and eternity, I realize that patriotism is not enough. I must have no hatred or bitterness for anyone."

These words, and her life's work, are her gift to you and to us all. Please do not allow her untimely and unjust death to extinguish your desire to do good in our poor world. We must, simply, carry on her work. In this way, she will live through us. So do not despair, my dear petite convict, but live now as she would want you to—in hope and love and the belief that every small good thing you do benefits all.

> God bless you,
> Mother Gonzaga

Marie-Thérèse placed the letter in a lavender-scented corner of her bureau. Sometimes she takes it out and rereads it.

Lately, she's been telephoning the Office of Refugee Registry at the Stadhuis to ask if the names Rudolph Fischer and Janine and Elli Arit have been added to the rolls. Each time, she spells the names with care. The clerk recognizes her voice by now, Marie-Thérèse senses, but is kind enough to hide impatience.

"Not yet. Perhaps try again in a day or two."

And she does.

Often, nightmare scenarios—Rudi facing a firing squad; Janine and Elli, hungry, wandering the streets of Brussels; the two of them huddled somewhere, trying to stay warm; the two of them wondering where *she* is.

With the help of the Stadhuis and various newspaper offices, she learns everything she needs to know. And then begins composing her own letter.

March 10, 1916

Herr Colonel Bruning,

On a January afternoon of last year, we met on an An-
twerp-bound train. You asked where I was going and why
and said that I appeared too much the student and should
beware of too much reading. You also told me about your
family's brewery in Cologne and kindly invited me and my
family to tour it one day. You said an interesting thing after
forgetting to introduce yourself. You said, "This war has
uncivilized me."

Much has happened since then. As I told you that day, I
was a student nurse at a clinic in Brussels. You mentioned
that you had heard of that place and that I might better
stay in the Netherlands and not return to Brussels. But I
did return. I returned in order to persuade our matron to
leave before she could be accused of treason and imprisoned. But she refused to save herself when so many others
needed help. She refused to abandon her duty, and for this
she was executed. There is nothing to be done about that
now. There is something, however, that you, as a civilized
and just person, can do, a small, good thing....

It takes several days to finally choose what she hopes are
the right words to tell him about Janine and Elli and how they
might be somewhere in Brussels, possibly at a patisserie owned
by Monsieur and Madame LaBreque or perhaps in that vicinity.
She asks if he would please make discreet inquiries and if approaching them, not be in uniform. She explains why, then goes
on to ask that he prevail upon the local authorities and see that
the two girls are brought to a refugee camp near Rotterdam,
which she names. She explains how, before her imprisonment,
she was their unofficial guardian. Finally, in a moment of bravado, or stupidity, she signs the letter with her full name.

But the letter remains there, tucked under a textbook.

Weeks later, clouds of blossoms appear in Rotterdam gardens
and orchards. In the camps, pea vines are climbing trellises, and
gardeners are harvesting green onions and asparagus—older

men with white mustaches and belted jackets who become, momentarily, Papa. She sees Janine in nearly every five-year-old little girl. And Elli in the older ones.

One day at a stationer's shop she buys red, old-fashioned sealing wax and a brass impress with the letter M in a circle. She buys red ink.

In her room she signs the letter, then inserts the pages in an envelope and seals the flap with the red wax. The letter M stands out in its circle. On the front face of the envelope she adds, to the left of Colonel Bruning's name and military address, the words, in red ink, *Dringend! Geheim!*

Urgent. Confidential.

It requires two more days to work up the courage to take the letter to the post office. The clerk looks at it and then at her. He weighs the letter and gives her the appropriate stamps. There is coldness in these actions.

She drops the letter into the slot for international mail and immediately wants to snatch it back. It occurs to her that she has just signed her death warrant.

But really, she tries to assure herself, why should she be terrified? The letter probably won't reach him anyway, for any number of reasons.

Days, then weeks pass. All her qualms and fears evaporate. It's as though she never wrote it and the girls are gone forever. Often, as if in compensation, she thinks of Rani. One of her volunteer assistants, Ingel, has the same red-gold hair and blotchy skin, and Marie-Thérèse sometimes finds it disorienting yet comforting. One afternoon the young woman's back is to her, and Marie-Thérèse calls her by Rani's name. When the young woman doesn't turn, Marie-Thérèse is momentarily annoyed.

Then she laughs. Rani has been telling her something all along. That they will see each other again. Somehow.

PIANO

She begins telephoning the Stadhuis again to inquire about the girls and a Rudolph Fischer. The answer is always the same: No, sorry. No one by those names. Could they be listed under different names?

That, of course, she cannot answer.

It seems pointless to keep telephoning, yet doing something is somehow better than nothing.

One afternoon, a donated piano arrives at the camp. The four men unloading it from the back of a truck are careful but, nonetheless, one of them loses hold of his end, and the piano tips, slides off the ramp, and hits the ground on its side, with a howling of all its keys. The young man can't stop apologizing. An assessment reveals that one of the piano's legs has cracked, so she goes to the infirmary for bandaging tape. When she returns, the young Belgian begins apologizing all over again. The other three offer a number of humorous comments as she wraps the tape around the piano leg. A craftsman will be found, she assures them, who will be able to create a new leg for the piano. When it's finally in the schoolhouse and she tests a few keys, she adds *tuner* and *simple sheet music* to her mental list. The rickety piano stool also needs repair. She's just relieved, though, that the piano didn't land on anyone's foot; getting a doctor out there often took some time.

After they leave, she ripples through scales and arpeggios. The Schubert waltz she tries next sounds like woolly music produced by some barely functioning gramophone. The cast-iron plate will have to be checked as well. She adds another mental note. Despite the awful sounds, she continues playing, stopping only when a child appears at her side. Marie-Thérèse's heart jolts, but the girl isn't Janine. She's older, with dark hair. Her slightly protruding eyes are luminous.

"May I try, Matron Hulbert, *s'il vous plaît?* May I?"

"Of course!"

Marie-Thérèse rises from the tippy stool, and the girl immediately sits and attacks, firing out the first of Johann Sebastian
Bach's Two-Part Inventions. This piece—Marie-Thérèse is sure
of it—has never in its long history been played with such force
and speed. The spinet howls and moans until the child finally
throws her small hands upward. "I know others too!"

"I am sure you must. What is your name?"

"Karena! I was given lessons in Brussels. May I have them
here? Please, Matron Hulbert?"

Marie-Thérèse adds yet another item to her growing list. "I'll
do my best to find you a teacher, mademoiselle."

"*Merci! Merci beaucoup!*"

Karena attacks the second Invention, and wanting to cover
her ears, Marie-Thérèse escapes the schoolroom.

An elderly woman is standing just outside the door, holding
an ivory-colored parasol to shade her from the sun. It occurs
to Marie-Thérèse that she might be related to Karena, a grand-
mother possibly, and that the two of them heard her playing
and stopped to listen. But then Marie-Thérèse recognizes petite
Madame LaBreque from the patisserie on the rue de la Culture.

"Madame! Are you here now? Is Monsieur LaBreque with
you? How good to see you! Do you have news of Brussels?
Mon Dieu, what a surprise!"

Madame LaBreque's mouth is quivering. Her pale blue eyes,
behind her eyeglasses, are blinking.

"Did something happen? Is it Monsieur LaBreque?"

She shakes her head. The parasol wobbles

"Let's go to my office. I'll get you some cold water, or coffee if you prefer. You can tell me everything. Today is awfully
warm, isn't it? It seems that it might storm, but the gardens
need rain."

Even then Marie-Thérèse doesn't suspect.

In her office at the front of the infirmary, she invites the
woman to be seated, then closes the door. Madame LaBreque is

using her handkerchief to blot each eye in turn. Marie-Thérèse
gets her water, but she's too upset to take it.

"Dear Madame LaBreque, you wish to tell me something.
One moment, please." Marie-Thérèse gets another chair from
the anteroom and sits near the woman. "Is it about your husband, or the patisserie? Did you lose the patisserie?"

The woman's entire body seems to be quaking, and then
Marie-Thérèse, trembling as well, understands. *Not Monsieur
LaBreque. Not the patisserie.* Blood drains away from her head.
Numbness is creeping in. "You can tell me, madame. Some-
thing has happened to the girls, hasn't it? But please, tell me.
Whatever it is."

Madame LaBreque averts her eyes and then begins apologizing like the man who dropped his end of the spinet. *Pardonnez-
moi, mademoiselle! Pardonnez-moi!* From a cinched bag looped
over her left wrist, she extracts a folded letter addressed to Marie-Thérèse.

"Where did you get this, madame?"

After a while, the woman is able to stifle hiccoughing and
tears and gain enough control for words. "He came to the
shop, a gentleman. A German gentleman. He asked…he asked
to speak with us in private. He said he knew we were caring
for two girls named Elli and Janine Arlt. He wanted to know
how they were, if they were healthy. I thought he must be their
parent, come looking for them. My heart broke, Mademoiselle
Hulbert. We feared the day, monsieur and I, we feared someone
would come to claim them. We would think about it and worry
and then we wouldn't. We would try to forget that it might happen. And then it finally did. I could see there was no point in
lying. He knew they were with us.

"I told him they are both healthy and happy. I told him how
they help us in the patisserie and are learning to bake. The little
one is even talking some. I told him they've been with us since
last October. At first, they were with Madame Kortman, but
she brought them to us. She said they were crying all the time
and she didn't know how to help them or what to give them

to do. She was afraid to send them to school because she was afraid they might run away somewhere. I don't know why she would think it but she did. She said she was not the right person to care for them. Perhaps, she said, we could take them and give them something to do in the patisserie.

"Monsieur and I opened our arms and, you know, it was such a gift because later that month we learned that our only son, Claude, was killed at the Battle of Loos, on the Western Front. Oh, we grieved, but there was so much to do to keep everything going and the two girls needed us, and we couldn't just let everything go while we wept. No! That is not our way. We kept on, we kept everything in order and did everything we could for the girls. Mademoiselle, we told ourselves not to, but we could not help it. We came to love them very much. And being cautious, we did not let it out that they were with us, but of course our patrons sometimes noticed them there, in the back. And then this man comes, this Herr Bruning, and he tells us they should be with you. I told him how happy they are with us and how much they have learned. He sent me here to tell you all this, as we told him. And he gave me the letter for you."

Madame LaBreque takes a long breath, then shuts her eyes but continues to dab at them.

Marie-Thérèse holds the glass to the woman's mouth. "Please take some water, madame. You've had a long journey, with so much on your mind."

"*Merci*," she whispers, then wipes her mouth with the crushed handkerchief. "It is like going through another death. Perhaps because we are older now, everything is so much harder. But you are young. It will be better for you to have them. I don't know how much longer we have, Monsieur LaBreque and I." Her mouth trembles. "I do not know how much more of this life we can take."

"Why don't you close your eyes for a few minutes and rest. Let me see what Herr Bruning has written."

It would only make it worse, Marie-Thérèse thinks, for her to know how her own heart has just been broken.

My Dear Nursing Student,

I have done what you asked me to do—for better or worse. Now it is for you to decide what is next. I have seen for myself how well the two children are doing. They were nicely clothed when I visited and obviously have been eating well. They both attend school and seem very bright. They told me they have been learning about baking gateaux and pastries. Madame and Monsieur LaBreque appear to deeply care about them. To spare the children pain, I did not reveal anything about you. But the baker and his wife told me the children believe that you perished in prison.

I told the LaBreques that you are to have the final word regarding the children. I have learned, you see, what you did for them when they first came to your clinic and how attached they were to you. This is all a tangle and I apologize. I should tell you that I also spoke with officials at the Office for Refugee Affairs in Brussels.

No one has come forward to claim the children, and since they are well settled with the baker and his wife, the official seemed satisfied. Evidently, the orphan situation is difficult and though the citizens of Brussels have been welcoming, there are only so many families able to take in refugee children now.

If you wish the children to be brought to you, tell Madame LaBreque. She knows how to contact me, and I will see to it that all is accomplished. Or, I can also arrange, instead, for their periodic visits. But then this may put the children in the position of having to—or wanting to—decide between you and the LaBreques.

I don't know which course will be best for everyone. I am out of my depth here but at least am on the way to relearning civilized behavior.

Warm regards,
Otto Bruning

Somewhere nearby, thunder. To Marie-Thérèse, it always sounds like siege cannons.

I should have gone back and tried to find them. Somehow. Taken that chance. Otto Bruning's letter falls to her lap. To ask the woman for more time to decide will just prolong her agony…and her own.

From the office window, she observes a wall of blue-gray storm cloud in the west. She turns. "Will you promise me one thing, madame? Will you promise that if you and Monsieur LaBreque become ill or incapacitated and can no longer care for them, you will have them brought to me in Rotterdam?"

"Oh, mademoiselle, *merci! Merci!* I promise. And Monsieur LaBreque will promise. Oh, God bless you. He will. He will for sure. I will write it down."

Marie-Thérèse doesn't know if she's referring to Monsieur LaBreque or to the Almighty. She stands and embraces the woman, assuring her that all will be well.

Then Marie-Thérèse watches her hurrying, with her parasol, to the waiting car. But just as she reaches it, Marie-Thérèse has a piercing thought. "One moment, please!" she calls, and hurries to the car.

Fear reclaiming her features, Madame LaBreque has paused and regards Marie-Thérèse while the driver holds open the door.

"Madame, you must do one other thing for me, please. You must tell them I'm alive and working in the Netherlands, in a refugee camp. I cannot bear to have them deceived. I cannot deceive them! If they ever learn that I've been alive all this time, living a life apart from them and not contacting them, it might seem the deepest betrayal and will be shattering, for I promised to take care of them. Do you understand, madame? It will be terrible after all that's happened to them. Janine might not remember so much, but Elli surely does. It might do great harm. I'm not putting it well, but surely you can see how they'll be hurt by the deception. Yes, they can stay with you and monsieur as I'm certain they'll want to. But please tell them that

you found me and that we talked. Tell them the whole story.
That I escaped from prison and am safe here but can't return
to Brussels just yet. Tell them they may be able to visit me here
one day."

Madame LaBreque gets herself into the back seat of the car
and raises both hands to her face. "No! They won't want to stay
with us! They will want to leave."

"I think not, madame. They love you and love their work in
the patisserie, and they're going to school and have friends and
have you both. No, they will not want to leave."

"It will be easier the other way, mademoiselle. For them to
think you are—"

"For now, yes. But what if I came to Brussels one day to
get them after you could no longer care for them? Or someone
brought them here? What would Elli think? It might break her
heart, no? How would you feel in her place, madame?"

The woman is shaking her head, tears wetting her fingers.

Marie-Thérèse uses her nurse's voice. "Madame, you know
how much they've been through. They have a sense of life and
will understand this, in their way. And they will appreciate honesty just as they appreciate your goodness. But if you don't tell
them about me and they later find out, they may turn against
you. I don't know but it seems possible. So be honest with them.
If they wonder where you went, tell them, simply. If they don't
ask, still speak to them simply and tell the truth. I will give you
a letter saying how happy I am that *they* are happy and learning
so much. They will have both of us, in a way. Their world will
be that much larger."

Madame LaBreque lets out a great sigh.

Wind whistles in gusts. Marie-Thérèse asks the driver to wait
for a few minutes.

In her office she writes:

> Dearest Elli and Dearest Janine,
>
>   Yes, I am alive. I escaped from prison and many people
> helped me get to the Netherlands. Now I am so happy to
> know that you are both well and living with Monsieur and

Madame LaBreque. I am also most pleased that you are learning so much at the patisserie and have been going to school. This is all wonderful news!

Dear girls, I have not forgotten you and now hope to see you one day soon for a good long visit. We will have our reunion after all.

Ever yours,
Mademoiselle Marie-Thérèse

She rushes through slanting rain to the car and hands the folded letter to the woman through the lowered window. Madame's face looks scoured and bloated. She has her handkerchief in hand.

"All will be well, madame. You'll see." Marie-Thérèse hopes to believe this herself.

Thunder breaks overhead, but she stands there in the rain and wind until the car jounces out of sight. From the direction of the schoolhouse comes the sound of piano music. Running through puddles to her office, Marie-Thérèse recognizes the piece. It's the lovely little Chopin Nocturne in E-flat Major but played *presto*, as if night lasts a mere minute.

A RATIONAL THOUGHT

Leaves fall like rain. The autumn sky is a gray slab or a roiled mass or vaporous with mist and fog. Then the heavy rains come, taking down the rest of the leaves. Marie-Thérèse isn't sleeping well, the hours before dawn the worst, her body rested enough and thoughts forming, usually sharp-edged and scraping at consciousness.

And then, October 12, and Marie-Thérèse's imagination presents it all, during those wakeful pre-dawn hours. The pockmarked prison wall. The blue suit and gray fur stole, the hair in its perfect coil, the blindfold in place, and a few meters away, the line of executioners raising their rifles. The eastern sky is pink. In imagination Marie-Thérèse halts the scene. There is a last-minute reprieve, thanks to all the international petitions. Or, failing that, one of the executioners lowers his rifle and shouts, "*No!*"—throwing everything into confusion; and then human decency and reason prevail. But no; instead, the others turn on that man and fire, and the traitor and his rifle fall to the ground. Then, a second order, and those others firing a second time, another rattling blast hanging in the air an instant before drifting away with the smoke from the guns. The figure in blue slumps forward and then to the stones. Without ceremony the body is conveyed to a burial ground outside the prison somewhere. Maybe there is a crude coffin. Maybe someone certifies death. A prison doctor, perhaps. Do they remove the blindfold? Maybe not. Without ceremony the box is closed and lowered into the earth. Dirt is shoveled in and then mounded up. Clouds overtake the pink light. Wind picks up. Yellow leaves tumble through the air, long slanting skeins of them, scattering over the graves of thieves and murderers and the fresh gravesite. Overhead, geese ride the north wind in their own long, wavering lines.

Almost as bad as the images are the *what if* thoughts in their excoriating loops. What if she had remained at the Académie? What if she had stayed in Rotterdam? What if she had been able to persuade the matron to leave? What if she had never met Rudi? What if, at this moment, she were a pianist? A real pianist? Living for music. And music living within her.

But at least I wasn't a coward.

And I experienced love. Deep love.

And deep sorrow.

Her very bones seem heavier. Which is odd, because she feels so empty.

Most of her time is spent at the camp, where Karena often searches her out and begs for help with a particular piece. Time and time again Marie-Thérèse will reach across the keyboard and still the girl's flying hands. At first Marie-Thérèse thought it was just nerves, and she saw herself in Karena, her younger self. But then she decided no, not nerves. The girl plays as a starved person eats.

On a clear, cold morning in December, people are entering the infirmary red-faced and huffing. Most have on a motley assortment of clothing donated by the aid societies. Marie-Thérèse has been getting reports of influenza cases, which are making her anxious. The infirmary won't have enough isolation rooms, should the situation develop into an emergency. She's at her desk, looking over plans for a new addition, but every so often her thoughts stray to the matron and how she'd been overseeing plans for the new clinic.

Someone taps on the glass of her open door, and she raises her head. This man appears to be a seaman in a heavy wool pullover and trousers. An eye patch covers his left eye. That side of his face is concave and misshapen.

"Please, come in," she says. "How may I help you?"

"You don't recognize me, Fräulein?"

Fräulein. She studies him.

"You are…Private Kohnert?"

"You remember my name! I'm flattered. Though now I'm Lance Corporal Kohnert. And you, of course, are Fräulein Hulbert, who once attended me at a Brussels clinic."

Slowly, she moves her hands to her lap and then safely under the desk. "Have you...are you a deserter, corporal?"

"No. I've come with sad news, I'm sorry to say."

Standing there, in front of her desk, he tells her that Lieutenant Rudolph Fischer was executed for treason. "Word has been circulating through the ranks, Fräulein. We were all told of his attempted desertion and subsequent execution, so that we would think twice before considering such an act. There has been something of a plague of desertions."

For Marie-Thérèse, the lance corporal's words take on the quality of distant echoes. Only the last few become clear. "They'd had reports of some fraudulent fishmonger and daughter and pieced it together after he was determined to be missing from your clinic."

Skepticism blocks horror. It might be some trap. He wants her to admit it, she thinks. As the matron was tricked into confessing.

"And how did you learn of this, corporal?"

With his right hand, he makes the same swiping impatient gesture he used at the clinic. She recalls picking up his notebook from the floor and then not knowing what to do with it.

"As I explained, Fräulein. Our officers made sure we learned of it...lest we stupidly entertain similar notions."

"Did he...confess?"

"They said he had."

They tortured him. She closes her eyes a moment.

"With your severe wounds, corporal, you might have been sent home. And yet—"

"They need men."

"But here you are, in civilian clothing, in another country, and you obviously spent time tracing me. You must think that I was that supposed daughter."

He looks down at her desk then at her again. "Your name

was mentioned, Fräulein. Also, I later heard of your remarkable escape from prison. A number of prison officials and guards were punished for that."

She thinks of the serving girl, Monica, who'd broken the rules by speaking French, and hopes she hadn't been among them. "You're taking a risk now. How were you able to cross the border?"

"I'm on leave. Finally! It wasn't difficult to get travel papers to visit my brother in Amsterdam. And not so difficult to find you...just a matter of a few inquiries."

"And you have such a brother."

"You don't believe me, do you? You think this may be some deception. I assure you it isn't. If I may offer advice...it's unwise to remain here. At least apply for citizenship if you haven't already. And possibly change your name."

"Lance Corporal Kohnert, forgive me, but I do have doubts. At the clinic you were rather...truculent. You demanded a different nurse. You threw your notepad at me, do you recall that? So why should you, of all people, make such an effort to come and tell me this when you might be in Germany or with this brother of yours? What if someone traces *you* here? You yourself might be accused of treason."

"I came because I know how hard it is to live in hope. Sometimes it's agony. I thought you would prefer knowing." At the door, he turns, hand on knob. "You may remember Gerhardt Haske? He had been bayoneted. He was my friend, and you were kind to him. My condolences, Fräulein Hulbert. I'm most sorry to have disturbed you with this sad news." He closes the door with care.

Through the pane of glass, she can see him putting on his seaman's cap and jacket and then winding a scarf about his neck. After he leaves, no one else enters the reception area, no one in German uniform. She takes slow breaths—one, then another, and still another. She tells herself that the pain is only the burning surprise of a gash parting flesh, muscle, and tendons. And then nerves simply conveying their futile messages from cell to cell. In time, the pain will end. And then, only its phantom will come to haunt. People survive pain. Some do. Private Schalk, the champion swimmer. Others do not. Yet their tragedies are catalysts in the equations, causing, possibly, some new and good rearrangement of matter. She forces herself to recall Madame Depage helping others get to lifeboats, which had been the case, as it turned out. But then the ship tilts, and she's standing amid a tangle of rope. How many nurses will remember her courage and goodness and strive to emulate her generosity? *There must be no bitterness,* the matron reportedly said the night before her death. *No bitterness.* She tries in vain to moderate emotion. She must not be bitter. She must not brim with scalding hatred. She tries in vain to convince herself that some good might come of this moment. Above all, she tries to dispel the nightmare vision of Rudi being interrogated and beaten.

Impossible. The vision won't dispel. Pain only claws in deeper.

Sometime later she's able to walk to the door, bolt it, and return to her desk. She's not aware of the wind, still whistling about the eaves and corners of the infirmary. The vision of Rudi being interrogated is losing its grip, for a different thought is forming. A perfectly rational thought. This thought, this decision, brings relief. She knows how she will do it. Morphine. Fast and painless. Painlessly she will thwart pain. Escape it as she did the prison. Otherwise, a prison of self-excoriation and despair. And that will be sinning, a lifetime of sin. Surely, God will understand. So will Our Lady and St. Gudule.

Making the plan feels constructive and positive. Tonight, after her assistant Inge leaves, she'll gather what she needs. She will leave a note and then will lie down on the cot in the anteroom and say a final prayer. Then she will descend into pure sleep—and peace. At the moment of Judgment right after death, she will say, *I did not want to commit the sin of despair.* Marie-Thérèse draws a piece of paper toward her, and her fountain pen. Sentences flow until loud knocking causes her hand to spring away from the paper. She looks up, expecting to see several German soldiers about to burst through the door.

But it's only Inge, skin flushed, eyes round and eyebrows raised. "Matron!" she calls. "Why is this door locked? Are you ill? Can you open it? We need you! It's Deiter Jahnke. He's having trouble breathing! Matron, please, we need you!" She keeps rattling the knob and knocking until Marie-Thérèse stands and goes to the door.

Later she will think that it wasn't her assistant at all but St. Gudule in disguise, scattering the demons with her lantern.

NOCTURNE

BRUSSELS, JULY 1920

In the Parc de Bruxelles, an avenue through beeches and oaks leads to a circular pool whipped into shivering wavelets by the wind. Marie-Thérèse pauses to watch the fluctuating play of metallic colors, the shimmer and opaqueness and illusion of depth. Then she walks on, passing broad cross avenues and narrower ones branching off in diagonals. At the opposite end of the park, there's another pool, smaller than the first. Again she pauses to admire the play of sun and cloud on its fitful surface. The wind-filled crowns of trees sound like a rushing stream. On the lawn, squirrels dash about in wavelets of their own. She draws a deep breath and continues along a rose border, its blooms bright as paint daubs in the flashes of sunlight. An elderly man in dark blue, his jacket belted, stands clipping off withered blooms and putting them in a cloth bag hanging at his side. "*Bonjour*, monsieur," she says. He partly turns, doffs his cap, and bows slightly. "*Bonjour*, madame." The resemblance is heartening, though bittersweet. Still, she takes it as a sign and walks on, finally leaving the park. In the Place des Palais, she must hold her hat. Raised high over the Palais Royal, the colors of Belgium flap like a flame in the wind.

After crossing the rue Royal, she enters the rue de la Régence. At no. 30, she hesitates before entering a courtyard embraced on two sides by the wings of a red brick and stone building. Five elaborate pediments hold sculptures honoring Orchestration, Composition, Performing Arts, Poetry, and Instrumental Music. As she stands there, students walk around her and continue on toward the entrance, satchels at their sides. Her heartbeat quickens. She breathes deeply, then proceeds through the open gate.

Inside the building, memory meshes with reality and finds no discrepancy. The parquet floor in the hall, the varnished doors, the dry churchy air—all the same. She ascends staircases and traverses a hall to its far end and stops before one of the last doors on the right. The bench alongside the door is also the same, its threadbare cushions a faded azure, its bowed legs cream colored with gilt veining. Suddenly she is sixteen again and terrified. She shakes her head to clear away the sensation, then sits, deliberately, where she always had, at the end farthest from the door, her music satchel on her lap. Oddly, fingers have retained warmth. There are no heart palpitations. And her senses are unblurred by incipient panic. Scuff marks on the floor resemble scudding clouds. Sunlight forms a golden splotch on the oak flooring at the end of the hall. Soon the muted notes of a Scarlatti sonata come through the door. Someone is doing well with it. The staccato exuberance, the balance and cohesion, clarity and assurance. The flow. *Bien. Très bien.* No despair accompanies this thought, as often happened in the past.

Soon the room is quiet. Madame, she knows, must be speaking. Her voice was always low and melodious but difficult to hear, at least to someone whose ears were blocked by terror. Marie-Thérèse remembers having to lean forward while being so afraid of missing any word, and then missing most of them.

Finally, footsteps, and the door opening outward. The student—a girl of about fifteen—glances at Marie-Thérèse without appearing to really see her.

"You did well, mademoiselle," Marie-Thérèse says just above a whisper.

This startles her and she hurries away without replying. Marie-Thérèse takes her satchel and knocks on the door.

"*Entrez!*" she hears.

The seated woman at the far end of the room says without turning, "You are ahead of schedule, Anton. When will you learn to tell time?"

"*Bonne après-midi*, Madame Gonczy."

The woman turns. She raises her gold lorgnette.

The leather armchair the same, but the woman is not. Marie-Thérèse observes that she has lost at least a quarter, if not more, of her mass. Slack skin drapes the facial bones. Skin appearing hardened in place, like dried clay. But the eyes…the eyes haven't changed. There is still the intensity Marie-Thérèse had always feared. And the censure. Her heart gives a flutter of recognition. Madame Gonczy, they used to say, regarded mistakes at the keyboard the equivalent of sins. But an elderly woman now, possibly ill and not having much longer to live. The sensation washing through Marie-Thérèse isn't fear, she realizes, or even pity, but something closer to—could it be?—love.

And as always, madame's right hand rests clawlike over the silver bird ornamenting the top of her walking stick.

"You are new? Are you lost?"

"Madame, *pardonnez-moi*. I am Marie-Thérèse Hulbert, a former student. I studied here before the war."

The eyepiece magnifies madame's eyes.

"What do you want?"

The woman's voice is still low, yet Marie-Thérèse has heard each disapproving word veneered with annoyance. "I wish to play for you and then, if you will allow, I have one question."

"What a mystery you present! If you wish to ask me something, ask, and then leave. I am expecting a student."

Marie-Thérèse extends an arm toward madame's Bösendorfer, its top closed and the surface a sheet of light. "May I, please?"

"Not anything long, then. I do not wish to critique anything long. Hulbert, you say? Hulbert. And your mother the ballerina? Am I correct?"

"You are, madame."

"If memory serves, you were only a mediocre pianist. I cannot imagine that you have improved in the intervening years. Have you?"

"Perhaps not. I don't know. But if you will allow just a few minutes?"

Madame Gonczy juts her chin in the direction of the Bösendorfer, assumes as much of her old upright posture as she can
manage, and slips into her legendary trance of concentration.

At the last moment, Marie-Thérèse decides against removing the sheet music from her satchel. Instead, she places the
satchel flat on the floor, next to the bench. She doesn't hurry,
as in the old days at auditions for madame's class, when she
had been so afraid of annoying the woman all the more. This
time her actions are focused yet languid. There's no need to
announce the title of her piece. Madame will know it from the
first note. She will also know when Chopin composed it and
when he had first played it and who was there to applaud his
new gift to the world.

Marie-Thérèse sits with head bowed for perhaps thirty
seconds, allowing emptiness to enter her, and then she begins
filling it with music.

They are all there—her audience of the living and the dead.
For them, she plays with a light touch, right hand offering the
simple melody, the left its repetitive ladder of ascending chords
in slow waltz rhythm, with demanding flats and naturals that
never sound demanding when played well, but rather something of utmost simplicity. *Multum in parvo*, Madame Gonczy
used to say. *Multum in parvo!* Do you understand? Marie-Thérèse
never had...before. Much in little; greatness in smallness. One
might think Chopin had offhandedly written this piece in a few
minutes. His genius had been to find a simple way into depth
and contemplation. Night comes, a simple thing, a beautiful
thing (those graceful mordents). A time of quiet. Of being in
darkness, in memory, in loss of the day, in acceptance. No py-
rotechnics, no rage, no bitterness, no glorious rapture. Those
found their way into other compositions but not this one.

And then, too soon all the same, the closing measures—
again repetitions: two of harmonious notes, pianissimo, with
right hand and left forming chords, and then three of full
chords, bright to dark, in a whispered double pianissimo, with
the final one held for six beats, time slowing, slowing, to the

point of nothing. The Bösendorfer hums its fading resonance.

She releases the final chord and then slowly raises her hands from the keyboard.

Madame is still sitting hunched forward, hand on cane. With her other, she raises her lorgnette. "With whom have you been studying?"

"No one, madame."

"*Impossible!*" Into this exclamation the woman puts all the volume she can command now, which is not much.

"No, madame. I have been…nursing. I am a nurse."

Judging by the woman's contorted expression, this might have been uttered in Greek.

"Nursing…*people?*"

"*Oui,* madame. I was a student of nursing after I left the Académie and now I am a nurse."

"Why?"

Marie-Thérèse smiles at the woman's childlike incredulity but has no answer. The why of it too large to be encapsulated in a few sentences, or even paragraphs, and in any case would only bore the woman.

"Madame, I have come to ask if you will have me as a pupil. Briefly. For six months. Perhaps eight. Once a week."

"*Je ne comprenez-vous!* You should come back here and study. And not just with me."

"I wish only six or at the most eight months, madame, with you. I have a certain…obligation to fulfill and must prepare."

"Can you tell me about this obligation of yours?"

"Later. If you agree. I will tell you then. At the end of my preparation."

"Are you planning to give a recital, mademoiselle?"

"In a way, yes. One could call it that."

"Why do you need me? You are a decent pianist already. Surely good enough."

"Because I wish to prepare some difficult Schubert, madame. Only you can help me."

"Ah. Schubert but not Chopin?"

"Possibly Chopin. Yes, I think so. The Grand Polonaise, for one."

"What made you chose the Opus 9, No. 2 today, mademoiselle?"

"I chose it because...I love it."

The woman stares for three slow beats. "*Bien.* Come next Wednesday at four o'clock."

"*Merci,* madame. *Merci beaucoup.*"

"Tell him he may enter now."

In the hall a young boy is sitting on the bench, kicking his short legs back and forth. Seven years old? Six? A pang of envy strikes, a small pang, before quickly fading.

"You may go in now, monsieur. Madame is ready for you. *Bonne chance!*" She holds the door for him.

He gives her a wide smile as if proud of his missing front teeth, grabs up his music, and clatters into the salon.

"Anton!" she hears madame scold. "Why must you *run* everywhere? Always in such a hurry! The pianoforte is not going anywhere. You see? It's right over there. It's not running away."

Marie-Thérèse stands outside the door a while as Anton begins Schubert's Allegretto *für das Pianoforte componirt.* Listening, she thinks Madame Gonczy must be in heaven.

The day's fitful clouds have disappeared, and the early evening air is still. Marie-Thérèse tips her small-brimmed hat slightly farther over her left ear and slows her pace. The pavement across the street is crowded with outdoor tables, most of them filled. A girl of about fifteen is carrying a tray of cups to one of them. Her honey-colored hair is gathered in a long plait. Marie-Thérèse walks on, her heart thudding. At a break in the traffic, she pauses, undecided, then dashes across the street and seats herself at a cleared table. When the young girl approaches, Marie-Thérèse, gripping her hands underneath the tabletop, smiles up at her. "*Bonjour,* Mademoiselle Elli."

The girl's eyes widen.

"I've come to visit as I promised. I'm so sorry to have

startled you. I should have telephoned. Please forgive me."

"Mademoiselle Marie-Thérèse? You are not a ghost?"

"A bit pale, perhaps, but no, not a ghost, *ma chérie*. Not a ghost at all! Could you possibly take a little rest? Is Janine here? Could we all have some *chocolat chaud* and a pastry?"

"I must ask Grand-mère, mademoiselle. One moment!"

The words hurt somewhat but still Marie-Thérèse smiles, and soon the three of them are seated at the outdoor table, eating bichon au citron Elli said they helped make. Janine, hardly recognizable at ten years old, says they want to become *pâtissiers*, like Grand-père. And all the while, Madame LaBreque keeps an uneasy eye on them from inside the shop. Marie-Thérèse has apologized to the woman for not telephoning first. It hadn't been an oversight, though. She'd been afraid madame would try to dissuade her, that there would have been words, tears, importuning. But now here at last, Marie-Thérèse is struggling to restrain her own tears of joy.

"Tell us, Mademoiselle Marie-Thérèse," Elli says in her young lady's voice, "exactly *where* you have been and *what* you have been doing. We want to know everything!"

"As I do, *mes chères*."

"Please tell us first. Grand-mère told us you were living in the Netherlands, and she gave us your letter, but, you know, we still couldn't be sure. We worried."

"I'm sorry you worried. So. I will begin first, as you wish."

The chairs' shadows lengthen, creating intricate geometric patterns in the low evening sun. The girls' faces are ruddy, golden, and intense as Marie-Thérèse narrates bits of her story and then they do, telling about school and the patisserie, Grand-père and Grand-mère, who survived terrible illnesses, and Donnie who came to live with them though not Jackie, who had died, sadly, and all the while the light deepens to lavender, patrons leave, and Monsieur LaBreque brings out omelets, coffee, and glasses of milk, then slips back into the shop, where the lights are on now, and Madame LaBreque sits reading her newspaper and resting her feet before the night's work.

"Phantasie"

May 1921

Private Schalk writes that he's married now and the father of a little boy. His innate exuberance surfaces in Berlin when Marie-Thérèse visits him there. He tells her how he's coaching a swim team, the same one that competed in the 1920 Olympics in Antwerp that year. "Imagine, Fräulein! Antwerp! Perhaps you attended?" She's ashamed to say that she hadn't, she'd been so engaged in other matters. But of more importance to him, it seems, is that he's also teaching his three-year-old son to swim and how much the boy loves the water. "A great gift! The greatest gift!" Yes, she thinks, and may it always be.

Her visit with Rani, now a nurse at St. Hedwig's Hospital, is more fraught. Their time together in Brussels, the duplicity, their arguing that last day—it's all there, in their embrace. Rani becomes tearful, over coffee and rolls, when Marie-Thérèse tells her about Papa, the matron, the prison, and her own escape.

"I shouldn't have left," Rani says after a silence. "I read about the execution and couldn't believe it. It was sickening. Terrible. A travesty. I should have stayed and helped somehow. It was wrong to have run away. I think about it all the time. And about Madame Depage and her courage. And yours, Marie-Thérèse."

Marie-Thérèse tries to console her by saying that it had been a hard time for everyone and that Rani had simply followed her heart.

"I followed only my anger."

Never argue with a patient. Marie-Thérèse reaches over and pats her arm, as in the old days. After a lengthy silence, she asks, in French, if Rani thinks the rolls are anything like those they'd had in Brussels.

"*Non! Pas aussi bon!*" Not nearly! It makes them laugh, finally. Rani accompanies Marie-Thérèse to the train station and waits while she purchases a ticket to Coblenz. It evokes that other time, but neither comments on it. This time there are no stretcher bearers and on handcarts, only luggage. And this time they promise to keep in touch.

Concentric rows of red and yellow tulips surround a pool with a stone cherub pouring water from a shell. A scented breeze sends white petals scattering over a brick walkway. Seated on a bench, Marie-Thérèse is thinking how beautiful spring is. She's also thinking that what she is about to do is the last thing in the world she wants to do. In an hour, however, it will be over. She tries to knead warmth into her fingers.

The fountain plashes. Tulips sway in the breeze. A sparrow alights. And then it's time.

The street door has beveled glass and gold lettering. *Fischer Pianos.* A bell tinkles as Marie-Thérèse steps inside a showroom where pianos in sizes ranging from spinets to medium-sized grands return glittering light from several chandeliers. A clerk enters from the back and wishes her a good morning. A younger man who doesn't resemble Rudi in the least but of course brings him to mind. At her hotel the night before, she had all but convinced herself that Rudi would be there. Somehow he escaped and would be working with his father. And it would be a joyful, tearful reunion. Seeing this young man now puts an end to that fantasy. Or nearly.

In German she gives her name and says she has an appointment with Herr Fischer.

"Ah. He is expecting you, mademoiselle. Please be seated if you wish." He indicates a grouping of chairs and a settee. "May I bring you coffee? Or tea?"

"*Nein, danke.*"

He bows and leaves the showroom. She sits at the edge of one of the upholstered chairs and squeezes her hands and fingers. She takes long deep breaths. The silence in the showroom is becoming ponderous. She thinks of leaving but then Herr Fischer is walking toward her, and she stands. He's a small man with white hair and Rudi's wide-set eyes but in a rounded pink face. The hair's comb marks reveal a pink scalp. Despite careful attention to grooming and clothing, he is a man in the shadows. Shoulders sagging, eyes dim. Had it not been for this appointment, she thinks, he might have been on the work floor with his pianos, where he could forget, for at least minutes at a time. Some promises perhaps shouldn't be kept.

"Please," he says. "Let us sit a moment. I believe you wish to tell me something more about my son. Since you corresponded, I was informed that they will not be returning his body to us. My son, they say, is buried somewhere in Belgium. I have been trying to learn where. One day I would like to visit the gravesite and, if possible, have the body brought home. Do you know anything of this matter?"

Even then she thinks it can't be true. Another part of her writhes with the agony of guilt and self-recrimination, all of which she confessed to Herr Fischer in her earlier letter.

"Sir," she begins, "I am sorry. I know nothing about that. I have come to tell you something your son wishes…excuse me, please…wished you to know. He asked me to promise that I would tell you something of great importance. I agreed, but putting it in a letter did not seem fitting." She takes another long breath. "Sir, he wished you to know that he…loved you very much and that he was so sorry for having disappointed you. He wanted you to know how much he admired you for your passion and how much he wished it could have been his own."

Herr Fischer sits there with lowered head, absorbing these blows. Marie-Thérèse forces herself on. "He asked me to play some Schubert for you and perhaps also some Chopin." Those might have been the worst words of all. He takes out a folded white handkerchief and blots his eyes. He's making gasping sounds. Marie-Thérèse can't prevent her own tears. With blurred vision, she goes to the nearest piano, one of the smaller grands, and then sits there, blinking to clear her eyes. She doubts she'll be able to play anything at all, with her stony hands.

But finally, she positions the bench, takes a long shaky breath, and pulls her shoulders back. And then there are the opening chords of Schubert's "Phantasie," strong as a heart pumping life-giving blood.

An impromptu follows the "Phantasie," then waltzes by Schubert, followed by several of Chopin's. Then the Grand Polonaise, a ballade, an étude, mazurkas, and finally the Nocturne in E-flat Major. After holding the last chord for several beats, she raises her hands and places them in her lap. They're tingling with life. She doesn't know how much time has elapsed. Later she will—nearly two hours. Several others are gathered around Herr Fischer, some in long aprons. Their applause sounds like rain splashing new leaves. After a while, she slides the bench back and stands. Herr Fischer, walking toward her, opens his arms. She's relieved to see that he's no longer weeping.

That was her first recital. Since then, there've been others. Herr Fischer had the piano sent to Brussels, where Marie-Thérèse is now living, in an apartment not far from her old home on the rue Belliard Stratt, and working three days a week at a hospital. That morning in Coblenz, Herr Fischer said some mystical things about how the piano must be hers now. It had claimed her and would refuse to give up its true sound for anyone else. Not wanting to argue, she accepted the extravagant gift. Also, she knew, Rudi would have wanted her to. But then, a strange thing. Soon after the arrival of the piano, she found herself in the vicinity of the Place des Palais and kept walking to the Académie, and then up to Madame Gonczy's salon. Madame, of course, had a pupil, and Marie-Thérèse waited on the same faded velvet bench with bowed legs. She tried not to think about what she was doing there. She tried not to think at all. Soon the pupil emerged, a girl, and Marie-Thérèse went in, once again disrupting madame's precious schedule.

"You are back? For good this time?"

"*Oui.*"

Madame was silent a moment and then raising her walking stick somewhat, struck the floor. "So. We will begin."

While leaving the Académie one evening, she notices a man seated on the bench in the courtyard. A thin man in a cream-colored suit. For Marie-Thérèse, old fears periodically surface at any unexpected breach of a familiar pattern. Usually, the bench is unoccupied at that hour or if not, then by young Académie students. Never a solitary older person just whiling away the time. *Rudi,* she thinks. Over the past months, she's been noticing him in various places. On a tram. At a café. Walking in a park. Of course, the figures always resolve into strangers. There's something in this man's hand. A piece of paper. He's holding a small piece of paper and studying it.

In imagination, he is Rudi, who looks up and says, I'm happy to see you've been practicing, mademoiselle. He waves the piece of paper, a recital notice. *Mademoiselle Marie-Thérèse Hulbert plays Schubert, Chopin, and Schumann.* In imagination they sit on the stone bench as evening comes on and white roses release their nocturnal fragrance. She tells him about her escape and then he tells about his, an improbable convoluted escape involving a fishing boat, a collision with a freighter, a night rescue and months spent in Portugal, and then working on yet another fishing boat, followed by a surreptitious journey home and learning about her visit and her playing, as she'd promised and as he'd known she would. After that lengthy word recital, he can't stop apologizing for all that happened as a result of his mistakes and Germany's aggression and, well, simply put, life itself. They go to a café where there's accordion music, and still he apologizes until their plates of cake arrive, strawberry cake, *gateau aux fraises,* the white frosting decorated with sliced fresh strawberries and reminding him, somehow, of the skating cap he wore at the pond that day when they first met, the one with the reindeer pattern around the border. He lost the cap, he tells her. It was very warm. She assures him they will find another.

On and on it goes, this bittersweet fantasy she fully recognizes as fantasy but indulges because…because why? Because we need our dead to be close? Matron, Papa, Rudi—while we live, we need them and, perhaps, they us? They not ready to fully depart until assured we can go on in what we need to be doing— for ourselves and, possibly as important, for them. And we? We needing also the depth of consciousness, the chord held in the lower octaves, held there and fading into nothingness, and still you hold it, certain that its sound exists somewhere even when you can no longer hear it.

"*Rudi*," she whispers, and walks on.

Afterword

Although a work of the imagination, *In the Fall They Leave* was inspired by historical events during the first two years of World War I in Europe. Several characters, portrayed fictitiously, are historical figures: the matron, based on the real-life Edith Louise Cavell, a British nurse and the matron of *L'École Belge d'Infirmières Diplômées* at the Berkendael Medical Institute in Brussels, Belgium; Madame Marie Depage, nurse, and wife of Doctor Antoine Depage, Belgian royal surgeon and founder of the Berkendael Medical Institute and Nursing School; Otto Mayer, head of the German Secret Police; and Georges Gaston Quien, a double agent. It is a historical fact that Madame Depage drowned when the *Lusitania* was torpedoed just off the southeastern coast of Ireland. King Albert, Queen Elisabeth, Cardinal Mercier, Philippe Baucq, and Louise Thuliez, mentioned in the novel, are historical figures. All other characters in the novel are fictional. Place settings, while generally true to geographic facts, are also imaginatively depicted. Regarding military matters as well as the arrest, execution, and prison burial of the matron, I strove for historical accuracy. Edith Cavell's body was exhumed from the St. Gilles Prison burial site in 1919, transported to England, and re-interred with full honors at Norwich Cathedral in Norfolk.

ACKNOWLEDGMENTS

Warm thanks to Donna West, RN, PhD, who read a version of this novel and made several helpful comments. I greatly appreciate her generosity in taking time from her full academic work and family life to read the manuscript. My gratitude to Deborah d'Courville as well for offering a number of valuable suggestions, and to John Vernon, Liz Rosenberg, Jerry Mirskin, and Sara-Jo Lupo Sites for their generous comments. Many thanks to Pam Van Dyk, my editor, for her keen eye and attention to detail, and to Elizabeth Lowenstein for her proofreading. I'm also deeply grateful to Jaynie Royal, editor-in-chief at Regal House Publishing, and to the RHP staff for their commitment to literature, writers, and social justice.

And to my husband and first reader, Jerry, a great hug for his patience in reading drafts of this novel and never failing to offer excellent critiques and suggestions which helped make this work stronger. I'm thankful as well for his unstinting encouragement over the years. Without it, I simply could not have gone on as a writer.

I was drawn to the story of Edith Cavell after reading a feature article by Peter Benesh in the *Investor's Business Daily* (March 1, 2005). At that time, the IBD featured portrayals of inspirational figures. The article about Edith Cavell is titled, "She Gave Her Life to Nursing," with the subtitle, "Help Humanity: Edith Cavell died trying to keep Allied troops alive in World War I." A striking black-and-white photograph accompanying the article shows a young nurse standing just behind a little boy of about four or five who is wearing a large round-brimmed hat, a cotton or linen jacket, dark breeches, white shirt, and bow tie. An ivy-covered wall is in the background. One can also see the creases in Nurse Cavell's white uniform apron, perhaps freshly put on for this photograph. Her pristine-white cuffs resemble long over-the-elbow evening gloves. The sleeves above the cuffs are dark. On her head is a small white cap. Under it, her waved hair is parted to the side and drawn back. The boy appears fretful, his elbows bent, hands held outward, the fingers parted. The photo was taken in 1903, sometime in the warmer months. She would have been thirty-seven years old, a beautiful woman with strong eyebrows, an oval face, and a gentle smile. Benesh's article recounts her contributions to modern nursing while summarizing her immensely productive, patriotic, and yet tragic life. Twelve years after the photograph was taken—and a month and a half before her fiftieth birthday—Edith Cavell was executed by a double firing squad in German-occupied Belgium.

Before reading Benesh's article, I had never heard of Edith Cavell. I didn't know that streets are named after her as well as hospitals, clinics, and schools, even a mountain. Nor did I know that several biographies exist as well as dramatic works, including at least one play and a film. I lived in London for a time but wasn't aware of the statue of Edith Cavell in central London's St. Martin-in-the Fields. So, the article in the *Investor's Business Daily* was a revelation. The photograph haunted me long after I'd clipped the article and tucked it into a notebook.

Some years later, still drawn to the story, I began doing research, beginning with a book for young adults, *Edith Cavell*, by Rowland Ryder (Stein and Day, 1975). Another publication that oriented me in the period was Barbara Tuchman's *The Guns of August* (alternatively titled *August 1914*), first published by Macmillan in 1962. Also helpful: Jack Batten's *Silent in an Evil Time: The Brave War of Edith Cavell*. Tundra Books: Toronto, Ontario, 2007. A number of online sources were helpful as well, including encyclopedia.1914–1918—online.net on the Occupation during the War; the librarie-immaterial.fr; windowstoWorld-history.weebly.com (on the spy Gaston Quien); the Diary of Constance Graeffe; the Diary of Edmond Picard, a Brussels magistrate; Cardinal Désiré–Joseph Mercier's Pastoral Address for the New Year 1915, "Patriotism and Endurance," (critical of the Occupation and daring in condemning the massacres during the invasion of Belgium); antique nursing books such as Charlotte Aikens's *Primary Studies* and A.D. Whiting's text on bandaging.

After reading for a number of weeks, I decided on a fictional protagonist, a young student nurse—Marie-Thérèse Hulbert—who serves not on WWI battlefields but in a small teaching hospital in German-occupied Brussels and who reluctantly, at first, becomes involved with Belgium's underground resistance movement. I thought it would be interesting to tell the story of Matron Cavell's heroic efforts through the point of view of a young nurse who idolizes her but also has her own story to tell.